Praise for Covenant of the Sword

Nagaro and his fellow galley slaves are free and safe on the remote , rustic island of Pakoa. The captured Mahuk war galley floats enticingly in the harbor, and he has a beautiful, deadly Mahuk sword under his bed, but neither seems likely to do him any good. He's famous all over the island for leading the slaves' escape, but he has no way to earn a living, and he's tormented by unanswered questions about the past he must conceal. Then when his friend Taru tries to "help" him, he ends up facing yet another challenge...

"Great news for readers who've been eagerly awaiting the next chapter of this engaging tale. Your wait is over and you won't be disappointed."

— Leslie Ann Moore, author of the award-winning *Griffin'a Daughter Trilogy* and the *Nuetierra Chronicles*.

"*Covenant of the Sword* is the second book of the epic literary fantasy series titled *The Nagaro Chronicle*, and is everything a reader looks for in a series, wrapped up in the main character of Nagaro, a man the reader will respect, trust, and think about long after they've finished reading. The author expertly allows us to see his humanity, but also his deep desire to do what's right. Wilde's intelligent and introspective prose reveals both the plot and the character of Nagaro a page at a time. I ended the first book of the series, *Gift of Chance*, greedy for the next book. *Covenant of the Sword* again gives me something to look forward to. I can't imagine ever tiring of reading about Nagaro, or any of the other deeply developed characters in *The Nagaro Chronicle*. If Carol Louise Wilde is writing, I'm reading it."

— G. M. Barlean, Nebraska author of eleven books, best known for her cozy mystery trilogy, *The Rosewood Series*.

Also by Carol Louise Wilde

Books of the Nagaro Chronicle

Gift of Chance (1)

Covenant of the Sword (2)

Return to Lankura (3)

Thief of Slaves (4)

Heir of Darion (5)

Brothers of the Blood (6)

The final title in this series,
Legacy of Loros (7), is forthcoming

The *Nagaro* Chronicle 2

Covenant of the Sword

Carol Louise Wilde

Rivulus Books Trade Paperback Edition

Covenant of the Sword is a work of fiction. Names, places, and incidents either are products of the author's imagination or are used fictitiously. Any resemblance to actual events, locales, or persons, living of dead, is entirely coincidental.

Text, maps, and internal artwork by Carol Louise Wilde

Published in the United States of America by Rivulus Books, Arcadia, CA. The Rivulus Books name and Rivulus Books logo are trademarks of Rivulus Books.

ISBN: 978-1-944492-07-6

Cover art copyright by Cherie Foxley

For my mother, who gave me so many things,
among them a love of reading

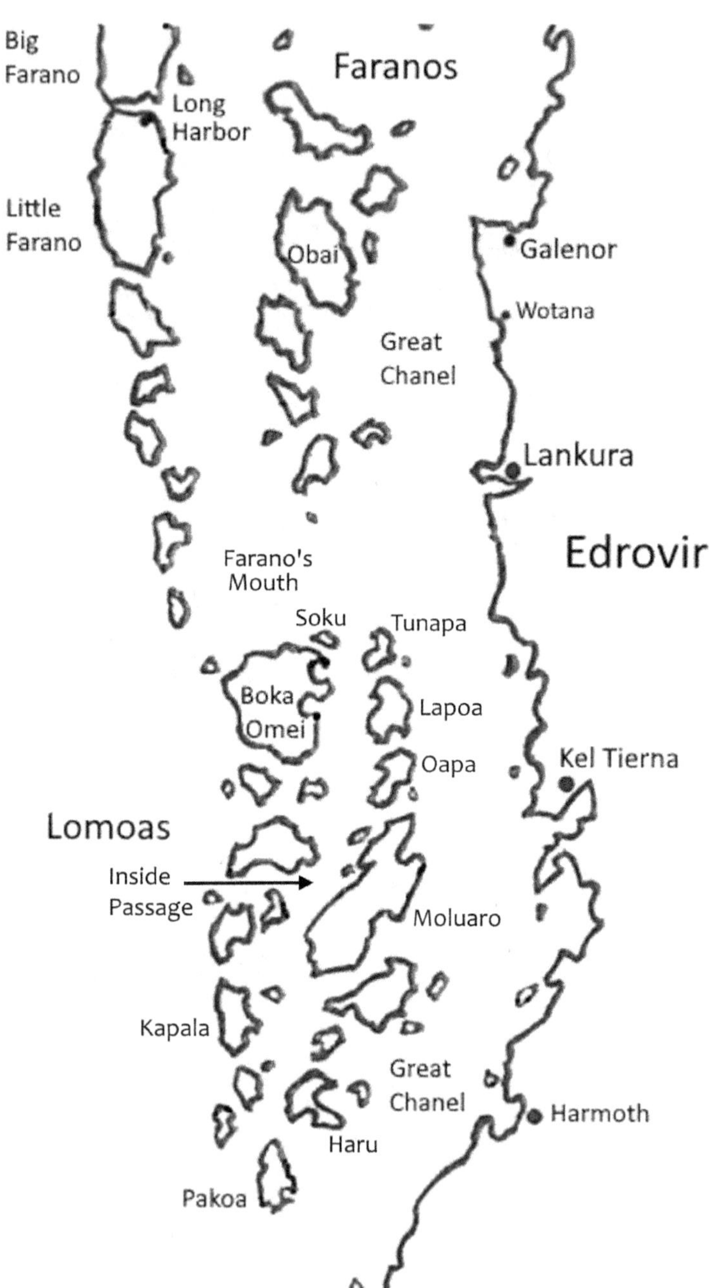

Big Farano
Faranos
Long Harbor
Little Farano
Obai
Galenor
Wotana
Great Chanel
Lankura
Edrovir
Farano's Mouth
Soku
Tunapa
Boka Omei
Lapoa
Oapa
Kel Tierna
Lomoas
Inside Passage
Moluaro
Kapala
Great Chanel
Harmoth
Haru
Pakoa

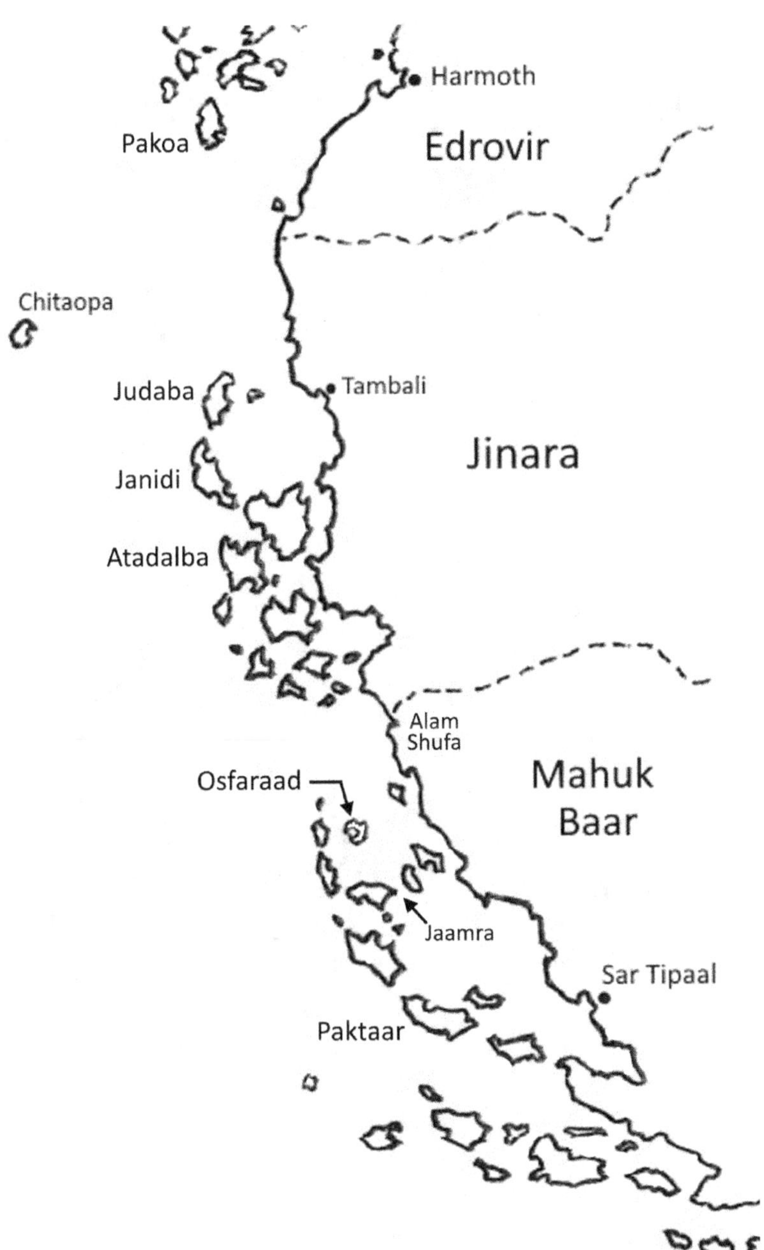
Harmoth
Edrovir
Pakoa
Chitaopa
Tambali
Judaba
Jinara
Janidi
Atadalba
Alam
Shufa
Osfaraad
Mahuk
Baar
Jaamra
Sar Tipaal
Paktaar

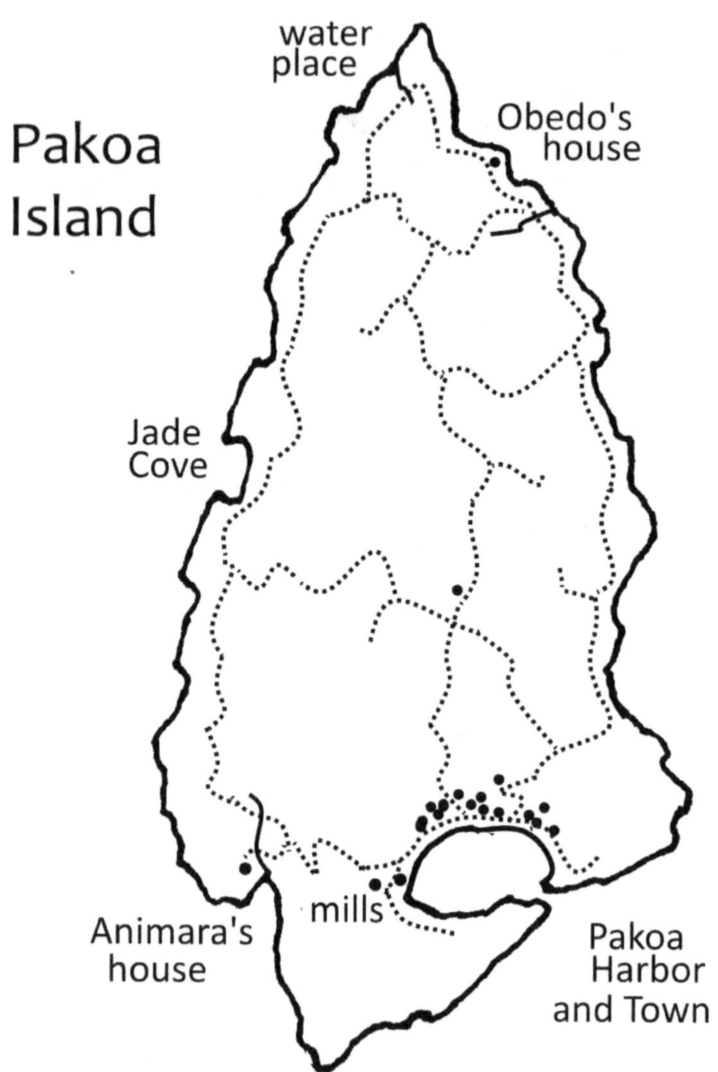
Pakoa
Island
water
place
Obedo's
house
Jade
Cove
mills
Animara's
house
Pakoa
Harbor
and Town

Chitaopa Island

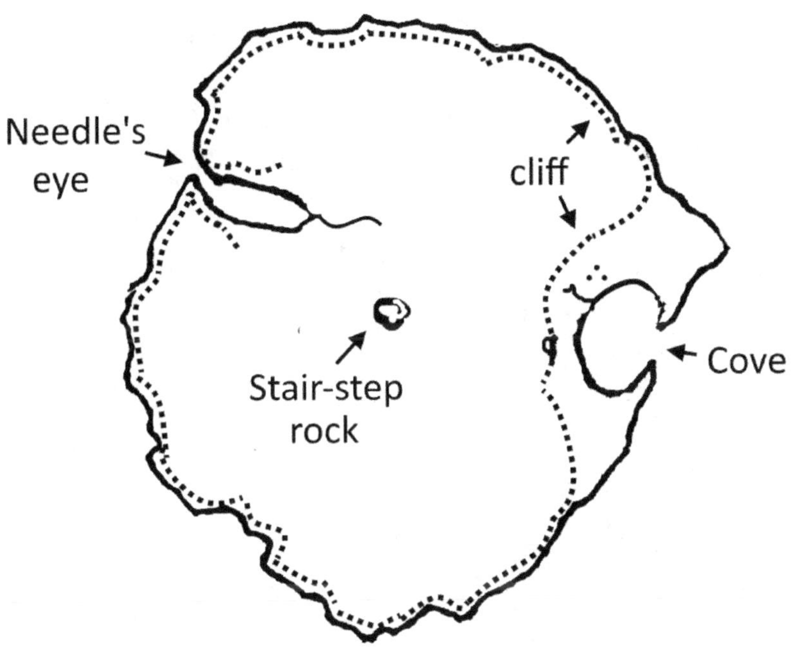

CONTENTS

Chapter 1

Shadows Of The Past

He was walking through Wotana's marketplace, moving among the stalls and booths until he came to the one that belonged to the blacksmith. And there she was... looking just as he remembered her, her yellow blouse a splash of color, her dark brown hair stirring in the breeze that blew in from the sea.

In his dream, he called to her. "Aramei!"

She turned towards him as he approached, but her clear gray eyes immediately grew clouded. "Nagaro? Why have ye come back?"

"I wanted to talk to you."

She frowned, and shook her pretty head, her dark hair dancing on her shoulders. "No. It isn't right for ye to talk to *me*. Ye should talk to *her*. To your *wife!*"

"She's not my wife! It wasn't a proper marriage—"

"*She* thought it was!"

And the blacksmith's stall was fading, disappearing into mist. Aramei was there, still, standing in front of it, but she was backing away from him, her eyes accusing.

He tried to follow her, but now there seemed to be things in the way, unidentified things that held him back, dragging at him. He couldn't reach her...

"Aramei, wait!" he cried. "I didn't *want* to marry her!"

But she was gone, and he was pushing his way through branches. Branches with thorns that caught at his clothing. There were roses... deep pink roses... their scent enveloped him, poignant and sweet.

Or it would have been sweet, except that he couldn't breathe...

He staggered free of the clawing thorns, and a marble bench appeared in front of him. Gasping, he sank down onto the cold, hard stone.

There came a new female voice, speaking right beside him.

"Why did you leave me?"

He turned to look at the young woman, who was sitting next to him. It was the princess. She was also just as he remembered. Her eyes were as green as an ocean wave with the sun behind it, her hair the color of dark honey. Her perfect eyebrows were knitted together in a frown.

"Why did you leave me?" She asked again.

"I... I'm sorry, Nevien," he stammered. "I didn't mean to—"

"Yes you did!" she said, with the gentle severity she sometimes used. "You ran away."

"I *had* to! They were hurting me!"

"But you left me to *him!*" Now *she* was accusing. "To Gillard. And *he* is hurting *me! Look!*" She extended her arms, the palms of her hands turned upwards, and there were bruises and red welts from her wrists to her elbows.

"No!" He recoiled in horror.

It couldn't be. They wouldn't do that. Not to her!

The image of her tortured arms seemed to fill his vision. He tried to stand up, but found he couldn't. He wanted to back away but suddenly he couldn't move.

Her face was right in front of him, tear stained, pleading. "*Why did you run away?* All you ever did was run away!"

"I was trying to die! I was *supposed* to die—"

"*Then why didn't you?*" She spat the words at him, her face contorted with an anger he had never seen there before.

He tried to speak, to answer her, but something was stopping his voice in his throat. And even if he could have spoken, what could he have said? He didn't know what had happened that night... after he had drunk the wine.

Why didn't you die?

The accusing question echoed in his mind, and he wanted to scream that he didn't know, but no sound came from his throat. He was floating, helplessly immobile, and darkness was beginning to press upon him. He struggled desperately against the terribly familiar paralysis. He tried to sit up, to move, to speak—

His own strangled cry jerked him awake, and the dream instantly evaporated.

He let out his breath in a ragged sigh of relief to find that he was awake and lying in a tangle of blankets on the narrow straw mattress of his bed, in the room he shared with Taru and Pavo on the upper floor of the Bay Tree Inn, in the town of Pakoa on the island of the same name.

Rough-hewn rafters supported the roof above him. The plastered walls around him were painted a faded yellow. The unvarnished wood planks of the floor were softened by three small wool rugs—one dark brown, one tan, and one that had probably once matched the walls but was now a kind of yellowish gray. The room was dry and clean and smelled of nothing worse than cedar, old wool, and wood smoke. The faint glow coming from the single curtained window suggested it was early morning. The sound of steadily dripping water indicated that it was either raining— again— or had been very recently.

Nagaro gave a low groan and sat up. He'd been sweating. His sheets were damp. But now he felt cold and the memory of the dream's disquieting images still lingered.

It could have been worse, he told himself. The previous night he'd dreamed that he had tried to fight Gillard Marchent, the Princess Nevien's current husband, with his sword—only to find that he couldn't move. He'd awakened just as the other man's blade was about to pierce his chest, with his heart pounding so hard it had frightened him.

The dreams were ridiculous, really. Just because Gillard had been sadistically unkind to *him* didn't mean the man would mistreat his wife. Gillard and Nevien had been married for a year and a half now, and Nagaro had heard nothing to support such fears. It was one thing, after all, to make sport of a youth who everyone had taken for the simpleminded bastard child of a disgraced noblewoman, and quite another to physically abuse the daughter of the current king and queen. And it was absurd to think that King Elgurn would ever try to manipulate his beloved daughter by injecting the will-controlling drug heskial into her veins with a bladder-thorn.

Just because the king had been willing to do that to him... to force him into a marriage against his will...

Nagaro hastily jerked his thoughts back from the precipice. The guilt that made him offer excuses to Nevien in his dreams was misplaced. He had nothing to apologize for. He'd been in terrible danger, completely helpless. Running away had been the only reasonable course— even if he didn't know how he'd been able to do it without dying... how the heskial's hold on him had been broken... *how he had survived having it withdrawn and had escaped from the palace of Lankura where the drug had been used to keep him enslaved...* Nagaro shuddered and shook himself. *Enough of that.*

But he knew he wasn't going to be able to sleep any more.

So he got up, wrapping the gray wool blanket around his shoulders against the morning chill. The bedroom was one of the largest the inn had, which meant it accommodated three narrow beds and three chests of drawers, spaced around the walls, and still had room enough in the middle for a table and three chairs. It also had a fireplace.

He approached the hearth and poked among the ashes of the previous night's fire. There wasn't an ember to be found, of course, so he went to the window, drew aside the faded yellow curtain, and looked out. It was indeed raining— a steady fine rain. There wasn't enough light yet to make out more than the general presence of the harbor beyond the branches of the huge, ancient bay tree that gave the inn its name.

Nagaro sighed. His thoughts crept back to the earlier part of the dream, the part concerning Aramei. The blacksmith's daughter had never even known about his marriage to the princess— let alone the circumstances surrounding it. Taking an interest in Aramei had been a mistake at a time when he couldn't remember his past. But while he wished he'd explained it to her better, the full truth wasn't something that he could tell, and he doubted she would care anymore, anyway. He couldn't even say he missed her—

His ruminations were interrupted by a rustle of blankets behind him, followed by the soft sound of bare feet on the floorboards.

Taru came to stand beside him, similarly blanket-wrapped. The young Turo peered hard at him, as if trying to read his face by the dim light. "Nagaro?" he said, questioningly. "Did ye have another dream?"

Grudgingly, Nagaro nodded. There was no use denying it.

"I don't like this." Taru sounded genuinely worried. "How many is that? Half a dozen since we moved off the ship?"

"I haven't been counting."

It was more than that, but Nagaro was in no mood to say so. His sleep had been troubled more and more frequently since he'd been spending his nights on dry land. During the voyage northward from the Mahuk Baar to Pakoa— after he and his fellow slaves had stolen a war galley and won their freedom— his dreams had been fleeting and forgotten upon waking. And before that? Of what does a slave dream? Nagaro knew: A slave dreams about the misery of his bondage, and despairs upon waking to find the dream is no different from reality. Or he dreams of freedom, and wakens to despair when he finds the dream a lie.

For a year and a half, neither Aramei nor Nevien had troubled his sleep. Now they both did so frequently, along with other things. It was as if his mind had picked up a thread it had dropped eighteen months before, when the Mautep had taken him and Taru captive on the shores of Wotana Bay. Perhaps it was because he now spent so much of his waking time thinking about what he was going to do, now that he was free. And every way his thoughts turned, they seemed to come up against his past.

"I don't like it," Taru said again. "It's getting to be just like... that *other* time. Back in Wotana."

Nagaro glanced quickly at the third bed to be sure that Pavo was sleeping. "No, it isn't," he said emphatically. "Those dreams were memories trying to come back. These are just ordinary dreams. They're full of things that never happened, all jumbled together."

"If they're just ordinary dreams, why were ye thrashing about and groaning?"

Nagaro scowled. "I didn't say they were *good* dreams."

"What was this one about, anyway?" Taru demanded.

Nagaro sighed. "It started with my telling Aramei I didn't want to marry Nevien, and ended with my telling Nevien that I don't know why I didn't die— *neither* of which ever happened."

"Aramei *and* the princess? Again? I tell ye, Nagaro, ye need t' find a woman!"

Nagaro turned back to the window to hide his annoyance. He should have expected that, and he didn't wish to start the argument again. It wasn't that Taru was wrong, it was just that it was beside the point. And of course Taru had a simple solution to the problem of finding a woman, whereas for Nagaro there was nothing simple about it whatsoever.

"If ye'd just come t' the tavern with me—" Taru began.

"*No!*"

Pavo turned over noisily at the other end of the room, and Nagaro glanced significantly in the direction of the young Hashtep. "I'm going to get dressed and go down to the common room," he said, carefully keeping his tone light. "You can join me there if you like, but I don't want to hear anything more about tavern women."

Taru gave him a hard look. "I'm coming with ye," he said pointedly.

Nagaro shrugged. "All right."

So they both set about getting dressed. Nagaro splashed his face with water from the basin that stood on his dresser and dried it hurriedly with a towel from a hook on the wall. The tiny square of mirror nailed to the wall above the dresser showed him a black-bearded young man with skin turned brown from kuma stain. The first thing he'd bought in Pakoa had been several months' supply of kuma ointment. He'd arranged to buy some even before they'd left the ship. Kuma was cheap and plentiful on Pakoa, since it was one of the island's chief exports, and the limited Kelorin population of the island used it heavily in the summer to avoid sunburn. Nagaro's decision to apply some at this late season had caused a few raised eyebrows among the former slaves, but no one had been inclined to be openly critical.

Together with his close-cropped beard and his hair tied at the nape of the neck, Turo-fashion, the kuma stain completed Nagaro's disguise. Few if any of the inhabitants of Pakoa had ever been to Lankura, and it was unlikely they'd ever set eyes on the missing idiot prince, Leyel Virden, but still he preferred to take no chances. For all that most of the townspeople knew, brown was his natural skin color.

Nagaro pulled on the pants and boots he had acquired from the Mautep when he and the other slaves had seized the war galley they'd been forced to row. He still chose to use these things, because they suited him. He'd bought two plain white cotton shirts, one of which he now donned, as well as a dark brown *tirka*, which he put on over the shirt. The latter was a sleeveless outer garment, thigh-length, opening at the front, and belted at the waist. He'd also bought another pair of pants— also dark brown— and a hooded cloak of gray wool for the cold weather. It was all the kind of solid, practical clothing he'd been accustomed to wear before his life had been turned upside down by an offer to wed the princess. It was an offer he'd had the temerity to turn down. Unfortunately, King Elgurn hadn't taken "no" for an answer.

Nagaro had simply chosen clothes he was comfortable in, but his choices had turned out to be the kind of clothing worn by Pakoa's more prosperous merchants and shopkeepers, most of whom were either Kelorin, or Turowans trying to look like Kelorin. Since Nagaro's appearance was more in the nature of a Kelorin trying to look like a Turo, he would have drawn stares on the street even if he hadn't also been the central figure in the much-told tale of the former slaves' miraculous escape. Taru and Pavo had also purchased clothing of a kind that made them comfortable. In their case, however, this meant fisherman's garb. Since there was nothing incongruous about this in Pakoa Town, both the young Turo and the young Hashtep now blended easily with the local populace.

Once Nagaro and Taru were dressed, they left the room, closing the door quietly behind them so as not to waken their friend Pavo.

In the hall, they encountered Simion. The Kelorin youth had been standing at the far end of the hallway, apparently looking out of the window at the head of the stairs, but when the two friends appeared, he turned and came quickly down the hall towards them. Nagaro gave Simion a friendly smile and a greeting as he always did, and received an answering greeting and a quick, shy smile in return. Taru looked away and stepped aside to give Simion a wide berth as they passed. The young Kelorin continued on down the hall and disappeared into a room at the far end of it.

"He manages t' be here every morning when ye come out," Taru muttered under his breath. "He gets up at the break o' dawn and waits for ye."

Nagaro was startled. "What do you mean, he *waits* for me?"

Taru gave him a sidelong look. "If I come out *after* ye've already gone, I never see him. But if I'm *with* ye, I see him every time. And what's he doing in that room at the end o' the hall, I'd like t' know?"

Nagaro frowned in annoyance. Simion had very often passed him in the hall in the morning, but why did Taru have to try to make something of it? After all, Simion slept on the second floor, too, in a tiny gable room a few doors down, facing the stable yard.

"The room at the end of the hall is the innkeeper's study, Taru," he said patiently. "Simion is helping him with the bookkeeping. Ramu says Simion is very good with figures, and he's very glad of the help."

"Bookkeeping? At this hour o' the morning?"

"I don't see why not."

Taru stopped at the head of the stairs and turned on his friend. "Are ye being blind on purpose?" he demanded. Then he lowered his voice. "Simion's always hanging about up here, when he knows ye're in, and finding ways t' get a word from ye, here, and a smile, there. And folk are starting t' talk! They were already startin' to wonder about ye, 'cause ye don't go to the tavern, and ye're not courting any o' the women in town. And now, anyone can *see* that crossy boy's in love with ye! Pretty soon they'll be thinking ye're as crossed as he is!"

Nagaro felt his face grow hot, and at the same time he felt a twist in his stomach. His first thought was to hope Taru was wrong about Simion's infatuation— though he had reason to fear his friend was right, based on Simeon's behavior while they were slaves. His second thought was that it wasn't *right* that his efforts to be minimally decent to Simion should be so misconstrued. Anger flared in him, and he turned Taru a dark scowl.

"*First,*" he said hotly, "Simion is not a *boy*. He's as much a man as you or I. *Second,* Vothra teaches that it's wrong to shun a man just because he's different. And *third,* if everyone else would just try to treat Simion like a human being, what I'm doing would be so commonplace that no one would get excited about it!" Then he turned away from Taru, who was looking stunned and hurt, and went on down the stairs, treading rather more heavily than was absolutely necessary.

***

The Bay Tree Inn's common room, with its rows of tables and stools, ran half the length of the inn's ground floor. Its fieldstone walls supported massive hewn beams and a plaster ceiling, and the floor was of well-worn planking. A row of windows along one long wall looked out onto a porch, beyond which lay the street and the harbor— a very pleasant view in fair weather. On this morning the scene was still very gray. Outside of the windows at the farther end of the room, the shadowy form of the great bay tree interrupted the grayness with its huge black trunk and overhanging branches.

Nagaro found the room deserted when he entered, although the innkeeper and his wife were clearly already astir since he could see that a fire was burning brightly in the fireplace at the opposite end of the room.

Nagaro strode between the two long rows of tables and approached the large stone fireplace. It was six feet wide and it pierced the thick stone wall between the common room and the kitchen so that the fire, and any pots hanging over it on hooks, were accessible from both rooms at once. On this morning, a kettle of sothiril hung there beside two cooking pots. The larger of the pots held porridge, bubbling vigorously, while the other contained a steaming brew of sliced apples in a syrup of sugar and cinnamon. The aroma of the stewed fruit made his mouth water.

Nagaro pulled up a stool and sat down. He frowned at the bubbling porridge.

Taru, who had entered the room behind him, approached a little warily. "Nagaro...?" He pulled up another stool and sat down, as well.

For a moment Nagaro continued to glower, but then he sighed and relaxed his brow. "I'm sorry, Taru," he said. "It's not your fault the world isn't a better place." He rubbed his forehead. "That dream I had put me out of sorts, and then you told me something I really didn't want to hear on top of it." Absently, he reached for the spoon protruding from the pot in front of him and began to stir the porridge.

Taru edged his stool a bit closer and lowered his voice. "Can't ye just tell him to stop hanging about?"

Nagaro's frown returned. "I don't see him 'hanging about,' Taru. Passing me in the hall and saying good morning is hardly a crime. And he never says anything else."

"At least ye can stop smiling at him, and—"

"And *what?* Start treating him like everyone else does?" Nagaro gave his friend a sharp look. "He isn't made of wood. He has feelings."

"Aye! It's his *feelings* that's the problem—"

Taru might have said more, but he was interrupted by the appearance of the innkeeper's wife. A short plump Turowan woman with her graying dark hair in a long braid, she'd been moving about at the other end of the kitchen and must have heard their voices, if not their words.

"Ah!" she exclaimed, as her broad, cheerful face came into view on the far side of the fire. "A very good morning t' ye, Tor Nagaro and Tor Taru!"

They both looked up guiltily. "Good morning, Tira Yuli," they responded, very nearly in unison.

"Here now! Ye stop that stirring, Tor Nagaro!" Yuli spoke with mock severity, leaning over and taking the spoon from his hand. "Haven't I told ye times enough already that ye're a paying guest, not hired help? It'll be time enough t' be stirrin' the porridge when ye run out o' rins!"

Nagaro sighed. "I'm sorry, Zirdyn—ah, Yuli. I keep forgetting."

"D'ye want t' know what else he *forgot* and did yesterday?" Taru put in archly.

Nagaro frowned at him. "Taru—" he began, warningly.

But the young Turo ignored him. "He mucked out the stable, Yuli. The whole thing! I guess he 'forgot' it's supposed t' be Habu's task."

The innkeeper's wife took a step back from the fire, and drew herself up to her full height— all of five feet two inches— as she regarded Nagaro through the arch of the fireplace. "Tell me ye didn't!"

Nagaro was too honest for the jest. "It wasn't much work," he said. "There are only two horses, and they were standing in water because some rain had got in. It's not good for horses to stand in water. They'll get foot-rot."

Yuli's expression turned genuinely severe, but her wrath was not for Nagaro. She put her hands on her hips. "And *where*," she demanded, "was that love-sick son o' mine?"

Nagaro looked uncomfortable. "Well... ah... chopping wood, I think."

"Aye," put in Taru gleefully. "Habu was chopping wood when Nagaro went out for his ride after lunch, and when he got back two hours later, Habu was still chopping—"

"And it was going to be dark in another hour, so I mucked out the stable," Nagaro finished quickly.

Yuli rolled her eyes. "That's my Habu," she sighed. "Stops after each chop t' stare at nothin' and dream about his 'sweet Sulani.' Ah well, I'll have a word with him. And I'll tell Ramu t' take three rins off your tab for the week, Tor Nagaro." She turned and bustled off across the kitchen, looking back over her shoulder to say, "Help yourselves t' some breakfast. There's dishes on the table."

So they helped themselves to large steaming bowls of porridge with spoonfuls of stewed apples on top, and mugs of hot sothiril tea, and went to sit at one of the tables near the window to eat their morning meal.

Nagaro frowned over his porridge as he stirred it to mix in the apples and cinnamon. "I don't feel good about getting Habu into trouble like that, just because he's in love with a girl."

Taru only shrugged. "He's in trouble most o' the time, anyway, Nagaro. If it hadn't been the stable, it would ha' been something else." He gave his attention to the porridge, but after several spoonfuls he paused to say, "I don't know ye're so bothered about not dying when they stopped giving ye that bloody drug, Nagaro. It seems t' me it must ha' just been that Spirit o' the White Flower, or whatever it was, that Vothra told ye about in the dream back in Wotana. It must ha' used its spirit magic t' help ye."

Nagaro had begun to eat, but his spoon came to a halt halfway between bowl and mouth. "Well..." he said slowly, "there surely must have been spirit magic in the... the heskial..."

He found it hard to talk out loud in detail about how he'd been drugged, even though the events were now more than two years ago. The passage of time had blunted his feelings somewhat, but the memories were still acutely painful. He paused to gather himself and to consider how to say what he wanted to say. At length he continued. "But there was a... a *how*, and a *why*, and a *who*— to the way it was..." he grimaced "...*administered*."

He paused again to shake the memory of the bladder-thorns from his mind, covering his discomfort by eating a spoonful of porridge, before saying, with an effort, "Dreigen... was the *who*— the one who made me drink the drug, or... or put it into my blood. He was working for King Elgurn, and they both had *reasons* for what they did." He swallowed. "The Spirit of the White Flower— or whatever it was that took my memories away for a year and gave them back again— surely had spirit magic in it, too. But there probably was also a *person* behind it... a person who somehow set it to working on me. And that person must have had a *reason* for doing it." He sighed. "And *none* of that helps me understand why I didn't die!"

Taru looked skeptical. "Maybe Dreigen was lying when he said ye'd die—" he began.

"He wasn't!" Nagaro's glance stabbed at his friend. "Dreigen and Bron *meant* to kill my Lady Maramine by withholding the heskial. They were showing me how it worked!" His mind shied away from the memory, but he managed to add, "They both believed it!"

"All right, all right!" Taru gestured with his spoon as if warding off a sword thrust, and applied himself again to his porridge. After another moment's thought, however, he said, "Maybe ye're just stronger 'n most folk. Ye were hardly sick at all with the plague compared t' the rest of us."

Nagaro frowned. The subject of the conversation was spoiling his appetite. "That's *true*..." he said, "but what bothers me most is that I can't remember what happened that last night in Lankura, when the Mautep attacked the palace. I hoped it would come back to me in time, but it's been a year and a half since I remembered all the rest of it, and the end is still missing!" He poked at a piece of stewed apple. "Something was different about that night. Every other time I tried to run away when the... heskial... started to wear off, the pain and the shaking hit me in a few minutes and just got steadily worse. But that *last* night, I somehow got all the way from Lankura to Wotana Bay. That's nearly twenty miles! And I was in a fever, too. There was never any fever any of the other times."

Taru had finished his porridge and now picked up his mug of sothiril. "What's the last thing ye *do* remember about that night in the palace?" he said. "Tell me again."

Nagaro shivered. "All right." He shut his eyes as he let his mind run back to that fateful time. "I was sitting with Nevien at the little table in her room," he began. "It was after dinner, and it must have been the night

I escaped because I was wearing that horrible purple shirt I had on when you found me near your father's house. She gave me some wine to drink. And I had to drink it, too— because she... she *insisted.* I remember putting down the empty glass, and half a minute later it was as if a light exploded in my head! I jumped up... grabbed my head... I think I knocked the chair over because I heard something fall. And that's *all!* There's the confused dream about running through the forest, but I don't remember anything else *clearly* until I woke up in your parents' house on Wotana Bay." He opened his eyes, frowning.

Taru frowned with him. "It sounds like there was something in the wine."

Nagaro heaved a sigh. "There *could* have been. Or maybe it was just the wine by *itself.* Or the wine mixed with the... *heskial...* Dreigen didn't want me to drink wine..." Nagaro swallowed, his throat suddenly dry. *Had Dreigen not wanted a drunken puppet, or had there been more to it?* "He gave me explicit instructions to turn down any offer of wine— which no one thought was strange because they thought I was keeping the Vothrin ban. The trouble was, I *also* had instructions to do whatever Nevien told me..."

His voice trailed. That part was particularly hard to talk about. He swallowed again and wet his lips. "It was one instruction warring with the other. Nevien had to really push me *hard...*" He stopped again, unwilling to relate more of that so-called conversation.

She'd insisted that it would make him more relaxed for what was to follow... for when they were supposed to lie together... He'd been given no instruction... no words... with which to answer such an argument.

Taru was swirling his sothiril thoughtfully. "Who poured the wine?"

Glad to redirect his line of thought, Nagaro frowned harder as he replayed the memory in his mind. "She did," he said at length. "And she had her back to me when she did it." He shook his head. "But Nevien didn't know about the drug! And the bottle came up from the kitchen with the cork already out of it—"

"So anyone in the kitchen or anywhere in between could ha' tampered with it." Taru blew a puff of air through his lips, then shrugged. "I don't know. Maybe ye were just drunk, Nagaro. Some men can't remember anything they did when they're drunk."

"I only drank one glass."

"Ye mean ye only *remember* drinking one glass. How do ye know she didn't give ye more after that, and ye just don't remember it?"

Nagaro had to admit that he couldn't be sure.

For a moment Taru stared thoughtfully into his mug. Then he raised his eyes. "Maybe if ye drank some wine *now* it'd help ye remember," he suggested. "Ye know... sort o' shake something loose?"

"Do you really think so...?" Nagaro found the idea both intriguing and disquieting.

"Well, aye," Taru said. "I think it could. It'd be like what we did that one time by goin' into the forest in the dark, ye remember? I'd say it's worth a try."

Nagaro chewed his lower lip uncomfortably. "It would mean breaking the ban."

"Aye, but ye said yourself the ban's only advice."

"Well... *ye-es...*"

It was true. Vothra's admonition to avoid fermented drink, and other things that "dimmed the light of reason," was not a rigid prohibition. Nagaro didn't really like Taru's idea, but he had to concede that it had some merit. He was trying to think if there was any valid argument against it when they were interrupted by the arrival of some of the inn's other guests— all former galley slaves from the Mahuk war galley, the *Fist of Death*— including their roommate Pavo Maat.

Chapter 2

Trouble At The Bay Tree Inn

Pavo quickly joined Nagaro and Taru with his bowl and cup. "Why you did not wake me?" he asked in his imperfect Common Speech as he sat down beside Nagaro.

"Ah, well..." Taru tried to sound casual. "It was early. We thought ye could use the sleep."

Pavo's narrow dark eyes flicked from Taru's face to Nagaro's and back again. "It is all right," he said very seriously. "I know sometime you two have thing you want to talk about."

Taru looked flustered, but Nagaro laughed. "Yes we did, Pavo," he said. "But I think we've talked about it enough."

Taru quickly recovered himself. "Are ye going t' be *sitting* with one o' your three sweethearts tonight, Pavo?" he inquired archly.

Pavo considered the young Turo through the narrow slits of his eyes, his spoon halfway to his mouth. "I do not have *three* sweet-heart," he said.

"But ye *have* been sitting with three different girls," Taru observed innocently. "At least ye *say* ye've just been sitting..." he added with more than a hint of insinuation.

Pavo swallowed his mouthful of porridge and pointed his spoon at Taru accusingly. "You are sometime not nice man, Taru," he declared. "Now you pretend Hashtep woman are not good woman. You maybe want them be like Turowan woman, who lie with man for money?"

Taru dismissed this with a shrug. "Only the tavern women do that, and if a woman's willing t' lie with a man for a few rins, and a man's got the money, what's the harm of it?"

Pavo shot a significant glance at Nagaro, knowing that his Kelorin friend shared his disapproval of tavern women. Nagaro, however, had no wish to revisit an old argument. "Are you going to see Tenepti tonight?" he asked. "I know she's the one you've chosen. Taru knows it too," he added with a quick, sharp glance at his other friend. "He just likes to tease. We both know you're not sitting with the other two anymore."

Pavo ignored Taru's wicked grin. "Yes, I am going to sit with Tenepti," he said, and his expression turned somber. "But I am afraid tonight be last time."

"But *why*, Pavo?" Nagaro asked in surprise. "I thought you really liked her."

Pavo nodded. "Yes. I like Tenepti very much." A wistful note crept into his voice. "She have most kind heart. And she smile like sunshine after rain. And she like me too," he added. "But now her father say she is too young to be married. He tell me come back— after two year."

"But that's ridiculous!" Taru's playful teasing instantly vanished in the face of such obvious injustice. "Why'd he ever let ye sit with her in the first place, then, if he's going t' tell ye she can't marry for two years?"

Nagaro was frowning. "How old *is* she, Pavo?"

"She is just have sixteen year."

"Well, that *is* young," Nagaro conceded. "But Taru's right. Her father shouldn't have let you sit and talk with her if he won't let you marry her for so long."

Pavo's face clouded. "I do not think he want me to marry her *ever*," he said quietly. "I think he say two year so that I will think it be too long, and I go to marry someone else."

"But why would he do that, Pavo?" Nagaro asked. "What has he got against you?"

Pavo turned his dark gaze to meet Nagaro's. "I was born in Mahuk Baar. When I speak Hashti, it is sound a little bit different. I pray to Sheptuum in little bit different way. Shupti father, he not mind. But Tenepti father, he do not like it."

"Well *bodjer* Tenepti's father then!" Taru had acquired a few choice words from listening to the old sea warrior Landros, whom he much admired. "Go marry Shupti! It'll serve Tenepti's father right if his daughter ends up with some weedy Pakoa boy, instead of a fine strong fellow like you!"

Pavo turned back to Taru. "Thank you for saying such nice thing," he said earnestly. "But I do not *want* to marry Shupti. I want to marry only Tenepti." He turned back to Nagaro. "What you think I should do?"

"Tell her father you'll wait." Nagaro said promptly. "If she's the one you want, don't let him get rid of you so easily. Maybe he'll change his mind when he sees how much you care for her."

Pavo's brow wrinkled in thought for a moment, then he nodded. "Like father of Minowei in story that Taru tell. I keep coming back, like Nevrath."

"That's not going to work," Taru protested. "It's just a story! *Real* people don't act like that."

Nagaro shook his head. "It's not just a story, Taru. It's history. Nevrath, Minowei, and her father, Takuma, were real people."

"Well, *ordinary* people don't act like that—"

Abruptly a raised voice cut across Taru's words. "Take yer bloody breakfast someplace else, ye little crossy! We're all men at this table!"

The voice belonged to the former merchant seaman named Moraga, and it was loud enough to stop every conversation in the room. Everyone turned to look.

The "table of men" in question was the table next to the one where the three friends were seated. Nagaro saw that Simion had intended to take an empty stool on the far side of it. The choice would have placed him closest to Mendorel, a middle-aged Kelorin, though still several feet away, and even farther from Moraga who was sitting across from Mendorel. Nagaro also noticed that Simion's chosen seat would have afforded the youth a clear view of *him* while being behind Taru's back, but he did his best to push that thought aside.

Simion's face wore a cringe of pain. He cast about for another place to sit, but he found nothing but hostile looks.

"Here now, Moraga!" Mendorel spoke reprovingly. "Ye've no cause to be so rude to him. Why, if he hadn't stepped between us and that Mautep warrior back at Jaamra, we might both be lying under the earth on Chitaopa with Potero and Hasaad. We both owe him for that!"

Moraga spat. "I don't need help from any bloody crossy boy! Who asked him to, anyway?"

"I did."

Nagaro had risen, and had spoken in a firm, level voice, ignoring Taru's frantic miming for him to be silent. Simion was also shaking his head at him, and mouthing "no," but Nagaro plunged ahead. "When Urchak's men came at us at the rail, I told Simion to look out for you and the other untrained men. He was the closest one who could have offered you that protection."

Moraga stood up also, and turned to face Nagaro. "Maybe I don't *want* protection from the likes o' him!"

Nagaro sighed. "You have plenty of courage, Moraga," he said earnestly. "But courage wouldn't have saved you from that Mautep. He was very skilled, and you have no training. Simion, on the other hand, is a trained Fleet warrior. It just made sense."

"Oh, he's a *fine* Fleet warrior." Gurd, a former Fleet man himself, spoke derisively from farther along the table. "'Except he can't finish a man!" The young Leithian was looking hard at Nagaro. "Truth is, I've never seen a crossed man what *could... Unless I'm lookin' at one right now!*"

The silence that followed the young Leithian's words stretched, taut as a drumhead.

Nearly all of the former slaves who were staying at the inn were in the room by this time, except for the two Fleet officers, Tredhold and Landros, and every eye was on Nagaro.

Simion was standing, frozen, wearing a look of desperate anguish.

Nagaro resisted his first impulse, which was to utter a heated denial. *It shouldn't matter so much*, he thought. *It shouldn't matter at all.*

It was Moraga who broke the silence. "Aye, now," he drawled. "Nagaro's still wearin' that ring what Roheed gave t' him. Seems t' me he was always a bit too friendly wi' that Mautep boy. Seemed they was both lookin' out for each other. What were ye doing there on Chitaopa, Nagaro, when ye went off where none of us could see?"

And now Nagaro had to resist the urge to look down at his left hand. The ring was still there, he knew, though he hadn't thought about it for weeks. Everyone surely knew what Roheed had said about it on the deck of the ship— that the ring had belonged to the slave woman, Emril, who had raised him, and that Roheed had wanted Nagaro to try to return it to her family. But what the men *believed* might be something else.

Moraga was waiting for his explanation, but Nagaro felt his anger rising at the very idea that he should have to explain any of it. When he spoke at last, his voice was hard and cold.

"What I do when you're not there to see, Moraga, is none of your affair!"

With that, he picked up his bowl and cup, turned, and strode deliberately past the silent men, making for the double doors that led out of the common room and onto the inn's covered porch. Shouldering the doors aside, he stepped out into the chill, damp morning. Behind him the room broke into a clamor of voices that was cut off as the doors swung to.

***

Nagaro stood on the porch outside the closed door for a long moment, seething.

It was still early, and there were only a few folk passing on the street or along the wharf in front of the inn. Several tables stood under the shelter of the roof that covered the porch. They were unoccupied except for one at the far end, where Habu sat with a bowl and a spoon and a faraway look in his eye. The innkeeper's son didn't even seem to have noticed Nagaro's arrival.

Nagaro drew a long breath. The rain had stopped, though water still dripped from the eaves and the air was cold and raw. There was a break in the clouds to the east, however, and a shaft of brilliant sunlight angled through it to strike glittering highlights from the surface of the harbor. The long, lean hull of the *Fist of Death* rode at anchor, there amid the glory, surrounded by Pakoa's fishing fleet like a single hawk in a flock of sparrows. Nagaro scowled at the ship, but in spite of his anger he found his thoughts inevitably going where they so often went when he beheld the captured Mahuk war galley.

Out onto the sea...

In moments of unbridled fancy, he imagined training a crew and sailing forth in that ship to attack other Mahuk warships. He could see himself striding through oar decks with his sword in his hand, cutting the hated leather cuffs, using his gift for swordsmanship to set slaves free. It was a wild fantasy that he had shared with no one, not even Taru. He knew that he and his fellow slaves had escaped from lives of hopeless misery and the fear of sudden death only by the whim of Lokundas. Even if many of the men didn't have lives and families to return to, he couldn't ask them to risk death or a return to bondage for nothing more than a wild hope of helping others who were less fortunate.

There was a ship in the harbor, and a sword under his bed, and neither one of them was doing him any good at all.

Nagaro wrenched his thoughts away and angrily dropped onto a stool at the nearest table, facing the water. He set down his dishes and began mechanically to spoon cold porridge into his mouth and wash it down with lukewarm sothiril while outrage still churned inside of him.

He didn't even look up when the door opened and Taru and Pavo quietly came to join him at the table. They sat down across from him and waited, while Nagaro ate, and the silence stretched between them.

Finally Taru could no longer contain himself. "What in the name of Hakura Kili did ye do *that* for, Nagaro?"

Nagaro shrugged without looking at his friend. "I don't have to explain myself to Moraga, or anyone else," he said tightly.

"But they're all going t' think that ye wouldn't answer him because ye're crossed! Couldn't ye just have said ye're not?"

Nagaro shot Taru a sharp glance. "What does it matter what I say, when they'll believe whatever they want?"

At this, Taru unexpectedly turned thoughtful. "There's some truth t' that," he said carefully. "Words do come cheap, they say. But actions are hard t' argue with."

Nagaro turned a smoldering gaze upon him. "What are you trying to say, Taru?"

It was Pavo who answered. "I think he mean you should try sitting with woman, Nagaro. So everybody see you are kind of man that like woman."

Nagaro felt his anger ebbing in the face of Pavo's simple earnestness. "You might actually be right," he conceded.

The truth was, he really didn't want everyone to think he was a crossed man, and not just because it wasn't true. After all, some day he'd find a woman who was right for him and there would be no more doubt. No, the problem was that he'd seen the abuse that was aimed at Simion by men like Moraga and Gurd. If Moraga could show Simion such ingratitude, Nagaro doubted that having doctored the men on Chitaopa or leading them to freedom would be enough in the long run to save him from the same treatment. And Moraga had influence with many of the others.

He shifted uncomfortably on his stool. "What happened after I left?" he asked.

Taru shrugged. "Simion bolted for the kitchen t' eat his breakfast. Yuli'll see that no one troubles him there. The kitchen's her place, and she likes Simion."

"Oh. Good." Nagaro smiled fleetingly at the mental image of Yuli fending off Moraga with a porridge spoon.

There was a little silence. Then Pavo asked, "Have you not see woman you want to sit with, Nagaro?"

Nagaro shook his head. In fact, the custom known as "sitting" rather put him off. It seemed to be a general custom on Pakoa rather than one belonging specifically to any of the three races on the island. A man who was interested in getting to know a particular young woman was expected to go first to her father and arrange to "sit" with her. The actual sitting was done on the front porch of the family dwelling— in full view of the neighbors and of any passers-by. It was also in full view of at least one of the young woman's parents who would be watching through the front window. In seasons when the sun set early, a lighted lantern was hung directly above the heads of the sitting couple to underscore the fact that privacy was definitely *not* intended. Taru's teasing insinuation that Pavo might have been doing anything other than sitting with his sweetheart was patently absurd.

When Taru had learned about the custom, he'd been thoroughly depressed and disgruntled for the better part of a week— until he'd discovered the existence of tavern women. Since then, his general practice was to express disdain for "sitting" at every opportunity. Pavo, on the other hand, had merely shrugged his broad shoulders and set about systematically going up and down the streets of the Hashtep quarter, observing from a discrete distance. Once he had identified the three most pleasing prospects, he'd arranged to sit with each one in turn, and thus had found Tenepti— only to be frustrated now, most unfairly, by her father's prejudice against him for having been born in the Mahuk Baar instead of on Pakoa.

Nagaro, alone among the three friends, had made no progress whatsoever with finding female companionship. He absolutely refused to avail himself of the tavern women, despite Taru's coaxing. And, while he certainly had no objection to observing proprieties, he was uncomfortable with the fact that there was no acceptable way to discover whether a young woman wanted to sit with *him,* short of arranging a sitting in order to find out whether she was more inclined to smile at him or spit in his eye.

Pavo was regarding Nagaro sympathetically. "It must be hard for you," he said. "Because there are very small number of Kelorin woman in this place."

In fact it was anybody's guess whether there were more Hashtep or Kelorin on Pakoa. The Hashtep were, however, all clustered at the island's southern end, in and around the town, whereas the Kelorin were scattered up and down the length of the island.

Nagaro shrugged. "She wouldn't have to be Kelorin," he said. "She could be a Turowa or a Hashtep if only she wanted to sit with me. But of course her father might not allow it," he added, with a commiserating glance at Pavo.

"Well, that's the sticky spot, isn't it?" said Taru, scratching his ear. "Folk don't see ye quite as one thing or the other, Nagaro. Ye're a bit too Kelorin-looking for the Turo, and ye've made yourself too Turowan-looking for the Kelorin."

Nagaro stared at his friend. "Is *that* why folk don't talk to me?" The tale of the slaves' escape had been told and re-told dozens of times since the *Fist* had sailed into Pakoa Harbor, with the result that Nagaro was embarrassingly famous in the town. He had supposed that his fame made him seem unapproachable and that this explained why so many of the townsfolk were polite but distant. It hadn't occurred to him that the ambiguity of his appearance might be to blame.

Taru was looking uncomfortable. "Well... *aye*... I'm afraid it is," he said. "Most folk like to keep t' their own kind. But I've been making a few inquiries—"

"You've been doing *what?*" Nagaro bridled.

Taru raised apologetic hands. "Just asking around some, that's all," he said hurriedly. "And... well... there's this woman named Panila. She's mostly Turowan, and her father's a Turo, but she's got some Kelorin blood on her mother's side so it stands t' reason her father wouldn't mind mixing in a bit more."

Nagaro was suspicious. "She's not one of the wanton ones you're always looking for, is she?"

"No, no! Not a bit! She's very proper. A very nice woman. Older, too..."

Nagaro frowned. "How much older? Not that I mind, but... I mean, is she older than *me*?"

"Oh, no. Not older than you. I don't think..." Taru shifted in his seat. "Ah... would ye like me t' arrange a sitting for ye?"

"Shouldn't I do it myself?" Nagaro wondered.

"No, no, ye can let me take care of it," Taru assured him hastily. "It'll be fine. Trust me."

They all sat in silence. Nagaro wasn't sure if he should let Taru handle this, but he didn't much look forward to doing it himself, either. *It's quite likely to turn out to be a disaster, either way*, he thought. *And all for the sake of appearances.*

At that moment, the door opened behind them, and Yuli emerged. She immediately approached their table and stepped around it to face Nagaro. "That was a fine thing ye did, Tor Nagaro," she declared. "Standin' up for Simion like that." She bent down and added in a conspiratorial voice, "Even if ye did let your own cat out the door, so t' speak. I want ye t' know that I don't think any the less of ye."

Nagaro stared at her with a sinking feeling in his stomach. "Yuli," he said, hollowly, "I'm not crossed."

Her eyes went wide. "Oh dear! I *do* beg your pardon, Tor Nagaro! I thought *surely*..." She wrung her hands. "Oh, I do *so* beg your pardon!"

Nagaro sighed. "It's all right, Yuli," he said gloomily. "Taru was just telling me that everyone probably thinks I am. I guess I really made a mess of this."

"Oh, now, 'taint as bad as all that." Yuli was clearly doing her best, now, to sound reassuring. "I'm sure it'll blow past. I know I'd never have thought it, if Simion hadn't told me what ye said." She patted his arm in a motherly way, and started to gather up his dishes.

Nagaro groaned. "Simion is repeating it?"

"I don't expect he's the only one," Taru said. Then he leaned closer and dropped his voice. "I'll just be setting up that sitting, shall I?"

Nagaro sighed. "I guess you'd better, but I—"

Yuli's voice interrupted him. "Now what's that lazy lump of a son o' mine doing still sitting out here?" She had apparently just noticed Habu.

The youth was indeed still sitting at the other end of the porch, staring straight ahead with a slack jaw and a vacant expression.

Yuli seemed to grow taller. "*Ha*bu!" She cried, in a voice that was completely impossible to ignore. "Get yourself up *this instant* and get t' work! Honestly, anyone 'd think ye hadn't a brain in your head, sittin' there lookin' like Leyel Virden!"

Habu jumped up as if he'd been kicked, dropping his spoon as he gave his mother a terrified glance before exiting the porch at a run.

Nagaro stiffened. “Yuli,” he said sharply, “You shouldn’t talk that way!”

Taru put a hand on his arm. “*Nagaro—*” he murmured.

But Yuli only shook her head as she stood watching her son’s retreat. “Oh, I know,” she sighed. “He’s not a bad lad, really. Always was a bit of a dreamer like his father, o’ course, but it was never this bad ‘til he got so stuck on Sulani.”

Nagaro was on his feet, shaking with anger. “That’s *not* what I meant, Yuli! You shouldn’t use that name! *You have no idea—*” He broke off, biting his lip at the sight of Yuli’s shocked face.

What had he imagined he was going to say?

Taru was tugging at his arm, trying not to be too obvious about it. “*Nagaro!*” he muttered urgently through his teeth.

Nagaro turned away from both of them. “I’m sorry...” he mumbled. He didn’t trust himself to say more. As it was, his voice shook. He felt he had to escape, before something inside of him just burst. Turning away, he strode from the porch, heading in the direction opposite to the one Habu had taken— around the end of the inn, making for the stable.

On the porch, Yuli stared after Nagaro’s retreating figure. “What did I say?” she asked in a stricken voice.

Pavo’s usually placid face wore an expression of mingled distress and bafflement. He looked questioningly at Taru.

Taru cast about, at a loss. “Nothing! I– I mean... I don’t know.” he licked nervous lips. “I’m sure it’s nothing, Yuli. He’s had a bad morning, that’s all.” Further words eluded him, and he muttered, “*Oh, bodjer it! I’d best go after him.*”

***

The stable yard was a rectangle of muddy gravel, flanked by arms of the inn on two sides and on a third side by the small stable and a pair of sheds for storing hay and firewood. The fourth side was separated from the road by a low wall with a gate that stood open at this time of day.

Nagaro was in the act of saddling the younger and livelier of the inn’s two horses. His hands jerked angrily as he cinched up the saddle girth, and the dainty sorrel mare swung her head around to eye him reproachfully. He glanced up when he heard Taru’s boots crunch on the gravel. “I’m going for a ride,” he announced, rather unnecessarily.

“Nagaro, ye can’t do things like... like what ye just did!” Taru voiced his exasperation.

Nagaro made no response. His gaze was focused on his hands, which were engaged in adjusting the stirrup leathers.

But Taru was not going to drop the matter. "I mean it, Nagaro! Ye can't just go stomping off looking like thunder every time somebody mentions Leyel Virden!"

Nagaro's hands stopped moving. "It wasn't just the *name*, Taru," he said through clenched teeth. "It was the way she used it! She has *no* idea who or what Leyel really was!"

"I know that! But it's gotten t' be just something people *say*. I've heard other folk say things like that. Ye're going t' hear more of it, so ye've got to learn t' let it go past your ear! What was I supposed t' tell Yuli?"

Nagaro turned around to face his friend— and stopped dead, staring past Taru, a look of horror growing on his face.

Taru spun around and saw instantly what the trouble was.

Pavo had followed him into the stable yard.

The young Hastep was standing a few paces away, still wearing that worried, baffled look. "What is wrong, Nagaro?" he inquired uncertainly. "Who is man with name Leyel Virden? Is it someone you know?"

Taru sagged as he turned back to face Nagaro. "Ye'd best explain it to him," he said wearily. "If he's going t' be our friend— if he's going t' keep sharing a room with us— it'd be a lot easier if he knew."

Nagaro tried to swallow. His mouth was suddenly very dry, his anger forgotten. *Taru was right, of course.*

Nagaro liked Pavo. When they'd needed a third man to share the room, the choice had been obvious. More than that, he trusted the young Hashtep. Pavo was honest, loyal, and good-hearted. And, other than Chaheel who also came from the Mahuk Baar, Pavo was possibly the only person in the whole country of Edrovir who could hear the story of Leyel Virden entirely without prejudice. The name meant absolutely nothing to him.

That should have made it easier, but it by no means made it easy enough.

"You tell him, Taru," Nagaro said brokenly. "I can't..." He drew a shuddering breath. "And neither of you is to tell *anyone* else! Unless I say it's all right. Do you understand?"

He looked from Taru to Pavo and back again. Both of the other young men nodded agreement. Taru was obviously relieved, Pavo still puzzled but willing to keep a friend's secret even if he didn't yet know what it was.

Nagaro's shoulders drooped. "I'm sorry..." he murmured. "Sorry to be like this. I just have to be alone for a while."

With that, he turned away and put his foot into the stirrup. Swinging lightly into the saddle, he gathered the reins and squeezed the mare with his knees, urging her into a gallop. Horse and rider exited the stable yard in a spray of gravel.

Taru looked at the still-baffled Pavo and heaved a sigh. "Come on then," he said. "There's a bench 'round the other side o' the stable. We can sit there and talk, and no one 'll hear us."

So it was that Taru told Pavo the tale of Nagaro's history, as best he could. It wasn't easy, but Pavo was good at understanding stories, even very strange ones. He asked a few earnest, halting questions, but mostly he just listened.

When Taru had finished, Pavo nodded solemnly. "So," he said. "Nagaro is this person with name Leyel Virden."

"He *was*. But not anymore. Now he's just Nagaro."

"And this is why he do not want to go to Lankura? He think somebody there will know him? King, or somebody else who do this bad thing to him with bad magic that make him look like stupid person?"

"He couldn't possibly go back to Lankura!" Taru was emphatic. "It'd be much too dangerous. Those men 'd surely kill him if they caught him again."

"And Nagaro is prince?"

"No, he's not a prince." Taru paused. "I mean... I suppose he would have been *called* a prince, because he was married to the princess. But he's not *really* a prince."

Pavo's brow furrowed. "Nagaro talk to Roheed like one prince talk to another."

"Well, don't tell *him* that. Nagaro doesn't want anything t' do with being a prince."

Pavo continued to look thoughtful. "I think Nagaro is very good man."

Taru was surprised. "Why?"

Pavo shrugged. "He do not want to be rich, like prince. He is kind to Simion when nobody else do it. He talk to me like friend when he first come to oar deck."

Taru snorted. "Nagaro treats everybody like that— like they're no better or worse than he is."

Pavo nodded wisely. "Yes," he said. "That is what I mean."

Chapter 3

Pakoa's By-Ways

Nagaro rode blindly through the town and took the Hill Road, up to the top of the ridge at the town's northern edge, and down into the patchwork of farmers' fields on the other side. He was still steaming as he turned the mare onto another road that swung east to intersect the coast once more. Arriving at last at the island's eastern shore, on a familiar stretch of windswept beach, he gave the sorrel mare her head. His anger finally ran its course in the wild, pounding gallop that followed, along the hard wet sand at the edge of the sea.

When the mare had run her course as well, she slowed, dropping briefly to a jolting trot before coming to a halt, snorting and blowing.

Nagaro leaned forward to stroke her neck. "Thank you for that run, Lady Cinnamon," he said. "Have you forgiven me, then, for being rough with you in the stable yard?"

Cinnamon tossed her head up and down as if in affirmative answer.

Nagaro sighed and leaned back in the saddle, content for the moment to let the mare breathe while he surveyed his surroundings. If he'd hoped to draw peace from that landscape, however, he was disappointed. The weather was as unsettled as his thoughts, the gray-green sea as restless as his heart. The wind that whipped his unbound hair was chasing great mountains of white and purple cloud across the sky, while in front of him the waves crashed and rolled, spreading lacy aprons of foam across the sand. Ragged patches of alternating sunlight and cloud-shadow moved over land and sea.

He was at that moment alone on the stretch of beach. To his right lay a headland that marked the entrance to Pakoa Harbor and became one with the range of low rolling hills that sheltered the town. To his left, the beach curved away, eventually disappearing around another jutting shoulder of land.

At length he heaved another sigh and picked up the reins. Nudging the mare with his knees, he rode back across the sand and through the beach grass to the road. He pulled the mare to a halt there for a moment, then turned her head to the right. He might as well continue to Obedo's house, since he was halfway there already. He could give the fisherman his share of the proceeds from the recent sale of a bundle of silk drawn from amongst the plunder of the *Fist of Death*. If Obedo was out in his boat, the fisherman's wife would surely take the money, and she would also likely offer him something to eat for his lunch. The prospect was much more appealing than returning to the town and facing the common room full of former slaves.

As he rode, he ran through the litany of his troubles. Upsetting Yuli was surely the least of them, although he was sorry he'd done it. Taru was right as usual: There was no sense in getting angry at Yuli for repeating what she heard others say. He would just have to get used to the fact that what had once been his name had become a synonym for "idiot." Those who truly deserved his anger were beyond his reach, and it was best not to think about them. The kind of anger their memory kindled in his soul frankly frightened him.

The unfortunate incident in the common room was a much more immediate concern. Nagaro frowned as the scene replayed itself in his mind. He was not very happy with Taru's solution, though he saw the necessity of it. He winced to think what was being said about him at the Bay Tree Inn at that very moment.

At least Taru's plan didn't involve tavern women.

Nagaro had ideas about how things ought to unfold between a man and a woman, ideas that came from stories like the one Taru had once told of Nevrath and Minowei. A man's and a woman's paths would cross, their lives intertwine, and love would blossom. That was how things were supposed to go. The difficulty, of course, was taking the right path and finding the right woman. He'd been telling himself he had plenty of time. He was only twenty, after all, but Pavo's rapid success in finding Tenepti, as well as Taru's talk of the charms of the tavern women and the stirring of his own blood, had lately combined to give him an increasing sense of urgency. Some of his dreams involving Aramei and Nevien had been much more intimate than the one that had awakened him that morning—although no more satisfactory in their resolution.

The debacle in the common room was pushing him along Pavo's path. He'd be taking his chances, "sitting" with this woman named Panila. Nagaro supposed it was possible that she might turn out to be someone he could love, but he had no particular reason to expect it. And what would he do if he didn't like her? He certainly wasn't going to keep sitting with a woman he didn't care for just for the sake of appearances. Would he have to pick another one at random?

As the road took him past a fisherman's hut, he noticed a woman standing in the open doorway, her face turned towards him. She was Turowan and she looked young, but she quickly withdrew into the house when she saw him looking her way and the door was closed by the time he came abreast of it. He'd seen such behavior before, both in the town and out of it. If a young woman lingered to watch him, he'd hear the mother call her daughter to come inside. He had supposed it was a matter of propriety— until hearing what Taru had said about people's reaction to his appearance. That revelation hurt. His appearance was his disguise and he had no intention of changing it. It made him feel safe, for one thing, and besides that, appearances shouldn't matter. It shouldn't make any difference whether he was Kelorin or Turo or a little of both.

He heaved a sigh. His thoughts were exacerbating a feeling that had been growing in him throughout the weeks that he had been on the island— a growing sense of *otherness*, of not belonging in this place. The feeling was a sum of many things. Things like riding. It had taken him only days to discover that the town's single inn had two horses for hire and he'd rapidly become acquainted with both of them. The older one was a stolid flea-bitten gray mare named Sugar, and the younger was Cinnamon. Within a week, he'd ridden every road on the island. Within two weeks he'd covered all of the more accessible farmers' tracks and goat paths as well. But as far as he could tell, he was the only person on the entire island of Pakoa who ever thought of riding a horse for pleasure.

Or there was reading. He missed it, so he'd sought all over the town for books that he might buy— and found none. Just an aged copy of the Book of Vothra in a shop window where it was obviously meant for window-dressing. It appeared that very few folk on the island even knew how to read. Pakoa was a trading port, after a fashion. Perhaps as many as a dozen merchant ships might stop there each year during the months of clement weather. And the sheltered harbor was also visited at irregular intervals by ships of the Royal Fleet of Edrovir under Lord Kuran Kel. Yet the place was scarcely more cosmopolitan than Taru's little village of Wotana.

Nagaro reined in the mare at the top of a rise, and looked to his left where a purple-black thunder head was massing above the rocky ridge that formed the island's spine. The misty gray shadow under it spoke of rain, and the wind was carrying it his way. Hurriedly, he squeezed Cinnamon into a long easy canter that carried them down the slope toward a cluster of fishermen's huts among which Obedo dwelt. He arrived just ahead of the downpour and left the mare sheltered under the eaves in the lee of the fisherman's house while he sought refuge inside.

Obedo came in soon after, drenched and dripping. The fisherman was indeed glad of the money Nagaro had brought. Being a recently escaped galley slave, he had missed most of the summer's fishing season. The two men waited out the rain together, eating a hearty soup of fish and potatoes while Obedo's two little children played on the floor at their feet. Obedo's wife kept offering Nagaro another bowl. The woman seemed almost in awe of him, which he didn't like, but had no idea how to counter.

"Have ye decided what ye'll do come spring?" Obedo inquired after the soup was finished and the rain had stopped and Nagaro was preparing to leave.

Nagaro shrugged. "Not yet." He tried not to let it sound as if it mattered.

"Well, ye know ye're always welcome t' come fish with me. Don't ye forget that." There was sincerity in the man's voice and in his broad brown face.

Nagaro thanked Obedo for the offer with some feeling, and thanked Obedo's wife for the soup. He looked past the fisherman to where the man's five-year-old daughter sat in a momentary shaft of sunlight, playing at string figures with a loop of fishing line strung between her fingers. He caught himself thinking it was too bad Obedo wasn't an older man with a grown daughter. He liked to think the fisherman would have let him sit with his daughter if she were of marrying age and agreeable to the idea.

Nagaro rode away from the fisherman's house through a world that was newly rain-washed and glistening. When the clouds broke and the sun came through, everything sparkled as if encrusted with diamonds. Ordinarily such a sight would have captured his eye and lifted his heart, but on this day he scarcely noticed it. All he could think about was Obedo's question: the same one he had asked himself over and over these past several weeks.

What was he going to do when spring came?

He didn't have to stay on Pakoa, not if he had the price of a passage on one of the merchant ships that would call at the harbor during the spring and summer. But where in Edrovir would he go?

He pulled Cinnamon to a halt once more when he topped the rise, and sat for a moment gazing out over the sea in the direction of the mainland. On a clear day it would have been visible from this vantage point as a long, low, blue-gray shape on the horizon. Today it was lost in the shadow of the retreating storm.

Nagaro sighed again and urged the mare forward. At the bottom of the next slope, he turned off of the road onto a narrow cart track that ran between a series of small farms on one side, and a plantation of kuma bushes on the other. He knew exactly where he was going. The track wound about and ultimately connected with the main inland road, which would take him back to the town.

Pakoa was roughly ten miles long from north to south and about half that in width at its widest point. It had a rocky spine running along near its western edge, and gently undulating hills that sloped gradually to the sea on its eastern side. Fishermen's huts dotted its shores. Its lower slopes were a patchwork quilt of farms and kuma plantations, while the higher, steeper ground was used to pasture little silken-haired goats called *givadi*. The island had ironwood trees whose wood was used for carving things, both useful and decorative, and there were large and small lumps of ice-green jade that could be taken from the rocky coves along the wave-battered western shore by men hardy enough to dive for them. The kuma mills, where the nuts were turned into ointment, were clustered just south of the town, on Pakoa Harbor. The economy of the island could be summed up very simply: Kuma stain, ironwood, and jade were its only exports. Its other products were for local consumption.

All of this Nagaro had learned in a few short weeks, and in the same time he'd gone from reveling in his newly won freedom to feeling like a wild deer in a fenced game park. He felt guilty about this resentment. He knew he should be grateful to be alive, free of his chains, and safe from those who had sought to do him harm, but he couldn't put aside the thoughts of what he'd lost. The dream that had been his at seventeen, the plan he and Taru had shared— to go to Lankura to join the Royal Fleet— had fallen in ruins with the return of his memory. He couldn't possibly go to Lankura.

When Nagaro had suggested that Taru go to Lankkura without him, his friend had instantly dismissed the idea. All his life the young Turo had expected to be a fisherman and so he now embraced his fate without deep regret. Taru also seemed quite content to pursue that fate on Pakoa rather than in Wotana. Pakoa had tavern women. Wotana had only painful memories of a mother and father murdered by sea raiders from the Mahuk Baar. Pavo was also content to find his future as a fisherman on Pakoa. This was entirely natural. If the young Hashtep couldn't find a place here in Pakoa's unique Hashtep enclave, there wasn't likely to be any other place for him in Edrovir.

Of the three roommates, it was only Nagaro who found this course unsatisfactory.

He was pulled abruptly from his thoughts when Cinnamon slowed of her own accord as they approached a roadside trough beside a grove of ironwood trees. He dismounted to let the mare drink. The trough was filled by water diverted from a little stream that flowed out of the grove and along beside the track for a little way. The stream served the local human population as a source of drinking water, and the trough was provided so livestock wouldn't foul the stream by standing in it to slake their thirst.

Nagaro idly ran his hand through the mare's coppery mane as she drank. Cinnamon raised her dripping muzzle and turned her head to regard him with a liquid brown eye. He stroked her head. "Ah, you are indeed a beauty, my lady," he said aloud, in the earnest, gentle , voice he always used when he spoke to horses.

"Good day t' ye, Tor Nagaro."

Nagaro started, and turned at the sound of the woman's voice, heavy with suggestion.

The owner of the voice stood just on the other side of the stream. She was a young Turowan with an earthenware water jug balanced on one shoulder, and she must have either emerged from the grove or have come around the end of it, for he'd seen no sign of her when he approached. She stood with her hips aslant and her shoulders back. The posture made her tightly-laced bodice seem scarcely able to contain her ample breasts.

"Good day, Zirdyn." He answered for the sake of courtesy, though he didn't find her behavior appealing. Curiosity then prompted him to ask, "How is it you know my name?"

"Oh," she said, with a flutter of eyelashes, "Tor Obedo has told everyone *all* about ye."

"He has?" Nagaro was dismayed to think that he might be as well known at the north end of the island as he was at the south end. "He probably exaggerated," he added. He wanted to be on his way, but the mare had lowered her head again to drink some more.

"Well, I'm sure I wouldn't know," she said in a tone that plainly said she didn't care. She bent to set down her water jug, taking her time about straightening up again. Nagaro couldn't help noticing that the drawstring neck of her blouse was rather loose.

"Are ye makin' for the upland road, then?" she inquired with an ingratiating smile.

"Yes." Nagaro shifted uncomfortably, increasingly anxious to end the conversation. Unfortunately, the mare was still drinking.

The young woman took a step forward so that her hips swung from one slant to the other. "I know a *better* way t' get there," she said, with another flourish of eyelashes. "Come with me an' I'll show ye."

At this point, Cinnamon finally raised her head and snorted wetly. Relieved, Nagaro moved quickly to gather the reins, set his foot in the stirrup, and swing astride. Turning, he looked down at the young woman, who was staring at him with mingled surprise and annoyance.

"No thank you, Zirdyn," he said as politely as he could. "The way I know suits me well enough."

As he rode away along the cart track, the young woman raised her voice to fling her words after him. "Ye think ye're so fine, Tor Nagaro?

Better 'n the likes o' me? Where's your '*lady*' then, that I heard ye talkin' to?"

Nagaro's face burned. The young woman had overheard him talking to his horse and had thought he was imagining talking to a woman! She would surely have laughed at him if she'd known the truth.

In due course, the cart track brought him to the upland road and he turned the mare's head to the left, back towards Pakoa Town. He rode on through the blustery afternoon, between goat pastures on either side. It seemed unfair when he thought about it. The young woman by the stream had been the first woman under the age of thirty who had spoken more than two words to him since he'd come to Pakoa. But she wasn't the kind of woman he was looking for at all. She was more the sort Taru always hoped to find— one who would lie with a man behind the woodshed without feeling any need to do any sitting on porches beforehand. She might not care what he looked like, but neither did she care what was in his heart.

As he approached Pakoa Harbor, Nagaro reflected bitterly that Simion might be the only person on the entire island who was prepared to offer him the love of his heart— a love Nagaro could in no way return and unfortunately did not want.

***

As he rode into Pakoa Town by way of a narrow unpaved back street, a fresh mountain of storm-clouds was gathering behind him, looming above the rooftops and visibly advancing before the wind. Folk passing in the street glanced at the sky and hurried for cover.

The street was flanked by small one-story houses built of wooden planks and fieldstones, separated by narrow yards enclosed by low walls or split-rail fences. In one of the fenced yards, a young Kelorin woman was snatching at the last garment pinned to a line strung between the house and an ancient apple tree. The shirt twisted and flapped in the gusting wind, briefly eluding her grasp. At last she caught it and added it to the bundle of laundry in her arms, just as the first large raindrops came plopping down. She immediately dashed for the door of the house, pausing under the sheltering eaves to scan the sky and the yard. For an instant, her gaze met Nagaro's before she turned to flee into her mother's kitchen.

Nagaro had reined Cinnamon to a halt at first sight of the young woman, but as he watched, the door of the house swung shut behind the girl. And Lokundas, the Turner of Worlds, apparently decided to add further insult, for the rain promptly began pelting down, peppering the cobblestones and splashing craters in the mud of the fenced yard. Nagaro muttered an oath and urged the mare forward again, pulling his hood up to shield his head from the downpour. As he passed the house, he deliberately kept his eyes straight ahead and didn't turn to look at the front window.

Cinnamon's hooves splashed on the wet paving stones as she rounded a corner into a wider street. Pakoa Town was nearly twice the size of Wotana, and its population was more diverse, both in occupation and in wealth. The outskirts were inhabited by fishermen and laborers, while the street Nagaro had just turned into housed the next tier of society: tradesmen and shopkeepers. Nagaro rode along the street, hunching over his reins and squinting at the buildings he was passing. Presently he bent lower still and guided the mare through a curtain of rainwater pouring from the edge of a wood-shingle roof. He drew rein on the other side of the small waterfall, under a sturdy timber shop-awning. There he dismounted and looped the mare's reins over a convenient hitching rail.

"Here you are, Lady Cinnamon," he said, stroking her rain-slick neck. "A nice sheltered place out of the wet. We'll just pass a little time here 'til this shower moves on."

He hadn't chosen the refuge at random. The shop he had stopped at was the one where he'd seen the book in the window. It was still there, a thick volume with faded gold lettering on the cover. The shop sold cloth, thread, and the like. He pushed open the door, causing a bell to jingle. The interior was dimly lit by a pair of dusty oil lamps and crowded with tables bearing bolts of fabric. Nagaro pushed his hood back and adjusted his wet cloak.

"How may I be helping ye, Zirda?" inquired the shopkeeper, a spare, stooped Kelorin in his mid-fifties who appeared miraculously from among his wares. "It's Tor Nagaro, isn't it? What would such a man as ye be wanting in my shop?"

Nagaro winced inside at being recognized yet again, but nodded in acknowledgment. "I noticed the book in the window. Might I look at it?"

The shopkeeper appeared taken aback, but he smiled ingratiatingly. "I don't see why not. Never say no to a customer, eh?" So saying, the man fetched the object from the window, wiped the dust off of it with a rag, and handed it over.

Nagaro received it reverently, lightly touching the words "*Book of Vothra*" tooled into the worn leather cover.

The shopkeeper cleared his throat. "Just wanted t' hold it, eh, Zirda? Ye've not seen one so fine afore, I'll wager. I put it in the window t' show what a fine shop I keep. That's the *first* Book of Vothra, though it doesn't say so. If it were the second, it'd say 'second,' ye see."

Nagaro shot the man a sharp look. “Yes, I know.” It seemed to him that he was being talked down to by a man who was clearly not in the habit of reading the book himself, judging by the amount of dust it had collected. The book was not such a fine specimen, either, compared to the one in the Lady Maramine’s collection. On impulse he opened it to the first page of text and read aloud, letting the familiar words roll smoothly from his tongue:

“The All That Is, is a circle, or like unto a circle in that it returns unto itself. I know not of a certainty that it is all that there is, but I have not to this time discovered any means or path of passing out from it into some other place. Nor can I perceive anywhere the existence of anything other than what I have called The All.”

He ceased reading and closed the book, raising his eyes to the shopkeeper’s stunned face. “How much do you want for it?”

The man swallowed visibly. “Well now, Zirda, ye see... I, ah, never really meant t’ *sell* it. But, seein’ as it’s *ye* that wants it, Tor Nagaro, what saved all those men, I suppose I could see my way t’ partin’ with it. Though I’m not sure how much t’ charge.”

Nagaro winced again. This was more of the hero treatment he’d seen so much of since his arrival on Pakoa. He supposed he deserved it this time. He *had* been showing off with the reading. *Or was the man just flattering him?* “I expect you’ll want to replace it,” he said quickly. “I’ll gladly pay you what it would it cost to get another.”

The shopkeeper made a show of considering. “Counting the cost o’ shipping t’ the island, Zirda, I expect I could get one for thirty rins,” he said at last.

Thirty rins! It was extravagant, and Nagaro had no idea whether it was a fair price. Still, he wanted the book, and it was hard to abandon a path after having come so far along it. “Very well,” he said, and the gleam in the shopkeeper’s eye told him he could have talked the price down if he’d tried haggling.

He walked out of the shop feeling a bit foolish and distinctly poorer. The leather-bound volume under his arm was wrapped in a piece of stout wool fabric the shopkeeper had supplied at no additional cost. The man had probably been salving his conscience.

The rain had subsided to a drizzle, though the eaves still dripped. Rainwater ran in rivulets among the cobbles, pooling in the low spots to form puddles that mirrored a lead-gray sky. Nagaro mounted Cinnamon and rode on along the street, picking a path that avoided the worst of the puddles. He hadn’t thought to bring a saddlebag, but he found he could manage the reins with his right hand while carrying the precious book in the crook of his left arm, under the shelter of his cloak. The streets were very nearly empty now, owing to the weather.

As he approached the harbor, the streets grew wider and the buildings larger, until he reached Front Street. It was the town's main east-west thoroughfare, a broad avenue running between the harbor quays on one side and a row of two-story dwellings on the other. The houses made up what was known as Merchants' Row. They housed some of Pakoa's most prosperous citizens, including the handful of merchants who made their living from the island's import and export trade.

The drizzle had completely stopped by this time, though the clouds had yet to blow over. Everything was sodden or slick, and the rain-fresh breeze warred with the salt air from the adjacent harbor. Nagaro drew rein when he came abreast of the house belonging to the Kelorin merchant with whom he dealt, Tor Gedras. He wondered if Gedras had any news for him. It was only two days since he'd last made inquiry, and little was likely to have changed, yet a sale could potentially happen at any time, and his own purse was lighter than he would have liked after his recent purchase.

The former slaves had left the captured Mahuk ship and taken up lodgings ashore only two weeks ago, prior to which they'd slept aboard the *Fist of Death* while eating the last of the ship's rations. Despite being in possession of considerable worldly goods in the form of the ship's assorted booty, they'd found themselves facing an awkward lack of negotiable currency. It had taken some time to find buyers in this backwater for enough of their trove to provide all the men with silver trokins and copper rins enough to serve their immediate needs for food, clothing, and shelter. The merchant Gedras had been instrumental in this process.

It was Landros who had brought Gedras to Nagaro's attention. The former Fleet second mate had known of the merchant because Lord Kuran, the Lord of the Royal Fleet of Edrovir, routinely did business with Gedras when the Fleet was in Pakoa Harbor and in need of provisions. Nagaro had been alarmed when Landros had performed the introduction and promptly stepped aside with the jaunty declaration that business was "captains' work," leaving Nagaro to deal with the details. The relationship had quickly become comfortable, however, owing in large part to the fact that Gedras had treated Nagaro with respect right from the start. Other folk on the island might be judging him by his appearance, but Gedras at least didn't seem to.

It was this fact as much as anything else that made up Nagaro's mind as he sat astride Cinnamon in front of the merchant's door. It had been a difficult day, and he badly needed something to lift his spirits.

Accordingly, he dismounted, secured the mare's reins to the ornate brass hitching post, and knocked at the impressive oak door. A moment later, the merchant's elderly servant took his cloak and ushered him through the entry hall into the wood-paneled study where Gedras conducted his business. The servant offered to hold the book Nagaro still carried, but Nagaro preferred not to be parted from it and declined.

The study was a sizeable room. It was tastefully furnished with leather-upholstered chairs, a pair of bookcases laden with bound ledgers, and a large elegant oak desk. A Jinari carpet, in tones of rust and gold, took pride of place in front of a fireplace where a fire burned to ward off the chill. On this overcast day, the two oil lamps mounted on the wall flanking the door were lit to supplement the light from the single tall window and the smaller lamp on the merchant's desk. The air smelled of leather and furniture polish.

Gedras was seated behind the desk when Nagaro entered. He was a middle-aged Kelorin, tall and thin with very narrow features and sleek black hair just beginning to gray. A pair of spectacles— a rare sight on Pakoa— perched on his high-bridged nose. He was dapperly dressed in a crisp white shirt and a formal tirka of deep burgundy that matched his britches. He rose as Nagaro approached, and reached across the desk to shake his visitor's hand.

"Please, Tor Nagaro, sit down." The merchant indicated one of the high-backed chairs before returning to his own seat. "What brings you here on such a wretchedly wet day?"

Nagaro sat down, placing the book in his lap. "I was out riding, and happened to come back this way. I wondered if you'd had any luck selling the rest of the iron fittings."

Gedras' face registered regret. "Unfortunately not. Neither of our smiths can yet be persuaded. The one pleads lack of funds— which to my mind is an excuse. The other, Tor Dakuro, expresses a reluctance to handle iron that was used to enslave men. While I can't quarrel with the sentiment, it seems a poor reason to let good iron go to waste."

Nagaro sighed. "At least he's honest. The other man may well feel the same way but doesn't wish to say so."

Gedras peered archly over his glasses. "That is my thought, as well. I'm making inquiries about the leather— without going into any details regarding exactly what it was used for. I have a harness-maker who has expressed interest in seeing a sample of it. There may be some hope there."

Nagaro chewed his lip. "It's rather thick and stiff for harness. I've thought it might make good shoe soles."

"Shoe soles? Ah, indeed." Gedras's lips curved in a satisfied smile. "Let me make a note of that." He dipped his pen and scratched a few words on a bit of loose paper among the ledgers on the desktop. "Is there anything else I can help you with?"

"No, thank you, Tor Gedras."

Since he had nothing more to say, Nagaro rose to go. As he juggled his purchased book in order to shake the merchant's hand again, the cloth came partly unwrapped.

Gedras quickly reached across the desk to help him with it. "What's that you have there? The Book of Vothra? How did you come by *that* riding around Pakoa in the rain?"

Sheepishly, Nagaro described his encounter with the shopkeeper. "I wanted it so much I just paid him what he asked. I miss having something to read— even if I've read it all before."

The merchant regarded him sympathetically. "Pakoa folk aren't very literate, I'm afraid," he said. "But I wish you'd said something. I can get books from the mainland if you just tell me your preference. I'm sure I can do better with the price, too."

"Thank you, Tor Gedras, I'll keep that in mind." Nagaro was thinking of the cost of his room and the other things he needed, and of the lightness of his purse. "Perhaps I'll make an order in the spring, when the ships come and some more of our goods have been sold."

Gedras smiled faintly. "Of course, Zirda. I understand. Though I would have thought it would be a little late by then, since I expect you'll be leaving in the summer for Lankura."

"Lankura?" Nagaro stiffened. "Why would you say that?" He tried to sound merely curious.

The merchant's eyebrows shot up. "I thought you would be joining the Royal Fleet. Your friend Tor Landros seems to believe you're officer material. He said he was prepared to provide you a letter of introduction to Kuran Kel himself."

"Oh, that." Nagaro relaxed. There was nothing new here. Before the former slaves had left the ship, Landros and Tredhold, the ship's doctor, had taken him aside and made a little speech about helping to get him a place in the Fleet. Gedras's information was merely out of date. "I had to turn the offer down," he explained. "I could never be part of sinking Mahuk war galleys, knowing that all the slaves on board would drown. I told Landros and Tredhold that a month ago."

"Ah, I see." Gedras's brows knit. "I confess I hadn't thought of that."

Nagaro sighed. "Neither had they, as it turned out. Once they *did* think about it, they felt the same way. Now Tredhold is talking about plying his healer's art on shore in Harmoth, and Landros says he'll retire from the sea and go to live with one of his two grown daughters near Lankura."

"Yes, yes. Quite, quite." Gedras was nodding. "Most understandable." He sighed. "Although very regrettable as well."

Nagaro took his leave of the merchant, going out the way he had come. Once outside, he mounted Cinnamon, feeling not the least bit cheered. Being reminded of the offer from Tred and Landros had only deepened his somber mood. It had been hard to say no to the two Fleet officers, though there had been no other choice.

He sighed. *A future he'd once dreamed of had slipped away that day.*

Chapter 4

Jila

It was late afternoon by the time he returned Cinnamon to her stall. The storm had at last blown over, and only a few ragged shreds of cloud still graced the deep blue vault of the sky. Nagaro gave the little mare a thorough rub-down and made sure she had both water and hay, just in case. He was relieved to see that Habu had at least mucked out the stalls this time. Crossing the stable yard, he heard hammering coming from the roof of the inn. He looked up and saw Ramu, the innkeeper, replacing broken slates. He raised a hand and called a greeting, which the innkeeper acknowledged in like manner. It was only as he lowered his gaze that he noticed the face at the gable window high up under the eaves.

Simion was watching him.

Suddenly reminded of the morning's events, Nagaro hurriedly pulled his gaze away and made for the inn's back door— the one that would take him directly to the bottom of the stairs without going through the common room.

Upstairs, he found both Taru and Pavo in the bedroom. The two young men were seated at the table playing a game of *kasadrin,* or King's Men, but they immediately put the board and pieces aside when he entered, and looked at him expectantly.

Nagaro greeted them awkwardly, uncomfortable under their eyes, knowing that Taru had talked to Pavo and that Pavo therefore knew his secret. He set down the wrapped book and reached under the bed for the small chest he used as a cash box. As he did so, his hand brushed a canvas bundle, and he did a mental flinch. The bundle contained the three Jinari scrolls they had found on the *Fist of Death.* He couldn't think about those scrolls without thinking of Dreigen, the king's Lore Master. *The master of the bladder-thorns...*

Hastily he moved his hand to the left, found the cash box, and drew it forth. Then he sat on the edge of his mattress to open it so he could replenish the coins in his nearly empty purse.

"What is it you have that is wrap in cloth?" Pavo asked with what sounded like uncomplicated curiosity.

Just for an instant, Nagaro thought Pavo was referring to the canvas-wrapped scrolls before he remembered that there was another cloth-wrapped object in the room and that this was therefore a safe question. "It's a book," he said quickly, picking up the thing he'd purchased that day. "The First Book of Vothra." He unwrapped it and showed it to them.

"What did ye buy that for?" Taru asked. "I thought ye'd already read it."

"Many passages are worth reading more than once," Nagaro said a little defensively. "Besides, it reminds me of my lady guardian and of home." He got up and put the book into his top dresser drawer, then returned to the bed and the cash box. He lifted out one of several drawstring bags, the one that held silver coins.

Taru cleared his throat. "Do ye want t' know what folk are saying about this morning?"

Nagaro's hands stopped moving, the open cash box and the bag forgotten. He'd hoped to avoid discussing the morning's events. *But he had to know...* "Has word already gotten about, then?" he asked, with a sinking feeling.

"Well, of course it has." Taru tilted his chair back. "Ye're already so famous that it's all over town— though folk don't seem to know quite what t' make of it. Some of our old crew from the *Fist* are in a stew 'cause ye laid hands on them on Chitaopa. But others say they won't get upset 'til they know something for certain. Mendorel says they should all be ashamed o' themselves, seeing as most o' them would ha' died if ye hadn't tended them through the plague."

Pavo had sat silently through this recitation, his eyes flicking back and forth between the faces of his two friends. Nagaro wasn't sure what to make of the young Hashtep's silence, in view of his newly expanded knowledge.

He put the drawstring bag down on the bed absentmindedly. "What about Tred and Landros?" he asked. As grateful as he was for Mendorel's support, it was the opinions of the two former Fleet officers that mattered most to him.

Taru gave him a searching look. "Landros says he knows it's not true 'cause o' the way ye acted when Simion made advances on Chitaopa," he said, and added reproachfully, "Ye never told me about that."

Nagaro returned his friend a hard stare. "I didn't see that I needed to tell anyone. Simion was in a fever, and I don't hold him responsible for it. Besides," he added. "I haven't repeated anything I heard anyone *else* say, either."

Taru started to say something, then caught Pavo grinning at him and closed his mouth. He scowled at the young Hashtep. "It's all right for *you!*" he said darkly. "Ye'd have been talkin' Hashti, and he wouldn't ha' understood a word of it."

"What does Tred think?" Nagaro prompted. He considered Tredhold Ferth to be one of the most sensible men he'd ever met.

"*We-ell...*" Taru looked uncomfortable.

Pavo stepped in. "Tred say he think maybe you are confuse."

"Confused?" Nagaro looked from one of his friends to the other. "Confused about what?"

Taru continued to look uncomfortable and Pavo apparently decided that pursuit of the matter was up to him. "What was that word, Taru?" he asked. "That Tred have talk about? That sound like 'catty-might'?"

"Oh, aye." Taru scratched his ear, sheepishly. "What does catamite mean, Nagaro?"

"What's a catamite?" Nagaro had read about it somewhere. He explained, frowning.

"Oh." Taru looked even more uncomfortable. He glanced at Pavo as if hoping the young Hashtep had more courage.

Pavo regarded Nagaro warily, but continued. "Tred say he think that maybe you were cat-a-mite," he explained, his face carefully expressionless.

"Years ago," Taru put in quickly. "And that ye didn't like it. He didn't say it, but I'm sure he thinks that's why someone had to—" He jabbed suggestively at his forearm with a forefinger.

Nagaro winced at this reminder of the way Dreigen had often put heskial directly into his blood. Tredhold had known about the bladder-thorn scars on his arms at least since Chitaopa... Feeling his thoughts slipping dangerously, he thrust the memory aside to focus on Tredhold's inaccurate guess. "Well, at least I'm safe, if that's what he thinks," he said wryly.

"Ye mean ye'd let him *believe* that?" Taru was aghast.

Nagaro shrugged. "It's no worse than the truth. And if he thinks *that*, he won't be looking for any other explanation."

Taru shook his head. "But ye don't *understand*," he said. "He thinks ye're confused because of it. He says maybe ye're not sure whether ye're crossed or not!"

Nagaro's stomach lurched. "How could I not be sure?" he asked in dismay.

"*I* don't know! That's just what he *said*."

This was not good. Nagaro shifted uneasily. "Who else heard him say that?"

"Well, there was me, and Pavo. And Landros. And Tego."

"*Tego!*" Nagaro's heart sank. "Tego shares a room with Moraga!" He groaned. "And Moraga is bound to make the worst of it." He put a hand to his brow. "What am I going to *do?*"

"Ye're going t' sit with Panila tonight… remember?"

Nagaro's hand jerked away from his forehead. He stared at Taru. "*Bishka!*" He swore in Hashti. "*Tonight?* You've already arranged it?" A knot of apprehension instantly began to tie itself in his stomach. He had more than half hoped the father's answer would be no.

"Oh, aye. I've got it all planned." Taru spoke with forced cheerfulness. "We'll go t' the Red Cask tavern for our dinner, and then—"

"The *tavern*?" Nagaro frowned. "*Why?*"

"Would ye rather eat in the common room downstairs?" Taru demanded.

Nagaro's frown deepened. He dropped his eyes to his hands and noticed Emril's little green-eyed salamander ring on the little finger of his left hand. He slipped it off and picked up a different drawstring bag from the cash box. "I thought maybe we'd have something sent up to the room," he said in a low voice as he tugged open the bag. It contained jewelry and other small gold items from the *Fist of Death* that had been entrusted to his keeping until they could be sold.

Taru dismissed this with a flick of his hand. "*That* makes it look like ye're hiding."

"And going to the tavern *doesn't?*" Nagaro shot Taru a look, then frowned distractedly at the bag in his hands and pulled the string tight.

"There'll be lots o' men at the tavern." Taru explained.

Nagaro looked up in dismay, the bag forgotten.

When Taru caught Nagaro's expression, he added hastily, "Don't worry. There's a back room. Lots o' folk 'll know we're there, but ye won't have to talk to anyone. And we can get ye some wine at the Cask, too, and—"

"*Wine?*" Nagaro had started to open the bag again, remembering that he'd meant to put the ring into it. His fingers jerked involuntarily on the drawstring.

"Well ye said ye wanted to try some t' see if it'd jog your memory, didn't ye?"

"Well, ye-es… But, *tonight?*"

"Why not? I mean, look at ye, Nagaro! The way ye're fussing with that bag!"

Nagaro looked at the bag in his hands. "I was just putting this ring away," he said defensively. He re-opened the bag and dropped the salamander ring into it. Then he pulled the string tight very deliberately and put the bag back into the cash box.

Taru was unimpressed. "Nagaro, ye've got nerves stickin' out all over like loose straw. A glass o' wine'll relax ye for the sitting, and ye may learn something from it besides. We'll catch two fish in one net!"

At this, Pavo spoke up. "I think Taru maybe is right," he said seriously. "Sitting go better if you be more relax."

"*Well...*" Nagaro looked from one encouraging face to the other. Some of the men had ale with their dinners. The changes he'd noticed in their behavior afterwards had never seemed very alarming. They laughed more easily, and they did seem more relaxed. *What harm could it do,* he wondered? And if it shed any light on the mystery of that night in Lankura, it would be worth it. Still, apprehension lingered... "I don't know what might happen," he muttered. "What the wine might *do*."

He glanced at Pavo. He'd detected no difference in the way Pavo had been looking at him since he'd returned from his ride, and there was nothing in Pavo's face now but earnest concern. Nagaro swallowed, deciding to risk a further revelation. "What if I remember something really *bad* from the wine?" he asked. "Or... or... what if the drug *changed* me somehow? The wine on top of that might..."

He couldn't finish. He had a vivid memory of light exploding in his head. And it was after *that* that he had lost his memory.

"Don't worry," Taru said quickly. "I'll be there with ye."

"But... I might not want to sit with Panila afterwards..." *He might not even be in any condition for a sitting.*

Taru had an answer for this, as well. "Ye don't need t' worry about that, Nagaro," he said. "I've told her father ye might come, or ye might not."

This earned the young Turo a deep scowl. "That makes me out to be rather rude, doesn't it?" Nagaro complained. "That I might just... *not come?*"

Taru laughed. "Not a bit! Girls' fathers 'round here are used t' nervous young men." The young Turo glanced pointedly at Pavo.

Pavo looked sheepish. "First time I ask to sit, I get so nervous I do not go," he confessed. "But I ask again, and second time I do it. Shupti father only laugh at me little bit when I ask second time."

"Ye see, Nagaro?" Taru put in. "I *told* ye I've got it all planned. Now, won't ye just trust me?"

Nagaro sighed, and gave in. "Oh, all right," he said. "I guess I might as well try it." He glanced at the open cash box and belatedly remembered that he'd gotten it out to refill his purse. He found the first bag on the bed beside him and took out three silver trokens and several half troken coins to replenish his supply of cash for the next few weeks.

Abruptly, Pavo stood up. "I think I go now," he said.

"You won't come with us then?" Nagaro inquired. He had hoped a little that his other friend might come.

The young Hashtep shook his head. "I am go to talk to Tenepti father, before any other man talk to him."

Taru frowned. "Ye don't think he'd let some other man sit with her? When he's told ye she's too young?"

Pavo's face was carefully impassive. "I hope it is not go to be that way," he said, and turned to go. At the door, he looked back. "Good luck to you, Nagaro," he said.

Nagaro smiled wanly. "Good luck to you too, Pavo."

***

Half an hour later, Nagaro and Taru were seated at a table in the dimly lit back room of the Red Cask tavern. Tor Sodo, the tavern keeper, stood before them. The paunchy, graying Turowan had taken their order for dinner and the request to eat it in the back room easily in stride, but Taru's request for a glass of wine had elicited a worried frown. He hemmed and hawed and finally said, "I'm afraid ye've come at the wrong season for wine, Tor Taru. I'll be gettin' more in w' the first ship in the spring, ye see, but right now there's only a little left o' last season's stock." The tavern keeper mopped at his round face with a corner of his rag and stuck the soggy thing back into his belt.

"But ye *have* got some," Taru persisted.

"Well... I've got a bottle or two o' Southern Borlundian." The man glanced from Taru to Nagaro and back again, gauging their response. "That's top vintage, that is," he added when he saw their blank looks. "I can't sell ye just a glass, either, mind ye. Ye'd have t' take the whole bottle."

Taru shifted in his seat. "How much for a bottle, then?" He was trying to sound confident, but there was a note of uncertainty in his voice.

"*We-ll*, now," Tor Sodo considered. "Ye're a good customer and all, Tor Taru, but I couldn't let it go for less than fifteen rins. I've my business t' think of."

"*Fifteen rins?*" Taru was too stunned to even try to dissemble.

"Aye. I'm afraid that's how it is." The tavern keeper had clearly been expecting this response. "Will ye just be wantin' two mugs o' ale, then?"

Taru looked flustered. "Well, all right... I..." He started to reach uncertainly for his purse.

"Let me take care of it, Taru."

Nagaro had spoken no more than a word or two since the two friends had entered the tavern, and the tavern keeper turned a startled glance upon him. Nagaro reached for his purse and the coins in it clinked together. He pulled out a silver half troken coin and laid it on the table. "We'll take the wine," he said quietly.

Tor Sodo covered his surprise with a little bow, then scooped up the coin, ignoring a small strangled sound from Taru.

"Of course, Zirda. Ye'll have it at once. And I'll bring ye your change."

The tavern keeper bobbed another quick bow and exited by way of the side door that led to the back hall and the kitchen.

"Fifteen rins, Nagaro!" Taru hissed as soon as the man was out of earshot. "Both our dinners together won't come t' five!"

Nagaro sighed. *It seemed a lot of money for wine, but...* "It's only going to be this once," he said. "And it wouldn't be a good test, otherwise. I don't know whether ale would be the same as wine."

Taru frowned. "It might not," he admitted.

"If the ale didn't do anything, I'd feel I had to try the wine anyway." Nagaro shifted nervously. "And I want to get this over with." His anxious anticipation had been growing ever since he'd made up his mind about the wine back at the inn. The hope of discovering what had happened on that final night in Lankura was a powerful enticement, despite his fears. He didn't want to wait for months to try again.

"A whole bottle might be more than we'll need..." Taru murmured thoughtfully.

"You *will* have some, won't you?"

"Of course." A movement from beyond the door leading to the tavern's large front room seemed to catch Taru's attention. The young Turo frowned a little. "Excuse me, Nagaro," he said. "I think, ah... someone... wants to talk t' me. Ye just wait here. It shouldn't take me a minute."

Nagaro shrugged and nodded. He watched his friend make for the doorway, only to note that Taru's disappearing figure was intercepted by another, smaller and more shapely. He caught a glimpse of a sweep of long, black hair and a swirl of turquoise skirts. He frowned and shook his head. Very likely Taru was making his own arrangements for later in the evening— arrangements that would certainly not involve sitting on anyone's front porch.

Nagaro heaved another sigh. He'd given up trying to change his friend's mind on the subject of the tavern women, since nothing he'd been able to think of had made any impression. "Ye don't have t' sit with them, or ask their fathers, or anything," Taru had told him. "Ye just pay them a few rins afterwards and everyone's happy. Surely ye can't object to that." Nagaro not only could object, but had objected, pointing out that there was a risk of getting a child. Taru had dismissed this, however. The women, he was told, had "ways" of preventing this, and in the rare case that it did happen, the woman would simply "take care of it." Pressed on the matter, Taru had been a little vague about what that meant, but the important thing seemed to be that the man needn't fear that anyone would come knocking on his door.

Nagaro's gloomy thoughts were interrupted by Tor Sodo's return with the bottle of wine and a large glass goblet. The tavern keeper extracted the cork from the bottle and filled the goblet with a flourish. The man then set the glass and the bottle down in front of Nagaro.

"There ye are, Zirda, your Southern Borlundian. I trust ye'll find it to your liking." The tavern keeper smiled unctuously.

Nagaro managed to smile back. "Thank you," he said. "And my change?"

"Oh, aye. O' course, o' course." The man fished in his pocket for a fistful of copper coins, and counted out thirty-five rins onto the table.

"Thank you, Tor Sodo. And we'll need a second glass."

The tavern keeper bobbed his head. "O' course, Zirda. I'll fetch ye one."

There was a shout from the kitchen at that point and Sodo made haste to excuse himself. He turned in the doorway to say, "Dinner's started cookin', Zirda. It shouldn't be much more 'n half an hour."

Nagaro found himself alone again. He shivered a little. The room was rather inadequately heated by a single small fireplace at the far end. It was not a very appealing place. The tables had benches rather than chairs, and no tablecloths. The only light came from two rather dirty oil lamps on either side of the door leading to the front room.

Taru had purposely arranged for them to sit side by side on a bench at a table facing that door so that they could be seen and identified by the Red Cask's other patrons. From where he sat, Nagaro could make out portions of several tables in the outer room. Nanu and Chaheel were seated at the nearest one. Nanu was facing him, and from time to time, the massive young Turo glanced in his direction. The front room was evidently beginning to fill up with customers, for there was a rising babble of voices punctuated by laughter and the clink of ale mugs. There had been only half a dozen men there when Taru and Nagaro had arrived. Nanu and Chaheel had been among them, not surprisingly, since the two men were sharing a room at the tavern. Both had raised hands in greeting as Taru and Nagaro had walked past. Tego had been there as well, although he roomed at the inn with Moraga. The gnarled little merchant seaman had given Nagaro a slightly forced smile.

Nagaro heaved yet another sigh and toyed with the stem of the wine goblet, wondering how much longer Taru would be. He never felt at ease in a tavern. The places existed primarily to allow men to engage in an activity that followers of the Path of Vothra were advised to avoid. Vothra valued the exercise of reason as the path to understanding and the surest way to bring about a good outcome. Anything that clouded the light of reason was therefore discouraged. A clouded mind was apt to make poor choices— so the Writings said. Misunderstandings or conflicts might ensue. Sometimes folk came to harm.

Nagaro frowned. He was only going to break the ban a little bit. Other men drank ale or wine all the time. Taru and his father, Jomo, had done it every market day, and he'd never seen either of them make any bad choices as a result. If Taru had been a little less sure-footed on the boat's catwalks, still he'd never fallen. And a glass of wine was smaller than a mug of ale, wasn't it? The goblet in front of him was larger than the glass the princess had given him, but still smaller than an ale mug.

His frown deepened as he thought about that night in Lankura— *the way she had watched him, as if waiting to see his reaction.* Soon Taru would be watching him that way. Nagaro squirmed. He didn't like the idea of being the object of such scrutiny. The more he thought about it, in fact, the less he liked it, and this train of thought led to another as the moments ticked by: Taru was taking a long time to return, and why shouldn't he begin the experiment while he waited? He began to make a mental calculation.

In Lankura, he'd felt as if his whole head were on fire after drinking an entire glass. Very likely the effect had been a result of mixing wine with the heskial in his blood and nothing like that would happen now. But even if it did, taking just a swallow would surely have much less effect... Gingerly he picked up the glass of wine and sniffed at the contents. There was that faintly sweet, musty smell that he remembered. Raising the glass to his lips, he took an experimental sip. The slightly astringent taste and the warm sensation of the liquid in his mouth were also familiar. He took a single swallow, feeling the warm sensation run down his throat, then set the glass down and waited a little.

The seconds ticked by, and nothing happened. There was no fire in his head. Not even a flicker. The taste of the wine evoked the memory of that final scene in the princess's bedchamber, but no new memories followed. Well, he couldn't expect a mere swallow to have much effect, could he? But at least it seemed to be safe. He stared at the ruby liquid in the glass and glanced at the doorway leading to the front room. Nanu was still sitting at the table, but there was no sign of Taru. Still, he thought, Taru would surely return soon, and he couldn't think why he shouldn't continue his experiment as long as he proceeded with caution. He picked up the goblet and drank about half of the wine remaining in it, then waited again to confirm that there was no explosion of light behind his eyes. Since there wasn't, he drank the rest of the glass.

Again he waited, but apart from the warmth that began spreading outward from the pit of his stomach, he didn't feel any different. Nor could he remember anything new about that fateful day. Wasn't it going to work? Had his hopes been raised for nothing? He frowned at the empty glass. Perhaps he still hadn't drunk enough. What he'd consumed so far was just a little bit more than he'd drunk that night, but there had been heskial in him then, as well, working together with the wine. Right now he was free of the drug. Perhaps he needed to drink more wine in some proportion to make up for it?

He reached for the bottle and poured a second glass. Then he hesitated, mentally taking the measure of the liquid in the goblet. After a moment, he nodded to himself. Two glasses would be only a little more than the volume of an average mug of ale. It should be all right. He picked up the glass and drank all of it straight off without pausing. Then he set the goblet down again, and once more he waited, trying to relax and let his mind drift, to let any memories come...

After a while, he began to feel a kind of soothing inner glow. The room no longer seemed so cold or dreary. The babble of noise from the front room receded, and he felt pleasantly warm and at ease. It seemed the wine had done nothing to jog his memory, but that no longer seemed so troubling. He didn't really need to know why he hadn't died, did he? It was just good to be alive... and safe... and warm...

He supposed this was what Taru meant by being "a bit relaxed." But was he relaxed enough to sit and talk with a woman he'd never met before... never even seen? With an effort of concentration, he examined his feelings on the subject. It seemed to him that there was still a small knot of worry there inside of him when he thought about it. Well, he knew what to do about that. He picked up the wine bottle and filled the glass again. Just a little more...

He raised the glass and drank.

***

Some time later, the thought drifted lazily across his mind that he was perhaps becoming drunk. The room seemed to be turning about him ever so slightly and the flames of the two oil lamps danced and swam in his vision when he looked at them. Well, if he was drunk, it didn't seem so bad. Certainly nothing to be worried about. And all of those things that had troubled him so? Simion, and what the men thought... sitting with Panila... his past and his future... None of them seemed very important now. Surely everything would be all right. He wondered vaguely where Taru was. His friend was missing all the wine. He should pour a glass for

Taru. He reached for the bottle, seized it... tipped it... tried to hold the neck of it steady above the rim of the wine glass so he could pour...

"Here, now, let me help you with that."

The voice was low and throaty, and unmistakably female. The hand that reached out to take the bottle from his unsteady grasp was slender and brown, with daintily tapered fingers and perfect, pearly nails.

Nagaro turned to stare at the strikingly beautiful Turowan woman who stood beside him. He watched, mesmerized, as she poured the remainder of the wine into the glass and set down the empty bottle. Then she turned to regard him.

Her heart-shaped face was dominated by a pair of large dark eyes of liquid brown. Just now, those eyes were half-veiled by her long, dark lashes. Above them, her eyebrows made two perfect arcs. Her exquisitely-formed lips were lusciously red and wet, as if she'd been eating cherries. Waves of shining black hair cascaded over her shoulders or lay softly against the smooth, brown skin of her throat. Nor was the rest of her any disappointment. The neck of her cream-colored blouse was cut just low enough to promise, without actually revealing, the round, ripe fullness of her breasts. Her laced bodice, sewn of a deep red fabric to match her lips, was tailored to accentuate the perfect hourglass of her figure. Above, the ruby-colored bodice cradled the swelling curve of her breasts. Below, it ended in the outward sweep of her hips. From there, a graceful black skirt descended to her daintily slippered feet.

Nagaro couldn't take his eyes off this stunning apparition. He might almost have believed she had materialized out of the air in answer to a young man's yearning. In fact she must have entered from the side hall door and come quietly up behind him. She seemed to be studying him with considerable interest, and he felt his heart beat more forcefully in his chest in answer. Presently she spoke again in that breathy voice.

"I don't believe I've seen you here before. I'm sure I'd remember ye if I had."

"It's the firs' time I've come," he told her. He frowned a little. It was hard to get the words out clearly. "An' I'm afraid I'm drunk."

A hint of a smile flickered briefly in her eyes. "Do you think so?" she asked, considering him with her head on one side. "Well, maybe ye are, just a little," she conceded after a moment, in a voice of purest silk. "But that's all right. *I* don't mind."

"Tha's very kind of you," he said, because it seemed to him that it was.

The smile flickered again. She leaned closer to him. "Do ye mind if I sit with you?"

Nagaro frowned in confusion. Wasn't that the wrong way around? "I don' mind..." he faltered. "But... shouldn' I ask your father?"

The woman laughed— a musical ripple of sound. She sat down on the bench beside him, so close that her thigh brushed his, and he felt his pulse quicken. Her eyes were suddenly serious. "But, I don't *have* any parents," she told him conspiratorially. "So I do as I please, and right now it pleases me to sit with *you*."

For a moment he could only stare at her. He could scarcely believe that this incredible creature was paying so much attention to him. When he finally found his voice, he said: "I don' have any parent's either."

She smiled, and her teeth were a row of perfect pearls. "Well there, ye see?" she said. "We have something in common. My name's Jila," she added, with another stunning smile. "What's yours?"

"N'garo."

She arched a delicate eyebrow. "What, don't ye want to tell me?"

He frowned foggily, until he remembered that his name meant "nameless man". "No," he explained. "N'garo is my *name*." *This was amazing. She hadn't even heard of him, and still she seemed so interested.*

She gave him a knowing smile. "All right, then ...*Nagaro*. Whatever you say." She studied his face for a moment. "Are ye Kelorin or Turo?" she asked. "Your eyes say Kelorin, but ye're so brown." And she reached out and ran a finger across the back of his hand where it rested on the table. A powerful thrill ran up his spine, and he drew in his breath.

"It's kuma," he managed to say.

"*Really?*" She smiled and leaned closer. "Do ye know that you're *perfect?*" she purred. "*Handsome...*" She put her hand on his shoulder and ran her fingers down his arm to his elbow, feeling the bulge of his muscles under his shirt. "...and *strong*, too!"

His blood rose hot in him at her touch. For a moment, he seemed to have no breath to speak.

"I've never seen a Kelorin man with a Turowan beard before," she went on, reaching out to run her finger along the line of his jaw.

He drew in his breath. "You don' mind it?" he asked. The room seemed very warm.

"Oh, no," she breathed, stroking his bearded cheek. "In fact, I think I like it."

His heart hammered. The world seemed to have closed in until it contained nothing but the two of them. Impulsively, he leaned forward and tried to kiss her. But she slid away, leaving him confused and chagrined.

For a moment she regarded him through the veil of her lashes. Then she leaned close to his ear. "Not *here*," she whispered urgently. "*Come to my room.*"

He wanted to say yes but an unwelcome thought was penetrating the fluffy haze in his brain. "I can't," he said with audible disappointment. "I'm s'posed t' wait for my friend Taru."

Jila looked at him with wide-eyed innocence. "The little Turo who was here?" she asked. "I saw him with Tulara. I'm sure he's forgotten all about ye by now."

"He *has?*" Nagaro blinked at her. That couldn't be right. He frowned. *Or could it?* He *had* seen Taru meet a woman in the outer room. "But... we had a plan..." he murmured. "An' I'm s'posed to meet..." He struggled for the name. "...P'nila... t'night."

Jila considered him through the veil of her lashes. "Ye're supposed to meet a *woman* tonight?"

"Tha's right. To... to sit..."

"Well, *I'm* a woman." Jila reached out to stroke his cheek again. "Won't I do?"

Nagaro felt hot and cold all at the same time. She was so beautiful... and so close... and so *female.* It was hard to think about anything else whenever she touched him. "I... yes... I mean..." he stammered. "I s'pose we could try to get t' know each other better."

"Oh, *yes.* I'd *like* that." She leaned even closer, her voice low and sultry. "I'd like to get to know you a *lot* better. But there's too many folk about down here. Won't ye come upstairs to my room?"

He found himself nodding. Yes, that would be much better. "All righ'," he said.

"Why don't you finish your wine first," she purred, reaching for the glass. "It'd be a shame to waste it when ye paid so much for it."

He nodded again, wordlessly. It *would* be a shame, wouldn't it? He took the goblet from her hand, raised it to his lips, and drained it.

She took the glass again and set it on the table.

"Now, come with me." She said, and rose, beckoning.

He stood up unsteadily. The room seemed to be moving a little. It was rather like being on a ship at sea, but he knew how to handle that. *Just focus on your destination and keep your feet moving...* He heard her laughter ripple again as she took him by the arm and steered him towards the side door. The hall beyond led to a stairway. He took the stairs in a rush, the way he took the ladders on the *Fist of Death* in rough weather. She laughed again, and this time he laughed with her.

The small room she led him to was dimly illuminated by the warm, yellow glow of a single candle. There wasn't much furniture... nothing to sit on but the bed. So he sat on the edge of it, and she sat beside him.

"What sh' we talk about?" he asked innocently.

She tilted her head to one side, and studied him through her lashes. "Oh, we can talk *later,* can't we?" she said. Then she leaned close to him and murmured, "Right now, I want *you*. And you want *me*... And what could possibly be wrong with that?"

As she spoke, she reached out and traced the line of his upper lip with her fingertip, and he gasped involuntarily at the thrill that jolted through him. Was there something wrong with it? If so, it couldn't be very important... because he couldn't for the life of him think what it could be...

"Ye *do* want me, don't you?" she breathed, her cherry lips close to his.

"*Oh, yes...*" he murmured. For, at that moment, it was true. He felt he had never wanted anything so much in his life.

"*Then here I am!*"

And she threw her arms around his neck and pressed her lips to his, long and hungrily. He embraced her in answer, drinking deep... pulling her to him... feeling her body against his... His blood rose like a tide of fire.

After that, one thing followed another in a seemingly inexorable procession. Jila had a way of removing clothing that was both an adventure and an education. She had to help him with the buttons on his shirt because his fingers stumbled. Once his shirt was off, she ran her hands over his bare back and asked him about the scars there, and about the brand on his shoulder. When he told her he'd been a slave, her eyes went wide.

"Were ye one of the men from that ship in the harbor?" she asked.

He nodded. "Tha's right."

"You poor man!" She murmured, tracing over the scars again with a finger and sending shivers down his spine. "It must have been *horrible.* I'm *so* glad you escaped."

A little later, she laughed to see that the kuma stain ended at his waist, saying that he was Turo above and Kelorin below.

As they lay side by side on the billowy feather mattress, she asked him: "Have ye done this before?"

"No," he answered with complete honesty, because it never naturally occurred to him to lie. There were some fleeting feelings associated with that admission— disturbing feelings left over from his un-willing marriage to the princess— but the memory was distant, the feelings remote, muffled in a fog of wine and overridden by his rising desire.

"What, *never?*" She was incredulous. "A fine, handsome man like you? Well, don't ye worry," she added indulgently. "*I'll* never tell."

And then she kissed him again and he forgot about everything else.

He filled all his senses with her. Not just the taste of her cherry lips, but the glorious vision of her nakedness, the musky scent of her body, the sound of her urgent breath in his ear, and the feel of her smooth, brown skin under his hands. Somewhere an inner voice was saying: *This is wrong! You don't love her... You don't even know her...* But the wine had muted it to the faintest of whispers, and the siren voice in his blood completely drowned it out.

And Jila knew exactly what to do— how to guide his inexperienced efforts so that he wasn't aware of any awkwardness. For that moment of time, he was her instrument, and she could have played upon him any tune she wished.

Later, as he lay with his head cradled against her breasts, half drowsing, his passion spent, she stroked his forehead with her fingertips. As if from a distance, he heard her soft, husky voice say, "Close your eyes now, and go to sleep, my pretty man. Your work is done."

Obediently he closed his eyes and drifted into dreamless sleep.

Chapter 5

The Morning After

He awakened to an aching head and a momentary confusion— until memory came washing back, to be followed immediately by a deep sense of shame.

Jila was gone— of course— and he was lying naked and alone on the disheveled bed, in a room that now seemed barren, dingy, and cold. The light of early morning was struggling to penetrate the dusty curtains on the window. He rolled over and sat up with a groan. The action made his headache ratchet up several notches. He was nauseous, and he had no words to describe the way his tongue felt.

He groaned again. However great his discomfort, he was sure he deserved it. The previous night's memories were blurred around the edges— especially towards the end— but clear enough to leave him no doubt at all about what he had done. He'd chosen to break the ban, had made himself quite drunk, and ended the fiasco by lying with a woman he had just met and knew nothing about. And he'd done the last for no other reason than to satisfy the desire she had stirred in him. He felt his gorge rise at the thought of it.

While marriage was not, in Nagaro's view, an absolute prerequisite to sleeping with a woman, love certainly was. Nevrath and Minowei, in the romantic tale, had lain together before they were married, but they had loved each other and hoped to wed. Mere pleasure was not a sufficient reason. The guilty memory of that pleasure came edging in to taunt him even through the pounding pain in his skull. Angrily he thrust the memory aside. *Of course it had felt good. But that wasn't the point.*

He sat on the edge of the bed with his head in his hands and continued to berate himself. He'd made a very stupid mistake, and it wasn't as if he hadn't been warned. The Writings were quite clear, but he'd chosen to ignore them. And so of course it had all gone wrong from beginning to end and he had no one to blame but himself. There might have been some small consolation if being drunk had brought him any of the memories he'd been seeking, but of course it hadn't. How, he wondered, could he have been so stupid as to imagine that anything useful could come from drinking wine?

He wasn't sure exactly how his experiment had gone so wrong. Perhaps he'd been in too much of a hurry with the wine? Hadn't waited long enough to feel the effect of the first glass before drinking the second? Or perhaps he just became drunk very easily? The one certain thing was that he'd been extremely stupid not to wait for Taru.

Stupid, stupid, stupid...

What eventually prodded him out of his cycle of self-castigation was the realization that he needed to leave this loathsome place. His clothes lay strewn about wherever he had dropped them. Jila had left nothing of hers behind. She must have rented the room for no other purpose than to serve for one night's pleasure. *And he had caught her eye...*

No! Enough of that!

Gathering up his clothes and beginning painfully to dress himself, he soon made another discovery. His purse was empty.

Humiliation was then added to shame, for now it seemed clear that Jila had never had any interest in him except to rob him! All the woman's deceit and mockery and manipulation were thus laid bare, and he cursed himself for an idiot and a fool. Thankfully, his ring still hung around his neck where he kept it on a loop of leather cord. Jila had at least left him that. But then, he recalled, she'd shown barely any interest in it the night before. He realized after a moment's thought that she would, of course, have had more sense than to take a treasured keepsake. Such a thing could be too easily traced if she tried to sell it. Coins, on the other hand, were quite anonymous.

There was half a pitcher of water on the nightstand, and a chipped basin. He drank some of the water straight from the pitcher, because there was no cup. It didn't help as much as he'd hoped. The rest of the water he poured into the basin and used to wash his face. That didn't help much either. He still felt dirty in a way he couldn't describe.

He left the room and descended the stairs, meeting no one.

He let himself out by the back door into an alley that ran behind the tavern. From there he made his way back to the Bay Tree Inn as much as possible by back ways, keeping his head down and not meeting the eyes of the few folk he passed. The early morning sunlight seemed too bright. It hurt his eyes and made his head throb painfully. When he reached the inn, he passed Habu in the stable yard with barely a nod of greeting. He went in by the inn's back door and slunk up the stairs. Grateful to find the bedroom deserted, he stretched himself on his bed with a moan, flung an arm across his eyes, and tried very sincerely and quite unsuccessfully to lose consciousness.

His anguished mind and aching head wouldn't let him sleep, and the longer he lay stewing about what he'd done, the angrier with himself he became. He realized that he had done exactly what Jila had wanted him to do, and the ease with which he'd been manipulated galled him. Being drunk was almost as bad, he reflected, as being under the influence of heskial. It didn't feel as bad while it was happening, of course, because you didn't realize how stupid you were being. But in another way it was worse. Unlike heskial, the wine hadn't *compelled* him to do anything. He could have said no to Jila at any time. But he'd lain with her because a part of him had wanted to— a part that he was not at all proud of.

Stupid, and worse than stupid...

An hour later Taru found him.

Nagaro heard the door open and the sound of footsteps on the floor, but he didn't move, even at the sound of his friend's voice.

"Nagaro, ye're here! Praise the Spirits! I thought ye might be lying somewhere in a fever like... like the other time..."

Taru's words trailed off as he came to a halt beside Nagaro's bed. The relief that had colored the young man's voice was replaced by concern when he spoke again.

"Are ye all right, Nagaro?"

"*No!*"

The word was spoken through clenched teeth, and there was an edge to it.

"What's wrong?" Taru dropped down, squatting on his heels beside the bed. He put a hand on the arm that Nagaro still held across his face. "Was it the wine?" he ventured hesitantly. "Did it... did it do something? Did ye remember something bad?"

Nagaro made a movement to shake off his friend's hand, without uncovering his eyes, and groaned when the effort made his head throb. "*No*, Taru," he said, biting the words off bitterly. "The wine only made me *drunk*. And I didn't learn *anything*. I'm *sick* and my head is splitting... and I feel completely wretched!"

There was a little pause, then Taru asked cautiously, "How much did ye drink?"

"The whole bottle. I was so *stupid!*"

"*Ai, Nagaro!* That's too much! Especially when ye'd had no dinner. Wine is stronger than ale— twice as strong— and it'll hit ye much harder on an empty stomach!"

Wine was twice as strong? An empty stomach made it worse?

Nagaro uncovered his eyes and turned his head to glower at his friend. "You might have warned me about those things!"

Taru looked uncomfortable. "I… I was *going* to. But it's no wonder ye feel so bad," he added hastily. "I'll just go downstairs and get ye a little ale t' drink. That'll make it better—"

"*NO!*"

This time the word exploded from Nagaro, and he winced at the resulting stab of pain. Shutting his eyes again, he put his hands to his aching head. When he went on, he spoke low to avoid aggravating his headache but his voice shook with barely controlled fury. "I don't want any ale. Or wine. Or anything of the kind! Not now. *Not ever!*" He clenched his teeth. "I don't *want* to feel better. I don't *deserve* to feel better! I want to remember *exactly* how bad this feels for a very long time so I won't ever be tempted to do anything like that again!"

There was a pause, and it lengthened.

Taru's next question, when it came, was spoken gingerly, as if he feared the answer.

"Where did ye go, Nagaro? Where have ye been all night?"

It was a question Nagaro had been dreading. He didn't want to answer it, but he didn't feel he deserved to be spared the confession. He massaged his throbbing temples without looking at his friend. "I went to a room upstairs. With a woman."

He heard Taru's intake of breath.

"*Hamanei…*" The young Turo spoke the word so low it was almost inaudible. "Who was she, Nagaro? Do ye know her name?"

Nagaro scowled at the ceiling. What did her name matter? She'd deceived him… manipulated him… *laughed at him…*

"Jila," he said through his teeth. "She said her name was Jila."

Taru groaned. "*Hamanei mata noa!* Not *Jila!* Nagaro, did ye lie with her?"

This time Nagaro was nettled by the pointedness of the question. He had no right to conceal his guilt, but considering Taru's history, what right had Taru to demand such a detailed accounting? "*Yes,* I lay with her," he said, turning a smoldering gaze on his friend.

Taru was still squatting on his heels, staring hard at him. "Are ye *sure,* Nagaro? It sounds like ye were very drunk—"

"Of *course* I'm sure!" It was easy to let some of his self-directed anger spill over onto Taru. "And, *yes,* I was very drunk! I wouldn't have *done* it if I hadn't been!" *At least he didn't think he would have.* "Now, are you *quite satisfied?*"

Taru was giving him a stricken look. The young Turo shook his head and groaned. "Ai, this is *bad,* Nagaro. Jila's *poison!* Ye've got t' try to forget her!"

This was so preposterous that Nagaro had to laugh. It came out as a harsh, humorless sound. "*Forget* her?" he said bitterly. "The most beautiful woman I've ever seen, and you want me to forget her? She said she wanted to get to know me, and like and *idiot*, I *believed* her. If I live to be a hundred, I couldn't forget her!"

"*Oh, no, no! Nagaro!*" Taru rocked back and forth. "They say there's young men mooning for Jila all over this island! She only ever lies with the young men once, and she leaves 'em dangling so they go mad over her!" Taru sounded nearly beside himself. "Please don't tell me ye still want her!"

It took Nagaro a second to grasp Taru's meaning, but when he did, he exploded. "*By the Eyes of Vothra!*" He sat up on the bed, heedless of his throbbing head. "Do you think I'm so weak that I'd want to lie with her again just because she's *beautiful?* Or because it *felt* good? *She's a wicked, lying, deceitful creature, and I want nothing more to do with her!*"

Taru sprang to his feet and backed away in dismay. "Nagaro! I... I'm sorry—"

But Nagaro's anger at his friend couldn't stand for long in the face of his own humiliation. Sitting on the edge of the bed, he took his head in his hands. "*Oh, Taru!*" he moaned. "I thought it didn't matter to her who I was. Or what I looked like. That I'm Kelorin, or the beard, or the hair, or the kuma stain. I thought she just liked me for *myself*. And all she wanted was the money in my purse!"

"Your money?" This time Taru sounded startled. "She *robbed* ye?" And then his voice changed, as he added, quickly, "Well, o' course she did! That's what Jila *does*..." His voice trailed and when he spoke again, the worry had returned to it. "How much money did ye have, Nagaro? How much did she take?"

Nagaro raised his head. He gestured vaguely. "Five trokins and the change from the wine."

"*Five hundred and thirty-five rins?* Did ye tell Tor Sodo?"

Nagaro scowled. "Do you think I care about the *money?*"

The fact was, he'd lost something he valued far more than silver. He struggled to find words to explain, words that Taru would understand. "That was the first time I ever lay with a woman," he said, at last, in a choking voice. "The first time I ever even really kissed a woman. And it was a woman who means nothing to me! That's not the way I wanted it to *be*, Taru. It's not the way it's *supposed* to be. I stepped so far off the Path last night that I might as well have thrown the Book of Vothra out the window! I've done everything wrong, and I'd give anything to take it back. *And I can't!*"

He stopped because his friend's face had become a mask of anguish.

Taru groaned and sank down hard onto the floor. Bowing his head onto his knees, he clutched at his hair. "*Oh no!*" he cried. "Nagaro, I'm *sorry!* It wasn't supposed t' be like that! I never should ha' left ye alone!

Why did Jila have t' pick *last night* of all nights t' come nosing around? *Ai! Ai! Ai! This is all my fault!*"

Taru's contrition was very obviously sincere, but Nagaro was in no mood at that moment to relinquish any of the blame. "You're not my nursemaid, Taru!" he grated. "*I* decided not to wait for you. *I* broke the ban! *I* made myself drunk! And *I* lay with Jila! How could any of it be *your* fault?"

Taru raised a wretched face. "Ye don't understand, Nagaro!" His voice broke on the words. "I *meant* for ye to go with a woman last night! But it was supposed t' be Tulara, not *Jila!* And I didn't tell ye about the wine on *purpose*, so I could get ye t' drink more of it. But I *swear* I never meant for ye t' get *that drunk!*"

Nagaro gaped at his friend. The pieces of the picture were frantically rearranging themselves inside his aching head, and he didn't like the implications of the new one *at all*. "What do you mean, it was *supposed* to be Tulara?" he demanded. And as other pieces dropped into place, he added, with an increasing edge to his voice. "And just exactly *how drunk* did you mean for me to be?"

Taru wrung his hands. "*Please* don't be angry! I was trying t' help! I couldn't bear having them think ye were crossed, and I thought if they saw ye go with a woman—"

"But I was going to sit with Panila!" With all that had happened, Nagaro had completely forgotten the other reason he'd gone to the Red Cask. "*Oh, Vothra!*" he exclaimed in sudden horror. "I have to go talk to her father—"

But Taru was shaking his head. "No ye don't, Nagaro! He wouldn't know what ye were on about. I never talked to him, because ye were *supposed* t' go with Tulara! Panila wouldn't ha' been enough! Don't ye see?" The young Turo was desperate to explain himself. "*Anyone* can sit with a woman. A *crossed* man can do it just for show! A crossed man could pay one o' the tavern women to spend an hour with him, an' for a few extra rins she'd tell any tale he asked. But when a man is drunk, he'll fall whichever way comes natural to him!"

Nagaro went rigid.

Fall whichever way comes natural...

"So you *arranged* for me to fall?" His voice came out low and fierce.

"Nagaro, I—"

"*That* was your plan? To trick me into getting drunk? *So I'd lie with a tavern woman?*"

"*No!*" Taru desperately shook his head. "Ye wouldn't have had t' *lie* with Tulara. Ye could've just sat and talked! Tulara wouldn't ha' minded, and she never would ha' pushed ye the way Jila did. She didn't like it that ye thought ye were going t' sit with Panila, and she was going t' have to change your mind. That's part o' what took me so long! I had t' talk her 'round to it again. And then, afore I'd finished with *that,* there was all the trouble with Pavo, an' I figured I had t' get *him* home while he could still walk—"

Nagaro had been struggling to follow this, trying to decide if it mattered what Tulara had intended, and then the last sentence penetrated the welter of his emotions. "*Pavo?*" he asked, his careening thoughts derailed by concern for his other friend. "What happened to Pavo? Is he all right? Was there an accident?"

Taru stared at him. "Ye don't know?" he asked. Then, seeing Nagaro's blank look, he added, "No, o' course ye wouldn't. Ye went with Jila, so ye wouldn't ha' seen that Pavo was in the Red Cask last night trying t' drown himself in ale."

"*What?* You're saying that Pavo got *drunk* last night?" Nagaro could scarcely believe this. He'd never seen the young Hashtep drink more than a single mug of ale, and so far as he knew, Pavo had never previously even been inside the tavern. "I don't understand," he said in utter confusion. "Why would Pavo do a thing like that?"

Taru rolled his eyes. "Something about Tenepti and another man," he said, with an air of exasperation. "He'll tell ye all about it if ye ask him. He's down in the kitchen right now. Yuli is feeding him soup."

Nagaro sat for a moment digesting this. But then he frowned, and the frown deepened. The news about Pavo's behavior was shocking, but Pavo was obviously all right, and he realized that there were further implications to this new development.

"So... you took Pavo home," he said slowly, feeling his way. "Because *he* was drunk. But you didn't stop to check on *me* or to let me know?"

"I'm sorry, Nagaro." Taru hugged his knees miserably. "But I had Nanu and Tego there t' watch ye. Tego said ye'd been at the wine, an' something about a woman that wasn't Tulara, but I thought it was just another one o' the tavern women. I didn't think it mattered *who* ye went with, so long as ye *went.* And when I came back from taking Pavo home, ye were gone! And Nanu and Tego were gone too! I swear I didn't know anything about Jila being there 'til this morning, when ye told me!"

This made the whole course of events clear, at least, but it also added more fuel to the flame of Nagaro's anger. "So you had Nanu and Tego there," he said, in a voice that was much too still. "To *watch* me? To see what I'd do with a woman? *Is that right?*"

"*Well... y-es...*" Taru's face registered apprehension.

And the answer was the last stick of kindling. The look Nagaro gave his friend was an ink-black thundercloud with lightning lurking in it. "*So.*" His voice had a knife-edge to it. "You set me up to fall. *And you made sure there were witnesses?*"

Taru cringed. "Somebody had t' see what ye did, Nagaro! There wouldn't ha' been any *point* if nobody saw it!"

"*Keshaal!*" Nagaro lunged to his feet, fists clenched and eyes blazing. His head was pounding, but he didn't care. "*Taru!*" he raged. "*How could you do this to me?*"

Taru scrambled to his feet and backed away. "*I wanted them t' see for sure that ye're not crossed!*" he wailed. "*I couldn't think of any other way!*"

Nagaro felt the reins of control slipping in his grasp. He was staring at the precipice, but fortunately, the look on Taru's face checked him. Taru was cowering away, the whites of his eyes showing, obviously and genuinely frightened.

For a long, pounding moment Nagaro just glared at his friend, fists clenched at his sides. Then, very deliberately, he unclenched his hands. Turning away from Taru, he flung himself down on the bed and put his arm across his eyes. "Go away," he said in a tight, hard voice. "Leave me alone."

"*Please, Nagaro...*" Taru's voice was pleading. "I didn't mean it t' end that way! I swear it by all the Spirits!"

Nagaro rolled over, turning his face to the wall. "*Just leave me alone!*"

After several heartbeats, he heard Taru's retreating footsteps, followed by the sound of the door being carefully closed.

***

Nagaro lay still, feeling the roiling storm of his anger slowly begin to dissipate. It took some time, but eventually the whirling maelstrom of his thoughts slowed enough to allow some reflection. By that time, he found his head didn't hurt quite so much. It probably helped that he'd stopped shouting.

He rolled over and cautiously sat up, then got up gingerly and went to retrieve the leather-bound volume of the Book of Vothra from the dresser drawer where he had stowed it. Sitting on the edge of the bed, he read the passages that dealt with making mistakes. The message was simple: Mistakes were an evitable consequence of a spirit having to find its way afresh in each new life. You should admit your mistakes, forgive yourself for making them, and learn from them so that they were not repeated. If your mistakes hurt someone else, you should offer apology and make amends if possible.

And if you were hurt by someone else's mistake? The answer was also simple: *Forgive.*

Nagaro put the book away. Then he sat on the bed and did some thinking. He wasn't going to make the mistake of getting drunk again. That went without saying, although forgiving himself might take a little time. Thankfully, he was fairly certain he hadn't hurt anyone except himself. He supposed Jila had gotten what she wanted. The chances of getting a child from one night's encounter were real, but small. And he thought Jila surely knew how to avoid conceiving, just like the tavern women Taru had told him about.

And Taru's part of it? He could see clearly that being left in ignorance of the wine's potency had contributed to his downfall, but he'd still been the one who'd done the falling. Taru's plan had been well-intentioned, if misguided, and it hadn't gone as Taru had intended. The woman named Tulara probably *would* have treated him better than Jila. And there probably would have been witnesses at the tavern even if Taru hadn't arranged for there to be.

At least there had been no witnesses to his actions in the room upstairs...

He winced and wrenched his thoughts away.

No matter how embarrassed he was by the whole fiasco, he realized that it would probably serve Taru's intended purpose. No one would now think him crossed. His actions downstairs had been quite unambiguous, he was sure.

Had he really tried to kiss her after she'd said only a few words to him?

Again he tried not to follow the thought.

It could have been worse. He might have gone out alone in his drunken state to try to find where Panila lived— seeking a sitting that had never been arranged. He shuddered to think how badly *that* could have gone. And the lesson, there, wasn't just that Taru shouldn't have lied to him. No, he really needed to take responsibility for arranging his own affairs. Actually, what galled him the most was how little of it Taru *had* done. Most of the harm he had done to himself— with considerable help from Jila. All in all, he found it easier to forgive Taru than to forgive himself.

And Jila? *She* surely had not been well-intentioned. And she surely was *not* sorry. There were passages in the Book of Vothra that dealt with how you should deal with people who wronged you knowingly, but he hadn't re-read those pages. He wasn't ready yet to try to understand Jila, or to forgive her. She was a deceiver and a manipulator, and the timing of her appearance the previous night had indeed been a colossal stroke of ill luck. He and Taru had both made mistakes, but they were also both victims of the whim of Lokundas, who had set Jila's path to cross with his. Not to mention sending Pavo a reversal that had put him on a downward arc...

It was thinking of Pavo that finally moved Nagaro to get up and leave the bedroom.

Taru had mentioned something about Tenepti and another man. Nagaro thought he could imagine what sort of thing it must have been. *Poor Pavo...* He ought to offer comfort to his friend if he could. Besides, he hadn't eaten since noon of the previous day. Sick though he was, he knew his body needed nourishment— and hadn't Taru said something about soup?

So he rose despite his aching head, washed his face again, and went downstairs.

Chapter 6

Of Wine, Women, And Consequences

When Nagaro stepped into the common room, it was empty save for two members of the *Fist's* crew who were sitting together at one of the tables, talking. From the way they immediately fell silent and avoided his gaze, Nagaro guessed he'd been the subject of their conversation. He stalked past them with his head up and his eyes straight ahead, making for the kitchen.

He found Pavo and Yuli there, but no sign of Taru. Pavo was sitting at the table in the middle of the room with a half empty bowl in front of him and a spoon in his hand. The young Hashtep gave Nagaro a wan smile when he entered the room.

Yuli turned as Nagaro stepped through the door and looked him up and down. "Well," she said carefully, "Here ye are at last, Tor Nagaro. I was worried when I missed ye at breakfast. And then Taru said—"

Nagaro interrupted her. "Yuli, I feel terrible."

She gave him a more thorough scrutiny. "Soup. That's what ye need," she declared. "Ye just sit over there with Tor Pavo, and I'll fetch ye a bowl."

Nagaro moved to the table and sank onto a stool across from Pavo.

The young Hashtep nodded a greeting, studying him a bit uncertainly with eyes that were noticeably red-rimmed. "It is good soup," he ventured after a moment. "I have two bowl already."

"How are you feeling, Pavo?" Nagaro asked as casually as he could.

To his surprise, Pavo looked relieved to become the subject of the conversation. "Not so good," he said. "I do stupid thing last night. I try to make pain go away from *here*." He put his hand on his chest. "But now I have pain *here*." He touched his head. "And still my heart is sore."

"What was it that happened to upset you, Pavo? Taru said something about Tenepti..."

Pavo's shoulders instantly sagged. He looked down at his soup. "Tenepti is go to marry other man," he said dejectedly. "Her father tell me not to come back any more."

"That's terrible, Pavo! I... I'm sorry." Nagaro frowned. "But I thought her father wouldn't let her marry for two years, because she's too young. He can't mean she'll marry very soon, can he?"

This did nothing to improve Pavo's mood. "She go to sit with other man for one year maybe, then marry," he said gloomily. "But her father have choose other man, and he tell me not to come back."

To Nagaro, this was patently ridiculous. "Her *father* chose the other man? Doesn't Tenepti have anything to say about it?"

At this point Yuli set a bowl of soup in front of him. "Ye're a man after my own heart, Tor Nagaro," she declared. "That's just what *I* said." She turned to Pavo. "Have ye even seen this other man, Pavo? Maybe her father made the whole thing up, just t' be rid of ye."

But Pavo shook his head. "I *have* see other man. He was sit with her last night."

Nagaro sighed. "Any man can sit with a woman just for appearances, Pavo," he said, speaking from very recently acquired insight. He took a spoonful of soup, then another. Then he put the spoon down, picked up the bowl with both hands, and drained its contents. "This *is* good soup, Yuli," he said. "Could I have another bowl, please?"

Pavo was staring at him. "You think maybe Tenepti father find man to sit with her, for me to see only? But he does not really want for Tenepti to marry this man?" His words held a rising note of hope.

"That's exactly what he's saying," Yuli observed, taking Nagaro's bowl. She crossed to the soup kettle, refilled the bowl, and brought it back to the table.

For a moment Pavo's broad face lit up, but then he sagged again and the light died in his eyes. "But her father have tell me not to come back! He do not even let me *talk* to her!"

Nagaro frowned as he applied his spoon to the second bowl of soup. The warm liquid felt wonderfully good in his stomach, and the pain in his head was subsiding. "What we need is someone to carry messages back and forth between you and Tenepti," he said, thinking aloud. "If we could just find a man that her father would let sit with her—"

"Who needs a *man?*" Yuli asked archly. "This is a task for a woman if ever I heard one."

Nagaro immediately saw the wisdom of this. "You're right, Yuli," he said. "A woman could act as a go-between, and her father wouldn't have to know anything about it. But we'd still have to find someone who could speak freely to both of them."

Yuli waved a hand. "That's easy as shelling peas! One o' my girls'll know someone— or someone that knows someone. Turowa or Hashtep, women talk t' each other. Ye just leave it to me."

"That's very good of you, Yuli." Nagaro smiled at the way she spoke of her daughters. Yuli's "two girls" were both grown women with husbands of their own.

Pavo was nodding. "Yes, is very good thing you do for me, Tira Yuli. Thank you." Then he frowned. "But I am afraid still Tenepti father will never let me marry her."

Nagaro put down his spoon with a decisive clink. "If you love each other, you should run away and be wed without her father's permission if you have to!"

Yuli and Pavo both stared at him open-mouthed.

Pavo managed to find his voice first. "Oh, no, Nagaro!" he exclaimed. "Good Hashtep woman never do *that!*"

Nagaro's face darkened. The soup was helping him to feel better physically, but he'd been through too much in the last day and a half. He was in no mood to be tolerant of things that made no sense to him. "A *good* father should want his daughter to be happy," he snapped. "If Tenepti's father won't let her be happy, then he's not a good father. And I don't see why a *good* woman should have to let a *bad* father ruin her life!"

This time Pavo was speechless. Yuli gave a low whistle. For the space of a dozen heartbeats, no one spoke.

Nagaro re-focused on his soup.

"I've half a loaf o' bread left," Yuli ventured as the silence stretched. "Would either o' ye lads be wantin' a slice?"

Nagaro looked up from his soup. "Yes, Yuli," he said with studied calm. "I would. Thank you."

Pavo released a pent up breath. "I would like bread also, Tira Yuli," he said quickly.

Neither young man spoke while the innkeeper's wife cut two thick slabs of bread and brought them back to the table. Then she pulled a stool up to one end of the table and sat down.

Nagaro took a bite of bread. He was uncomfortable under Yuli's gaze. She was studying him intently. At length she spoke.

"For weeks I've been wonderin' how ye came to be captain o' that ship, Tor Nagaro," she said. "But now I know. I'd heard the tale, o' course," she added, seeing his startled look. "But I just couldn't see it t' look at ye. Ye have such polite, quiet ways. But now I see that ye've a commanding way about ye when ye've got something t' say as really matters to ye."

Nagaro studied his bread. "I'm sorry," he said after a moment, looking up to meet Pavo's eyes. "Other folk have their own customs. I should remember that."

"Now don't ye go backin' away from it!" Yuli chided him, wagging a finger. "What ye said was exactly right. And the women 'round here have been sayin' it for years. I just don't know that I've heard a *man* say it before, and that's a fact!"

Nagaro gave her a dismayed look. "It comes out of Kelorin law," he protested. "The Writings say the same thing, but Kelorin law is older. It says men and women are equal, and neither should have dominion over the other. And when children come of age at seventeen— male or female— they should be free to make their own choices. But," he added, "even Kelorin men don't always seem to follow the law these days." He was thinking of how the Lady Maramine's father had forbidden her to marry the man she loved, with devastating consequences.

"How d'ye know all that?" Yuli asked.

He shrugged. "My lady guardian had books."

Pavo had retreated into the stoic impassivity his people seemed to affect when uncomfortable or unsure of their course. Now he spoke guardedly. "Do you mean, Nagaro, that I should not run away with Tenepti until she have seventeen year?"

Nagaro turned to him. "I *hope* you won't have to run away with her at all, Pavo," he said earnestly. "I hope her father will come to see what he must do to make her happy and will change his mind. And you should give him every chance to change it, too, because it's far better to have her father's blessing than not. By all means wait until she's seventeen— or even longer— as long as he doesn't try to make her marry someone else. But, if he *does* try that, I think you should be ready to do what you have to, for her happiness and yours."

Pavo regarded him thoughtfully for a moment and then said, "I think maybe this is not so bad plan. Maybe is all right, sometime, to do bad thing for good reason."

"A bad thing for a good reason..." Nagaro's voice trailed off and he dropped his eyes, frowning as he examined the half-eaten slice of bread in his hands. *If only he could say there had been a good reason for what he'd done...*

Yuli spoke as if in answer to his thought. "Doin' one bad thing doesn't make someone a bad person, Tor Nagaro, whatever the reason."

"No, it doesn't," he said tightly. For a long moment he concentrated on eating his slice of bread. But he was aware of the way Yuli was looking at him, and Pavo's wary manner suggested the young Hashtep was anticipating an explosion. "What did Taru tell you?" he asked at last. "About me?"

Yuli and Pavo exchanged glances. The innkeeper's wife spoke first. "He said ye were upset... about what ye did last night—" she began.

"And angry," put in Pavo. "He say you are very angry with him. He say he was afraid you go to hit him!"

"*Hit him?*" Nagaro bridled. "I would never have hit him! But I'm afraid I did shout at him a lot. I was *really* angry. Did he tell you what he did?"

"Oh, aye," said Yuli. "There were some bad parts to it, I know. But everyone'll know ye're not crossed after last night."

Nagaro winced. "Does everyone already know about it?"

Yuli eyed him. "*We-ell,*" she said carefully. "If the men from the tavern missed telling anyone, I expect Taru won't."

Pavo nodded seriously. "Taru have go to tell every-body, Nagaro. He go to say it is all his fault. He say maybe you never talk to him again, but he be sure that it not be wasted."

"*Bishka!*" Nagaro bowed his head. Which was worse? Having them think he was crossed, or having them know what he'd done?

After a moment he heaved a sigh and straightened. "The truth is best," he murmured. "And I have to live with it. But Taru shouldn't tell them it was all his fault, because it wasn't."

Pavo looked puzzled. "Why you think it is bad for everyone to know you lie with woman?" he asked. "Lying with woman is not bad thing."

Nagaro was puzzled in his turn. "It goes against the teachings of Vothra for a man to lie with a woman he doesn't intend to marry, Pavo," he said seriously. "And I surely do *not* intend to marry Jila."

"You do not have *faasha*?"

Nagaro frowned. "What is 'faasha'?"

"It is what you call test... proof... for young man. My brother Taal take me to faasha woman when I have sixteen year."

Nagaro stared at the young Hashtep. "Are you saying," he said slowly, "that your brother took you to lie with a woman when you were sixteen?"

Pavo nodded. "Oh, yes," he said brightly. "Faasha is good thing for young man!"

Nagaro shook his head. "Kelorin men don't do that," he said flatly.

Pavo considered this. "But if they have no faasha, when they go to be married, how do they know what to do?"

Nagaro felt suddenly sick. Memories of his marriage to the princess rose unbidden in his mind. Memories of things he would much rather have left forgotten. *The heskial had complicated things with Nevien, but there had also been a certain element of not knowing what to do.* Feeling the blood in his face, he glanced hurriedly at Yuli, thinking she would also be embarrassed by Pavo's words. Instead, he found she was sitting with a hand over her mouth while her shoulders shook with silent laughter. She gestured for him to answer Pavo's question.

Frowning, Nagaro turned back to Pavo. "I expect," he said stiffly, "that they figure it out."

Yuli emitted a small choking sound.

"And new wife?" Pavo asked. "She do not mind that her husband not have practice?"

Nagaro was trying not to look at Yuli. He could tell she was still laughing, and he hoped she wasn't laughing at *him*. Again he had to answer, so he fell back on what he'd always believed. "If a woman loves you, Pavo, she won't mind whether you've had any practice or not." *And would it have been different if he and the princess had loved each other?*

"Oh." Pavo considered this thoughtfully. "Yes," he conceded after a moment, "I think this is maybe true."

Yuli coughed. She appeared to have mastered her mirth. "Tor Nagaro," she ventured, "I can see that your lady guardian raised ye t' be a very proper young man. But ye really needn't worry about what the men 'round here will think o' what ye did. They won't call it *faasha*, o' course. They'll just say ye've proved your manhood."

Nagaro flushed under his kuma stain. He didn't think he should get off so lightly. While he *was* secretly relieved to know that he could "do a man's work" in bed— especially after his complete incompetence with Nevien— the fact did nothing to change his self-judgement. He swallowed painfully. "And what will the women think?"

"The women?" Yuli asked. "Why do ye want t' know what the women think?"

Nagaro frowned. "If I'm ever to win the heart of one, I'd better give heed to what they think."

She studied him with her head on one side. "I believe ye mean that," she said. "So I'll answer it. I can't speak for *all* the women, o' course, but it's likely that most will blame Jila. The mothers with sons that are prey t' Jila surely will. And any young woman that likes ye at all would blame Jila in a minute." She laughed shortly. "The men'll blame Jila, too, for that matter. If they think there's any blamin' t' be done, men *always* blame the woman. Though the truth is, when it comes t' Jila, there's plenty o' blame to be had. Ye're not the first young man she's taken for a tumble."

Nagaro shifted in his chair. After what Taru had said, this wasn't news. "Who *is* Jila, Yuli?" he asked. "She doesn't seem to be one of the tavern women."

"Not now, she isn't. But she started that way," Yuli told him. "Jila was always a wild one. She lost both her parents 'fore she was grown, and her sister couldn't keep a hand on her. So Jila started workin' as a tavern woman when she barely *was* a woman, and she kept it up 'til she figured out she could live a lot more comfortably by gettin' her hook into one o' the merchant captains that come t' Pakoa every summer. She's had one after another o' them, over the years. I hear the one she's got right now keeps her in a nice house over on the west shore, near Jade Cove, so's he can see her without havin' the folk here in town be any the wiser."

"You mean she's a sea captain's *mistress?*" Nagaro was more than a little disturbed to hear this.

Yuli leaned back on her stool. "I've heard that word, an' I guess that's what ye'd call her. But these merchant captains come an' go, ye know," she went on. "They're not in port for more 'n a few days at a time— with months in between. Jila has time on her hands and she gets restless, I suppose. So she goes fishin' sometimes, and it's the young men she fishes for. She's only interested in two kinds o' men: the captains, with plenty o' money, that she keeps on her hook, and the young lads that's green as grass— too green t' see what she is. Those she tumbles for a lark and whatever they've got in their pockets." Yuli paused. "Oh, she enjoys it too, I'm sure," she added, reading Nagaro's face. "Ye needn't think she didn't fancy your looks just 'cause she robbed ye. Jila's eyes are wide enough t' see what a handsome man ye are."

Nagaro felt his face burning. He looked down. *Handsome... and green as grass...* "Taru said she only lies with the young men once."

Yuli nodded. "Jila don't care a bit what she does to a man's heart. She just chews men up and spits 'em out."

Nagaro sighed. *Spits them out.* That was pretty much the way he felt. *Spit out, like a cherry pit...* At least he didn't have to worry that she'd ever trouble him again... except— "What will happen when the sea captain comes back, Yuli?" he asked, aware that men had been known to kill each other over a woman.

Yuli waved the question aside. "I don't think ye need worry he'll come after ye, Tor Nagaro. It was Jila that hooked ye. There's others saw it. Ye'd no idea who she was, and ye were drunk, besides."

"I shouldn't have been drunk!" Reminded again of his shame, Nagaro spoke with sudden bitterness. "I shouldn't have broken the ban. I was stupid, and the wine made me more stupid. Why does any man want to drink it, anyway?"

"Oh, well," Yuli replied sagely. "A little ale only makes ye a little stupid, and there's times that a man wants t' be just stupid enough to forget his troubles for a few hours."

Nagaro considered this. He turned to Pavo. "You said you were trying to make your heart stop hurting last night. Did it work? For a while?"

Pavo shrugged his broad shoulders. "I think, maybe. But I do not remember most of it. Taru have told me I was go to fight with man who insult all Hashtep woman— only he stop me. I do not remember that. Also I do not remember I get sick in street coming home. Taru say that was good thing, because some of ale that go down come back up. Otherwise today I feel even more bad." Pavo shook his head. "I do not think I am go to try that again."

Nagaro sat silent, remembering that Taru had told him that some men couldn't remember what they did when they were drunk. Either Pavo was one of those, and he wasn't, or else he hadn't been as drunk as Pavo. Either way, it seemed unlikely that the gap in his memory of that last night in Lankura was the result of being drunk. It wasn't much, but perhaps he *had* learned something, after all.

Yuli must have still been thinking about what Nagaro had asked her. "There's some men as think too much, Tor Nagaro," she said. "And it stops 'em from *doing* things. Things they ought t' do, or want t' do, but are afraid o' doing. A couple o' mugs of ale sometimes'll get a man past those fears."

Nagaro remembered how he'd been trying to cure his nervousness with the wine. It had worked, after a fashion. Too well. *He hadn't known when to stop.* "I think it's better to face things, in spite of being afraid," he said seriously.

"Well maybe it is— for ye at least, Tor Nagaro," Yuli conceded. "But it wasn't for my Ramu when it came t' marryin' me. I think I'd still be waiting if our fathers hadn't put their heads together. His father got a couple o' mugs of ale into Ramu, and sent him off t' speak t' mine, and... well... Ramu asked for me that night, and I don't think he's ever regretted it. And that's a fact."

Nagaro stared at her in astonishment. "Ramu's father got him *drunk* so he'd ask if he could wed you? And *your* father was in on it?"

She laughed. "Only a little drunk. They both knew he wanted to, ye see. It's just that he kept thinking *what if*, and *maybe*, 'til he got himself all tied in knots." Yuli sighed. "That's my Ramu."

Nagaro considered this revelation. From what he'd seen, Yuli and Ramu adored one another. So it had obviously turned out all right. *Strange were the ways of the world.*

Yuli was studying him, and Pavo was watching them both in the silent, secret way of his people.

"There's some men as can't find where they keep their hearts without a pint or two o' ale in 'em," Yuli said at last. "But ye're not one o' those, Tor Nagaro. Nor are ye, Tor Pavo," she added, giving the young Hashtep a smile, which he returned shyly. "No, Tor Nagaro," she went on, turning back to him. "Go ahead and keep your ban. There's nothing I can think of that ale or wine could do for ye."

Nagaro wasn't sure whether he'd just been told that he was very nearly perfect or completely hopeless. *More likely the latter,* he thought, and decided not to embarrass himself by asking. Glancing down, he rediscovered the remains of his bread, and took a bite. He drew in a long breath. "I suppose I'd better go find Taru," he said into the silence. "I have to tell him that I'm still his friend. And see if I can get him to stop saying it was all his fault. Do either of you have any idea where he went?"

“I’d look for him at the tavern,” Yuli suggested. “If ye don’t find him sooner.”

The thought of going back to the tavern made Nagaro cringe, but he was resolved to do whatever he had to. He finished his bread, and Yuli cut him another slice to eat as he went. He thanked her and left the kitchen, passing out by way of the common room into the street. The soup, the bread, and the talk had all helped. He no longer felt sick and his headache was much diminished. And he also felt easier at heart than he had when he’d come downstairs. The day was still bright, but had grown blustery, so he put his head down into the wind, and set off up the street.

***

Nagaro had no sooner left the kitchen than Pavo rose to leave as well. “I think I go to maybe sleep now,” he told Yuli.

“Aye, ye do that,” she said. “And I’ll find ye a go-between— a woman t’ carry your words to Tenepti. Don’t ye worry.”

“Thank you, again, Tira Yuli.”

She brushed it aside. “Ye remember what Tor Nagaro told ye, now,” she admonished. “About givin’ her father time t’ change his mind— and runnin’ away if ye have to, but *only* if ye have to. That’s the best piece of advice I’ve heard in a long time.”

After Pavo had gone, Yuli stepped to the little kitchen window and surreptitiously drew aside the curtain. The window offered a view of the street outside. Down near the end of the block she could make out Nagaro’s retreating figure. For a moment she lingered, watching him striding along, taking bites of the bread she’d given him and pausing to look into each shop window he passed. “If only I had another daughter o’ marryin’ age,” she said aloud. Then she sighed and drew the curtain back across the window. “Jila thinks she’s played him for a fool, I don’t doubt,” she added. “But the only fool I see is Jila.”

Chapter 7

Tredhold's Offer

Nagaro was sitting with Taru and Pavo at their favorite table on the covered porch in front of the Bay Tree Inn. For the first time in days it wasn't raining, and they'd come outside with their mugs of hot sothiril to get some fresh air and admire the view of the harbor spread out before them, awash in watery morning sunlight. Unfortunately the topic of conversation was hindering Nagaro's enjoyment of the scene.

"I wish they'd let it be!" he said in exasperation. "Why can't they do that? It's been a week now!"

Taru shrugged. "A lot o' the island folk would like t' see Jila get her comeuppance, and ye've given them an excuse t' say so."

Nagaro glowered. Making up with Taru had been the easy part. He'd found his friend at the tavern, just as Yuli had suggested, engaged in heated discussion with Sodo the tavern keeper in front of a small audience. The audience had begun to grow alarmingly as soon as Nagaro made his appearance. The discussion had been interrupted long enough for Taru to be reassured that Nagaro had gotten over his anger and did not intend to punch him— which had put everything straight between them as far as the young Turo was concerned. And then Nagaro had been pressed to verify the details of his encounter with Jila, including the amount of money taken from him, and the fact that Jila had made no mention of any price for her "services."

Sodo had claimed he'd believed that Jila was just a tavern woman plying her "honest trade." He'd professed to be unaware that she had been robbing young men in his establishment for years. Apparently, none of the other victims had ever complained. Sodo had proceeded to declare that he would never rent a room to Jila again. All of the tavern staff had then been gathered and questioned, and one of the kitchen women had been reprimanded because she'd been overheard telling Jila there was a young man in the back room who'd just paid a lot of money for a bottle of wine. Nagaro had endured the mortification with what grace he could, reminding himself that it was no worse than he deserved. And of course the story had run the whole length and breadth of the island within two days time. So Nagaro's reputation as a "straight-sailor" had been secured at the price of a public shaming.

He'd dared to hope that would be the end of it, which, of course, it hadn't been. Nor was it just that the island folk couldn't seem to put the matter down. There was also the way Jila haunted his dreams. On one recent night, he'd dreamt that he was lying next to a weeping Nevien, had reached to embrace her, and had found himself holding Jila instead. He'd awakened feeling very hot, and thoroughly disgusted with himself. The next morning he'd asked Pavo about his experience with the faasha woman. Pavo had looked thoughtful. "I think maybe is not such good thing to have very beautiful faasha woman," he'd conceded. "Faasha woman I have was much more old and had teeth like horse. I do not dream about her at all." Which didn't help.

Nagaro realized that Taru was still speaking.

"Wouldn't ye really like t' get your money back?" Taru was asking. "Ye say ye don't care about it, but isn't that cash box o' yours getting a bit light?"

Nagaro avoided his friend's eyes by studying his sothiril. "I can manage," he said.

Pavo turned his own narrow dark eyes on Taru. "Why you do not understand, Taru? Nagaro do not want people to talk about it anymore."

"It doesn't matter what he *wants*." Taru gestured so vigorously with his cup that the contents nearly sloshed out. "We can't stop them from talking. And they'll go right on talking about it until something better comes along."

Nagaro scowled into his cup. Leering grins and conspiratorial winks were the typical responses of most of the men he knew, and many had congratulated him on having lain with the most beautiful woman on the island. They were all indignant about the theft of his money, while his having gotten drunk occasioned no more than benign indulgence. Since none of this did anything to diminish his sense of shame, Nagaro could only wish for it to stop. He feared, however, that Taru was right.

"I wish they wouldn't try to track Jila down," he muttered. "She's probably already spent the money anyway."

"That she hasn't!" Taru was smug. "Not in trade with any honest merchant at any rate. That's what Yuli says."

"Maybe there are merchant that are not so honest," Pavo volunteered.

"Well, maybe there are, but I tell ye, Jila must be hiding. Nobody knows where she's gone."

Pavo lifted his broad shoulders. "Jila sometime do not come to Pakoa town for three or four month. That is what Hashtep say."

Taru was unimpressed. "She hasn't been back t' the house her captain keeps for her over on the west shore either. Even her sister hasn't seen her. Tego says she's afraid t' show her face!"

Before Pavo could respond, a new voice spoke from behind them, from the direction of the door of the common room.

"Tego is right. Jila's dived deep."

Nagaro recognized the voice as belonging to Landros, and turned on his stool to see that Landros and Tredhold had stepped out of the inn and were approaching the table where he and his friends were seated. The two former Fleet officers were both smiling broadly. Landros, a grizzled Kelorin with a sea warrior's weathered face, was wearing a dark blue tirka that could almost have been part of a Fleet uniform. Tred, the former ship's doctor, was a younger man, a stocky sandy-haired Leithian clad in pants and tirka in the plain brown wool favored by the local tradesmen.

Landros continued. "She's shut herself away someplace like a clam in its shell, Nagaro. She should ha' known better than t' hook a fish o' your size."

Nagaro winced. "She hadn't even heard my name, Landros."

"Well she must ha' been the only soul on Pakoa who hadn't."

Nagaro sighed. "She knew about the *Fist*, and the freed slaves," he said. "Enough to guess I was one of them, but—"

"But ye didn't tell her that ye were the captain," Landros guessed. "Because ye don't like to boast."

Nagaro gave Landros a sharp look. "Are you saying she'd have left me alone if I'd boasted about captaining the ship?" It was a bitter thought.

The sea warrior shrugged. "Only if she *believed* ye, lad," he said. "Which isn't likely. I'd never have believed it myself if I hadn't seen it with my own eyes. That a man o' your slim years could do what ye did—"

"*Don't*, Landros. *Please!*"

Pavo shifted in his seat. "That is another thing Nagaro do not want people to talk about," he said. "That he be captain of ship."

"They *have* stopped talking about that," Taru pointed out. "They'd much rather talk about Jila."

"Don't pay them any mind, Nagaro," Landros advised. "Just set your course and steer it."

"But I don't have a course!" All Nagaro's pent up frustration rang in the words.

Landros cocked an eyebrow. "Would ye like to change that?" He glanced significantly at Tredhold.

The healer cleared his throat. "I have... ah... something I'd like to discuss with ye, Nagaro. If ye've a few minutes."

"Why? What sort o' thing?" Taru's glance flicked avidly from Tred to Landros.

Tredhold started to say something, but Landros cut in. "I'm sure Nagaro will tell ye all about it *later*, Taru, if he's a mind." The Kelorin's gaze came back to Nagaro. "If ye've time right now, our room is a good place to talk privately."

"Of course." Nagaro glanced at his friends. "If you'll excuse me, I'll rejoin you later."

Pavo nodded with his usual deadpan. Taru looked mildly annoyed but unchastened as he shrugged his acquiescence.

Nagaro rose and moved to follow Landros back into the inn, with Tred bringing up the rear.

As the Leithian closed the door behind them he said, "It's really not a secret."

"Of course not," Landros tossed over his shoulder. "But I don't care for Taru's meddling."

Nagaro paused just inside the door, thinking he should defend his friend. "Taru means well," he said. "He's just looking out for me."

"Oh, aye," Landros muttered, "The same way he was with that tavern business."

"He's promised not to try anything like that again."

Landros turned around to give Nagaro a hard look. "Gave ye his solemn promise, did he? What makes ye think he'll keep it?"

Nagaro was indignant. "He swore it! By Hakura Kili and all the Spirits!"

Landros' expression softened. "Well..." he conceded, "that *might* be worth something. But his scheme lacked sense. I'd have had something t' say about it if that young fool had let on what he was planning." The grizzled sea warrior turned and started forward again, then nodded in the direction of the main room. "There's some o' the lads in here," he said. "Moraga and his lot."

Nagaro steeled himself to run the gauntlet. As he stepped forward into the room, several of the men who were seated there rose and approached him.

Moraga was at the front of the group, but he seemed to be holding back until Tego pushed him from behind. "Go on," the older Turo hissed in a stage whisper. "Ye've been tellin' us what ye wanted t' say. Here's yer chance t' say it!"

Moraga cast his roommate a look of annoyance and muttered something under his breath, but then he squared his shoulders and stepped up to Nagaro. He cleared his throat. "I've been meanin' t' tell ye," he said gruffly, "that I'm sorry for what I said t' ye in here t'other day. 'Twas nothin' but guessin'. And, as ye say, it weren't none o' my affair. I wish I'd kept me gob shut."

Nagaro was mildly impressed. This was better than he'd expected from the belligerent merchant seaman. "That's very decent of you, Moraga," he said. "I accept your apology."

Gurd had been hovering behind Moraga and he now stepped forward. "We should ha' known ye weren't crossed from the way ye did Simion's work for him," he said. "No crossed man can fight like ye do!"

Nagaro's glance stabbed the young Leithian. "When it comes to fighting, I understand Simion's reluctance far better than I understand your enthusiasm," he said coldly. "I'd rather I hadn't had to kill five men to get us free, but there didn't seem to be any other way. And in any case, a crossed man has as much right to walk under the sun as anyone else." Poor Simion, he knew, had scarcely been seen in public in the last week.

Having spoken his mind, Nagaro shouldered his way between the stunned men, making for the door at the other end of the room that led to the hallway and the stairs. Gurd was left standing with his mouth open.

Behind Nagaro, Landros coughed and added, "That's what the Writings say. Isn't that so?" He was addressing himself to Mendorel who was Kelorin, and was sitting at a nearby table

The graying former shopkeeper made haste to answer. "That it is, Landros. I've heard men say it more 'n once."

Nagaro didn't bother to turn back, but continued through the doorway and stopped in the hall beyond to let Landros and Tredhold catch up. As the door closed behind Tred, the healer said, "That was well done, both of ye, speaking up for Simion. The lad's been taking the blame for what happened. He's been taking his meals in his room, too, and Yuli gave me an earful on the subject just yesterday."

Landros looked embarrassed. "I was just trying t' keep Nagaro from undoing what little good came out o' Taru's scheme," he confessed, as he started down the short hallway that led to the inn's ground-floor guest rooms. "Though it *is* wrong for Simion to suffer, of course. He can't help being what he is, and I'm sure the Writings have *something* to say on the subject."

"They do," Nagaro said pointedly, and then quoted the text as he remembered it: "'Since we know not what the next life will make of us, we should be tolerant of others in this one'. Of course," he added, "except for Mendorel, those men out there aren't Vothrin."

"Nor am I," said Tred. "But I still think it's good advice."

Nagaro bit his lip. "I got too worried about what other men thought of me," he said. "And I talked myself into doing something stupid."

They had reached the room that Landros and Tred shared. Landros pulled out his key, unlocked the door, and opened it. "It's a common failing," he said as he ushered Nagaro through. "Don't ride your own back about it."

The room was similar to the one Nagaro shared with Taru and Pavo, except that it was a little smaller, containing only two beds and two dressers. There was also a table and two chairs. Landros went to his dresser and busied himself with something. Tred offered Nagaro one of the chairs and sat down across from him, fixing him with his bright blue gaze.

What's this about?" Nagaro asked, with some misgivings.

"Something simple, really," Tred assured him. "And nothing that couldn't have been said out there under the sun. Ye know how I've talked of practicing my healer's trade outside the Fleet?"

Nagaro nodded. "In Harmoth, you said."

"Yes, and I hope to go there in the spring. But it now looks like I'll be working here on Pakoa this winter.

Nagaro was surprised. "I would have thought Pakoa had plenty of healers."

Tred shook his head. "The island only had two, and the older one died last spring. The other man— Master Pedril— hadn't yet bothered with taking an apprentice. When I last spoke to him, he admitted that he may have more than he can handle and it might not be a bad thing to have someone t' take up the slack in his rope."

"Oh, well, that's good for you, Tred, but I don't see what it has to do with me." Nagaro glanced at Landros who had taken a seat on one of the beds and was leaning against the wall, fingers laced behind his head.

"Keep listening," Landros drawled. "He's not done casting his line."

Tred coughed to reclaim Nagaro's attention. "Hearing Pedril go on about needing to find an apprentice set me to thinking," he said. His tone was light, but he was watching Nagaro keenly. "I realized I'd be needing one too some day, and maybe sooner than later. And *that* set me to thinking about what sort o' lad I'd be looking for." Tred paused, his expression almost wary. "And the person that kept coming t' mind was *you*, Nagaro. Ye may recall that I said on Chitaopa that I thought ye'd make a good one. And I thought... well... since ye've nothing better to do all winter, maybe ye'd like to try your hand at it."

For a moment Nagaro could only stare in shock. "I... I'd never even thought about it," he stammered. "Anyone could have done what I did on Chitaopa after all. There wasn't much skill involved."

Tred's eyes had remained on him and there was still tension in the way the Leithian held himself. "What ye did there needed both care and patience," he said. "And not everyone would have wanted to do it, either. But ye took it on willingly. Ye've got good hands, a quick mind, and the right temperament. The rest is just knowledge and experience."

Nagaro dropped his eyes. The praise embarrassed him. Tredhold wouldn't speak so if he didn't mean it, but... could he really become a healer?

The idea was attractive. It was certainly a way of doing good in the world... He frowned. "I think I'd like to try, but I don't know about going to Harmoth..." he said, thinking aloud. "My friends mean to stay here."

Tred relaxed visibly. "Well, ye needn't decide about that until the day comes. Master Pedril would likely take ye on after ye've worked with me for a bit, if ye show promise— which I expect ye will. And if ye find that ye don't fancy the work, ye needn't ask him."

That sounded all right, but there were other considerations. "I don't know how the Pakoa folk would take to me." Nagaro was thinking of all the doors that closed when he rode by.

Tredhold spread his hands. "I don't know how they'll take to *me*. Leithians are as scarce as fish-feathers on this island. But sick folk will often take what they can get."

"I see..." Nagaro had no other reservations that he could think of, and he'd just been lamenting his lack of direction. He made up his mind. "Then I would like to try it, Tred," he said. "And I'm very grateful for the offer." He extended his hand.

"Good." Tred took the hand and shook it warmly. "Come to me First Day of next week then, and I'll start with some basic things ye ought to know before we begin seeing patients." He stood up, and pushed back his chair. "And now, if ye'll both excuse me, I've an appointment with the barber."

"And I guess I'll go back to my friends." Nagaro rose to follow Tred from the room.

Landros stood up quickly, however, and came after him. "Stay a moment, Nagaro," the older man said, "I'd like a word with ye."

"All right." Nagaro turned back, frowning a little, uncertain what Landros might intend.

The door closed behind Tred, and Landros slid into the chair the healer had vacated motioning Nagaro back to the other seat. The former first mate leaned forward as Nagaro sat down. "Ye're taking what happened at the tavern much too hard, lad." he said. "Am I right in guessing that ye never broke the ban before?"

Nagaro dropped his eyes. The question was problematic because of the single glass of wine he'd drunk that fateful night in Lankura. He didn't dare mention it, of course, and the truth was it had yielded him no useful experience because he couldn't remember what had happened. He swallowed, offering Landros no answer, hoping the old sea warrior would take his silence as an embarrassed affirmative.

"I thought so." The satisfaction in Landros' voice indicated that the older man had done exactly that. "And it does ye credit," Landros continued. "But since ye didn't know what ye were doing, ye got yourself drunk, and got rolled by a woman who knew *exactly* what she was doing. And that's nothing that hasn't been going on for as long as there's been dishonest doxies and green young sailors. Ye were brought up by a lady, having no father t' teach ye the ways o' the world— like the dangers o' sitting alone in a tavern with a bottle of wine, not t' mention flashing your silver about. That sort o' behavior draws women like Jila the way old meat draws flies. I'd ha' warned ye about her kind myself, if I'd known what ye were planning. We warn all the new Fleet recruits, and there's still always some that gets taken." Landros paused, turning a little red. "Truth is, I got taken that way once myself."

"You *did*?" Nagaro was so astonished that the words slipped out before he could catch them.

"Aye." Landros coughed. "It was years ago, and it didn't turn out as well for me as it did for you. I'd had a mug or two of ale and this little she-cat was acting all soft n' sweet. But she must ha' slipped something in my drink that put me out afore I could get me trousers off. So *I* never got what I thought I was gettin', and *she* got all my money."

Nagaro could feel the blood in his face. He shifted in his seat. "You... don't keep the ban, yourself?"

Landros studied the table top. "I used t' break it pretty reg'lar, when I was a young buck. Sailing men are inclined t' be drinking men, I'm afraid." He raised his eyes. "I do much better now, though, and getting rolled like that was part o' what set me on a straighter course— that and meeting the woman I married. Now, o' course, my wife is gone, and my daughters have husbands o' their own, but I've just gotten used t' steering clear o' the taverns."

Nagaro digested this. "I appreciate your telling me this, Landros," he said after a moment. "And I'm grateful for your advice, although I have no intention of breaking the ban again. I think I'd rather my experience had ended the way yours did."

The older man gave him a solemn look. "Coming from you, I believe that. Ye may find there's those that don't understand keepin' the ban, but ye've got your reasons, and we both know what Vothra's advice is. *My* advice for right now is what I already told ye: Pay no attention to what folk are saying. Just set yourself to finding that course o' yours. This storm'll blow by." He smiled crookedly. "Now go back out there and satisfy your friends' curiosity."

Nagaro rose and thanked the former second mate again. He left the room with a real hope that his luck might at last be turning.

Back on the inn's front porch, he watched his friends' faces as he described Tredhold's offer. Pavo was impassive as usual, merely nodding at several points.

Taru, however, quickly began to frown, and his frown darkened. "So ye're going t' do this?" he asked when Nagaro stopped speaking.

"Well... yes. It seems like a good opportunity."

Taru leaned back, gripping the edge of the table to steady his tilting stool. "I thought we were all going t' be fishermen."

At that Pavo stirred. "This is work like he do on Chitaopa island," he said. "It is better work for Nagaro."

Taru rounded angrily on the young Hashtep. "What's wrong with being a fisherman?"

"Is nothing wrong with it," Pavo replied calmly. "But Nagaro do not seem like fisherman to me. I do not think that is how his story go."

For a moment Taru could only gape.

Nagaro had listened with amused embarrassment. "It's not as if anything is certain," he protested. "I may not do well at the work, or I may not like it. I may very well end up a fisherman after all, and it's not as if I wouldn't still be your friend, whatever happens."

Taru scowled. "If ye go t' Harmoth, ye'll be leaving us behind— or Pavo, at least. There aren't any Hashtep in Harmoth— or anywhere else in Edrovir besides here on Pakoa."

Pavo shook his head. "Nagaro must do what he must do," he declared solemnly.

Nagaro raised a silencing hand before Taru could make a retort. "The earliest Tredhold would go to Harmoth would be in the spring," he said. "Which is months away. And he may not be ready to go even then. If I haven't finished my training whenever he goes, I can possibly finish it here with Master Pedril. Or I could go to Harmoth to finish it with Tred, and come back here to practice the art. So there's no need to assume anything."

Taru appeared to be mollified by this. His gaze turned speculative. "If ye're going t' be doing work with the healer..." he mused, "maybe Pavo and I should look for work with the fishermen."

"That's a fine idea, Taru." Nagaro grasped gratefully at the dangled thread. "If you can earn some money towards buying a boat, it would be all to the good. There's no telling exactly how much your shares will be from selling the rest of the *Fist*'s cargo, or how long it will take to find buyers— especially for the gold."

Pavo flashed one of his brief, brilliant smiles. "Yes," he said. "This is good plan."

To Nagaro's relief, Taru sat up straight and declared, "All right, then, let's do it! And since Nagaro's set t' begin with Tredhold next week, we should get up early on First Day so we can all get started."

Chapter 8

First Steps

It would have been easier if there had been even one medical text in Tredhold's little bag, or anywhere on the island of Pakoa for that matter. Nagaro was used to learning things by reading. He considered himself fairly good at it. But there weren't any books, which meant there was nothing Nagaro could do to prepare on his own and Tredhold had no recourse but to either explain things himself or demonstrate them.

The healer began the first day by going over the items in his satchel and describing their uses.

"I've gotten together a fairly complete kit," he began as he laid out the trove of objects on the table in his room, to be examined by the light that penetrated the small glass panes of the single window. "Some of this I found in the infirmary on the *Fist of Death*. The rest I've added here on Pakoa. I've had to make my own bandages and dressings." He indicated two rolls of cotton cloth torn into strips and a thick package of the same stuff cut into squares and folded. "And I bought needles and thread." He opened a small folded leather book-like object that contained two cloth pages with several needles of assorted sizes thrust in-and-out of the fabric. There were also two wooden spools, one bearing thinner and the other thicker thread.

Nagaro understood the use of these things, but others puzzled him. "What's this?" he asked, picking up a wooden tube about eight inches long. It had a two-inch diameter bell at one end and a quarter-inch diameter rounded opening with an odd little flange around it at the other.

"That's a listening trumpet." The healer took the object from Nagaro's hands. "Ye put the wide end against the patient's chest and your ear to the other end, like this." He demonstrated as if he were listening to the table top. "It amplifies the sounds of heart and breath."

"To get the pulse, or tell if the person is breathing well?"

Tredhold dismissed this with shake of his head. "Much more than that. Ye can tell the *quality* of both heartbeat and breath. There's much that can be learned about the state of a man's health from those sounds. But I'll have to show ye when we have a patient. There is no other way."

Nagaro reached out to touch a fat leather bundle. "Are these the tools you use for treating wounds?"

"Aye." Tredhold took the bundle, undid some strings that secured it, and unrolled it on the table. A series of neatly sewn pockets and loops of leather held a bewildering array of metal objects.

Nagaro saw several small knives with long handles and blades of different shapes, two pairs of scissors, and a number of things like small tongs or tweezers. These things were the most identifiable. The rest were quite mystifying. Tredhold immediately launched into a piece-by-piece, detailed explanation of the uses of the things, until he looked up and noticed his pupil's lost expression. He stopped in mid-sentence. "Never mind," he said with a sigh. "It'll all make sense when ye see the things used. We'll go over it a bit at a time as it comes up."

Nagaro swallowed. "All right," he said. He couldn't help feeling he had disappointed his mentor, despite Tred's encouraging smile.

Tredhold turned to some of the simpler things on the table. There was a small basin and three nesting metal cups whose purposes were obvious. A small, shallow dish was for making up salves and the contents of poultices. A small wooden box held several straight-sided glass tumblers of graded sizes with markings on the sides for measuring things, and a series of delicate glass tubes that Tredhold called droppers.

"These I can teach ye the use of here," the healer said, taking one of the tubes out and laying it on the table. He then took one of the cups to the washstand and poured a small amount of water into it from the pitcher there. Returning to his seat at the table he picked up the dropper. "Now watch carefully," he said. Holding the tube vertically between thumb and fingers, he lowered the bottom end of it into the water and moved his forefinger to cover the top end. When he withdrew the dropper from the cup and held it up, Nagaro saw that there was water retained in the tube.

Tred grinned at Nagaro's startled look. "It'll hold the water as long as I keep my finger over the hole," he explained. "Now watch how I measure drops."

So saying, the healer picked up one of the tumblers and held the tube over it. Carefully he rolled his forefinger to one side and a single drop of water formed at the tip of the tube, swelling and quivering until it fell into the little glass. Tredhold then quickly rolled his finger back over the hole to stop the flow. "That's one drop," he said. "Now I'm going to measure out three more." And he proceeded to do so, uncovering the hole long enough for three drops to form and fall before covering it again. "Here," he said, with a tight smile, as he handed the dropper to Nagaro. "See if ye can measure three drops."

The trick lay in holding the hand very still while precisely controlling of the movement of the finger that covered the hole. After some initial frustration Nagaro managed to dispense exactly three full drops without letting a fourth begin to form. Tredhold then asked for two drops, and finally for one, and Nagaro managed to comply.

Tredhold nodded appreciatively. "That was well done," he said. "It is as I said. Ye have good hands."

Nagaro relaxed, feeling he'd redeemed himself.

After the contents of the satchel, came the medicines. These Tredhold kept on a shelf over the washstand for want of any other place. Some were tinctures or infusions in small stoppered vials, others were dried herbs or powders in paper-wrapped packets. "This is where I'm still lacking," Tredhold confided. "There's things I'd like to have that I've not been able to find— or couldn't afford, to tell ye the truth. And some o' the dred herbs could be prepared in advance, but I've no way to do it here in this room."

"It looks like more than will fit in the bag," Nagaro observed.

"It is. There are some basic things I like to carry all the time, but mostly I'll have to decide what I'm likely to need after I get a call."

The healer spent the rest of the lesson explaining the uses of what he considered the most basic medicines. Tred had labeled all the packets and vials in a clear, precise hand, so Nagaro could read the names and repeat them aloud along with their uses to fix them in his memory. "For pain, there's willow bark. For an emetic, rue," he recited. "For a burn, lavender oil. For fever, *batari* root. For swelling, turmeric. For stings and rashes, *komforei...*"

When he had the ten most common remedies committed to memory, Tredhold took pity on him and let him go. "Come back tomorrow morning," the healer said. "I'll take ye to meet Master Pedril."

Over dinner that evening in the inn's common room, Nagaro confessed to Taru and Pavo that all he had learned so far were the names and uses of ten herbs, and how to measure drops of liquid— only to find that his two friends were much more disgruntled than he was. They had talked to quite a number of local fishermen without finding anyone in a position to offer them work for pay.

"It's not that some o' them wouldn't mind having another pair o' hands," Taru explained, spearing a chunk of roasted carrot with his fork. "But it's too late in the season t' be taking boats out much, so there's precious little money coming in. And whatever money they've got, they'd rather keep for their own needs, seein' as they don't know what the winter might bring." He thrust the piece of carrot into his mouth and chewed morosely. The dinner had consisted of roasted chicken and potatoes in addition to the carrots, but Taru had already finished his meat and potatoes, leaving what he found least appealing for last.

Nagaro poked among the chicken bones on his plate. "Well, you can't blame them for that," he said. "Maybe you should look for other kinds of work."

"That is what I think," Pavo interjected. "Fisherman tell us we should ask for work at kuma mill."

"The kuma mills?" Nagaro looked questioningly from one of his friends to the other.

Taru gave Nagaro a suffering look. "It's *hulling,*" he said. "Cutting the husks off the nuts, and cracking the shells. We're too late for the kuma harvest, but just in time for hulling. That's no work for a man."

Pavo leveled a well-chewed drumstick at the young Turo. "I do not see why not. If they pay you money."

Nagaro sighed. He was inclined to agree with Pavo, but he knew Taru would only become more adamant if he argued the point. "Well," he said, "tomorrow's a new day. If you keep asking, maybe you'll turn up something."

***

Tredhold began their next meeting by giving a verbal lesson on his expectations of a healer's apprentice, delivered over a light breakfast eaten at the table in his chamber. The morning sun was flooding in the window, illuminating their repast, which consisting of a pot of sothiril and a plate of scones with a small dish of honey and a knife to spread it—all fetched from Tira Yuli's kitchen.

"Your task will be mainly to watch and listen," Tred explained between mouthfuls of scone. "And learn as much as ye can from my example. I won't always be able to explain what I'm doing while I'm doing it. Sometimes it's better that patients not know things. They'd only be confused. Or frightened."

"I can understand that," Nagaro observed cautiously. "But I thought I was to be your assistant."

"Ye will be, but to begin with, ye are not to do anything unless I explicitly tell ye to."

Nagaro paused, cup in hand. "Not even fetch a cup of water? Or... or open a window for more light or air?"

Tredhold swallowed another bite, and shook his head. "Ye've no way of knowing what might be the wrong thing to do," he said. "Something quite innocent-seeming can sometimes harm a man that's sick or injured. Ye wouldn't want to be the cause o' that, would ye?"

"No, of course not, but—" Nagaro was imagining himself hovering in the background, resisting the urge to put his hands to good use.

The healer raised a warning finger. "This is how it must be in the beginning. I'll tell ye when I judge that ye're ready to act on what ye've learned."

Nagaro frowned. "I understand," he said. "It's just that I think I'll feel rather useless, that's all."

Tredhold sighed. "Trust me to make sure ye're not useless."

Somewhat reassured, Nagaro picked up a second scone and started to spread honey on it. "Can I at least ask questions?"

This, surprisingly, seemed to give the healer pause.

"*Ye-es*," he said slowly. "If ye've any uncertainty about whatever I've told ye to do. But if it's curiosity about what I'm doing, I'm afraid ye'd best not ask while we're with the patient for the same reason I just told ye. Ye'll have to save *that* kind o' question 'til we're alone."

"All right," Nagaro sighed, inwardly. The logic at least was clear.

When they'd finished breakfast, they gathered up the dishes and returned them to the kitchen, then set out to walk to Tor Pedril's house. Their way took them first along Front Street beside the harbor, then up one of the side streets that radiated out from the bay like spokes of a wheel. The second street was called Butcher's Lane. Nagaro privately thought it an unfortunate address for a healer, but he refrained from saying so.

The morning was bright and cold, with a stiff salt breeze blowing off the bay. A massing of clouds to windward threatened rain before the day was out. The two men wore their cloaks and set a rapid pace to ward off the chill. The other folk they passed were similarly bundled up and in a hurry.

As they walked, Tredhold continued the lesson.

"There's certain rules that all healers must keep," he said. "The first being to never do anything that will harm your patient."

Nagaro tugged his cloak closer and frowned. "What if it isn't clear?" he asked. "What if the treatment that could cure a person could also kill him, and you can't be certain which?"

Tredhold came to a dead stop in the street, fixing his sharp gaze on Nagaro's questioning face. "Now why do ye ask such a question?" he demanded. "I mean, certainly it *can* happen, but it's hardly common. Where did ye get such an idea?"

Nagaro looked away. He shivered. "Something I heard once," he said. "When my Lady Guardian was tending to one of the householders."

"Oh. I see." Tredhold started walking again. "I don't want ye to worry unduly about that possibility," he said, keeping his voice low. "But if there *is* a hard choice t' be made, ye must let the patient make it. And if the patient's in no state to choose, ye give the choice to the next o' kin. And if there's no one to ask, ye do what ye think is best and pray to the gods that no one curses ye for it."

They walked on, heads down against a particularly strong gust of wind. A wagon rumbled by, the driver hunched in his seat. When it had passed, Tredhold continued. "It's your duty to serve anyone in need, or anyone who asks, no matter who it is or what ye may think of him. No matter what his politics, or who he prays to, or whether or not ye think he's honest, or a good man, or whether he can pay your fee." He cast Nagaro another look as they turned from the main street into a side street, as if fearing he would be handed another hard question.

Nagaro obliged him. "What if someone refuses your help? What if he'd rather die?"

Tredhold gave him a dark look, then turned his face away, into the wind. "If that is his wish, it is his right," the wiry Leithian said curtly. "And may Solbrid forgive him."

Nagaro nodded his acceptance. Vothra always allowed such choosing without judgement, but a Leithian would object, of course, to what amounted to suicide. "Is there anything else?" he asked.

Tred laughed shortly. "Never speak ill of another healer. Not for anything that's short o' criminal. That's not an official rule, but it's understood between men of our trade. We're only human, and nobody is always right. So if ye disagree with a treatment or a diagnosis, ye do it privately— or at least politely. Ye let the other man save his face if he's wrong. The next one who's wrong could be you."

Nagaro could see the advantage in this, though he couldn't help hoping it wouldn't come up.

***

Master Pedril's house was a modest two-story affair, constructed mostly of wood. The front window looked into a combined office and examining room, into which Pedril ushered them after answering Tredhold's knock. The room was dominated by a large desk at one side and an examining table at the other. The latter was shielded from the window by a screen for privacy. The examining table was heavily varnished, though the fresh coating couldn't conceal the evidence of old stains and abrasions. New scratches already marred its surface. The wooden floor looked as if it had also recently received a new coat of varnish and there was a taint of turpentine in the air. Faded yellow paint on the walls and mustard-colored curtains gave the room a faintly jaundiced appearance.

Master Pedril turned out to be a short, well-dressed Kelorin man in the very middle of his middle years. He had sleek dark-brown hair, watery gray eyes in a face already tending towards jowls, and the beginnings of a comfortable paunch. Nagaro guessed the man must be doing fairly well for himself.

After an exchange of greetings, Pedril looked Nagaro up and down. "And this is the one ye've picked for an apprentice? Tor Nagaro, if I'm not mistaken. I thought he was a warrior— that, and... other things."

Nagaro felt the blood in his face.

"I'm a warrior, too, if it comes to that," Tredhold responded tartly. "Ye seemed pleased I was a Fleet man when I spoke to ye before."

"Oh, tut, tut. I meant no harm." Pedril waved the matter aside, then spoiled the effect by adding, "Although now that ye mention it, I've always wondered how Fleet healers put the two together. Killing men on the one hand, and healing them on the other."

"It's not complicated," Tred answered, stiffly. "When the order is to fight, I'm a warrior. When it's to cease fighting, I'm a healer. And since the Mahuk warriors always fight to the death, I've never had to practice both arts on the same man."

"Ah, I see." Master Pedril apparently decided to take Tred's testy response as humor, for he smiled broadly as if it were a jest. He turned to Nagaro. "Well, young man, I'm pleased to make your acquaintance. Whatever ye may have been— or done."

"What he's *done*, Tredhold put in quickly, "was to nurse three dozen galley slaves through the plague. I was one of them, and he did it under the sky on a desert island with nothing but water and an inadequate supply of food."

"Really?" Master Pedril's eyebrows shot up. "How many did he lose?"

"Five." Nagaro answered for himself before Tredhold could speak. "And there was one who chose to refuse food so he could die in the open air. And I'm pleased to meet you, too, Zirda," he added.

Pedril's eyebrows danced upward again. "Well, he's polite, I must say," he said to Tredhold. "And losing only five under such conditions isn't bad. Would ye like to see my infirmary?"

It was as good a way as any to end an awkward moment.

The infirmary was a small room at the back of the house, rather plain, though not unpleasant. It smelled of soap and vinegar. There were two windows, one looking out into an alley running beside the house and the other into a tiny fenced yard with a number of bushes, all leafless owing to the season. The room's floor was bare wood and the furniture consisted of two narrow beds, each with a chair and a little chest of drawers. The beds, currently unoccupied, were supplied with sheets, pillows, and patchwork quilts worked in squares of faded fabric. The walls were whitewashed, and the only color in the room besides the quilts was the yellow edging on the window curtains. The room was across the hall from the house's kitchen where they could hear Master Pedril's wife involved in some activity that involved a clatter of crockery.

"How often do ye have occasion to use it?" Tredhold asked.

Pedril shrugged. "Not more than once or twice a season when a patient comes to my door in such a state that it would be a risk to send them home, or they've a condition that needs constant tending. I've found most folk are more comfortable at home."

"Where they do their best healing," Tredhold affirmed. "I expected we'd be seeing patients in their own houses, and I've nothing like this to offer them. I trust ye'd allow me to send them here if there was need?" He gave the other healer a questioning look.

"Of course, of course!" Pedril was expansive. "And as for who'd have the care of them, and the payment, I'm sure we can work that out if it comes up."

"Yes, yes." Tredhold was clearly anxious not to argue.

They returned to the office and sat down on opposite sides of the desk. The talk turned to the matter of how to divide the potential work.

Tredhold began with, "I hope ye'll have the kindness to send some work my way— at least in the beginning— since I'm not known to the Pakoa folk."

Pedril tilted back his chair. "Yes, yes. To be sure. I thought I'd start by sending ye cases of bodily injury. I think folk will consider ye for that when I tell them ye were a Fleet healer." He smiled a little condescendingly. "And of course I'll tell all of old Keros' regular patients ye're available— the ones who were in the habit of going to him rather than to me."

Tredhold nodded, his expression neutral. "That seems reasonable. And thank you."

"Of course I don't know how many will choose to have ye see them... I, ah, can't *make* anyone do that, after all..." Pedril let the sentence dangle.

"I understand," Tred put in quickly. "And I wouldn't expect ye to do anything that would cut into your own livelihood."

"Well, naturally not." Pedril looked relieved and a little embarrassed. "I've my wife and children to think of."

"Is there anything else I should know about practicing the healer's art on this island?"

Pedril pursed his lips. "Hmm... I've already told ye about our two apothecaries— their merits and their weaknesses. Is there anything else? Let me see now... Ah!" He abruptly brought his chair back to earth and leaned across the desk. "This is important: Don't do anything to cross Zomora."

"Zomora?" Tredhold looked blank. "Who is Zomora?"

"Tira Zomora, she likes to be called." Master Pedril's watery eyes had come sharply to focus. "She's Pakoa's medicine woman, and the Turowan folk set a lot of store by her. They may find uses for my skills or yours, but they'll not hear a word said against her. Even some of the Kelorin folk call on Tira Zomora for some things. Not that she doesn't have knowledge, and skill, mind ye." Pedril added hurriedly. "She has her ways. Her special remedies." He made a vague gesture in the air. "I don't know where she gets half the things she uses. Just don't get on her bad side if ye want any Turowan customers."

Tredhold had listened to this with a very serious expression. "While I don't know a lot about the Turowan medicine women," he said, "I know enough not to discount them. I'm grateful for the warning, since I didn't know there was one on the island. Does she have a particular territory?"

Pedril shrugged. "She doesn't live in town," he said. "But she does venture here sometimes. Her house is part way up the length of the island, I believe, along the main road. The town folk often go to her rather than expecting her to come to them— but she gets about when she chooses on a piebald pony. If ye once see that pony, ye won't forget it, either. She rides it on a kind of side-saddle the like o' which I'll warrant ye've never seen."

Tred raised an eyebrow. "I'll have to keep an eye out for her," he said. "Thank you again."

At this point, Tredhold rose to go, and Nagaro stood up as well, but before they could take their leave, Master Pedril spoke again. "Ye should know that she does midwifery," he volunteered, still seated at his desk. "There are several other midwives on the island, and they're like a sisterhood with Zomora as their queen. Myself, I'm just as glad to leave them to it. Keros delivered all three of Gedras' daughters, but I can't think of another birth on the island that was handled by a healer."

"I'll bear that in mind." Tredhold had paused beside his chair. "Is that everything we need to know?"

"Yes, I think so. And if ye have any trouble, don't hesitate to stop by, and I'll be of any help I can." Pedril stood up at last and offered his hand to Tredhold, across the desk. Tred stepped up to take it, thanking the other healer again.

With that, they bid the healer farewell, and Tred and Nagaro were soon outside again on the street, clutching their cloaks once more about their shoulders.

Tredhold turned to Nagaro as they started up the street, and asked over the wind, "What did ye think of him?"

Nagaro chose his words carefully. "I'm sure I could learn to work with him. But I'm glad I'll be learning from you."

Tred laughed shortly. “I’ll take that to mean ye prefer my company. And I prefer yours, if it comes to that. But I’ve no reason to think Pedril isn’t knowledgeable or well-trained.”

“Nor have I,” Nagaro put in quickly. “It’s just that he seemed more concerned with his business than with his patients. And he clearly thinks a medicine woman inferior to a healer.”

Tred paused at the corner where Butcher’s Lane emptied into Front Street. “And you don’t?”

The healer’s gaze probed him, and Nagaro was glad when a gust of wind in his face gave him an excuse to put his head down. “We had no trained healer where I grew up,” he said, pulling up his hood. “But there was an old Turowan medicine woman who came at need and who spent a whole month with us every autumn. My lady guardian had great respect for her. She bought medicines from her. And learned their use from her. And when I broke my arm, it was old Luka who set it—” He caught himself with a jolt of alarm. He hadn’t meant to mention Luka’s name. He glanced up worriedly at Tredhold and caught an avid gleam in the healer’s eye that made his stomach clench, until the man spoke.

“Ye broke your arm?” Tred asked. “Which one? How long ago?”

“Ah... the right one.” Nagaro went limp with relief. “I think I was seven or eight.” He raised his arm, flexing it.

“Let me see.” Tredhold reached for Nagaro’s arm. “Where was the break?”

“Just below the elbow. On the outside.”

Tredhold gripped Nagaro’s forearm, feeling along the bone through the shirt sleeve with practiced fingers. “Ah, yes,” he said. “There’s a little bump, here, on the shaft of the ulna. A fairly clean knit. And since I’ve seen what ye can do with that arm, it was obviously well set. It speaks well of the woman. The forearm can be tricky, with the two bones and the complex movement for rotation.”

His professional curiosity satisfied, Tredhold relinquished Nagaro’s arm and began walking once again.

A few raindrops spattered the cobblestones as Nagaro made haste to follow. He was glad to drop the subject.

They spent the rest of the day in the common room, talking and drinking sothiril. They speculated on how soon Pedril might send a patient their way, but since they really had no idea, the conversation was not very productive. Tredhold drilled Nagaro on the basic medicines he’d memorized the day before. When they’d exhausted this exercise and Tred could think of nothing else relevant to do, Nagaro suggested they pass the time with a game of King’s Men.

Tredhold readily agreed, and so Nagaro went upstairs and fetched down Taru’s board and pieces. It was an inexpensive set, though it had been a bit of an extravagance even so. The pieces were carved from cedar instead of ironwood, and the board was of hardened leather with the dark squares painted in ink and the light squares left the natural leather color. It was cut into four hinged pieces so that it could be folded up. The folded board and pieces all fit into a canvas bag.

Nagaro and his friends were still new to the game, equally unskilled, and thus well-matched. Tredhold was more experienced, and the healer quickly toppled Nagaro's king with more than half the pieces still on the board. They played a second game with much the same result. After that, Tredhold gave Nagaro some pointers on game play, and they were just setting up for a third game when Taru and Pavo finally walked in.

Tredhold was discerning enough to realize that the three friends would wish to talk, so he excused himself. "Tomorrow morning ye needn't sit with me here, like this, to wait for a call," he told Nagaro in parting. "Only see that ye're somewhere close by where I or Yuli, or that son of hers, can find ye quickly if a call comes in."

There was a hint of smugness lurking behind Pavo's deadpan as the other two young men sat down across the table from Nagaro, but Taru had been frowning since he entered the common room. He continued to frown as he poked at the playing pieces.

"You've had no luck yet?" Nagaro asked cautiously.

"Oh yes, we have luck," Pavo immediately volunteered. "We have got work!"

Nagaro was pleasantly surprised. "You've found work? That's wonderful."

Taru looked up at that. "Well, not exactly," he began. "It's at one o' the kuma mills, and they only had work for one person."

"We are go to share it," Pavo put in. "I work one day and Taru work next. It is not so bad. There are many man that do this work."

Taru shot the young Hashtep a disgusted look. "It's dirty, and it's dull," he said. "But it was all we could find. We'll share it the way Pavo said, or maybe I'll work mornings and he'll work afternoons. I don't think I could stand a whole day of it. It's that boring. At least whichever one of us isn't working can keep looking for something better."

Nagaro did his best not to smile, though he now understood Taru's surly mood. "Well," he said diplomatically, "at least you'll be earning something."

"Oh, aye. Rins are rins." Taru managed a wan smile. "Anyway," he added. "Tell us how ye fared with Master Pedril."

Nagaro did, and when he finished, Taru asked, "D' ye think he's jealous of his territory?"

"A bit," Nagaro conceded. "Though it's probably only natural that he would be."

Pavo straightened on his stool. “But he have say you do well with plague on Chitaopa?”

“Well, yes,” Nagaro agreed. “He did seem to be favorably impressed by that.”

Taru gestured his annoyance with one of the playing pieces. “But will he really send ye any work?”

Nagaro sighed. “I hope so. For Tred’s sake if not for mine.”

There seemed nothing more to say, so they played King’s Men in the common room until dinnertime, and continued their games upstairs in their room after the meal was over.

Nagaro lay awake for some time that night reflecting on the recent changes in his life and the lives of his friends. There was no telling where any of it would lead, although he was looking forward to learning how to care for patients. And at least his conversations with Tredhold seemed to be providing harmless fodder for his dreams, for which he was grateful. The only thing he truly regretted was that being a healer’s apprentice would put an end to his daily rides on Cinnamon. The freedom of those rides— going whenever and wherever he chose— was something he was going to miss.

Chapter 9

Healer's Apprentice

It was two days later that they got their first call. A Kelorin girl of about twelve rushed into the common room while Tred and Nagaro were sitting at one of the tables, finishing their midday meal. She was white-faced and breathless and spoke first to Tira Yuli who pointed her in the direction of the new healer and his apprentice.

"Master Tredhold?" The girl gulped air as she bobbed a curtsy to Tred. "Can ye come right away? My brother fell off the roof an' broke his leg, an' Papa said that Master Pedril said t' go to the inn and fetch ye!"

Tred was already on his feet before she'd finished speaking. "Of course I'll come, child. Is your brother bleeding at all?"

The girl wrung her hands. "Yes, Zirda. His f-face. And his... his... l-leg. Here." She leaned down to touch her ankle, brushing at tears with her other hand.

"I'll get my bag." Tredhold turned to Nagaro, who had risen in alarm. "Stay with her while I get what I need." He then dropped his voice and spoke for Nagaro's ears only. "Keep her talking. Get any details ye can, but don't distress her."

Nagaro nodded and turned back to the distraught girl, who was wiping her wet cheek with the back of her hand. Her dark brown hair was mussed and her gray eyes reddened from crying.

"Why don't you sit down," he suggested, and added, "What's your name?"

She collapsed onto a stool. "S-S-Salinda..." she said. "But everybody calls me Sali." Leaning her elbows on the table, she covered her face with her hands and sniffled. "Oh, Zirda, I'm so s-scared!"

Nagaro sat down on the other side of the table, trying to think how he could keep the girl talking. "What's your brother's name, Sali?" he asked.

She peaked at him through her fingers. "N-Neved."

And how old is he?"

"Nine."

"So he's your younger brother?"

Sali dropped her hands and sat up, nodding. "I'm almost twelve." She gulped. "When I left, Neved was crying— so *much!* He *n-never* cries like that!"

Nagaro nodded earnestly. "A broken bone hurts a lot," he said. "But a healer can fix it. When I was eight I fell out of a tree and broke my arm. I cried like a baby, but the medicine woman fixed it. Here, I'll show you." He quickly pulled up his right sleeve. "It was right here. Can you feel the little bump?" He leaned across the table," presenting his forearm.

Sali tentatively reached out to feel the place he indicated. "Oh!" she said. "I *can* feel it! Was it really broken?"

"Yes, and look," Nagaro flourished his arm. "Good as new. If it's broken, Master Tredhold will lay the bone straight and—" He stopped as he saw her expression change.

Tears were starting in Sali's eyes again. "B-b-but I *s-saw* it! It was all b-b-bloody... an'... an'...*crooked*... and it was turning purple!" Her eyes screwed up and she hid her face in her hands again, awash in a fresh deluge of tears.

Nagaro's stomach dropped at her description of the injury. He prayed his alarm didn't show in his face. "Then Tredhold will wash it," he said, keeping his voice calm and remembering what Luka had done. "And he'll stitch it, and straighten it, and bind it. Master Tredhold knows about these things."

Sali's sobs eased. She lowered her hands. "Do ye think so? Will it be all right?"

"Yes, I think it will." Nagaro hoped he wasn't misleading her. Surely "almost twelve" was old enough to understand that sometimes there was something unusual or unforeseen that made a difference?

Tira Yuli had approached the table to clear off the dishes and she now produced a handkerchief from a pocket of her skirt. "Here ye are, dearie," she said, offering it to the girl.

Sali took the square of cloth and wiped her eyes and blew her nose. Yuli began stacking plates and cups.

"I... I was t-teasing Neved when it happened." Sali sniffed. "He'd gone up on the roof t' fetch his arrow. He's done it a *hundred* times. B-but I teased him. I s-said he was *clumsy*... an' just when I said it— he p-put his foot wrong... an'... an' he f-f-fell!"

Hearing this, Yuli cast Nagaro a *say something* look over her shoulder as she made for the kitchen, dishes in hand.

Nagaro frantically ran through his memories of the householders' children that he'd known when he was growing up. "You mustn't feel bad because you were teasing him," he said quickly. "Brothers and sisters do that, but they don't really mean it. I'm sure Neved knows you didn't."

Sali sniffled again and gulped air. "D-do ye really think so?"

"Yes, I do."

She managed a weak smile at that, and asked, "Who are ye, Zirda?"

Nagaro shrugged. "I'm Master Tredhold's apprentice. My name is Nagaro."

The girl's eyes widened. "*The* Nagaro? That was captain of that big ship out there in the bay?"

"Well, yes." He wished he could erase her worshipful look.

"*Oh my!*" she breathed, and then she added earnestly, "I'm really sorry that bad woman tricked ye and took your money."

Nagaro nearly choked. *Was that what parents were telling their children about it?* It was much too kind to him, and he was trying to think how to correct her mis-impression when Tredhold returned with his bag in his hand and a bundle of splints under his arm.

They had cut the splints the morning after visiting Master Pedril, remembering the tale of Nagaro's broken arm. They'd borrowed the innkeeper's axe and spent an hour splitting wood, followed by two hours of whittling the resulting rough sticks smooth with pen-knives.

There was no point in saddling the horses because Sali said her house wasn't very far away. Accordingly, they set out on foot, walking briskly. Sali trotted ahead to show them the way, holding her skirts up about her knees so she could go faster without entangling her feet. Tred carried his bag and Nagaro carried the splints.

The day was neither as cold nor as windy as when they had last ventured into town. As they went, Nagaro described, between breaths, what little he had learned from his talk with Sali.

Tredhold shook his head at the description of Neved's injury. "I hope the bone isn't through the skin if it's actually broken," he puffed, "It could be a simple break, or even just a bad sprain with some laceration."

"Was I too reassuring?" Nagaro asked, worriedly. "What's the worst that can happen?"

Tred shrugged as they followed Sali around a corner into a lane. "An open wound's a risk of infection," he said, "which could cause him to lose the leg, or even kill him, though that's unlikely with good care. Or, if it's a bad break... the leg may heal crooked. Or too short."

Nagaro winced, thinking of a boy whose life might be changed forever, and a girl who might blame herself.

He could think of nothing to say, however, and in any case they had reached the house. It fronted on the lane and was not very large, being one story, a wood frame faced with clapboard. The infamous roof was covered with split cedar shingles and had a pitch so low that nothing except water would have rolled off of it. Therein lay young Neved's downfall, quite literally. His arrow had stayed where it had fallen and lay there still. The house also had a small fenced yard, which had acquired an impressive crowd of people.

Tredhold shook his head. "Look at that," he said. "Misfortune draws folk like flies t' manure."

The injured boy was presumably somewhere inside the knot of about two dozen adults who were clustered at one side of the house, their voices raised in a confused babble. Half a dozen children stood at the outskirts of the group, wide-eyed and whispering, their expressions a mix of dread and guilty excitement.

Sali had stopped at the gate that led into the yard. For a moment she stood as if gathering courage, then she pushed the gate open and dashed inside, crying, "Papa, Papa! I've brought the healer! The new one that's good with broken things!"

Tredhold cast his eyes heavenward, then raised his voice as he went after the girl. "Stand aside! Let me through!"

Nagaro followed, trying to stay close to Tredhold while remaining unobtrusive.

The crowd fell silent, parting to let them pass, and Nagaro soon found himself looking down at a boy who lay sprawled on the ground near the side of the house. His arms were wrapped tensely around chest, his face contorted in pain. The lad moaned softly, a small, pathetic sound, strangely loud in the sudden hush that had followed Tred's arrival.

There was blood on the boy's cheek, though Nagaro judged that the wound there wasn't serious. Much worse was the leg. Someone had slit the boy's right pant-leg up to the knee, exposing a nasty red gash near the ankle, running right down to the top of his shoe. The foot was bent at an odd angle, and the ankle looked bruised and swollen. Nagaro felt queezy. The ankle *looked* broken and his heart went out to the boy.

He dragged his eyes away to sweep the scene, trying to reconstruct the accident. It wasn't very difficult to imagine what had happened. The boy lay not far from a stone cistern, covered with planks, that had been built against the wall of the house. Beyond that was a low woodshed, also built against the wall. Nagaro could picture young Neved climbing from the cistern, to the shed roof, and from there up onto the roof of the house in quest of his arrow. It was the sort of thing he might himself have done at that age.

A tall, stoop-shouldered man stood at Neved's side. From the way Sali was talking to him as she gestured at Tredhold, Nagaro concluded that he must be the children's father. Like all Kelorin, he was dark haired and pale skinned. Anxiety made his face paler still. He towered over the wiry yellow-haired Leithian healer, but showed no inclination to look down on Tred in any but the most literal sense. Though obviously worried, he met Tred's glance with a steady gaze. "We haven't moved him, Master Tredhold," he was saying. "Master Pedril said we shouldn't."

"That's sound advice," Tred responded. "And ye did well to follow it." Another moan drew the healer's attention back to his patient, and he knelt beside the boy. "Could someone fetch some water?"

Neved's father spoke to a gray-haired woman who stood stolidly at Neved's head. "Leina, could ye see t' that?"

She nodded curtly, turned, and pushed her way into the crowd.

Tredhold had his satchel open on the ground and was rummaging in it. "Nagaro," he said. "I need your hands." He looked up as Nagaro knelt beside him. Addressing the boy's father, he said, "I'm going to give him something for the pain. It will make him sleep, and he'll be less likely to move while I'm working."

The man nodded understanding.

Tredhold must have located the wooden box he had shown to Nagaro on that first morning, and opened it inside the bag, for he now produced a small glass tumbler and one of the fine glass tubes used for measuring. He handed them to Nagaro, who carefully took one in each hand, glad that he already understood the use of them. If he hadn't been there, Tred would have been forced to call on someone without even that experience.

The healer moved closer to Neved's head. Reaching out he placed his hands firmly on the boy's temples. Neved's eyes flicked open at the sudden touch.

Tredhold leaned closer until the boy's gaze came to focus on his face. "Don't be afraid," he said. "I'm going to take care of you."

"*O-oh... Mama...*" Neved's words were scarcely audible.

Tred looked up at the boy's father. "Where is his mother?" he asked.

The father grimaced. "In the house. She's taking it hard."

At that moment, the gray-haired Leina returned with a pitcher of water and Tredhold promptly released Neved's head and returned to his bag to rummage again. "Fill the glass to the top mark," he directed.

Nagaro held the glass, watching carefully while Leina poured, and telling her when to stop.

In the meantime, Tredhold had extracted a small vial from his satchel and uncorked it. He held the vial in his left hand, expertly palming the cork, and reached with his free hand for the glass tube that Nagaro held.

Nagaro understood immediately and handed the tube over, then watched as Tredhold dipped it into the vial, placed his finger on the top, and withdrew it with a small amount of clear liquid trapped inside. Knowing what must come next, he held out the glass tumbler and watched as Tred carefully dispensed a single tiny drop of liquid into the water.

"Swirl it around," Tredhold instructed him. "And don't spill it!"

Nagaro carefully swirled the glass while Tredhold re-corked the vial and returned it to his bag.

The healer then reached for the glass. "Could ye all please step back?" he said loudly, addressing the onlookers, who had begun to inch in while he worked.

There was some murmuring, and some of the people moved.

"Ai, now. Give the man some room!" Neved's father waved his hands at the crowd, and this time they all fell back, their murmuring at least temporarily hushed.

Tredhold ignored the crowd. He guarded the glass in his hands as he looked from the father to Nagaro. "I'll need ye two to lift his head. He'll have to drink this without choking."

Nagaro managed to raise the boy's shoulders, while the father cradled his son's head and tilted it forward. Tredhold gingerly offered the glass, touching it to Neved's lips.

"Drink it, son," Neved's father urged, but the boy only whimpered, his eyes and lips clamped shut in pain.

Feeling Tred's frustration, Nagaro had an inspiration."Sali, can you talk to him?" he asked, speaking without stopping to think that he was violating Tredhold's earlier instructions.

The girl had been standing a little behind her father, but she met Nagaro's eyes with a brave smile. She got down on her knees beside her brother and took his hand. "Please, Nev," she said firmly. "Just open your mouth. They're goin' t' help ye."

Neved's eyes flickered open and he focused first on his sister's face, then on the glass. When Tredhold brought it to his lips again, he drank awkwardly and then closed his eyes, his head lolling in his father's hands. Carefully they lowered the boy back to the ground. Sali retreated with a look of relief, before flashing Nagaro a quick smile that contained both hope and gratitude.

Tredhold hadn't missed the girl's reaction, and he shot Nagaro a look of approval. He returned the glass to his satchel and stood up. "All right," he said. "Now we *are* going to move him. Into the house. Very carefully." He located Leina at the edge of the crowd. "Could ye bring a blanket, please? A good strong one?"

Leina gave him her silent nod and once more pushed her way out through the circle.

Tredhold scanned the ring of neighbors. "*You*," he said. "And *you*. And *you*," as he pointed in turn to each of three of the men. "Ye'll help us carry the stretcher. The rest of ye can help best if ye keep clear and don't hinder us!"

The last words caused a few resentful looks, but no one ventured to voice a complaint.

While they waited for Leina to return with the blanket, Nagaro took stock of the men Tredhold had chosen. One was little more than a youth, and the other two were well into their middle years, with the weathered faces of fishermen. They weren't the largest or strongest-looking men present, but they seemed steady and serious— which was more than Nagaro could say for some of the others. He guessed that Tredhold had read their faces and liked what he saw.

One of the two older men boldly returned Nagaro's glance. He was Kelorin, with a narrow, neatly trimmed beard that was going to gray and a fading hint of kuma stain on his face. He stood very straight and looked Nagaro up and down with a challenge in his gray eyes. "I don't know this lad," he said, addressing Tredhold and jerking his chin at Nagaro. "How does he come to be part o' this?"

Tred gave the man a hard look and answered shortly. "Tor Nagaro is my apprentice."

"Tor Nagaro, ye say?" The man's gaze became even more measuring.

The other two men, both Turowan and with enough similarity in their features to suggest they were father and son, gaped at Nagaro and he was alarmed to see that the younger one appeared to be working up the courage to say something. Fortunately Leina returned with the blanket before the young Turo could find his tongue.

Moving the injured boy turned out to be much easier than Nagaro had expected. Tredhold directed the process with confident precision. The blanket was rolled up lengthwise and laid on the ground beside Neved, and the five lifters were positioned, kneeling, with their hands slipped under the boy's body. Nagaro held the lad's head and two of Tredhold's chosen men were placed on either side of his torso. The third man's hands were placed under Neved's good leg and the boy's father had the task of managing the injured one. On Tredhold's cry of "lift," they raised the boy's body about a foot above the ground, and Leina and Sali quickly unrolled the blanket under him. Once the blanket was placed, the lifters lowered Neved onto it. After that, the lifters had only to grasp the edges of the blanket firmly and stand up, using the blanket as a stretcher.

Whatever drug Tred had given Neved had already taken affect, for he made no protest as they lifted him. He lay cradled limply in the blanket, his eyes closed in a slack face. The most difficult part of transporting the boy was getting everyone through the narrow back door of the house, but again Tredhold's experience was evident. He got them through by having the men on opposite sides advance alternately past the door posts.

The room they entered turned out to be the kitchen, and its atmosphere was laden with the rich, spicy aroma of freshly-baked apple-cinnamon cake. Nagaro inhaled deeply as he entered, grateful for that incongruous gift amid the tense drama of the task at hand. It was a rustic, homey kitchen of modest size, simply furnished with plain wood cupboards, shelves, and a table and chairs. The cake that scented it was plainly visible cooling on a shelf over the ample hearth.

They laid Neved on the kitchen table and Tredhold instructed the men to lift the lad again as they had done outside while Leina whisked the blanket away. Tred then thanked the three men he'd chosen and assured them that their services would not be needed further.

"Once the leg is set, the boy's father can safely carry him to his bed," he explained. As the three men filed out, Tredhold moved close to Nagaro's ear and said, "See if ye can get the gawkers outside t' go home."

Nagaro nodded, with more confidence than he felt, and said, "All right."

Outside in the yard, the crowd was even bigger than it had been when Tred and Nagaro had arrived. A press of bodies descended eagerly upon the healer's three lifters with craning necks, peering eyes, and mouths clamoring for news.

Nagaro frowned and stepped forward, raising his hands and voice.

"Good people!"

Annoyed, startled faces turned towards him, and he found himself in a circle of hostile eyes. He plunged on. "Thank you all for the concern that you have shown for Neved and his family."

He saw glances shift away and heard feet shuffle.

"Master Tredhold will need time now to do his work, which will proceed best without distraction or interruption," he continued. "You should all return to your own tasks. If you come again this evening, or tomorrow morning, you can get news and show your care for the family."

Some of the people were looking at the ground when he finished speaking, embarrassed and chastened. Most of them began to move away, but one woman who was standing quite close to him said, "And who are ye to be tellin' us what t' do?"

"Aye." Another woman spoke up, as if emboldened by the first. "Ye're no friend o' the family. I've known that boy's mother since she was a babe!"

Nagaro was taken aback, but before he could respond, one of the lifters— the bearded fisherman— addressed the women.

"He's Master Tredhold's apprentice, and he speaks for the healer," the man said, and added pointedly, "Rather sensibly, to my mind."

The second woman who had spoken seemed satisfied by this. "Well that's all right then, Tor Timegar," she said. And she gave Nagaro a nod before turning to go.

The first woman was less gracious. "Well, if that's how it is, I guess I'll be going," she said stiffly. Without even glancing at Nagaro, she stalked off.

Nagaro turned to the bearded man. "Thank you, Zirda," he said quite sincerely.

The man shrugged. "I stood back to give ye a chance," he said. "But I stayed close, because I thought ye'd have trouble— more than you did, in fact. They know me, ye see, and they don't know you— and ye're young. But ye spoke well, with a captain's voice. Most o' them took your words t' heart and followed orders." He nodded after the departing townsfolk, who were still filing out through the gate.

Nagaro frowned. "I only tried to say what seemed needed," he said, uncertain what to make of the "captain's voice" comment.

The fisherman gave Nagaro an appraising look. "Ye reminded them of why they *should* ha' been here. There's more than a few that know they were hanging about out of idle curiosity." He sighed, then added, "I'm just glad I could be of some use with the boy. And I'm glad he'll live." His eyes shifted, looking far away. "Ye do everything ye can for your children, and sometimes Lokundas takes 'em anyway." He shook his head somberly and turned away to follow the other departing folk.

Nagaro stared after the man called Timegar, thinking that he should perhaps follow him, that there was a tale in those last words that might need telling. But he had another duty that called him. He was a healer's apprentice.

He turned about and went back into the house.

Inside he found a number of changes. A piece of oiled canvas had appeared from somewhere and been placed under Neved's injured leg, offering some protection for the tabletop. Leina was boiling water in a pair of pots hung over the fire, and the boy's father was sitting on a chair, tearing an old shirt into strips.

Tredhold was carefully cleaning the cut on Neved's face with a moistened cloth. He looked up at Nagaro's approach. "Any trouble out there?" he asked.

Nagaro shrugged. "There were two women who didn't see why they should listen to me. The man named Timegar explained it to them."

Neved's father looked up. "Everyone respects Timegar. He used t' be with the Fleet."

Nagaro looked around. "Where is Sali?"

"I sent her to comfort her mother." The father sighed. "She has no need t' see this. And my wife is... well... she's not strong about this sort o' thing. Kindest woman in the world. But she's not strong."

"Kind is good," Tredhold offered judiciously.

"Aye." Neved's father was glad to accept this. "How does that cut look?"

"It's not much." Tredhold squeezed out his cloth into a basin. "It'll heal with just a bit of a scar. Less if I put a stitch or two in it. But I'll worry about that after I've dealt with the ankle. For now, I've got it clean."

When they turned their attention to the ankle, there was so much to be done that there was no danger at all of Nagaro feeling useless. His first task was to empty the basin, rinse it, and refill it with some of Leina's boiled water. Then he watched Tredhold carefully examine the ankle. The healer squeezed and pressed with his fingers, and very gently attempted to straighten the foot while Nagaro held his breath.

He let the breath out when the healer muttered, "The ankle bone isn't broken, just dislocated," then tensed again as Tred added, "But there may be a fracture of the fibula."

The healer looked up. "Could one of ye bring Sali in here, please? I need the history of the accident."

Nagaro and Neved's father both went, and the father stayed to speak some words of comfort to his wife while Nagaro brought Sali back to the kitchen. When the girl gave him a worried look, he returned her a reassuring smile, and said, "Master Tredhold only wants to ask you a few questions because you're the one who saw what happened."

Tredhold proceeded very gently with his questions, and the tale soon emerged. The cut on the boy's face had been inflicted by a loose shingle at the edge of the roof, while the injury to the ankle had come from Neved's foot striking the corner of the cistern as he fell. Neved had tried to stand up immediately after falling but had taken only one step, screamed, and fallen down again. Sali had started screaming too at that point, bringing her mother out of the house.

Neved's father returned to the kitchen and picked up the story at that point after sending Sali back to her mother. He explained apologetically that his wife had run, not to Pedril, but to him where he worked at the local ships' chandlery. He'd sent the distraught woman home again and gone to Pedril himself. "But Master Pedril said we should fetch *you*, Zirda. And that the boy shouldn't be moved," he added. "So thought I'd best go home and take charge o' things. Once I was *here*, I sent Sali t' find ye, and ye know the rest."

Tredhold listened gravely to this tale of confusion and lost time, but all he said was. "I don't think the delay has done any harm, and with all that crowd out there, it's a good thing ye were here."

After that, Tredhold began cleaning the gash on the boy's leg and bathing the area around it. "Look here, Nagaro," he said. "The skin is torn, see, and the muscle under it bruised, but the bone isn't exposed. That's good."

Nagaro leaned close, making careful mental note of the injury's appearance— which was less alarming with the blood cleaned away.

Tred then put aside the cloth and began to probe around the cleaned wound. "Ah!" he exclaimed, after a moment. "Put your finger right *here.* Can ye feel that? There's a break in the small leg bone, the fibula. But it's pushed in, not out. It wasn't standing on a twisted foot that did that. It was the blow from the cistern."

Nagaro reached in very gingerly to feel the place Tredhold indicated. "Yes," he said after a moment. "I can feel the break. Just as you described."

After that, it was a matter of gingerly removing Neved's shoe and stocking, and very carefully pulling on the leg while pressing and teasing things back into place. Tredhold made liberal use of Nagaro's hands throughout the process, to assist with the clothing and to steady the boy's leg while the healer manipulated the foot. He then had Nagaro feel for the broken bone again, to see how it had moved back into place, after which he had Nagaro steady both the leg and the foot while he cleaned the wound again, calling for more hot water, which was supplied by Leina. Finally, the healer made several stitches to close the wound, applied a salve containing salt and garlic to repel infection, and bound the leg with bandages from his bag, followed by more bandages to stabilize the ankle joint with the foot in its proper position.

By the time they got to the bandages, the afternoon was waning and Neved's father had to fetch and light an oil lamp and hang it on a hook over the table so that Tred and Nagaro could see what they were doing.

With the ankle bandaged, Nagaro finally found his hands free. "What about the splints?" he asked, then bit his tongue as he belatedly remembered Tred's request that he not ask questions.

The healer offered no rebuke, however. "Splinting is a bit tricky with the break this close to the ankle," he said. "But I think there's something we can do. It's called a stirrup splint."

So Neved's father was set to cutting one of the splints into two short pieces about six inches long while Tred and Nagaro chose two more splints of the right length and bound them firmly to either side of the boy's calf, using the strips of cloth the father had made. Tred positioned the splints so they extended two inches past the sole of the boy's foot. Once the side splints were firmly in place, the two short sticks the father had cut were lashed across between the free ends of the long splints to form the "stirrup" under the boy's foot.

"Ye want the stirrup just under his heel and instep," Tred explained, "to protect the foot. But not right against it. Ye don't want him to be able to put any weight on it." He looked up to find the father's eyes. "He should be able to hobble about with this a bit, ye see. But not too much. And a crutch or a stick t' lean on to steady him wouldn't be a bad idea."

The boy's father nodded. "I'll see t' that." He rose and came over to look down at the bandaged leg and splint. "Ye've done a fine piece o' work there, Master Tredhold," he said. "And ye've been hours at it. I'm in your debt, and I'll see ye're paid fairly for it. I must owe ye sixty or seventy rins at least for your time and your skill."

"Let's say sixty," Tredhold said quickly. "Since Neved is my first patient. And we've yet to see the outcome."

The boy's father nodded. "It won't all be today, and it won't all be in coin," he said, "but I'll see ye get what's due t' ye, one way or another." He looked at Nagaro. "And ye made yourself useful, too. I'll tell anyone that asks that ye're a fine healer's apprentice."

Nagaro ducked his head and thanked the man for his words.

Tredhold finally returned his attention to the cut on Neved's face, cleaning it again and closing it with two stitches. Then he and Nagaro watched the boy's father gather Neved up and carry him to his bed. Once the boy was comfortable, they all set about cleaning up the kitchen with Leina's help. Tredhold thanked the quiet woman and she returned him a few words of humble acknowledgment. Nagaro had imagined her to be a relative but she turned out to simply be a neighbor whom Neved's father trusted for her good heart and cool head. She must have been a close family friend, though, for she served them each a slice of the freshly-baked apple-cinnamon cake with scarcely a glance at the man of the house to be sure that her offering met with his approval.

By the time they'd finished their cake, the afternoon was completely spent. Tred paused at the door. "We'll stop by tomorrow," he told the father. "And probably every day for the first week. "I'll want to see how the boy is faring, and the dressing will need to be changed."

The man pulled out his purse, dug into it and held out a handful of copper coins. "This'll be an earnest for the rest," he said gruffly.

Tredhold counted the coins as he and Nagaro walked back to the inn through the twilight streets. Talebra in her first quarter showed raggedly through a drift of cloud and a handful of stars pricked the deepening cobalt sky. The yellow glow of oil lamps warmed the windows of the houses they passed. "Fifteen rins," he said with some satisfaction. "A quarter of my fee. It's a beginning." He handed Nagaro three of the coins. "And that isn't much, I know," he said. "But at least it's something to show for your part in this. "I can't offer ye room and board, as a master should, but I can give ye something towards what ye're paying the innkeeper."

Nagaro thanked him and pocketed the coins. They were passing by the harbor, where the distant shadowy shape of the *Fist of Death* rode on a light swell. Seeing it reminded Nagaro of Tredhold's Fleet experience. "Have you dealt with many broken bones?" he asked.

Tredhold shrugged. "A few," he said. "It's not the most common injury ye see in the Fleet. Compared to sword cuts. I've dealt with a couple o' falls from the rigging and a handful of injuries taken on shore."

"But you're confident of what you did today? You certainly seemed so."

Tredhold shot him a look. "I'm confident I handled it as well as, or better than, any person on this island. Because most o' them wouldn't have the first notion what t' do. And as for *seeming* confident... I'd better seem confident! The patient and the family need to see that, Nagaro. The patient needs to be able to get over being afraid and get on with healing." He sighed. "Ye asked me earlier if ye'd been too reassuring when ye said I'd fix the leg 'good as new.' Well, it may not turn out quite as good as new, but we'll go back as often as we need to t' see that ankle healed the very best it can. And that's a damn sight better 'n what would ha' happened if we hadn't been here."

They walked on in silence for a bit while Nagaro digested this. As they approached the steps leading to the Bay Tree Inn's front porch, he asked, "What about Master Pedril? Do you think he would have done as well?"

Tredhold paused on the bottom step. "I can't be sure, of course, but I fancy he just might ha' thought this sounded a bit nasty."

"You think he gave us a task he didn't want?" Nagaro was shocked.

Tredhold laughed shortly. "I *said* I wasn't sure, and he said he'd send us the cases of bodily injury. Whatever it was, he may just have given us a gift— assuming the ankle heals well and doesn't fester. What happened today will be all over the island by week's end. And there's nothing like having handled a tricky case to bring in patients."

***

The common room of the Bay Tree was full of men and boisterous conversation, and redolent of fresh bread and roasted pork. Nagaro's stomach growled in spite of the apple-cinnamon cake. He parted with Tredhold at the door and went to get himself a plate of dinner before finding Taru and Pavo at a table near one of the windows.

He expected Taru to laugh at his paltry three rins, but his friend gave him a nod of restrained congratulation instead.

"Three rins for half a day's work doesn't sound half bad t' me," he said. "Pavo and I get just eighteen rins a week, and that's t' be split between us. At twelve rins a week for our lodgings here, my wages wouldn't even keep me if I didn't have some money put by." The lesson in everyday economics was clearly proving more than a little sobering.

Pavo paused in diligently cleaning his plate with a piece of bread. "If you work whole day instead of half, it be enough," he pointed out. "And you could save some rin for your boat, too."

"Aye, but we can't *do* that. We still need to find another job t' work!" Taru slapped the table. "Even the one we've got 'll run out when the hulling's done," he added gloomily. "Then we're out o' work again. Unless we want t' stir the vats for two rins a day."

"Have you tried talking to Obedo?" Nagaro asked. "He said he was willing to take me on to help man his boat."

Taru brightened for a moment, but then shook his head. "He made that offer to ye that was our captain, Nagaro. Ye're the one who wielded that sword and led us all t' freedom."

Nagaro frowned. "You wielded a sword, too, Taru. And Pavo held that fending pike in the face of all those Mautep trying to come over the rail."

"Well, maybe..." Taru looked unconvinced. "We might try Obedo. But he's not likely t' have any real work 'til spring." He sighed, shaking his head. "Just think o' Tredhold asking sixty rins for an afternoon's work! Seems we should all be studying to be healers."

This time Nagaro sighed. "Don't forget that some of what Tredhold takes in he'll have to spend to replenish his stock of medicines and supplies. And we're not through with this patient either. We'll be going back to tend him— quite a few times, by the sound of it. There's no telling when we'll see the rest of the fee either. *And*, if the wound festers, or something else goes wrong, Tred'll have to deal with *that*. Besides, we can't expect patients to come at regular intervals. We just had two days with no patients at all, and we don't know when we'll see the next one."

Taru rolled his eyes. "Aye," he said. "It's a hard world."

Chapter 10

Tira Zomora

As it turned out, Tredhold and Nagaro had to wait three days before they got another patient. On each of those three days, they looked in on young Neved just as Tredhold had promised. On the first day, they found the boy sitting up in bed and smiling. He sat patiently while Tredhold removed the splint, changed the dressing, and put the splint back on again. The wound's condition met with Tred's approval and the healer used the opportunity to give Nagaro a brief lecture on the signs of infection. This process was repeated on the second day— without the lecture. By the third day, they found Neved hobbling about the house. All still appeared well with the wound, and Neved's father inquired as to whether Tredhold would accept part of his payment in the form of fresh eggs. These would come courtesy of Neved's mother's sister, who kept a few chickens. Tredhold graciously accepted, knowing the innkeeper would accept them in lieu of coin. Tira Yuli could surely find a use for fresh eggs in the Bay Tree's kitchen.

Their second patient was a middle-aged Turowan shopkeeper, a former patient of Master Keros, who suffered from gout and had suddenly been taken with a bad bout of it. Tredhold dosed him with turmeric and prescribed a tonic made from ingredients that could be purchased from the local apothecaries. Then he gave the man a lecture about diet, advising reduced consumption of fatty meat and also of certain fish— mackerel and haddock. Wine and ale were also to be strictly limited. When Tred and Nagaro left, the man was looking chastened. Apparently Master Keros had said much the same thing, but the man had dismissed the advice as "old-fashioned" because of Keros' age. The man's wife followed them to the door and paid Tred's entire requested fee of fifteen rins on the spot. Again the healer handed three of the coins to Nagaro.

The next day, Sali appeared at the Bay Tree with half a dozen eggs in a basket. They were duly delivered to Yuli and valued at one-and-a-half rins apiece. Two rins of this total was counted towards Nagaro's lodgings.

Their third patient was a two-year-old child whose distraught mother brought him to the inn cradled in her arms. "I heard how ye fixed that boy's leg, Master Tredhold. The one that fell off the roof," she said. "So I came here straight away." She went on to explain tearfully that her little boy had said his stomach hurt and was acting "not like himself." Under Tred's questioning she further confessed that she'd seen him chewing on something while playing in the yard, but since she'd given him a little piece of salt-fish for a treat, she'd thought nothing of it.

Tredhold wasted not a moment after that, and Nagaro knew the healer must suspect some form of poisoning. He felt his own stomach knot at the thought of the boy's plight and the sight of the mother's very obvious anguish.

Tred's examination included holding the child where the light from a window shown into his eyes. When the pupils failed to constrict, he promptly sent Nagaro to tell Yuli to brew some sothiril and burn some toast while he set about administering an emetic.

After being induced to vomit and coaxed into eating some of Yuli's burned toast and drinking a generous cup of sothiril, the child looked noticeably better and Tredhold sent the mother and son home with the rest of the toast and instructions that the boy should be watched carefully and made to drink plenty of liquid for the rest of the day. The healer further directed the mother to teach her son not to eat, or chew on, *anything* that wasn't given to him as food or medicine.

Mother and child were no sooner out the door than Tred collapsed onto a stool by the fire and called for a large mug of ale, which he downed half of without stopping for breath. When he set the mug down, he mopped his brow with his sleeve and said with feeling, "The Gods be thanked, we were in time. And I pray they don't send me another case like that any time soon!"

"What do you think happened?" Nagaro asked. "What did he eat?"

"It could ha' been any number o' things, and we'll never know for certain." Tredhold took another long swig of his ale. "There's plenty of poisonous plants with pretty flowers that folk like to see in their gardens." He made a helpless gesture. "If I went to their house and looked about their garden, I *might* be able to pick out the culprit, but I'm no master of herb lore. And even if I found it, the child could find something else t' chew on tomorrow that's as bad or worse." The healer very deliberately downed the rest of his pint. "*Sweet Solbrid's teats,*" he muttered. "*Send me anything, but not a poisoned child!*"

Nagaro understood that they had been in the presence of the shadow of death that day, and he knew that a healer couldn't always expect to be so lucky. For a moment, he was back among the slaves he'd tended under the cedar trees on Chitaopa, kneeling beside the still, cold body of Laash.

He remembered the sting of that death, the sense of having failed, and he heard again the healer's words to him at the time: "*Ye can't possibly save them all...*" Tredhold had lost patients, he knew, and the man had clearly learned to accept the death of sea warriors, but his heart was not so calloused as to be immune to the horror of possibly losing a little child.

Their next case put Tredhold on more familiar ground. A local farm worker, clearing corn stalks with a couple of mates, had taken an ill-aimed scythe cut to the leg. A neighbor arrived at the inn about an hour after breakfast on a sweating horse, calling loudly for "the Fleet healer." While Tredhold stocked his satchel, Nagaro saddled Sugar and Cinnamon in record time, and they rode out as fast as the messenger's weary mount could be made to go.

They arrived to find that their patient was already in the farmhouse kitchen and that someone had known enough to apply a tourniquet. Tredhold praised this action and set Nagaro to managing the boiling of water and locating of clean cloths, while he measured out the appropriate dose of the soporific drug he'd given young Neved— *dedrel*, he called it. Nagaro watched, occasionally refreshing the water in the basin, or cutting suture thread, or fetching another piece of clean cloth, while the healer cleansed and stitched, and then poulticed and bandaged the wound. They left the farmers duly impressed, returning to Pakoa Town with a handful of rins and the promise of a five-pound sack of corn to be delivered when the shucking was done.

***

It was two days after they'd taken care of the man with the scythe cut, and they were in the kitchen of Neved's house finishing a routine change of the dressing on his ankle, when a Turowan boy of about nine appeared at the front door with an urgent plea.

"Come quick, an' look at my mama, Zirda," the boy begged when Tred went to see who was asking for him, leaving Nagaro to finish re-wrapping the bandage. "She's hurtin' real bad!"

"Where does she hurt, lad?" Tred inquired over his shoulder as he started to re-pack his bag.

The boy put his hands to his head, clutching it and grimacing in illustration. "She gets these spells, Zirda, an' this one's a bad one! An' Tira Zomora's not at home, so I came t' find ye. Can ye come quick?"

Nagaro had emerged from Neved's room, with the injured boy curiously hobbling after him on his splinted leg. "Is it Tira Zomora that usually tends your mother when she has a spell?" he asked the boy at the door.

The young messenger nodded vigorously. "But Mama was taken sudden, an' Tira Zomora's gone up-island, and I don' know when she'll be back!"

Tredhold had his packed satchel in hand. "We'll come right away," he said. Then he turned to Neved's mother, who was hovering. "The leg's healing well, Zirdyn. The next time we come, I think we'll be able t' take the dressing off for good." The woman's thanks were effusive, and she handed Tred a few more rins as he started for the door. He pocketed the coins without bothering to count them.

They retrieved their cloaks from the peg beside the door, and Tredhold told the boy who had summoned them to lead the way. Outside, the intermittently gusting wind smelled of rain, and they were glad of their cloaks. It was near midday, though the sun that broke through the trailing clouds was riding low, owing to the advancing season, and the houses cast long purple shadows across the wet cobblestones.

As they hurried along, Tredhold questioned the boy about his mother's "spells," getting broken answers. After a few of these, the healer dropped back a little to stride along beside Nagaro. "It sounds like a sick headache," he confided in a low voice. "I've read about them. Some folk are just given to them, and there's no cure. They're not dangerous but they can lay a body up— for a day or more at a time."

"What can you do, then?" Nagaro asked. "If there's no cure?"

Tredhold looked uncomfortable. "Nothing but try to ease the pain."

Their destination turned out to be just two streets up and one street over, at the edge of the town, where the cobblestones straggled off into muddy dirt. It was a small house, with no fence around it. A Turowan girl of about six, with tangled hair and tear-stained cheeks, stared at them warily from the open doorway. The boy gave her a reassuring pat on the arm. "See, Kadi?" he said. "I told ye I'd bring the new healer."

The girl made no answer. Her eyes followed the two strangers as they entered the house.

The boy took their cloaks, hanging them on the usual peg just inside the door.

They found themselves in what appeared to be the dwelling's main room, which served for everything but sleeping, judging by the furnishings. The fire was burning low on the hearth, and the room was drafty with the door standing open, but before Nagaro could note any other details, his attention was arrested by a sound, a low, intermittent, rhythmic moaning.

It was a suffering sound. An expression of pure misery.

Tredhold paused, head up, ear cocked to it. “Is there anyone else here besides ye and your sister?” he asked the boy.

The lad shook his head. “Papa’s gone t’ the fields. He’s cuttin’ the old wood from the kuma bushes. Ye have t’ do it this time o’ year, or ye won’t get any nuts next summer. It’s *very* important.”

Tredhold frowned. “All right,” he said, although Nagaro thought he would probably have preferred to deal with the man of the house. “What’s your mother’s name?”

“Lunani.”

“Show me, then.” Tredhold gestured for the boy to lead the way.

The boy took them through a door that opened directly off the main room. The room it led to wasn’t large, and was dimly lit because the curtain was pulled halfway across the glass panes of the only window. It smelled faintly of cedar and wood smoke, and was simply furnished with a double bed, a bedside table, chest of drawers, and two stools. The bed’s headboard was placed against the wall opposite the window. The bed had been made up, and the woman Lunani lay on it, fully clothed. Her dark hair straggled across the pillow, and there was a folded cloth laid across her eyes. Her hands were clutched at her breast and her chest rose and fell with rapid shallow breaths in time with her moans.

The boy advanced to within a few feet of the bed. “I’ve brought the new healer, Mama,” he said in a low voice.

The moaning stopped, and the woman stirred slightly and spoke, her voice barely audible, the words wrung out one by one. “*Thank... ye... Tobei.*”

Tobei, dipped his head in acknowledgment, though his mother couldn’t have seen the gesture, and backed out of the room, leaving Tredhold and Nagaro to do their work unwitnessed. After a moment, they could hear the voices of the two children, speaking low to each other in the outer room.

Tredhold muttered, “I’ve no experience with this,” under his breath, but he advanced upon the bed nevertheless. Nagaro followed, moving gingerly.

“Good afternoon, Lunani—” Tred began, but the woman cut him off with a moan even as she winced at the sound of his voice.

“*Merciful... hamanei...*” She raised one hand feebly to her brow, but let it fall back to her breast with a little groan, leaving the cloth untouched.

Nagaro noticed a basin of water on the little bedside table and he silently indicated it with a gesture, giving Tredhold a questioning look.

Tredhold put out a hand to gently touch the cloth, and nodded, indicating that it was damp. Lowering his voice to the barest murmur, he asked the woman, “Shall I re-wet the cloth?”

Mutely she made the slightest of nods, moving as if her head were fragile and might break.

Tredhold sat down on the stool that was next to the bedside table, and reached for the cloth.

Nagaro remained standing, though he drew nearer. As Tred's apprentice, he wondered what, if anything, there might be for him to do.

As Tredhold lifted the cloth from the woman's face, her eyelids fluttered and she murmured, "*Oh... mercy... please...*"

Nagaro saw that she was about thirty, and she would have been quite pretty if lines of pain were not etching her face.

Tredhold dipped the cloth into the basin, squeezed out just enough water so it wouldn't drip, and laid it gently back across Lunani's brow and closed eyes. "Is there anything else I can do for ye?" he asked, his voice scarcely above a whisper.

"*...sss... ssa... bah...*"

Tredhold frowned. "I don't understand. I have willow bark—"

But Lunani shook her head slightly, impatient, wincing at the pain the movement caused. "*No use! Sah... sah... bah...*"

"Ah! *Sasaba!*" Tredhold spoke more loudly in his excitement at having understood, and the poor woman moaned again. "I'm sorry," he murmured hastily. "Does Tira Zomora give ye sasaba?"

The question elicited a tiny, brittle nod.

"I'll see what I can do."

Tredhold rose from the stool and moved back towards the doorway that led to the outer room, beckoning for Nagaro to follow him. Standing at the doorway, he spoke in an urgent whisper. "I've heard of sasaba, but I don't have any. We call it *wintervine*, and I wouldn't expect it to grow this far south."

"Would nothing that you have work?" Nagaro asked. "She seemed to think willow bark wouldn't, but you still could try it. And what about dedrel?"

Tredhold shook his head. "I expect the willow bark isn't strong enough. It seems she's tried it and found it no help. And I wouldn't risk dedrel. That drug often causes headaches when it wears off. No, I'm going to have to go to the apothecaries to look for sasaba." He paused to glance at Lunani. The woman wasn't moaning, but her rapid breathing betrayed her distress. "I mean to leave ye here with her," the healer continued. "I want ye to try some distraction while I'm gone."

"Distraction?" Nagaro was surprised. "But it hurts her every time anyone even speaks too loud."

"I don't mean that ye should try to make conversation." Tredhold was quite serious. "She's very sensitive to sounds, and light, too, I expect. But touch should be safe. I want ye to try this:" The healer held up his left hand, palm down, and began to trace simple figures on the back of it with his right index finger. "Tell her to try to follow your finger. Draw circles, squares, crossed lines or zig-zags— anything a person might be able to picture from the feel of it. Can ye do that?"

"I can certainly try."

"Good. Ye can draw on the back of her hand, or the back of her lower arm. Whatever is easy, and comfortable for her." Tredhold met Nagaro's eyes. "The children will be your chaperon if anyone should come by, but see that ye don't touch her anywhere that might be seen to be taking liberties, ye understand?"

Nagaro felt the blood in his cheeks. "Of course," he said quickly.

So Nagaro sat down on the stool beside the bed while his master ventured forth in search of the herb called sasaba.

"I'm going to try to distract you from the pain, Lunani," Nagaro told the woman in the softest voice he could manage. "Can you move your hand, please?"

She winced, and stirred a little when he touched her hand. She resisted, just for a second, when he gently tried to move it, but then allowed him to guide the hand to a place beside her on the bed quilt where he could more easily reach it.

Nagaro took a deep breath. "Try to follow my finger," he murmured. "See if you can tell what I've drawn." And he began with a simple circle traced on the back of her hand. Then he traced a triangle, then a square, two crossed lines, a spiral.

Lunani remained silent throughout this exercise. She continued to hold herself very still, except for her tense breathing. Since everything the woman said or did seemed to hurt her, Nagaro decided not to take this amiss. At least she'd made no protest. So he continued to repeat the figures, in varying order.

After a time, it seemed that the woman's breathing had begun to slow to a less troubled rhythm, and this Nagaro interpreted as a good sign even though she still didn't speak. He continued to provide the distraction, but the repetitive task was very tedious, and he began to amuse himself while his finger moved by studying the room's contents.

Now that his eyes were fully accustomed to the dim light and he had leisure to study the furnishings, he found the room less plain than it had seemed. A small rug that occupied the patch of floor between the bed and the window was made of rags braided into a spiral coil with colors of dark brown, red, tan, and yellow. Atop the chest of drawers there was a vase of red-brown glazed ceramic. There were no flowers at this season, but the vase contained some interestingly twisted twigs and three large gull feathers, surrounding a dried branch bearing several clusters of ripe kuma nuts with the husks stripped off. The nuts were the color of polished mahogany, ovoid but flattened a bit at the base and coming to a point at the tip.

The kuma nut motif was repeated elsewhere in the room as well. The headboard of the bed had protrusions at each end that were shaped like a kuma nuts, and the knobs on the drawers in the chest of drawers were carved in the same shape. Even the curtains on the window were decorated along their hems with a row of kuma nuts cut from brown fabric, done in applique.

The window had a dozen small panes of glass set into two separate wood frames that could be opened independently. Both sides were presently closed to keep out the cold, and the left side was covered by one of the curtains. The right-hand curtain was tied back, however, letting in a little light and yielding a view across the muddy dirt road.

It was while Nagaro was studying the window that he witnessed the arrival of Tira Zomora.

Master Pedril had said that they couldn't mistake Tira Zomora's piebald pony, and it was true. The beast that drew up outside the window could best be described as white with black spots on one side, and black with white spots on the other. Nagaro couldn't get a clear view of the medicine woman's unique side-saddle, but he saw plainly that she was sitting with her yellow skirts all on one side of the pony, and he watched her dismount as if descending steps. She wore a dark green cloak with the hood up, so he couldn't see her features as she passed out of his field of view on her way to the front door.

Nagaro sat waiting in apprehension, remembering everything that Pedril had said about this woman. He heard the front door open, and voices came to him from the outer room, speaking low so he couldn't catch the words. He briefly considered getting up and going to introduce himself, but it seemed that Lunani might be dozing, and he was reluctant to stop providing the distraction of his touch. So he stayed where he was at the suffering woman's side.

The conversation in the outer room seemed to go back and forth between the medicine woman and the boy, Tobei. Nagaro heard Tira Zomora say something that ended in the rising inflection of a question, though her voice was unusually low-pitched for a woman's and he couldn't tell what she had asked. However, he very plainly heard Tobei's indignantly defensive reply:

"What was I t' do, Zirdyn? She was makin' that noise again, an' Kadi was crying! And they said ye'd gone up-island!"

From her tone, Nagaro deduced that Tira Zomora's response was meant to be conciliatory, though again he couldn't make out the words. Either the words or the tone must have worked, however, for Tobei's response was a much less defensive "Go on in, then."

There followed the sound of approaching footsteps.

The woman who came to stand in the bedroom doorway was very striking, although she was of only ordinary height for a Turowa and certainly not beautiful. The lines on her brow and around her eyes said that she had known forty summers or more, yet the unbound hair that framed her face was ink-black without a trace of gray. The face framed by the hair was broad and square-jawed, with a nose like a flattened eagle's beak and piercing jet-black eyes. Besides her imposing physical appearance, there was the supremely self-assured way she carried herself. This was a woman who knew what she knew and would not be afraid to say any of it.

Her clothing reminded Nagaro instantly of Luka, the medicine woman of his childhood, for she wore a pale green blouse with long loose sleeves, gathered at the wrists, and a yellow skirt that sported at least a half a dozen ample pockets, several of them bulging noticeably.

The woman paused only for a heartbeat in the doorway and then advanced deliberately across the floor to within two paces of where Nagaro sat, regarding him fixedly all the while with those penetrating dark eyes. Halting again, she addressed him, speaking very low in her commanding contralto.

"*I* am Tira Zomora," she announced. "Who are *you*? And what are ye doing here?"

Nagaro found his mouth suddenly dry. He swallowed. "My name is Nagaro, Zirdyn, and I'm Master Tredhold's apprentice." He kept his voice low also for the sake of the woman on the bed, and inclined his head a little as he spoke to show his respect.

Her glance didn't waver, but he thought her eyes narrowed ever so slightly. "And what are ye doing *there?*" Her glance stabbed at where his finger was still tracing circles on the back of Lunani's hand.

"It's for distraction," he explained. "Master Tredhold told me to do it while he went to the apothecaries for some sasaba. Tira Lunani said that's what you've given her that's worked in the past."

Tira Zomora snorted. "He won't find it. Neither one o' them keeps it." She said this with just a trace of smugness. And then, before he could think how he might possibly respond, she said, "And what is your *other* name, Tor Nagaro?"

His breath all but stopped in his throat, even as his heart began to pound. Momentarily forgotten, his finger stopped moving, and Lunani stirred and gave a low moan. Immediately he gave his attention back to providing the distraction, keeping his eyes on his moving finger, avoiding Zomora's gaze. *What did the woman suspect?* But, no, he told himself, it must be only that she was Turowan and knew the meaning of his name. All the Turo seemed to know some of their old tongue, and they used it to make names, though they didn't speak it anymore.

"Have ye forgotten it?"

Nagaro swore silently. He'd kept the medicine woman waiting too long. He thought everyone on the island must surely have heard his carefully edited tale of being a foundling, raised by a noble lady, now dead. This woman could hardly be an exception. If she kept asking questions, it must be because she wasn't satisfied with the tale. He had to somehow put her off, but he sensed she was not a good person to lie to. "No, I haven't forgotten it," he said, still without looking at her. "Nor the woman who gave it to me. But she is dead, and there's no good that can come to me from speaking it."

"I *see*." She stepped a little closer. They had both been speaking softly for the sake of the woman on the bed, but Zomora spoke more softly still as she said, "Some men change their names to hide a misdeed."

That stung, and he did look at her then, a sharp glance that held her eyes. "The misdeed was not mine!" He still spoke low, though he couldn't keep the anger from his voice.

This time it seemed that her eyes widened ever so slightly.

And it was just at that moment that they heard Tredhold's voice in the outer room.

Nagaro let out a long breath as Tira Zomora turned and stepped away from him. *What else might she have asked if given but a minute more?* He stayed on his stool and kept his finger moving, alternately tracing little squares and zig-zags.

The medicine woman intercepted the Leithian healer at the doorway. The face Tredhold presented to her was carefully open and neutral, but Nagaro could read the tension in the man from the stiffness of his shoulders. "Well met, Tira Zomora," the healer said, speaking softly, and with respect. "I know she's usually your patient, but the lad was distressed and very insistent. As a healer, I couldn't refuse to come."

"Of course not, Master Tredhold." Zomora inclined her head to him with gracious dignity. "I'm sorry ye wasted your time with the apothecaries, but ye seem t' have left Lunani's care in good *hands*, at least."

The last words were accompanied by a pointed glance in Nagaro's direction.

Tredhold immediately looked past Zomora to where his patient lay. "How is she?" he asked.

Zomora answered him before Nagaro could speak. "The distraction is good. I taught her to put the center of her spirit outside the pain. But when it's very bad, she can't do it. She has centered her spirit on her hand now, I think. Where he touches it."

"Ah, good." Tredhold sounded impressed by the medicine woman's understanding.

Zomora smiled thinly. "Of course ye must sit with her the whole time t' make it work," she pointed out.

Tredhold allowed his weariness to show. "Which is why I went to look for sasaba. I've brought back *opa*, because it was all they had, but I'd rather not give her that. With the dreams it causes, we'd still have to sit with her for the sake o' safety."

Tira Zomora shook her head. "No, opa is not good for this." Plunging her hand into one of the bulging pockets of her skirt, she drew out a fat packet wrapped in homespun cloth. She unwrapped the packet to reveal a generous fistful of leaves. They were long and narrow, and dark-green in color despite being dry and crackling in her hands.

"Sasaba." Tredhold sounded both disgusted and relieved. "I'd like t' know how ye came by it!"

Tira Zomora arched a brow at him. "I'm sure ye would, Master Healer. The fact is, my people make a trade between the islands that your folk never see, and have done so since long before the coming o' your kind to this land." She carefully drew four leaves from the bundle and held them out to the healer. "A gift from one healer to another," she said. "If the lad seeks ye out, ye needs must come. And if ye come, it's best ye have what's needful."

Tredhold gravely accepted the gift. "Thank you, Zirdyn."

"Ye can finish here now. Do ye know how to prepare it?"

Tredhold shook his head. "No, Zirdyn," he said humbly. "Ye must instruct me."

"Brew one leaf in a cup o' fresh-boiled water," she told him. "Steep it long, 'til no more color comes out. That should be all she needs for one of her spells. And don't let the children touch it. It's very strong."

"Thank you." Tredhold actually bowed. "I'm honored to have met ye, Tira Zomora."

The look this earned the healer was benignly regal, though it seemed to Nagaro from where he sat that she was flattered. "I'm pleased to have met ye, too, Master Tredhold," she said, and her voice betrayed no hint of anything but sincerity. She turned to go, then paused to cast a glance back over her shoulder at Nagaro where he still sat at Lunani's side. "And you too, *Tor Nagaro*." Her black eyes locked on his for just an instant before she turned again and swept out in a rustle of skirts.

Through the window they watched the medicine woman remount her pony, tucking up her long skirt just enough to free her feet for mounting by means of two hanging steps, then turning and settling into her side-saddle. She picked up the reins, and the piebald began to move, carrying her out of their field of view.

Tredhold sagged against the doorframe. "Well," he said, "I guess we weathered *that* squall."

He then set about seeing that water was boiled, and steeped one of the sasaba leaves in a cup of it. And when it was properly brewed, they roused Lunani and raised her head enough so she could drink the infusion. At that point Tobei, who had helped with boiling the water, declared that his mother would now sleep for an hour or two and then she would be, "right enough t' cook for us." Since the boy seemed confident that all was now as it should be, or as nearly so as was possible, Tredhold decided he would worry later about collecting his fee. Nagaro showed Tobei how to do the distraction, and then he and Tredhold took their leave.

Walking back to the inn through the waning afternoon, under a sky that looked much less threatening than it had earlier, Tredhold actually whistled a bit of a tune. "That wasn't as bad as I'd feared," he said, interrupting the tune. "From what Pedril told us, I expected worse. And there's a lesson in it for ye about dealing with other healers, even touchy medicine women. Show respect for what they know, and let them see that the patient's more important to ye than your pride. Any healer that's the right sort o' healer should warm t' that."

He whistled another few bars, and when Nagaro still said nothing, he added, "Ye must ha' done all right before I came in, since she spoke well of ye."

Nagaro shrugged his shoulders under his cloak. "I was... polite," he said carefully.

Tredhold was in a high humor, and he merely laughed at this. "I can hardly imagine ye being anything else," he said, and resumed his whistling.

Nagaro was glad to let the matter rest. He was not at all sure what kind of impression he had made on Tira Zomora. Her questions had unsettled him deeply, and he had to wonder why she'd asked them. The tale of Tredhold's successful treatment of Neved's injured ankle had more or less supplanted the one of Nagaro's misadventure with Jila, and he hadn't thought about the beautiful Turowan temptress for days, nor dreamt of her. But now all he could think of was that Zomora, who was a significant figure among Pakoa's Turowan population, might know where Jila was, and might have spoken to her. Jila had seen the truth of his kuma-stain disguise, and Tira Zomora had shown far too much interest in his history.

Had Zomora spoken to Jila? And, if so, what might the temptress have revealed?

Chapter II

A Door Closes

When Nagaro told his friends about the way Tira Zomora had questioned him, Taru was quick to reassure him.

"Ye worry too much, Nagaro," he said. "She's a medicine woman. So she worries about the care of her people— which, I hear, means all o' the Turo in the southern Lomoas. If she had a good word t' say about ye when she left, she must think ye're all right."

Nagaro hoped his friend was right, though he was thinking that Jila would be one of Zomora's people, while he most certainly was *not.*

He didn't want to speak to Tredhold about it again, but he couldn't prevent the healer from bringing it up— which Tred did the following day.

"Pedril thought we had uncommon luck with Tira Zomora," the healer confided. "He thinks she's fickle and unpredictable. But I say we just took the right tack with her, and we'll prove it the next time our courses cross."

Nagaro nodded in response to this and offered no comment, though the thought of crossing Zomora's path again still made him uneasy.

The days went by, however, without any further encounters with the medicine woman, and Nagaro saw no obvious consequences of their having spoken with her. He and Tred continued to be sought out by patients from within the town of Pakoa, and occasionally the lands around it. Perhaps a few more of the patients were Turowan than before, but there was no way to know whether it had anything to do with their having met Zomora.

It was just as Nagaro had begun to relax, that they got another request to see one of Zomora's patients. This time it was brought by a Turowan youth who arrived at the Bay Tree Inn on an aging plow horse. The patient was his mother's sister, the wife of a farmer who lived a few miles outside of town along the Main Road. Tira Zomora had been treating her for a chest cold, and she'd seemed to be recovering, only to take a turn for the worse during the night. The medicine woman was again somewhere "up-island," tending to a birthing.

Tredhold listened quietly to this, and promptly sent Nagaro to saddle the horses while he packed his bag. Nagaro's apprehension had stirred at the first mention of Zomora's name, but he tried to put it from his mind as he focused on readying their mounts.

The day was cool, overcast, and damp, though no rain was actually falling as they set out. During the ride, Nagaro tried to think about what might have caused the woman's downturn. Unfortunately, he knew too little about her ailment to have any thoughts of his own on the subject and Tredhold set a rapid pace that precluded conversation. Nagaro tried to tell himself that the medicine woman had surely lost interest in him. When that didn't work, he reminded himself that a birthing could take hours. What was the chance that he would even see Tira Zomora on this call?

Their destination turned out to be a squat stone farmhouse flanked on one side by a small stand of nearly leafless trees and located at the bottom of a hillside that still bore the stubble of a harvested crop of grain. The road ran within a dozen yards of the dwelling's front door.

The day's mood continued to be very somber as they approached the house, although the heavy gray clouds still disdained to rain. Tredhold and Nagaro quickly dismounted and tethered their horses to a low-hanging branch of the nearest tree. Their guide left them there to return to his work, and he had no sooner gone than the weathered front door burst open and a middle-aged woman appeared, beckoning urgently. Tredhold immediately approached her and inquired about the state of the patient. The woman launched into a confused and frantic tale of woe even as she ushered the healer and his assistant into the main room of the house.

The woman who had let them in turned out to be the sick woman's sister, a thin, angular Turowa who kept wringing her hands and who introduced them to their patient's husband, a stolid, graying Turo with a crooked nose and a limp. It quickly became apparent that the sister and the husband had been at odds over whether to send for Tredhold at all. The sister's fear for her only sibling had won out over the husband's distrust of the skill of an unfamiliar Leithian Fleet healer— compared to that of the island's revered and trusted medicine woman.

Tredhold was polite and businesslike. "Just let me look at her," he said. "And I'll see if she's in any danger. Perhaps I'm not needed here, and ye can safely wait for Tira Zomora. I'll not charge ye just for the looking," he added.

"Well, all right then." The farmer said, relenting. "That seems fair enough."

He led them to the closed door of the sickroom. When opened, it revealed a small, dim chamber where the patient could be seen lying on a narrow bed, swathed in blankets.

Tredhold uttered an exclamation as he stepped through the doorway, and Nagaro, close behind him, soon discovered why. Walking into the room was like walking into an herbal steam-bath. The window was closed and tightly shuttered, and the only sources of light in the room were a candle on a bedside table and the ruddy glow of the fire burning on a small hearth. A kettle hung there over the fire and its seething contents were clearly what was filling the air with a miasma of pungent vapor. Tred immediately asked the reason for the boiling pot.

“Tira Zomora’s orders” was the husband’s terse response.

The sister, who had followed them into the room, hastily elaborated. “She told us t’ boil it for an hour whenever Mira said she couldn’t breathe, but we’ve been boiling it steady since morning because we’ve not been able t’ rouse her enough t’ ask.”

Tredhold cleared his throat. “Ye might be overdoing it just a little,” he said carefully. “Why don’t ye take the kettle off the fire for a while and let the air freshen a bit?”

This earned him a scowl from Mira’s husband. “I’ll not do that,” the man said sullenly. “Tira Zomora said it was good for her. And besides, ye said ye were just going t’ take a look.”

Tredhold cast Nagaro a glance that was equal parts resignation and exasperation, and moved quickly to the bedside.

Nagaro came up beside the healer, pushing thoughts of the medicine woman out of his mind to focus on the patient. The wheezing of the woman’s breath sounded disturbingly loud in the quiet room, and now that his eyes had adjusted to the dim light, he saw that she plainly didn’t look well. Her face was slack, her forehead slick with sweat. She was covered by a linen sheet and woolen blanket that were pulled up to her throat, and she lay very still under the covers except for the rise and fall of her chest in rhythm with her labored breathing.

While the husband and sister hovered behind him, Tred bent over the woman. “I’d like to use the listening trumpet,” he muttered to Nagaro under his breath. “But I doubt the husband would let me touch her t’ turn down the bedclothes.” Frowning, he spoke to the sick woman, calling her by name. There was no response. He tried shaking her gently, placing his hand on her blanket-wrapped shoulder, still to no effect. Finally, he touched her brow, and winced. “How long has she been this hot?” he asked sharply.

The sister stepped forward to touch Mira’s brow. “I found her so this morning,” she said, wringing her hands.

“When was the last time she woke, or spoke to ye?”

The husband and sister exchanged glances, and it was the sister who answered. "Yesterday evening."

Tred's lips pressed together in a hard line and he shook his head. "Her fever is dangerously high," he said. "And with the room this warm and steamy, she can't cool herself. I recommend that ye strip the covers off of her, take that kettle off the fire, and open the window t' let in some air."

The husband immediately shook his head. "Tira Zomora said th' fever was good for her, and she can't breathe cold air."

Tred was clearly restraining himself with difficulty. "The air needn't be cold," he said patiently. "Just *cooler*. And a moderate fever *is* good. But if Tira Zomora saw how the fever has risen, I'm sure she'd tell ye the room is too warm. A very high fever can do harm." He paused to look hard at his listeners. "Haven't ye heard the tale of Leyel Virden?"

No one was looking at Nagaro, which was fortunate, because he flinched sharply at the name. *Why did Tred have to use that example?* The tale wasn't even true, though Tredhold couldn't know that and Nagaro was in no position to enlighten him.

The truly depressing thing was the way the healer's words evoked matching looks of alarm from the sick woman's husband and sister. Clearly neither wished Mira to suffer Leyel Virden's terrible fate.

Nagaro's struggle to keep his own expression neutral had cost him his concentration, and he'd missed what Tred was saying. Now the healer turned and addressed him directly, saying, "Nagaro, could ye please fetch some water?"

"Aye, and hurry," put in the husband. "Ye'll find the well out behind the house."

Nagaro shook himself. "Of course," he murmured, turning. "Right away." He was only too glad to escape, to get out of the smothering atmosphere of the sickroom and have time to further compose himself while doing something useful.

Despite the lowering sky, the world outside seemed all light and air compared to the dim closeness of the room he had left. Nagaro found the well, and a bucket beside it, and drew water with hands that shook only a little. He took a moment to guiltily scan the stretch of road that curved away northward between the hills. There was a man moving along it, driving a half dozen silken-haired givadi, but no sign of Tira Zomora's piebald pony. He heaved an internal sigh of relief, then mentally kicked himself for fretting so much about it. The medicine woman's first concern would be for her patient, and it was Tredhold, the master healer, who had the most to fear from her wrath. *He* was only the apprentice. Being thus reminded of the suffering patient, he hurriedly made his way back to the house with the sloshing bucket.

He found Mira's sister and husband in the main room of the dwelling, engaged in a whispered debate that was pointedly suspended as soon as he appeared. Nagaro inclined his head respectfully to them, getting stiff nods in return. He drew a preparatory breath as he approached the sickroom. Thrusting the door open, he slipped through into the over-heated, humid gloom and immediately noticed some changes.

The pot of herbs had been removed from the fire, and the woman's blanket stripped from the bed. The sheet had been turned down, as well, exposing her upper body, clothed in a simple cotton nightdress. The window was still tightly closed, however, and Tredhold was fanning the woman's face with his handkerchief. The healer's metal basin stood on the bedside table, a folded piece of cloth lying beside it.

Nagaro crossed to the table and poured some water into the basin, setting the bucket down on the floor. He gestured at the window. "Can't we open that?"

Tredhold frowned darkly as he stuffed his handkerchief into his pocket. "The husband won't hear of it," he muttered with suppressed anger. "He's determined to 'keep out the chill.' So we'll have to manage without cool air. See what ye can do with a wet cloth," he added as he sat down on the only stool. Reaching for his bag, he began to rummage in it. "At least they're letting me tend her."

Nagaro knelt and wetted the folded cloth in the basin of cold water, then sponged the woman's forehead. Her face twitched slightly in response, but that was all. He put his fingers to her temple and found her indeed alarmingly hot.

Tredhold had in the meantime gotten out his listening trumpet. Putting the narrow end to his ear, he placed the broader end of it against the woman's chest, listening attentively and then moving to a second spot, and a moment later to a third and then a fourth. "There's fluid in the lungs in several places," he muttered.

Nagaro dipped the cloth again and dabbed at the woman's temples, but saw no reaction at all this time. He sponged her forehead again, then leaned down and blew on it. Still there was no response. "She may be as bad as the men were with the plague," he murmured. Since they were alone with the patient, and she was clearly unconscious, there seemed no reason why he shouldn't share what he was thinking.

Tredhold offered no rebuke. "It's only a moderate pneumonia, on the right side," he said. "The real danger right now is from the fever— which *wouldn't* be a danger if only we could cool the room. And blowing on her won't help because the air's too damp. The water can't evaporate. Here," he added, holding out the listening trumpet. "Try listening. Notice the difference between the upper right side where there's fluid, and left side which is clear."

Nagaro moved to the side of the bed and took the trumpet, using it as Tred had done, and he was indeed able to hear a difference in the sounds made by the air in the different areas of the patient's lungs. He nodded excitedly at Tred, forgetting everything else for a moment in the pleasure of gaining new knowledge.

Tredhold was rummaging in his bag again, and presently he retrieved one of his little bottles. As Nagaro returned to his place at the basin, the healer got up from the stool and knelt on the floor beside it, placing the bottle on the stool's seat. He watched for a time as Nagaro sponged the woman, who remained disturbingly inert. Finally he bent close to her ear. "Mira," he said urgently. "Mira!" He tried shaking her gently again, but shook his head when there was no response. "I want to give her this to bring down the fever," he muttered, touching the bottle.

Nagaro mentally sorted through the list of common medicines he had learned. "A tincture of batari root?"

Tredhold nodded, his hand still on the bottle. "Yes. I was hoping to rouse her enough to safely take a dose by mouth, but—"

"Do you think we could get her to swallow it the way I did with the men on Chitaopa?" Nagaro asked, referring to the Lady Maramine's method of stroking the throat to elicit a swallowing reflex.

Tred shook his head. "Too risky. She might breathe some of it, and there's already fluid in her lungs. Besides, if she didn't swallow all of it, I couldn't be sure of the dose." He reached for his bag again. "No, I'm afraid I'm going to have to use a bladder-thorn."

Nagaro's hand froze in midair above the basin.

A bladder-thorn...

Sudden fear made his stomach clench. He understood the need. Tred's explanation made perfect sense. But acutely unpleasant memories were pushing their way to the surface of his mind. With an effort he forced them back down, focusing on the cloth in his hand. Deliberately he immersed the folded cloth in the water and lifted it out. He wrung it with hands that shook, forcing himself to pay attention to where the water fell so that it landed in the basin and wasn't wasted.

The feverish woman coughed just then, feebly, though her eyes remained closed. Nagaro glanced eagerly at Tredhold. *Was she getting better? Would the thorn not be needed after all?*

Tred met his eyes briefly, but shook his head. "That's just a reflex," he said, and gave his attention back to his collection of glass tumblers.

Nagaro's apprehension returned as hope died. He wiped the woman's forehead, trying to concentrate on controlling the movements of his hands. He felt the woman's temple again. "She's still very hot," he reported unnecessarily, hoping speech would help cover his agitation. Instead, he heard the tremor in his own voice.

Tredhold merely grunted without looking up. The Leithian was continuing to use the stool in place of a table. He had put the smallest of his glass tumblers on the seat and now began to pour some of the contents of the little bottle into it, paying close attention to the markings on the side of the glass. "*Three quarters of a dram*," he muttered under his breath, then turned again to the contents of his bag. "Now where are those bladder-thorns..."

Nagaro jerked his gaze away, shifting position uneasily.

He had completely forgotten about the bladder-thorns. They must be the very ones that Tred had rescued from the cabin floor aboard the *Fist of Death* after their box had fallen from Nagaro's nerveless fingers. Tred had said even then that they were useful in the healer's art. But Nagaro had always found that the best defense against troubling memories was not to think about them. Apparently he'd been so good at it that he hadn't thought of that box of bladder-thorns when Tred had offered him the apprenticeship... *nor in the days since then.*

Silently he cursed himself and wiped Mira's forehead again with the wet rag, keeping his eyes on his hands rather than watching Tred.

It was just as the healer had said. The air in the room was so saturated that nothing could evaporate. The water from the rag was trickling down the sides of the woman's head onto the bedclothes. *This is useless,* he thought, as he mopped the perspiration from his own brow with the back of his hand. His own sweat wasn't cooling *him* either. The room seemed so unbearably hot and close that it was hard to breathe.

He risked another glance at Tred's preparations and saw that the healer had found the bladder-thorns and was carefully inspecting one of them by the light of the candle on the bedside table. The little wooden box sat innocently on the stool.

It was definitely the same box, and just as definitely it had *not* been in evidence on that first morning when the healer had spread the contents of his bag out on the table at the Bay Tree Inn. *Surely that was no accident?* Tredhold had seen Nagaro's reaction to the contents of the box. The man must have hidden it somewhere... or left it in the bottom of the satchel...

Stop it, he thought. *Just try to get through this.*

He watched in sick fascination as Tredhold finished his inspection and wiped the bladder-thorn with a clean cloth, then turned to meet his eyes.

"Now watch carefully," the healer instructed him, seeming not to read the tension that knotted Nagaro's entire body. Turning his attention to the small glass tumbler on his makeshift table, the healer continued. "Ye squeeze the bladder and put the tip o' the thorn well into the liquid... *like this...* and then ye release the bladder very slowly..."

Nagaro frowned. The room was so hot that his shirt was sticking to his back, the herb-laden air clogging his nose and throat. If Tred would just get *on* with it... "I know how they're filled," he said, irritated.

Tredhold shot him a piercing glance, without moving his hands. "Do ye want to show me then?" he asked mildly.

Nagaro bit his lip. "No... I... I've seen it done, that's all." *And Tred surely had guessed that. Was the man playing with him?*

Tredhold turned back to the filled bladder thorn. "Then perhaps ye've seen this as well," he said easily. "The medicine is all inside now, but there's likely some air as well. Ye don't want to be putting a bubble of air into the vein. That could harm or even kill your patient. So ye hold it with the thorn pointing *up*, like this. And tap it, like *this*. And then ye squeeze until ye can see a drop *just* starting t' show..."

The words seemed to echo in Nagaro's head as he watched in horror. He had seen Dreigen go through *exactly* those motions— dozens of times— without knowing the reason for them. *The Lore Master could have killed him accidentally so many times!* A sudden shiver wracked Nagaro's body.

If Tredhold noticed, he gave no sign. The healer's voice seemed to come from far away as the man continued his running commentary.

"Ye have t' give it another little squeeze just before placing it. But first ye need to find a good vein." Still holding the bladder-thorn in his right hand, Tredhold reached out with his left and began to run his fingers along the inside of the woman's forearm where it lay upon the mattress.

Nagaro was kneeling, rigid, his eyes riveted on Tredhold's moving hand. His heart had begun to pound heavily against his ribs and sweat trickled down his sides under his shirt. The air seemed so thick he could scarcely draw it into his lungs... It felt as if some invisible force were pressing on his chest...

The arm...

It loomed large even as the stifling air around him seemed to dim and his vision to fade at the edges— until the world was reduced to that arm and those probing fingers.

It was Maramine's arm... It was his arm... He could feel the fingers...

The healer's relentless voice still reached his ears: "If ye press, just below the spot... like *this*... it'll make the vein stand up, d' ye see—"

The room was growing darker; the walls closing in...

"One more little squeeze t' the bladder, and then... ye place the point, like *this*... and slide it *right into the vein...*"

Tredhold's hand thrust the needle-sharp point of the thorn through the skin—

—and Nagaro felt a stab of pain, spiking up his arm to his shoulder. He emitted a strangled cry, tried to draw a breath, and choked. He staggered to his feet and blindly backed away, his arm still throbbing... his heart seeming about to burst out of his chest. Something was in his throat—

"*I can't breathe!*" he gasped.

Turning away, he bolted for the door... fumbled with the handle. Then, somehow, he was out of the bedroom and into the room beyond.

Mira's husband and sister were sitting at the table eating soup and bread. They looked up, alarm in their eyes. "*What's happened?*" The husband's spoon clattered on the table. The sister jumped to her feet.

"N-nothing," Nagaro managed to stammer, hot shame flashing through him. "I... just... need air..."

Embarrassment briefly warred with panic and lost. *He had to get out of there... away from their eyes... away from that thing in the other room... away from this terrible house...*

He lurched to the outer door, flung it open, and fled without looking back.

Somehow he got down the two front steps without falling. He squeezed his eyes shut against light that was too bright as he blundered along the wall of the house, his shoulder scraping the fieldstones, until he came to a halt, leaning against the wall while the world spun around him.

He was still clutching his throbbing left arm... panting for breath... The air was cooler here, but he couldn't seem to get enough of it into his lungs, and when he tried to open his eyes, the world spun so badly that his knees threatened to give way.

He was never sure, afterwards, how much time passed in this way—but suddenly Tredhold was there, grasping his right wrist and wrenching his hand away from his arm.

"For the Gods' sake, man, breathe *slowly*," the healer's voice was urgent. "*Slowly,* if ye don't want to faint!"

Nagaro struggled to comply, drawing a long shuddering breath. Letting it out... Drawing another...

After a dozen such long breaths, with Tred still gripping his wrist, the air at last came more naturally and Nagaro's vision began to clear. He steadied and straightened his body, though he still leaned his shoulder against the wall for support. "I'm sorry, Tred," he murmured, unable to meet the healer's eyes. "You shouldn't leave your patient."

At the sound of his voice, Tredhold released his wrist. "It's all right," he said lightly. "I got the medicine into her, and sent the sister in to sit with her. There's nothing more I can do for the moment, and air sounded like a good idea. It *was* pretty thick in there."

The news about the patient was a relief, but Nagaro shook his head. *He had to say something. He couldn't let Tred brush this off like that.* "It wasn't the air, Tred. I... I can't do that..." With an effort, he brought his eyes up to meet Tred's gaze and found that the Leithian was studying him intently.

The healer's blue eyes were worried. "I confess I had hoped it would help ye to see the thing used that way," he said. "But I guess it was too much, too soon. We can practice, though, without a patient. I'll let ye handle a thorn some, and watch me use it. And after ye've seen it done a few times, I'll have ye practice on my arm."

Nagaro shuddered and looked away again. The thought of trying to put a thorn into the healer's arm threatened to rekindle his panic. He shook his head emphatically. "No," he said with complete conviction. "I will *never* be able to do that. I... I can't be a healer, Tred."

"Let's not be hasty." Tredhold spoke reasonably. "There's healers that don't use the bladder-thorn. It's rather a new thing, and some o' them haven't picked up the skill."

Nagaro's eyes followed the course of the road where it ran past the trees. "And what would I do when I had a patient who needed it?" he asked. "Like this one? I'd have to watch the patient suffer... maybe even *die*... because my head wouldn't let my hands do what was needed. I could never live with that."

"Nagaro, I tell ye, we can work on this. If ye'll come back inside—"

"*No!*"

Nagaro flung himself away from the wall of the house and stumbled across the bare ground to the tree where Sugar and Cinnamon were tethered.

Tredhold caught up with him as he stood beside the sorrel mare, unnecessarily adjusting the stirrups.

"Nagaro," the Leithian tried, gently, "It would help if ye could just tell me what was done to you—"

"*No!*" Again the word jerked out of him. "*I can't...*" Nagaro studied his hands on the stirrup leathers, desperately casting about for some way to explain— something to tell this man who so clearly wanted to help him. "I'm sorry, Tred," he said at last. "This is *my* trouble, and it's nothing you can help me with. And there were some... powerful people... involved... So *please* don't ask me again."

There was a pause. "All right then, I won't." Tredhold's voice was carefully even. "But have ye at least talked to someone about it?"

"With Taru... a little..." Nagaro frowned, and he made a show of checking the buckle on the saddle girth, though he knew it was secure.

"Well, that's good. As long as there's *someone*." Tred sounded sincerely relieved. There was another pause and then he asked cautiously, "What about... Vothra?"

"*Vothra?*" Nagaro was so startled to hear a Leithian speak the name of the Kelorin guiding spirit that he turned to stare at the man. Tredhold's face was etched with concern, and Nagaro remembered that Tred had been present when the Benevolent Spirit had come to him, on the ship, to reassure him about the way he'd used his gift for swordsmanship at Jaamra. "How could Vothra help?" he wondered aloud. "There's nothing *I* did... Nothing I don't *understand*. It's just something bad that happened..."

Some things are better not remembered. Vothra had said that. And also, *There is wisdom in the Spirit of the White Flower.* That spirit, Nagaro believed, had taken his memories and given them back again, even if he didn't understand exactly how or why. It had been a long time since he'd thought about Vothra's words, which had come to him in that first dream more than two years ago in Taru's house on Wotana Bay.

"I'm all right as long as I don't think about it," he said. "But *that*—" He jerked his head towards the farmhouse. "That *made* me think about it. Would *always* make me think about it! I can't be a healer, Tred."

Tredhold sagged. "What will ye do instead?"

"I don't know... Be a fisherman—"

Tred waved a hand. "Ye're no fisherman, Nagaro."

Nagaro gave the healer a reproachful look. "I studied it for a year. I know how to do it."

"I don't doubt that. But it's a waste o' your talents. Have ye thought about the Palace Guard?"

Nagaro shifted his feet uncomfortably. Eventually someone had been bound to think of that. "I, ah... I'd best stay away from Lankura," he said guardedly.

"Ah. Yes. I see." Tredhold digested this tidbit and nodded. "I guess all the lords come to Lankura sooner or later."

Nagaro made no answer, thinking it best to let that stand. "Could I go now, Tred?" he pleaded. "If you don't need me, I mean? I feel such a fool, after running out like that. I don't know what those people must think of me." The truth was he had no desire to go back into that room— or even into that house— and he was afraid Tred would try to persuade him to, just to prove he could.

Tredhold hesitated, then sighed. "Oh, aye, go on," he said resignedly. "I'll make some excuse for ye. Try not to dwell on this, Nagaro. And promise me ye'll let me know if ye change your mind."

"Of course I will, Tred. And, please don't say anything about... what we've just talked about... to anyone?"

Tred gave him a look of genuine sympathy. "Don't worry, I won't."

"Thank you." Nagaro shivered in a sudden gust of wind. He was suddenly aware of how cold the day was. *How could it have seemed so bright to him? It was still quite overcast and gray.* He reached for Cinnamon's reins, then put a foot into the stirrup and swung up into the saddle. "I'm grateful for what you've tried to do, Tred," he said earnestly, looking down into the healer's eyes. "Trying to teach me your trade."

"I wouldn't have offered if I hadn't thought that ye'd make a good healer—" Tred began, and stopped when the door of the house burst open behind him.

The sick woman's sister stood on the doorstep, radiating excitement. "Mira's awake, Master Tredhold!" she cried. "She just spoke to me! *Praise the Sprits!*"

Tred cast Nagaro a wry look. "So the spirits get the credit for the miracle?" he muttered. "Ah, well, I expect the husband will be willing to open the window *now*." He laughed mirthlessly as he turned back towards the house. "And it'll give me some satisfaction to hear Tira Zomora tell him I was right all along, when she gets here."

***

Nagaro rode hurriedly away, urging Cinnamon into a brisk trot. He was glad that the woman, Mira, was doing better, and was anxious to put the house and what had happened in it behind him. At the first turn of the road he looked back.

Far away, on the stretch of road beyond the house, he glimpsed a black-and-white pony, a splash of yellow skirt. Sucking in his breath he pressed Cinnamon into a canter. In his mind he could see the medicine woman's challenging stare, hear her probing question: "*And where is your apprentice today, Master Tredhold?*" What would Tred say to her? The man would make up some excuse for him, of course, but Tira Zomora was not a woman to be lied to. She wouldn't be easily deceived. At least he might not have to worry so much about her in the future if he wasn't trying to be a healer.

Once he was well out of sight of the house, he reined in the mare and rode on more slowly. He needed time to think. He was still feeling shaky, and shaken, and his thoughts were in a turmoil. He had never experienced anything quite like what had happened in that house— and he sincerely hoped he never would again. Clearly he had imagined the pain in his arm. *He must have remembered it so vividly that it had seemed real...*

He shivered and pulled his thoughts away, only to have them settle on his parting conversation with Tredhold.

He knew that Tred had seen the scars of bladder-thorns on his arms while they were slaves, on Chitaopa if not before. The healer thought he had been an unwilling catamite, and Nagaro had just deliberately played to the Leithian's misconception. Purposeful deception always made him acutely uncomfortable. He tried to tell himself that he hadn't said anything actually *untrue*. In fact, he hoped he hadn't said too much. *If only he hadn't been forced into saying he couldn't go to Lankura...*

Again he deliberately redirected his thoughts.

He wondered why Tred had pressed him so hard to talk about his past. He could understand the man being curious, but he couldn't understand why the healer thought it was a good thing that he had talked to Taru about it. Surely it was best to put the thing out of his mind? Wasn't that what Vothra had meant about things best forgotten?

At least Tredhold had agreed not to ask about it again. It was a relief to have that promise— to know where he stood with Tred.

Tredhold was a very decent man— one of the best that Nagaro had encountered in his life— and he felt fortunate that the Leithian still seemed to hold him in good regard after all that had happened. *Especially after today*. Tred, it seemed, was a man who didn't judge people for things that shouldn't matter. It was a principle that figured in the Vothrin Writings, and one that Nagaro tried to follow. Tred wasn't Vothrin, but the man seemed to have found a parallel path. Nagaro smiled somberly. The healer would doubtless have treated him no differently had he been a crossed man, and he admired the man for that.

Nagaro came out of his thoughts long enough to find that he had topped the rise above Pakoa Town. Here, the road he was on became the Hill Road, which descended in two long switchbacks to disappear among the houses that straggled up the slope from the harbor. Since he still didn't feel ready to be back among folk, he decided to stop at a place he knew— a place he'd come to think of as the "stone seat."

It was near the turning of the first switchback, next to a boarded-up house, where there was a stand of ironwood trees. Rising above their branches was an outcropping of weathered rock, into which the actions of wind and water had sculpted a hollow. It was more than an alcove but less than a cave. It was also a place where a man could sit and inconspicuously look out over the town and the harbor.

The place reminded Nagaro of a similar one on the small estate of Averwin where he had grown up. It had been a place where he had gone as a boy whenever he wanted to be alone. That other stone seat was a wind-sculpted hollow in a cliff that the river had cut from the side of a hill. He had been accustomed in those days to tie his horse under a great oak tree beside the water, to cross the river by means of a footbridge and climb a narrow stair-like path to reach his special place. From there he'd been able to look out over the Lady Maramine's little domain— the woods and the pasture— all the way to the house, with its garden and stable. He'd even been able to see a bit of the road where it showed between the stable and the house. It had been from that vantage point that he had seen

Elgurn ride up to Averwin on the fateful day that had changed his life three years ago... *the day he had said no to the king of Edrovir.*

Which was another thing he tried not to think about as he tied Cinnamon's reins to a low-hanging branch of one of the ironwood trees and walked to the place where a weathered crack in the rock formed a slanting groove that could be easily climbed to reach the hollowed-out place above.

Settled in the seat, he heaved a sigh that came from the bottom of his soul. The day was still every bit as gloomy— cold, damp, and dismally overcast— as it had been when he had left the inn. The sky was gray, and the water of the harbor reflected the gray sky. Whatever other colors there were in the landscape were muted by the wan, gray light.

The relief he had felt at escaping from the farmhouse and a possible confrontation with Tira Zomora had by now been replaced by a gnawing emptiness— the hole left by the loss of a hope and an expectation. He had been offered the chance to become a healer, a chance that Lokundas had dangled and then snatched away, leaving him with nothing to show for it but a few rins. It might not have mattered so much except that he'd felt a genuine affinity for the work. He had helped to heal half a dozen patients, and had truly felt that he was learning things— ways to help people. Healing folk was a way to do good in the world, and he had hoped it might be his future. But the door to that potential future had just slammed shut.

Because of his past.

No, he thought, *don't dwell on it.* Tred was right about that.

He frowned and shifted position on the cold rock, drawing his knees up in front of him and encircling them with his arms as he'd been accustomed to do as a boy sitting perched on the cliff above the river. A chilling wind gust swirled into the rocky hollow, and he shivered. It was really too cold to sit for long in this place. The stone beneath him seemed to suck the warmth from his body. He knew he would have to move soon.

He remembered that he had an errand he could run in town. Gedras had sent a written note to the inn requesting that Nagaro see him on a matter of business. There was no hurry about it, but he unexpectedly had the rest of the day before him and no excuse not to make use of it. Perhaps the merchant might have more money for distribution from the sale of additional spoils from the *Fist of Death.*

The thought of the ship's cargo drew his eyes to the captured Mahuk war galley where it lay anchored in the harbor. The ship rode there like a great slumbering bird, a dark gray shape on the pale gray water. Even the black-and-scarlet diamonds painted along her side looked like two shades of gray at this distance, dimmed by the misty dampness of the intervening air.

An ironic smile twitched the corners of Nagaro's mouth. The men had given the ship to him the day they'd all come ashore and taken rooms in town. It was an awkward trophy for which none of them had any use, and it had been Nagaro's idea to take it in the first place. So there it was: his ship, anchored in the harbor, and there was nothing to be done with it. Landros had explained that a war galley couldn't be refitted and sold as a merchant ship. It wasn't just that the prow was made for ramming: The *Fist's* hull was designed to be propelled primarily by oars. Though the oar ports could be sealed, her draft was too shallow to hold much cargo, or the ballast she would need if she were to carry more sails than she already had— which simply weren't enough for a merchant vessel.

No, the *Fist of Death* was a ship of war. Nagaro frowned as his dream stirred again, that wild dream of sailing forth in her to free more galley slaves. But it was only a dream. He heaved a sigh. It wasn't as if he'd even be allowed to *keep* the ship. Gedras had told him that when the Royal Fleet next blew into Pakoa Harbor, Lord Kuran would likely seize the *Fist* for Edrovir as a prize of war. The best Nagaro and the other former slaves could hope for was to get some modest reward for having captured her.

He sighed again. There *really* was no excuse for sitting here since it wasn't even comfortable. He stood up, stiffly unfolding his legs. As he turned to go down, he caught a view of the abandoned house and its grounds and wondered, not for the first time, whether the ironwood grove and the rocks where he was standing belonged to whoever owned the house. It was a very modest wooden house, though larger than those of most local fishermen. A currently leafless fruit tree of some kind nestled against the back of it, and it had a small walled garden, completely gone to weeds. There was also a good-sized fenced pasture running up the hillside behind the rocky outcropping where he stood. A wooden shed intended to shelter livestock adjoined the fence directly below him.

As he was surveying this scene, a movement caught Nagaro's eye. A man had just turned off the road from the town and was approaching the house with a rolling gait. He was an aging Turo with hair and beard quite gray, bent under the weight of a ladder balanced on his back and a large sack slung over his shoulder.

Nagaro ducked from sight and hastily descended the weathered crack in the rock. His first thought was to steal quietly away, but as he was untying Cinnamon, another idea struck him. He led the mare out of the grove of trees on the side facing the house and hailed the man.

The old Turo was just leaning his ladder against one end of the porch roof. He turned, startled. In his prime, he must have been a powerfully built man, but he had grown a little bent with age. Sharp black eyes peered at Nagaro from out of a weathered brown face.

The old man raised a gnarled hand and hailed him in return. "Hoy, matey! Tor Nagaro, is it?"

Nagaro heaved an inward sigh. It seemed everyone on the island could identify him either by sight or by description. He crossed the remaining space that separated them, still leading the mare, and came to a halt in front of the man. "Yes, I am Nagaro," he said. "But I'm afraid I don't know *your* name, Zirda."

The old man grinned broadly, showing stained teeth. "I be Ulapa," he announced. "Soon or late, everybody what stays on Pakoa comes t' know old Ulapa."

Nagaro extended his hand. "Well met then, Tor Ulapa. Does this house belong to you?"

The man took Nagaro's hand and shook it, but at the same time his shoulders shook as a dry chuckle rattled in his throat. "*This* house? Belong t' the likes o' *me?* No chance o' that, matey. I'm just the one what sees that the rats an' the rain don't get in." The old man spat without malice. "Fine job for an old salt dog, ain't it? Gedras pays me three rins a week, and I does it proper."

"Oh. I see. You're the caretaker." Nagaro nodded. "And you've come to mend the roof, I'd guess," he added, eyeing the ladder and the sack. "So the house belongs to Gedras?"

Ulapa leaned against the ladder and put his head on one side. "Ah, no-o..." he drawled. "Gedras ain't the one she *belongs* to. That 'd be old Fendorin what used t' live in 'er, but moved over to the main close t' two years ago. Gedras is lookin' after her for Fendorin. Only he doesn't do the lookin-after *himself* o' course— not a fine, fancy gentleman like Gedras. That's where *I* comes in."

"I... see." Nagaro's eyes swept over the house again. "What's it like on the inside?

Ulapa scratched his bearded chin with a sly grin. "Empty."

Nagaro laughed in spite of himself. "I mean, how many rooms?"

Ulapa covered his smile with a cough. "Oh, *well* now, ye should ha' *said*." Turning toward the house, he pointed with a gnarled finger. "That window's the kitchen, and that one's a room for sittin' and eatin' in. And there's two bedrooms on t'other side, and a *par-lar* in the front. D'ye know what a par-lar is, matey?"

"A parlor?" Nagaro grinned. "It's a useless sort of room that you keep tidy just for guests but never use yourself."

Ulapa stared at him, a hint of approval in his glance. "Well, now, I suppose I should ha' knowed ye'd know that," he said. "Seein' as they say ye was raised like a lord's son."

Nagaro laughed to cover his unease with the topic. "I was raised like a lord's son if you imagine a lord's son spending his whole life in a small house in the country."

"A house in the country, eh?" The old man eyed him narrowly. "A house like this one, ye're sayin'?"

Nagaro shifted a little, awkwardly, but it wasn't as if the details would mean anything to this man. "We-ell, it was a *bit* bigger," he admitted. "But it had a parlor." A childhood memory suddenly came vividly to his mind, and it made a good distraction. "When I was a boy, I used to sneak into the parlor and play 'storm the castle' under the table with two different colors of pebbles for soldiers," he said, smiling at the memory. "The housekeeper caught me at it several times, and chased me out of the house with a broom. I kept going back though, day after day, because the carved center leg of the table made such a wonderful castle." He sighed. "The housekeeper was fit to be tied, of course, but I couldn't see what all the fuss was about. It wasn't as if we ever *used* the room since we never had any guests—" Nagaro stopped.

Ulapa's shoulders were shaking again with laughter and there was a more than approving twinkle in the old man's bright black eyes. "Were ye a bad boy then, matey?" He chuckled. "A proper-seemin' man like ye, an' all? Who'd ha' thought it!"

Nagaro smiled the most wicked smile he could muster— white teeth contrasting sharply with his black beard. "That's not the half of it," he said in a conspiratorial tone. "I used to keep birds' nests and fish bones under the stairs, and leave sticks and stones in the back hall." Though he had gotten along better with Hinda— who'd served as cook and housekeeper— as he'd grown up, Nagaro suspected the woman had never fully forgiven the Lady Maramine for bringing a boy into her house. His smile died as he returned his attention to the house in front of him. "Do you know if it's for sale?" he inquired seriously.

Ulapa wiped his eyes and stifled his mirth. "For sale? I suppose she just might be, at that. It'll be two years come Evrel that she's been empty, and I don't reckon that old man Fendorin is a-comin' back." The old Turo cocked his head again. "Would ye be thinkin' o' buyin' 'er then, Zirda?"

Nagaro sighed. "I wish I could— if I'm going to live on this island. I can't stay at the inn forever, and this is the first empty house I've seen." He frowned. "But I probably don't have enough money."

The old Turo was instantly sympathetic. "Aye, that was a rough go, mate. Jila robbin' ye like that. Still, I've seen the woman." He gave a low whistle and winked at Nagaro. "It might just be worth it, bein' robbed, fer a night with *her!*"

Nagaro winced inwardly. Though there was nothing new about the sentiment, it still embarrassed him. He had hoped he was done with Jila.

Not liking the direction of the conversation, or his thoughts, he cast about for a way to end it. He'd let go of Cinnamon's bridle, and he now saw that the mare had wandered off— conveniently— while he was talking. She was cropping grass along the muddy dirt path leading from the house to the road.

He hastily murmured something about needing to catch his horse, and bade the caretaker farewell.

Chapter 12

Choices

When Nagaro arrived at the stable, he saw that the stalls needed mucking out again and there was no sign of Habu. He grimaced. Since he wouldn't be working with Tredhold anymore and still needed money, he decided to ask Tor Ramu if he could keep the stable clean to pay for part of his board. The innkeeper would probably be willing and wouldn't be likely to ask what had become of Nagaro's apprenticeship. Having thought of this way to ease his financial situation made him feel a little better at least. But he still left Cinnamon in the stable and set out for Gedras' house on foot. It wasn't far, and walking was significantly less conspicuous than going on horseback. He had no desire to be noticed and possibly questioned about why he was in town when Master Tredhold was not.

On reaching the merchant's house he found that Gedras was closeted with another client. The servant who answered the door instructed him to wait in the downstairs hall, a square, wood-paneled room with a stairway leading up to an open second-floor landing. The furnishings consisted of two small tables, bearing matching china vases, and a brocade-upholstered couch set against the wall across from the foot of the stairs. The couch was clearly intended for the use of waiting clients, so Nagaro sat down on it after hanging his cloak on a peg beside the door. Trying to relax and compose himself, he leaned back and laced his fingers behind his head while stretching out his legs and crossing his booted ankles.

To occupy himself, he began mentally reviewing what was left of the part of the ship's cargo that had been stored in Gedras' warehouse. He'd been at this for less than a minute when he became aware of a rustling sound above him at the top of the stairs. He tried to ignore it, but the rustling was followed by a distinctly feminine giggle, and the giggle was in turn followed by a hurried exchange of female whispers.

"Oh *my!* Isn't he handsome?"

(This was followed by another giggle.)

"*Shh!*"

"If only he weren't so *brown!*" (The first voice, again).

"*Shh!* Father says that it's just kuma stain," said a second voice, disapprovingly. "And besides, Father says he has a good head on his shoulders."

"Oh, *yes*, I see his head." (Again the first voice.) "*And* his shoulders!"

Yet another giggle followed. It seemed the giggler represented a third person.

"*Shh!*"

By this time Nagaro was blushing crimson under his kuma stain. The shush-er, he surmised, was the second speaker, the one who'd mentioned the kuma stain. It was obvious that none of the speakers realized that he could hear every word they were saying. As casually as he could, he unlaced his fingers, uncrossed his legs, and turned his head to look up in the direction of the voices. To his shock, his eyes met the startled gaze of the oldest of three dark-haired, fair-skinned, young women who were leaning on the railing of the second floor landing, looking down at him.

Not knowing what else to do, he inclined his head politely and said, "Good afternoon, Zirdyn."

The one whose gaze he held, who might have been twenty, frowned and put a finger to her lips as if to tell him he shouldn't have spoken. She was tall, and very slender, with very dark hair pulled severely back from a high forehead. The second young woman wore her hair in loose waves. She looked to be seventeen or eighteen, and when she now put her hand to her mouth and said, "Oh *my!*" her voice identified her as the one who had pronounced him to be handsome. The third, a girl of no more than fifteen with braided hair, stared unabashedly at him and giggled.

There was another rustle of skirts, and a woman Nagaro recognized as Gedras' wife suddenly appeared behind the three girls.

"Good afternoon, Tor Nagaro," she said, inclining her head to him with cool formality. "I'm sorry if my daughters disturbed you." Without waiting for a response, she turned to the three, and spoke rather severely. "Come away now, Berenil," she said to the eldest, then turned and addressed the other two in order of descending age. "Gesrin, Lissel, come!"

Mother and daughters all promptly withdrew in a flurry of skirts, though Nagaro quite distinctly heard one of them— probably Gesrin— say, "He called you *Zirdyn!*" in a loud whisper that was followed by, "*Shh!*" and another giggle.

Nagaro had met Gedras' wife once before, and had been aware that the merchant had three daughters, though he'd never so much as glimpsed the girls, let alone had any idea of their names and ages. He had no time to digest this sudden feast of information, however, because the women had no sooner disappeared than Gedras' other client emerged from the merchant's study and Nagaro was promptly ushered in by Gedras himself.

Nagaro entered and sat down in front of the merchant's desk while Gedras fetched the appropriate ledger from a shelf and then sat down across from him.

"I've sold the bale of leather to one of the cobblers," Gedras began, without preamble. "The man saw that it would make good shoe soles as you suggested. And Tor Dakuro got over his squeamishness and bought the iron— the chains, the brands, and the brazier. He said he'd decided it didn't matter what it had been used for, since it can all be reworked into something else."

Nagaro nodded, curbing his impatience. "Which is quite right, of course," he said. "What does the total come to this time?" It was probably too much to hope that it might make a difference to his circumstances.

"It's right here, Zirda." The merchant opened the ledger to a marked page, turned it about, and pushed the book across the table for Nagaro's inspection. "I've totaled it up, calculated my fee, and subtracted it as usual. The total you'll have for distribution is there at the bottom."

Nagaro leaned over the ledger, checking the arithmetic as he always did. There had never been an error...

...until today.

He frowned. "You have written two thousand, six hundred, and forty-five rins," he said. "But it should be two thousand, *five* hundred and forty-five. The mistake is here." He pointed. "Where you subtracted your fee." He looked up and was surprised to find that Gedras was smiling a tight, satisfied smile.

"Yes. Quite so." The merchant turned the book around, dipped a pen, and made the correction with a flourish. "I thought you would catch it, and I'm pleased that you chose to point it out, considering the error was in your favor."

Nagaro's brows came together sharply. This "mistake" had been made on purpose? "I hope you don't think I would try to cheat you, Tor Gedras," he said stiffly. Until this moment he'd been very inclined to like the merchant.

Gedras was instantly apologetic. "Indeed not, and I beg your pardon, Zirda. It was a test, but one I believed you would pass. It's a common practice in the trade, I assure you, when one is about to offer a man a position."

Nagaro gaped at him in astonishment. "A position...?"

"Yes. I'm prepared to offer you employment, Tor Nagaro, if you are interested. And if I can persuade you to forgo your apprenticeship to Master Tredhold."

Nagaro's thoughts spun wildly. This development was completely unexpected. And, given the morning's events, quite fortuitous. "Actually, the apprenticeship isn't... ah... working out..." he stammered. Then, collecting himself, he asked more cautiously, "But tell me, please... what sort of position?"

It had seemed that Gedras had smiled ever so slightly at the news regarding the apprenticeship, but the man quickly smoothed his features. "Do you know what a merchant's agent is?" he enquired blandly.

Nagaro knitted his brows. "I believe it is a person who accompanies a shipment of goods to its destination... to assure safe delivery and collect the payment."

"Well done!" Gedras beamed. "That would certainly be part of it, as well as some routine bookkeeping when you were here in Pakoa. And in time, of course, I'd expect you to conduct other business on my behalf at the ports of destination— Harmoth, or Kel Tierna. The position requires a man who is scrupulously honest and good at arithmetic. If he is also comfortable on ships, so much the better. And of course," the merchant added, "since you have such great skill with a sword, you could also defend the ship in the event of a Mahuk attack."

Nagaro's frown deepened. "One man would not be much use against a whole ship-full of Mautep warriors," he said seriously. "No matter what his skill. There were other men fighting with me when we took the galley, and most of her crew were elsewhere."

"An excellent answer." Gedras smiled another satisfied smile. "You recommend yourself well, Tor Nagaro. You're an unusual man," the merchant went on, studying Nagaro over his spectacles. "A man of action, we're told, but also a man of some education. Someone taught you how to keep books, if I'm not mistaken?"

Nagaro shrugged. "My lady guardian showed me how it was done. But it's mostly common sense and simple arithmetic."

"And who taught you the arithmetic?"

"She did."

Gedras's eyebrows went up. "Herself? You had no tutor?"

Nagaro frowned, puzzled by the merchant's reaction. "No, Zirda. My lady taught me all my lessons."

"Unusual..." the merchant murmured. "And this lady adopted you? I believe that's your story?"

Nagaro shook his head. "No, not formally. I was a foundling, and she raised me. That's all." He wasn't entirely happy about being so interrogated, but Gedras was offering him work, and he supposed it was reasonable that the man wanted to know more about him.

"I see." Gedras rubbed his chin. "So, you don't feel entitled to use the name of this lady's House?"

Fortunately Nagaro had given thought to how he might deal with this kind of question. "I don't even choose to speak it," he said, allowing some of the bitterness that he felt to enter his voice. "Her family would have none of her, or of me. So I decided to make my own name for myself after she died."

This was true as far as it went. The members of the House of Virden had certainly done all they could to distance themselves from the "idiot prince" when he'd been in Lankura. There were a number of significant details he had left out, of course, but Gedras had no need to know them.

The merchant was nodding sympathetically. "That's certainly understandable. But why, ah... choose a Turowan name?"

Nagaro had an answer for that, as well. "It was a Turowan family— Taru's family— that took me in when I was in need. I chose to honor them." Also true, though not the only reason.

"Ah, yes. I see." Gedras coughed politely behind his hand. "Very commendable." He took off his spectacles, polished them, and put them on again. "And the unfortunate recent matter involving the woman at the tavern...?"

Nagaro winced at the way the merchant let the sentence dangle, but he didn't drop his eyes. "Breaking the ban was an experiment," he said firmly. "One that went rather badly wrong, and will not be repeated. I don't intend to repeat the rest of it either."

"Yes, yes, of course." Gedras had the good grace to look apologetic. He straightened his glasses unnecessarily. "Well, the position is open if you choose to take it," he said briskly. "The wages would start at four trokins a month. But don't feel you need to decide at once," he added quickly. "You have until Madrel to think it over."

Nagaro looked down at his hands, clasped on the desktop, to hide his emotion. *Four trokins a month?* He could scarcely believe such good fortune. "Thank you, Tor Gedras," he said. "I will certainly consider it."

Gedras got out the cash box then, and counted out the agreed-upon total in an assortment of silver and copper coins that could be divided evenly among the number of former slaves. Nagaro frowned as he transferred the coins to the bag he'd brought for the purpose. The bag was heavy, but it amounted to little more than a hundred rins apiece. Still, it would help him, some, to get through the winter, and he knew the men who wanted to leave Pakoa in the spring would be grateful for any amount. The price of a passage was several hundred rins, depending on the destination, and a man had to wait for a ship that was bound for wherever he wished to go. The longer he waited, the more of his money would go for other expenses.

"What else is left in your warehouse to sell, Tor Gedras?" He asked, though he was fairly sure he knew the answer.

The merchant made a wry face. "Just the ship's own stores— rope, tar, canvas, timber. You should be able to sell some of it when the ships start coming in the spring. And you still have the gold. I estimate its worth at several hundred trokins."

"Ye-es..." Nagaro chewed his lip. The gold was a huge windfall, but unfortunately there was little market on Pakoa for jewelry or anything else made of the stuff. "I'll have to see what I can do with that in the spring too, when the ships come."

Gedras eyed him shrewdly. "You might try dealing directly with the merchant's agents that come with those ships," he suggested. "They may agree to sell things on the mainland for you— for a ten or fifteen percent fee, of course. They might also purchase items outright, though only if they have enough cash in hand."

Nagaro nodded, trying not to let his worry show. While its value was impressive, there was no telling how long it might take to sell the gold. And the only other assets he had were the captured Mahuk sword, which he didn't intend to sell despite the fact that he had no use for it, and the three Jinari scrolls tucked under his bed. He didn't intend to sell them, either. It might be foolish, but he couldn't rid himself of the fear that the scrolls would somehow find their way to the king's Lore Master, Dreigen, who would put them to ill use.

Nagaro rose, and thanked the merchant. As he turned to go, however, another thought occurred to him, and he turned back. "There is one more thing, Tor Gedras."

"Yes?" The merchant remained standing, having just finished putting the ledger back on its shelf.

"There's a house near some ironwood trees, where the Hill Road takes its last bend. The caretaker said you were looking after it for the owner. I wondered if it were for sale." Nagaro felt a fool for asking, since he knew it would be beyond his means, but he very much wished to know.

"The Fendorin place?" The merchant crooked an eyebrow. "Yes, it is. Tor Fendorin was asking forty trokins, but he'd probably take thirty by now, since it's been empty for some time."

Nagaro had been prepared, but his heart still sank. *Thirty trokins.* Three thousand rins. On a wage of four trokins a month, how long would it take him to save that much, after expenses? Even his share from the sale of the gold wouldn't come to so much.

"Thank you," he murmured. "Good afternoon, Tor Gedras."

Wrapped in his thoughts, he passed out through the entry hall, pausing just long enough to retrieve his cloak and not thinking to look up at the upstairs landing to see whether any eyes were watching him.

***

Gedras stood at the large bay window and watched Nagaro make his way up the street. He turned at the sound of footsteps.

"Ah, Delmanei. Did the girls get a good look at him?"

His wife nodded curtly. "They did. *And* he, them." She sighed. "Gesrin could *not* hold her tongue, so naturally Berenil had to answer her, and Lissel *will* giggle." She paused. "He spoke to Berenil. He wished her good afternoon, called her Zirdyn. She had the good sense not to answer, but I had to intervene."

Gedras turned back to the window. "Well, he was at least polite, and it was really quite harmless for him to speak to her under such circumstances."

She frowned. "Of course it's harmless. But it's just as well there was no one to see it. One can't be too careful... after what happened at the tavern."

Gedras made a dismissive gesture. "He's learned his lesson as far as breaking the ban is concerned. The rest was that woman's fault. And he had to do something about the rumors. I confess I'd begun to wonder myself."

Delmanei knit her brows. "I suppose you're right." She sighed. "And it's not as if Pakoa offers many choices for our girls."

Gedras conceded the point with a nod and a shrug. "He's considering settling on the island. He asked about the Fendorin house."

"Well... that's a start, I suppose." Delmanei wrinkled her nose. "Though if he married one of the girls, I would hope they would find a place in town."

"Of course." Gedras sighed. "Though we might have to offer some assistance there. As I feared, he expects no inheritance. Whatever he will have in his life will be of his own making. Still, I don't think it will be so mean, for all that. He's well educated, and his honesty runs deep. My little test offended him. He thought at first that I distrusted him."

"You've offered him the position then?"

"Yes. If he's sensible, he'll take it. What did Berenil think of him?"

Delmanei sniffed. "Berenil doesn't deign to say. Gesrin seems to think he would be quite handsome if he weren't trying to look like a Turowan."

Delmanei paused. "Do you think you could persuade him to forego the kuma stain and to cut his hair?"

Gedras shrugged, a slight lift of the shoulders. "One can hope."

***

When he got back to the inn, Nagaro immediately sought out Tor Ramu since Gedras' offer, even if he accepted it, would not solve his current shortfall. The innkeeper gladly accepted his proposal regarding the stable, and Nagaro promptly went out and set about the task.

The physical activity of mucking out the stalls was welcome. It busied his hands while leaving him free to think, something he very much needed to do.

It had been an eventful day, bitter disappointment followed by an unlooked-for opportunity. The wages Gedras had offered had initially thrilled him, but he now found himself having second thoughts. The position did have attractions compared to being a fisherman— sailing on merchant ships, for one thing. It would also mean that he could live on Pakoa where his friends were, even as his work took him to mainland ports, like Harmoth, the place of Tredhold's origin, or Kel Tierna, which was Mendorel's home. He had never set foot in either city, so his face wouldn't be known in those places. It *should* be safe, in that sense. Now that he thought about it, being a healer was a rather conspicuous trade. Being a fisherman, on the other hand, was not. Being a merchant's agent struck him as falling somewhere in between.

The real trouble was that he wasn't sure how he felt about making his living conducting business for Tor Gedras. Being a merchant's agent didn't appeal to him in the same way as being a healer. The idea of using his gifts to do good in the world was central to Vothrin teaching and had been thoroughly instilled in him by the Lady Maramine. Tredhold had apparently seem some gift in him for healing, and healing was obviously a good thing. Gedras apparently thought he would make a good merchant's agent, but Nagaro wasn't sure what good purpose would be served by that activity.

He supposed it was good that there was trade between Pakoa and the mainland, since it brought things to Pakoa that the island folk couldn't make or grow for themselves. It also offered a market for the island's products— which brought in money that allowed some people to live more comfortably. Yet Nagaro now knew how poorly-paid the men and women were who worked in the kuma mills. Why should he be paid so handsomely for seeing products like kuma stain get safely to market?

Simply because the kuma farmers couldn't do it themselves? Or because he could do arithmetic? Who would he be serving as a merchant's agent? The kuma farmers, the owners of the mills, or mainly just himself and Tor Gedras?

Night was falling by the time he finished making sure that both horses had their ration of hay and plenty of water. His thoughts were still churning as he washed at the pump and crossed the stable yard to the inn's back door. He entered and passed quickly into the common room, looking for Taru and Pavo. He was curious to see what they might make of his dilemma.

The tables were already laid with dishes and cutlery, and the men were beginning to gather in anticipation of dinner. The innkeeper had lit the row of oil lamps mounted on the wall opposite the windows, and he was in the process of lighting candles set in earthenware candlesticks scattered along the lengths of the tables. An enticing mix of aromas wafted from the kitchen, suggestive of rabbit stew among other things.

Neither of Nagaro's friends were there yet, however, though he did see Mendorel sitting alone near one of the windows, staring moodily into space. He approached the Kelorin shopkeeper.

"What's the matter, Mendorel?" he asked, taking a seat across the table from the older man.

"Ai, Nagaro, ye'll never believe it." Mendorel passed a hand across his eyes. "One o' my nephews is here on the island! My wife's, sister's oldest son. Came just last summer t' learn the kuma trade, and I never knew he was here 'til today when I met him in the street!"

Nagaro frowned. "That doesn't sound like a bad thing. Why are you so downcast?"

"Ah, well, it's the news, ye see. From home."

"What news? What has happened?" Nagaro's own troubles were forgotten in an instant. "Is it your family? Are they all right?"

"Oh, aye." Mendorel reassured him. "They're well enough, or at least they were in Duleyin, when my nephew saw them last. My wife and my youngest boy were sick with the plague, but they got better, and that's all past." He drew a long breath. "But they had t' sell the candle shop last year t' pay their debts. What with losing me, and the plague and all, they just couldn't make the ends meet in the middle. They're still dipping candles the same as before, and living in the rooms upstairs, but someone else owns the house and they're paying rent to him! My father built that house, Nagaro. When I think o' my poor wife paying rent t' live in my father's house, it fair makes me sick!"

Nagaro's heart ached for the man. "I'm really sorry, Mendorel. That *is* hard." After a moment, he added, "But you can buy the shop back, can't you?"

Mendorel sighed. "That's easier said than done. They had to sell it cheap, and the landlord want's ninety trokins! That's double what he paid for it, the villain! Even when I get back there t' help, it could be years before we can save enough."

Ninety trokins! Nagaro tried to think of something to say. It was depressing to realize how often things came down to money. "When the ships come, I'll sell the gold jewelry," he said, as confidently as he could. "That should raise quite a large sum. One share won't be enough, but it's a start."

Mendorel nodded, but without enthusiasm. "We both know it could take years t' find buyers for all that gold, Nagaro. And ye'll have to send me my share. I mean to be on the first ship to Kel Tierna."

Nagaro swallowed. "If it will help, you can have my share from the first gold sale."

But Mendorel shook his head. "I can't let ye do that, lad. Ye'll be needing it yourself."

Nagaro leaned forward and lowered his voice. "Maybe not," he said. "Gedras just offered me work as a merchant's agent— at four trokins a month." The work seemed more acceptable when he thought of using some of the windfall to help others.

"He *has*?" Mendorel instantly brightened. "Now that's a fine job for ye! And a steady wage is better 'n being a healer's apprentice—"

Mendorel might have said more, but his words were interrupted at that point by the noisy arrival of a large group of former slaves coming in by the front door. The troop was led by Moraga and was mostly made up of Turowans, although Gurd's blond head stood out above the crowd. They all seemed to be talking at once as they gathered around one of the tables near the kitchen. Nagaro was surprised to see Taru among them. Taru had never been close to Moraga and his cronies.

In fact, Taru remained standing when the others in the group took their seats. His gaze eagerly swept the room, and when he spied Nagaro, he immediately left the group and hurried over, his eyes bright with excitement. "Ye have to hear this!" he burst out as he reached them. "Moraga's got a plan. Come on," he added, beckoning to Nagaro. "He wants t' tell ye about it!"

Nagaro glanced at Mendorel, who shrugged. "Go on," the shopkeeper said gloomily. "I'm not fit company tonight."

As Nagaro followed Taru back to the table where the men were sitting, he couldn't help noticing that they seemed to be eyeing him expectantly. Moraga was watching him the most keenly of all. Two of the men moved their stools aside, and one rose, gesturing for Nagaro to take his seat, directly across from the gap-toothed merchant seaman.

Nagaro nodded to the man who had offered and sat down on the stool, while Taru hovered behind him. "What's this about, Moraga?" he asked warily. "Taru says you have some sort of plan."

Moraga cleared his throat. "Aye, well, ye might say so," he began. "Ye see, mate, I been thinkin.' An' talkin' with some o' the lads. And it seems we're all o' the same mind."

Nagaro frowned. Moraga's discourse was usually more to the point. "All of the same mind about your plan, I assume," he said dryly. "Are you going to enlighten me as to what it is?"

Moraga cleared his throat again. "Aye, well, it's about the ship—"

"*Your* ship," Tego put in pointedly. He was sitting a little farther along the table, his eyes fixed avidly on Nagaro.

Moraga shot a glance at the weathered seaman. "Well, o' course," he said quickly. "*Your* ship, Nagaro. That's what I meant. The point is, she's just sittin' there, goin' t' rot and ruin. So I got t' thinkin'. It'd be better if she were put t' some use..." He let the sentence trail, watching Nagaro's eyes.

Nagaro had no idea where this was heading, and the fact that Moraga was being so cagey made him suspicious. "I'd be happy to see the ship put to use," he said. "And although you all gave her to me, I won't hold you to it—if that's what this is about." He glanced around at the men's faces, but he was evidently off the mark, judging by their expressions. He frowned in bafflement. "I... ah... still haven't heard your plan."

Gurd was growing impatient. "We want t' fit her out and go after merchant ships. *Mahuk* merchant ships o' course," he added hastily when he saw Nagaro's deepening frown. "*That's* the plan. And we want *you* t' be our captain! We got so much loot from one war galley. Can ye imagine what a merchantman would bring? We'll all be rich!" He came to a halt, eyeing Nagaro, whose look was darkening by the moment. "So... what d' ye say, Nagaro?" he asked uncertainly.

Nagaro's brows knit sharply. "I'm sorry," he said, "but I have to say no. What you're talking about is piracy."

There was a murmur among the gathered men, who were now frowning in their turn and exchanging angry glances.

Gurd was indignant. "It's not piracy!" he exclaimed. "Not if they're *Mahuk* ships. We're at *war* with the Mahuk Baar. And besides, they took us for slaves!"

But Nagaro shook his head. "It's the Mautep— the warlords— that take slaves," he said. "The captains and crews of the merchant ships are common folk, *Hashtep*. They never did us any harm, and we shouldn't be stealing from them."

Moraga's anger had been visibly growing throughout this speech, and he now cut in. "It didn't trouble ye t' be stealing things when ye took the ship!" he said pointedly. "*And* everything in her!"

Nagaro shook his head again. "Actually, it *did* trouble me," he answered. "I don't mean taking the *ship* and sailing away in it. That gave us our freedom, and it made sure the ship couldn't be used to take more slaves. But it troubled me to keep the *cargo*. Most of it was plunder from merchant ships— ships from Edrovir or Jinara. Some of it belonged to Utabala's master, for example. But Utabala said we should keep it, that his master would have written it off as a cost of doing business. And since there was no easy way to return any of the rest of it, I decided to accept it as 'finder's gold,' because we had need—"

"Oh, we had *need* all right," Moraga cut in, scowling. "We had *need*, 'cause the bloody Mautep robbed us of everything we owned! *And* they beat us. *And* branded us. An' made us row their bloody ship! It's only right they should pay us back for all o' that."

This speech elicited vigorous nods and exclamations of agreement from all along both sides of the table.

Nagaro swept the circle of faces with his eyes, and let out a long breath. "Well... *yes*..." he admitted. "I agree there *is* justice in the idea of recompense— payment for what was done to us and for what we lost."

Moraga spat. "*I* don't count the debt paid," he growled. "Not by half! Not after what they done t' me! It was close-on t' three years o' me life they took! And the bloody rowin', and the beatin's, an' livin' in filth—"

Gurd spoke up again. "What d' ye say, Nagaro? Will ye join us?"

Nagaro sighed. "If this is what you all want to do with the ship, I can't stop you," he said, glancing around at their hopeful faces. "But I won't join you. If you rob Mahuk merchant ships, you'd be taking your recompense from the *wrong people*."

"The Mautep do it to *us!*" Tego protested. "They rob *our* merchant ships all the time!"

Nagaro faced the older merchant seaman. "It's piracy when they do it to us. And it's wrong," he explained patiently. "And it's just as much piracy— *and just as wrong*— if we do it to *them*."

"Then ye're saying ye won't be our captain?" Gurd spoke in dismay.

"That's right, I won't."

Moraga had been nursing a deepening scowl and now the Turo sprang to his feet. "I should ha' *known!*" he cried. "We all should ha' known he'd be too high-minded! He's always been too high-minded for the likes of us!" He spat on the floor for emphasis. "Who does he think he is? *The bloody Prince o' Pakoa?*"

There was dead silence.

For the space of several heartbeats Nagaro sat frozen. The words were like a dagger in his heart. When he stirred, the glance he leveled at Moraga was pure ice. He stood up, the scrape of his stool's legs on the floorboards painfully loud in the hushed room.

Instinctively Moraga stepped back, but Nagaro only turned his back silently and stalked away, back to the other end of the room where he'd left Mendorel. Behind him there rose a babble of angry voices.

Mendorel was still sitting at the table by the window, but the older man was no longer alone. Pavo was sitting beside the shopkeeper, having apparently come in unnoticed by the back door.

The young Hashtep clearly knew all about Moraga's plan, for as soon as Nagaro dropped, glowering, onto a stool across from him, Pavo leaned urgently across the table.

"Nagaro, you will not do this thing Moraga have plan to do?"

Still frowning, Nagaro shook his head. "It's piracy," he said flatly. "I will not be a pirate."

"You see!" Pavo exclaimed, turning to Mendorel. "It is what I tell you."

Footsteps sounded behind Nagaro, and Taru dropped onto a seat on the stool beside him. The young Turo glanced uncertainly at Pavo and Mendorel, who eyed him warily. He then turned to Nagaro and cleared his throat. "I'm sorry about that 'Prince o' Pakoa' nonsense, Nagaro," he said with evident sincerity. "Ye mustn't take Moraga seriously when he says things like that. He's just a dog waitin' t' growl, and he doesn't hardly think afore he opens his mouth."

Nagaro considered Taru, his gray eyes stormy under the sharp black line of his brows. "Moraga knew what he was saying," he said coldly. "He meant that I think I'm better than other folk. And sometimes it seems to me that *you* think so too!"

Taru's eyes registered alarm. "I never! I know ye don't think ye're better than the rest of us. Ye just go by a different book o' rules than we do, that's all."

"Not *all* the rest of you." Nagaro turned to Mendorel. "You're Vothrin, Mendorel," he said. "Would *you* go after Mahuk merchant craft?"

Mendorel shook his head. "Not me. It's piracy, like ye say. It's just a kind o' thievery."

"And you, Pavo? You don't think I should do it either, do you?"

Pavo shook his head vigorously. "That is true, Nagaro. Merchant is maybe rich man, but all those sailor on ship are not rich. If ship lose all her cargo, sailor not get paid."

Nagaro turned back to Taru. "You see!" he said with satisfaction. "I'm *not* the only one."

Taru threw up his hands. "All right!" he said. "But it doesn't matter anyway. None of us'll be doing it if ye'll not be our captain."

Nagaro scowled. "I don't know why not," he observed bitterly. "I've said you could take the ship. Why can't Moraga be your captain?"

"Moraga?" Taru gave a short laugh. "There's not even a dozen men would follow Moraga. But they'd all follow *you*, Nagaro— and that sword o' yours— if ye'd just say the word."

"I've *said* my word," Nagaro muttered. But then he shook his head and uttered a short, mirthless laugh. "And anyway, I'm sure you're exaggerating, Taru, about the men. They thought well of me right after our escape, but you saw how quickly they turned against me when they thought I was crossed."

"Aye, but they've got over that since the thing with Jila."

Pavo spoke up. "It is not only because they know that you are not cross-man, Nagaro," he offered. "They know now that you are man like every other man— because you make mistake."

Nagaro stared at Pavo. "Of course I make mistakes," he objected. "Surely they always knew that! And besides, half of them don't even seem to think it *was* a mistake."

"No, Pavo's right." Taru jumped back in. "When ye *acted* just as proper as ye *talked*, it put them off. But now that ye've gone and put a hole in your own boat, everyone's much easier with ye on account of it. I tell ye, they'd follow ye in a minute."

"But there *must* be others!" It wasn't that Nagaro wanted the men to pursue Moraga's plan; he just couldn't believe what he was hearing.

"It wouldn't matter, even if there were! *I'd* never go without ye, Nagaro," Taru protested. "Ye should know that! Better we all just stay on Pakoa and be fishermen. Or I'll go an' be a fisherman in Harmoth, if ye want t' be a healer there—" He stopped abruptly, embarrassed by his own words.

Nagaro looked from one face to another. He was touched by Taru's loyalty— and sensitive to his friend's embarrassment. Pavo and Mendorel were both watching him closely.

"I'm sure we all want to keep the friends we've made," he said, quickly. "Let's hope Lokundas doesn't scatter us too far."

"Hear, hear!" Mendorel's voice was gruff with emotion.

And at that moment Habu arrived with stew in a big earthenware bowl, which he set on the table and left for them to help themselves. A pitcher of sothiril followed soon after, and for some time the four men were all busy ladling and pouring, and chewing and swallowing.

After a time, when the edge was off their appetites, Mendorel brought up his distressing news. Taru and Pavo immediately expressed sympathy and outrage.

Mendorel did his best to put on a brave face. "I'll just have t' go home on the first ship," he said. "I'll set t' work and save every rin. However long it takes, I'll get my father's house back! But Nagaro has better news," he added. "Gedras offered to hire him as a merchant's agent, today."

"He *did*?" Taru gaped.

Pavo's broad face registered mingled surprise and confusion. "I thought you were go to be healer, Nagaro," he said. "Like Tredhold."

"I was—" Nagaro squirmed under their eyes. "But I don't think that's going to work." He couldn't say any more in Mendorel's presence.

"Well, that's all right." Taru had recovered his aplomb. "Being a merchant's agent has t' be better 'n being a healer. I expect the pay's more regular for one thing."

And then of course Mendorel had to volunteer what he knew about the pay.

"*Four trokins a month?*" Taru nearly choked on his sothiril. "Nagaro! That's a hundred rins a *week*, for nothin' more 'n sailing around in a ship an' collecting money! And here's me an' Pavo slaving over a vat o' stinkin' kuma stain for *five* rins a week. I tell ye, there's no justice in this world!"

And it was true. Nagaro was sure he'd been offered the job because his lady guardian had seen fit to give him the gift of an education. It helped, too, that he was a Kelorin, and fair-spoken, but it was no fault of Taru's that he'd been born a Turowan fisherman's son and had no education beyond the imperfect knowledge of his letters that he'd gotten from Nagaro's teaching. Nagaro was suddenly acutely aware that becoming a merchant's agent would put him in a class above farmers and fishermen. "I don't know that I'll take the job," he said hastily. "Gedras only just made the offer and I needn't decide until spring."

"*Ye mean ye didn't say yes?*" Taru was all but apoplectic.

Fortunately, Pavo was more understanding. "Money is not only important thing, Taru," he ventured. "Nagaro have to decide if it is right thing for him to do."

Taru might well have argued about that, but Mendorel started to weigh in on Pavo's side, and Nagaro hastily changed the subject. "I'm glad you didn't try to talk me into Moraga's plan, Taru," he said. "I was afraid they'd sent you over here to do that."

Taru gave him a rueful look. "They *did*," he said. "But I told them it was no use. Not when ye've made up your mind that something is just *wrong*."

Nagaro studied his sothiril. "If only they'd wanted to go after warships," he murmured. "*That* I would have been glad to try."

"Warships?" Taru frowned. "But Lord Kuran and the Fleet do that."

Nagaro shook his head. "Kuran *sinks* warships," he said. "I'd just board them and free the slaves. But of course no one would get rich doing that," he added with a sigh. "And it would be terribly dangerous besides."

"*Dangerous...*" Taru murmured, still frowning. "Aye. It would be that." He and Pavo exchanged glances across the table.

Yuli came around just then with dessert on a tray: fresh hot buns stuffed with yellow raisins and dried apricots. They reminded Nagaro of ones that Hinda had used to bake at Averwin, and he took two. Soon after finishing the buns he excused himself, pleading that he was tired—which was quite true. He went upstairs, leaving Taru, Pavo, and Mendorel to their talk.

It wasn't until he had undressed that he realized he'd forgotten to distribute the money Gedras had given him. Well, it could wait until tomorrow. *It wasn't as if it was very much, anyway.*

He lay down in bed and tried to imagine what it would be like to be a merchant's agent. Before long, however, he was yawning. The day had been long and trying and he was more tired even than he knew. He closed his eyes and slept.

His sleep was haunted by dreams of blond men brandishing bladder-thorns.

Chapter 13

The Covenant

"What do you mean they like *my* plan better than Moraga's?"

It was the following morning and the three friends were sitting together in one corner of the common room enjoying plates of fried potatoes. It was early and they were almost the only ones in the room. Taru and Pavo had been exchanging knowing looks ever since they'd gotten up. After ignoring their behavior all the way to the breakfast table, Nagaro had finally demanded an explanation. Now he sat staring at Taru with his fork suspended halfway to his mouth.

"What on earth are you talking about, Taru?" he demanded.

"He mean your plan to take Mautep warship, and make slave be free," Pavo offered helpfully.

Nagaro put down his fork and stared at the young Hashtep's broad, impassive countenance. "But I don't have a *plan*," he protested. "It was just an *idea*." He swung back to Taru. "What exactly have you been telling them?"

Taru shifted uncomfortably in the heat of Nagaro's gaze. "Just that ye're willing t' captain the ship if we go after Mautep warships to free slaves," he answered with an obvious effort to sound casual. "And... and that we'd take whatever booty from them that we could, t' live on. Maybe we wouldn't be *rich*, but we wouldn't be poor either," he added a little defiantly. "Just look what we got from one warship! If we took more than one in a season..." His voice trailed when he saw Nagaro's frown, and he sat looking like a man waiting for a sword stroke.

In fact, Nagaro's frown reflected the urgent thoughts passing behind his eyes. *Was it possible this could work?* He had imagined doing it many times, but he'd thought it was an idle daydream. And he hadn't thought about how it could be financed. Freeing slaves wasn't piracy. He felt sure of that. Men had no right to own other men. But taking plunder from the warships was another matter. Could *that* kind of theft be justified for the sake of a just cause? Apparently the men thought so. But he had never dreamed that they would be willing to take the risk! He wondered if they'd thought about what would actually be involved.

Still frowning, he refocused on Taru. "They'd all have to be trained in swordsmanship," he said seriously. "And they'd have to be prepared to row into close quarters with another galley— risking being crushed by their oar if its outboard end was struck. That's a danger they've seen before, but they'd also have to *board* the other ship. And *fight*. They could be killed. Or taken for slaves again. Did you point out all of that?"

Taru licked his lips nervously. "I'm sure they know it, Nagaro," he said quickly. "When we talked about taking merchant ships, they were saying that Mautep warships would likely come after us, and we'd have t' fight. And of course we could be captured. We just have t' make sure we aren't, that's all."

Nagaro looked at Pavo. "You are willing to do this?"

Pavo grinned. "Oh, yes," he answered cheerfully. "If you are captain. If we take all of rich thing that warlord have, he will not be able to pay his warrior. Then maybe his ship cannot sail!"

"I see." Nagaro sighed. Pavo's views on theft had always been somewhat different from his own. He picked up his cup of sothiril, took a swallow, and set it down again, frowning once more. "We'd need at least forty men, and we only have twenty-two that were slaves on the *Fist*," he pointed out. "And those twenty-two wouldn't all come. Landros and Tred have made other plans. Obedo has his wife and children to think of... and Mendorel's going home to his family." He doubted if Simion would come either. The young Kelorin rarely even showed his face in public anymore.

"But Mendorel say he *will* come," Pavo interjected. "Last night he say maybe he can get enough silver that way to buy back house."

"He did? *Really?*" Nagaro was more than a little surprised, and not at all sure how he felt about the shopkeeper taking such a risk. "But that's still not close to forty."

Taru gestured impatiently. "There's men all over this island that have lost fathers or sons or brothers t' the Mautep," he said. "Tego and Moraga'll be going out right after breakfast t' spread the word, and we'll see how many come to the meeting."

Nagaro nearly choked on his sothiril. "*Meeting?* What meeting?"

"The meeting we're going to have here in the common room after dinner tonight, so ye can tell everybody about your plan." Taru's face was all innocence.

Nagaro set down his cup and put his hand to his forehead. "Taru," he said very quietly from behind his palm. "Didn't I ask you *not* to get me into things without telling me first?"

"And did not *I* say it is better to tell Nagaro first and make meeting after?" Pavo put in chidingly.

"Well I'm telling him right now!" Taru protested. "And it's *hours* before the meeting. Besides, this is different. This is something he *wants* to do." There was a pause. "It *is*— *isn't* it, Nagaro?"

The last question sounded a little desperate. Nagaro studied his friend for a long moment. Taru looked so worried that he finally took pity on him. "Yes, it *is* something I want to do. And I suppose I *do* have all day to think about what to say. But it's still rather sudden, and Pavo's way would have been better." Then he smiled his most wicked-looking smile. "And if I decide I don't like the idea, I just won't go to the meeting, and I'll leave *you* to explain it to them!"

Ignoring the horror in Taru's face, Nagaro picked up his cup again and took a long, slow swallow. When he set the cup down again, there was a distant look in his gray eyes. "We only have eleven swords," he murmured. "We'll need more. That may take some doing. But we can make wooden ones for practice, and begin training with those..."

***

The three friends spent most of the morning searching the groves of trees closest to the town for likely sticks that could be used to make practice swords. Nagaro had suggested the activity, and Taru and Pavo had eagerly agreed. Nagaro suspected his friends took the suggestion as an indication that he expected the sticks to be needed. In fact, he thought that gathering the sticks was premature, but it occupied his hands while leaving his mind free to think.

After lunch, they returned to their room, and Nagaro and Taru pulled their Mautep swords from under their beds. There had never been any thought of selling their captured blades. By unspoken agreement all the men who had borne swords on the day of their escape had kept them as prizes.

Nagaro sat down on the edge of his bed with the sword across his knees in its black leather sheath. He admired again the gold tracery on the curved guard and the smooth green stone set into the pommel. The other men had dubbed it the "sword of freedom," and it looked the part. As his fingers closed around the leather-wrapped handgrip, he felt a sharp little thrill run along his nerves. He drew the sword, and it slid out with barely a whisper. The blade was long and slightly curved, still sharp and shining.

It had come to him by the hand of Lokundas, and he had no idea how one went about making such a thing. So beautiful, so potentially deadly. With a shiver, he re-sheathed it. He set it aside and went to take a closer look at Taru's blade. Pavo, who had stood silently watching through his inspection of the elegant weapon, padded after him.

Taru's Mahuk-made sword was of a design similar to Nagaro's but without ornamentation. The blade, though sharp, was less shiny, and the scabbard, which was of slightly battered brown leather, didn't fit as well.

"Yours is much finer, Nagaro," Taru said as they examined his captured weapon.

"Yes," Pavo agreed. "Other sword is much more beautiful."

"This one did its work well enough," Nagaro observed. "Gold filigree is nothing more than show, and this sword looks more like a thing our town blacksmiths might be able to fashion. Let's go see what Tor Dakuro has to say about it."

"You bring your sword also," Pavo suggested.

"Aye, ye must, Nagaro." Taru seconded the notion. "I want t' hear what Dakuro says about our sword of freedom."

Nagaro acquiesced with a shrug.

The three friends found Tor Dakuro, the older and more experienced of the town's two blacksmiths, at work at his forge. The smith was a Turowan in his sixties, who also served as chief of the Town Council. A great bear of a man with beetling brows, he nevertheless turned out to have a ready smile. "What can I do for ye and your friends, Tor Nagaro?" he asked as they gathered around him.

Nagaro had felt some misgivings about revealing his idea to the Town Chief for fear the man would think it was ridiculous— or even forbid it. But Dakuro was known to have an appreciation for knives as well as skill in making them. He was their best hope for making swords, and without enough swords, the whole scheme was likely to collapse.

As it turned out, Dakuro had already gotten wind of what was afoot. "That fellow Tego was here this morning," he said as he examined the blade of Taru's sword. "Talking t' two o' my customers about a meeting tonight at the inn— to talk about freeing slaves from Mahuk war galleys. I'm too old for such work myself, not to mention having my smithy t' run and the Town Council besides, but I don't mind seeing someone go after those devils— if ye think ye can do it."

"Did any o' the men say they meant to go t' the meeting?" Taru asked, a touch of worry in his voice.

"Aye, there was one that said he'd like to hear what Tor Nagaro had to say." The blacksmith looked up from the sword into Nagaro's eyes. "I think I could make one o' these, Zirda. I could use some of that iron o' yours that I bought."

Nagaro returned him a grim smile. "I'd say that's only fitting."

"I'd have t' make one as a trial, first, to be sure I could do it to your liking— and t' see how much work went into it— afore I'd know how much to charge. How soon would ye want it?"

Nagaro frowned. Things were getting a little ahead of themselves. "I can't have you start work yet," he said. "Right now there are no funds to cover it. I might know more after the meeting."

Dakuro cocked an eyebrow. "What'll ye do? Take up a collection?"

Nagaro's glance didn't waver. "I've considered it."

Dakuro started to laugh, but his mirth dissolved when Nagaro's expression didn't change. He sheathed Taru's sword, but held onto it. "I've made long knives and plowshares," he said. "And I like to think I could make a sword. If ye don't mind leaving this with me for a model, I *might* just have some spare time... Just t' satisfy my own curiosity, mind ye," he added, and he winked at Taru.

Taru grinned back. "Aye, keep it for now," he said. "I'm not using it."

Pavo stirred. "You must look at other sword, Tor Dakuro."

Taru poked Nagaro. "Aye, go on. Show it to him."

Nagaro shrugged and handed over the filigreed weapon for the smith's inspection.

The old Turowan's eyes and fingers lingered long and caressingly over the elegant weapon. He shook his head and sighed. "Now this is a work o' art," he said. "And I've no such art in these hands— though I wish I did. It's a sword to conjure by, and no mistake."

***

The hour for the meeting came all too soon.

Dinner was nearly over, and the three friends were sitting together in the common room, feeling the tension gather with the evening's gathering gloom. Outside the windows, the sky was deepening from blue to purple. Inside, the ruddy light of lamps and candles glowed on men's faces and cast shadows among the rafters. Taru had chosen a place for the three of them at the table closest to the kitchen, with their backs to the fireplace so they could survey the entire room.

Men had been coming in all during dinner, filling up the stools and sitting on the edges of tables. More men stood leaning against the wall. Nagaro noted that all of the former slaves were there, both those who had rooms in the inn and those who roomed at the Red Cask. Chaheel and Nanu were at a nearby table. Moraga, Tego, and Gurd sat together at another. Mendorel was farther back. Landros and Tredhold were seated near the door, and young Kunoa stood near the two sea warriors. That last troubled Nagaro. Kunoa was not yet eighteen and had a mother who had lost him once and only gotten him back by a miracle.

There were also about a dozen island men, most of whom Nagaro didn't know by name.

Altogether, Nagaro had counted thirty-three men, including Taru, Pavo, and himself— thirty-four if one included Simion, who he knew was in the kitchen. Ramu the innkeeper was hovering about near the kitchen door. The innkeeper made thirty-five, but he surely wasn't going to take to sea in a war galley.

Yuli was moving about among the tables, retrieving dishes from those who had finished their dinners. Both of the inn's proprietors had been informed of the intended meeting and had raised no objections. Now that the time had arrived, however, Ramu looked worried, as if he hadn't expected such a crowd— or maybe it was because a number of the men had brought swords.

This last had been Taru's idea, and several of those present had taken it upon themselves to wear the weapons rather than merely carrying them. Taru had left his own sword with Dakuro, of course. Nagaro's lay unobtrusively at his feet, under the table.

"Perhaps we should wait a little longer." Taru nervously chewed a fingernail as he surveyed the assemblage. "A few more might turn up."

Nagaro was in a somber mood. He knew what he meant to say to these men, but he was by no means sure how it would be received. He truly hoped the evening would go well. He heaved a sigh. "There are more than enough for such short notice," he said. "We might as well begin. Anything we say will be all over the island within a few days' time in any case."

He had told himself that he would captain the ship if there were enough men who still wanted him to after hearing what he had to say. If there weren't enough... well... then he would have to choose between being a merchant's agent or a fisherman. He had told himself that either of those callings would be acceptable. He'd been telling himself so all day. But in the course of the passing hours since his friends had first informed him that he had a meeting and a plan, he had come to realize that neither trade appealed to him very much when compared to the noble work of freeing slaves.

He surveyed the room again, the array of tense, eager faces revealed in the glow of the oil lamps. These men were waiting to hear him speak, and he needed to sway their minds. But he had no idea how to manipulate or persuade them. All he knew how to do was be honest.

If honesty didn't serve...

But the evening was now deepening into night, and waiting wouldn't help him. A stillness settled in his mind. It was time to get this over with. He turned to Taru.

"Are you going to introduce me?" he asked. "Since you called this meeting."

Taru looked startled. "There's no need for that, Nagaro," he muttered. "Everybody knows who ye are. And what ye're going to say."

Nagaro frowned. That they knew who he *was*, was probably true, but he hadn't even told Taru and Pavo his exact intentions. He knew he shouldn't let Taru wiggle off the hook so easily, but the readiness he felt might evaporate if he delayed too long. So all he did was give Taru a look that made the young Turo squirm. Then he rose to his feet and rapped with his knuckles on the table.

All conversation immediately ceased.

There was a rustle of clothing and scraping of stools as men turned to face him and shifted position for a better view. Every eye in the room was turned his way. There was a time when he might have been unnerved by this, but now he could remind himself of how he'd once stood before many of these same men in the ship's fore-cabin the day after leading their escape from bondage.

He cleared his throat.

"Taru says that you all know who I am," he began. "But perhaps he exaggerates. My name is Nagaro. Nagaro Nareyo, since Taru has given me leave to use his family name and I have no other." He paused. All the men were still watching him expectantly. "Taru also tells me that you know what I am going to say. I hope you haven't been misled."

This brought some murmurs and unsettled looks. Beside him, Taru stirred uneasily.

Nagaro smiled a little, grimly. "Yesterday I told some of you, quite publicly, that I would not lead you in pursuit of Mahuk merchant ships because it was piracy." He could see Moraga scowling. "And afterwards, I told Taru, Pavo, and Mendorel privately that I would be willing to do it if we went after Mahuk warships, with the aim of freeing galley slaves."

He took a moment to survey the faces. There were many nods and appreciative murmurings, but there were a few worried frowns as well. He cleared his throat again. "It seems to me that we could only make our living that way by plundering the warships whose slaves we freed."

This drew enthusiastic grins and cries of "Aye! Aye!" from several quarters.

Nagaro waited, frowning, until the noise died down. "Whatever *you* may call that," he said in a lower voice, but still one that carried, "*I* still call it piracy. It's a kind of theft. *But*," he added quickly when he saw their looks of dismay and heard Taru's indrawn breath, "It is a *kind* of theft that I consider to be justified by the circumstances. We will need to finance the continuation of the good work we do and also provide some recompense to the slaves we free for the losses they have suffered— at least enough to help restore their livelihoods. I believe it's appropriate that the Mautep should pay for undoing of the harm they have done, using the wealth they've seized, even if some of it came originally from Edrovir or Jinara."

It took a few seconds for some of them to work out what he meant, but then a ragged cheer went up, and Nagaro had to wait again for it to subside. His frown only deepened as he waited, and those who saw this soon ceased their cheering and waved those around them to silence.

"Therefore," Nagaro continued, "I am willing to captain the ship that lies in the harbor, for the purpose of freeing slaves— provided, of course, that enough men can be found for a crew, *but—*"

He was interrupted by a real cheer this time. But his brow didn't relax, and when the noise didn't quickly abate, he raised his voice to be heard over it. "*But,*" he shouted, "*I will do so only on one condition!*"

That silenced them, and brought back many worried looks as well.

Taru poked him with his boot under the table.

Moraga raised his voice. "What's yer 'condition' then?"

Nagaro looked straight at the merchant seaman. "Just this: If I'm to be your captain, things must be done *my way.*"

That brought a new scowl to Moraga's face and a darker murmuring from the assembled men.

"*What are ye doing, man?*" Taru hissed.

"And what is *your way?* Nagaro Nareyo?"

The words rang with a note of challenge. The speaker was one of the townsmen near the door, a Kelorin of middle years, with cool gray eyes, a neatly-trimmed graying beard, and a military bearing. A sword in a well-worn scabbard hung at his hip. His face seemed familiar, though Nagaro couldn't place it.

Everyone had stopped speaking. The room was so quiet one could hear the floorboards creak as men shifted their weight.

Nagaro regarded the man with a measuring gaze. "Those who were with me at Jaamra have some idea, I think," he said levelly. "I mean to slay the smallest number of Mautep necessary to persuade the rest to lay down their arms. I will ask them to surrender, and if they do, I intend that they shall not be harmed. Any man who follows me must swear that, if I say 'halt,' or 'put up your sword', he will do so."

There were looks exchanged, and muttered words, and then the room broke into a jumble of conversations.

The man with the well-worn sword looked skeptical. He raised a hand for silence and got it as soon as the men's attention came back to him. "So y mean t' ask the Mahuk to *surrender?*" he asked with dripping sarcasm. "Just what makes ye think the devils will do that?"

And all eyes returned, expectantly, questioningly, to Nagaro.

Before Nagaro could answer, however, Landros stood up, folding his arms across his chest. He also wore his sword conspicuously at his hip. "I saw nine o' them do it at Jaamra, Timegar," he drawled. "They knew they couldn't win, and living looked better to 'em than dying, I expect. Besides," he added significantly. "Ye've not seen Captain Nagaro wield a blade. He's bloody wonderful to watch if ye're on *his* side— and I imagine he's bloody frightening if ye're on the other!"

The name Timegar jogged a memory. Nagaro realized with a jolt that this was the man whose authority had sent two sharp-tongued women on their way the day Tredhold had tended Neved's broken ankle. Nagaro opened his mouth to protest that he wasn't "Captain Nagaro" yet. Nor, he hoped, so frightening as all that. But Taru kicked him hard under the table and shook his head.

And in the next instant Moraga was on his feet. "Now look ye here!" the merchant seaman cried. "We all know Nagaro's good with a sword. And he's good at talkin' fancy words too. But that don't give him the right t' tell *me* I can't kill the bloody Mautep!"

This time Nagaro cut in before anyone else could speak. "You're right, Moraga. Skill with a sword, or with words, doesn't give me the right to command you— or anyone else. And I *won't* command any man who doesn't freely choose to follow me. You've a right to know what kind of captain I would be, and I've just told you what to expect."

This time a wild babble erupted as soon as he ceased speaking. Some of the men were for Moraga's point of view, some against.

Nor would Moraga be silent. He waved his arms and shouted over the din. "It ain't *reasonable*, what he's askin' us— not t' kill as many Mautep as we please— just 'cause he's captain! Some of us was slaves ourselves. An' the rest have lost kin t' those rotters!"

Some of the men were nodding. Many were muttering. As if on impulse, Moraga seized the homespun tirkyl he was wearing and stripped it off over his head, baring his upper body. He slapped at the brand on his left shoulder. "See *that?* That's where they put their bloody mark on me! And look at me back!" He turned around to display his crisscross of whip scars. "And what about *this?*" He turned back to face the room, jabbing a finger at his scarred lip. "There's me good looks spoiled. What woman's goin' t' look at me now?"

Feeling the drama of the moment, Moraga paused to bask in it.

There was more muttering and nodding, and Nagaro feared he would lose a good number of them if he didn't think of something to say.

Before he could speak, however, Yuli broke the spell. She'd been collecting the dishes all the while they were talking, and she had obviously been listening as well. She wasn't far from Moraga where he stood, brandishing his shirt in the air. "Well, there's Panila, for one," she said matter-of-factly as she leaned across a table to retrieve a plate. The room was not so noisy that her voice didn't carry to its farthest corner.

Nagaro started at the name, but no one noticed since every eye was on Moraga.

Moraga was caught completely off guard. "What d' ye mean, 'there's Panila?'" he demanded, lowering the hand that clutched the tirkyl.

Yuli straightened. "Oh," she said blithely, but quite loudly enough in the now-deafening silence. "I have it from her mother that Panila fancies ye, that's all."

Moraga's jaw dropped. "But she's near as tall as I am!" he blurted, and promptly turned scarlet.

Yuli took his measure with her eyes. "I think she just might be taller," she said calmly. "And she's a sight prettier, that's certain. But she fancies ye all the same, and I suppose there's no accounting for taste."

The now-flabbergasted silence held for a pregnant moment. Then came the laughter.

Someone said, "Aye, she's a lot o' woman t' love, Panila is." Another voice said, "She'll give ye tall sons, Moraga!"

There was more laughter as Moraga sank onto his stool. He sat with his tirkyl in his hands, very red in the face. Yuli gave Nagaro a wink over her shoulder as she made for the kitchen with a tray full of dishes.

Nagaro looked hard at Taru, whose answering look said plainly that Panila's interest in Moraga was news to *him*. Nagaro was suddenly very glad he'd never managed to sit with her. Clearly his attentions would have been unwelcome.

Grateful though he was for Yuli's intervention, however, he didn't really like to see Moraga so embarrassed, so he rapped loudly on the table to regain the men's attention.

"I'm sure you've all suffered something at the hands of the Mautep," he said seriously, when their eyes came back to him. "You wouldn't be here tonight, otherwise. And I can't tell you that you shouldn't be angry." He swept their faces. "I know I'm asking a hard thing. I'm asking you to put aside your anger and forgo vengeance if you sail with me. Because I would be sailing to free slaves. *Not* to slaughter Mautep."

There were uncertain whispers from several sides, but it was the man named Timegar who spoke up first. "Will ye at least tell us," he demanded, "*why* ye'd be so gentle with those murdering swine?"

"Aye, tell us!" It was Gurd. He was immediately echoed by several others.

Nagaro ran a hand through his hair. "There are two reasons for seeking their surrender," he said. "First, I want to bring as many of you safely home as possible. The sooner the fight is over, the fewer of our own are likely to die in it." He paused, frowning. "The second reason is that I hope to show them that men of Edrovir have honor. Mautep don't slay other Mautep who surrender. It goes against their honor—"

"Now ye're being daft, man!" The words burst from Timegar. "To speak of honor and the Mahuk in the same breath!"

This time it was Pavo Maat who sprang to his feet, erupting in a stream of rapid Hashti in which the word *kajadeem* figured prominently. When at length he had to catch his breath, he mastered himself with a visible effort, and leveled an accusing finger at Timegar. "You do not know one thing about honor of my people!" he declared. "Man should not speak of thing he do not know!"

Timegar looked affronted at first. His face grew red and he seemed about to say something heated, but then he appeared to reconsider, and his expression turned apologetic. "I beg your pardon, Zirda," he said carefully. "I'd forgotten that ye and your countryman were here." He nodded to Chaheel. "Of course ye'd know better than I what the Mahuk know of honor. I take back my words."

Pavo bent his head to Timegar in acceptance. He sat down, mollified.

Nagaro bowed an acknowledgment to his friend, then addressed the room at large.

"I know most of you aren't accustomed to thinking of Mahuk honor," he said. "And some among the men of the Baar have more honor than others. I think I've seen the best and worst of it, and if you sail with me, you can judge for yourselves. But in any case, the first reason I gave should suffice. I mean to keep you as safe as I can."

Moraga had put his tirkyl back on while the men's eyes were elsewhere, and apparently he'd recovered from his embarrassment. He now sprang to his feet again. "What if ye say 'halt' and one o' them comes at me when me sword's down?" he demanded. "Am I t' stand an' be butchered?"

"Of course not." Nagaro answered quickly. "I would forbid no man to strike in his own defense. And I wouldn't call for a halt until we had them cowed." He looked out over their faces. "Men may die in a fair fight. That's the fortunes of war," he continued. "But, if any Mautep slays a man who follows me, through treachery or by any dishonorable act, that Mautep's life will be forfeit, and I will slay him with my own hand. *But mark this*:" He paused for emphasis. "If any man who follows me, in *his* turn, kills a Mautep through treachery or dishonor, I'll consider that man's life to be forfeit to the Mautep if they demand it. The sword of honor must cut both ways, or it means nothing."

It was very quiet when he ceased speaking. Many of the men looked stunned.

Nagaro raised his hand as if swearing an oath. "This is the covenant I offer you," he said into the silence. "If you will swear to follow me upon the path of honor, for the purpose of freeing slaves, I will do everything in my power to bring you home safe and whole— even to laying down my life if that will serve."

Those of the former slaves nearest to him were staring at him now with awe in their faces, their eyes aglow.

"Does he truly mean what he says?" Timegar wondered aloud. It was so quiet that his words were heard by all.

It was Tego who answered. "Every word of it, mate! Ye can depend on it. If ye'd been with us at Jaamra, or on Chitaopa, ye wouldn't have t' ask."

Afterwards Nagaro could only look back at what followed with amazement.

Mendorel was suddenly on his feet. "The sword!" he cried. "The sword that won our freedom! We'll swear on the sword!"

Taru must have anticipated something of the kind, for Nagaro found the black leather scabbard immediately thrust into his hands. The moment seemed to have a kind of magic that carried him. He drew the sword in a sweeping gesture, holding it aloft. The blade sang as it left the sheath, and flashed gold fire in the light of the oil lamps.

A gasp and a murmur went up from the gathered men.

Nagaro turned the sword and held it before him by the hilt with both hands, the blade pointing downward. He spoke in a firm, clear voice. "As I have spoken, so will I do. In Vothra's name I swear it, upon this sword and upon my honor."

Tego was the first to move. The gnarled little Turo jumped up and strode forward. Drawing the sword he bore, the former merchant seaman laid it on the table in front of Nagaro. Then, placing his right hand on the hilt of Nagaro's sword, he raised his voice. "I pledge my sword t' Captain Nagaro!" he cried. "By all the Spirits, I swear t' follow him on the path o' honor, wherever he chooses t' lead!"

And after that, the men kept coming— some brought swords, others knives, to lay before their chosen captain. The room rang with their cries:

"Captain Nagaro!"

"Captain Nagaro and the sword of freedom!"

Nanu and Chaheel rose and swore on the sword, the latter invoking the name of Sheptuum, the god of the Mahuk Baar.

Taru and Pavo did the same after them, placing their hands together on the sword's hilt. Pavo bowed his head to Nagaro before he sat down again. "I always know you go to do something like this," he said. "Because you are Kiraam Shaku-Tal!" Nagaro knew those Hashti words. They meant *Thief of Slaves.*

Mendorel came next, and one by one the other former slaves came— even Gurd and Moraga. The scar-lipped Turo gave Nagaro a look of grudging respect as he grasped the sword hilt and said rather gruffly, "I'll say just what Tego did. I'll keep yer honor, and go wherever ye choose t' lead. Sometimes I think ye're daft as a dune-beetle, but daft or not, I think the Spirits love ye!"

Gurd laughed outright at that. "The men of Leith have a saying," he said. "That boldness is next t' madness. But they also say the gods favor the bold."

At another time, hearing such words would have troubled Nagaro, but in that moment his heart was too full.

Among the last of the *Fist's* old crew came Landros. The grizzled sea warrior laid his captured Mahuk blade on the growing pile. After swearing, he winked at Nagaro and said out of the side of his mouth, "That was well done, lad. I wouldn't ha' missed this for all the land an' sea together!"

Tredhold came behind Landros. "Could ye use a good ship's doctor?" he asked with a crooked smile.

Nagaro was so overwhelmed he could do no more than nod to the two sea warriors. He only found his voice at last when Kunoa tried to lay his fisherman's knife with the other blades. Then he reached out, took the youth's knife, and handed it back with a shake of his head. "Not yet," he told the disappointed youth. "I'll not take any man that's not yet twenty. If we return— if this doesn't prove to be a dangerous folly— and you still wish to join us when you reach twenty years, I'll be proud to accept your service."

After Nagaro's old comrades, came the townsmen. Eleven of the thirteen present swore themselves to him that night. Most surprising to him was the last of these, the man named Timegar. The bearded Kelorin stood sternly as if to attention while he swore on the sword. Afterwards he met Nagaro's gaze and spoke very seriously.

"I used t' be a Fleet officer," he said. "That's how Landros comes t' know me. I left that service half a dozen years ago t' teach my son the fisherman's trade, that my father taught to me." His eyes grew hard. "But the Mahuk took him— my only child, not seventeen— the first time he took the boat out alone."

It was as if someone had punched Nagaro in the gut. He remembered that this man had said something when their paths had first crossed. Something about children, something suggesting he'd suffered a great loss. "I'm very sorry..." It felt utterly inadequate. "How long ago?"

"A year, last Sedrin."

Nagaro shook his head. "I'm very sorry," he said again. "I can't offer you much hope. Most men don't live long in the galleys. Your son may be alive yet, somewhere, but there are so many slaves... so many ships..."

Timegar only nodded. "I know," he said quietly. "I don't expect to find him. The truth is, I came here tonight seeking a path to vengeance.

But ye've offered me something better— a chance to do some good in the world before I die."

Nagaro met the older man's gaze. "I mean to try," he said grimly. He could feel the magic beginning to slip away. "But I know that death may overtake us all. Or worse, we may end in chains. This sword—" he took the elegant blade and sheathed it, "—was a pure gift of Lokundas. I can't expect such a thing to come to me a second time."

"Still, it was well spoken. I heard your captain's voice again tonight."

Nagaro remembered the reference. He hadn't understood it before. "And I heard yours," he said. "You have a voice of command as well."

Timegar shrugged. "Perhaps," he said. "And I might try my hand at using it one day. But for now, I'm content to follow your lead."

***

There was a great deal more that passed that evening— talk of sword training, of what stores the ship would need, and how they could win at least ten more men to their cause. It was close to two hours later that the meeting finally broke up and the three friends at last ascended the stairs to their room.

Exhausted, they undressed without speaking and threw themselves on their beds. Taru and Pavo were snoring within minutes, but Nagaro lay long awake. The magic on which everything had turned had long since faded. The flush of success had run its course and left him with a sense of shock, even dismay, at what the night had wrought. In the chill darkness of the bedroom, his doubts began to multiply. Could this thing really be done? Could *he* do it? What would be the cost? And what would he do if that cost were more than he was willing to bear?

At last he sat up, swinging his bare feet out onto the cold wood floor. "Vothra," he said aloud, addressing the darkness, but keeping his voice low. "Are you there?" He waited for several heartbeats, not really expecting anything. And indeed, nothing happened. So he lay down again, and tried once more to sleep. Eventually he did drift off.

And it seemed that he dreamed.

The sign of Vothra glowed as if with a silver light, two circles, the smaller inside the larger, the tops of their rims touching, their bottoms joined by a straight vertical line. The sign faded slowly, and behind it the silver figure stood with open hands.

Yes, I am here, said the musical voice. *As I have said, you have been called upon by others who have seen you use your gifts. And you have chosen to answer the call. To take up the sword. But you are troubled, Spirit called Nagaro. Tell me why.*

Nagaro's thoughts were a tortured tangle, and he struggled to identify the ugly truth at the heart of the knot. "I'm afraid," he confessed.

What do you fear? The voice was very gentle.

In his dream he frowned. He wasn't afraid of death. Not his own death, at least... but the deaths of others? "I'm afraid the choice I've made is the wrong one, I guess."

Ah. The figure nodded. *But there are no wrong choices that are made in good faith. Men only choose wrongly when they knowingly choose to do harm.*

Nagaro frowned again. "Well, not a *wrong* choice, then, but I'm afraid it will turn out to be a *bad* choice."

Vothra seemed to smile, though sadly. *And how shall we tell a bad choice from a good one, except by its outcome? But we can never know what the outcome would have been had we chosen differently. Fate might have sent us something worse.*

Nagaro's trouble remained. "That may be true," he said. "But it will be of little comfort to me if very many of those men are slain— or if we all end in chains!"

There was a ripple of soft laughter. *I might have known you would not make this easy. But consider: These men are all fishermen, or seamen of some kind. How easily may they be taken as slaves while going about their usual work? Or how easily may the sea take them? Though you saved some of them once, you cannot keep them safe all the rest of their lives, no matter what you do.*

"But they think I have the protection of the spirits! And the favor of the gods! They expect too much of me! Some of them even seem to think that my sword has some sort of magic in it! But it's just a sword."

Midnight eyes considered him. *Have you misled them?*

"No, of course not! At least I haven't meant to. But they've misled themselves!"

Then correct them.

Nagaro shook his head in frustration. "I mean to. But I doubt they'll listen. Even Pavo believes this is my destiny."

The figure produced a sigh like a breath of air in a still place. *You can only tell them the truth, whether they believe it or not, Spirit called Nagaro. Be honest always. Be true to yourself. And know that they will believe what they need to believe, and that it will give them courage.*

For a long moment Nagaro didn't answer. "You wish me to do this thing?" he asked at last. "You believe it can succeed?"

The figure shook its head. *I believe that you will try. For so you have promised, if only enough men will follow you. And I believe there will be enough men, though I do not know it. Nor do I know what the outcome of this venture will be, for the future is as dark to me as to any living man. This undertaking may prove a glorious disaster, but I know one thing: Such a noble venture is surely worthy of the effort. It is worthy of you, Spirit called Nagaro.* The figure smiled, an expression both sad and gentle. *There. You called, and I answered. Have you found comfort in my words?*

Nagaro considered. "Some," he admitted. "I'm still afraid of what may happen if I do this. But I'm no longer afraid to do it."

That will have to be enough. The spirit sighed again and the eyes seemed to look right into his soul. *Is there something else you would ask, before I go? Something else that troubles you... or that you do not understand?*

It seemed as if the spirit expected there to be something. Nagaro searched his mind. No, nothing to do with Jila. He knew that had been a mistake. He'd forgiven Taru, and was trying to forgive himself. He didn't need to hear words of forgiveness from Vothra. "No, I don't think—" he began, then stopped. Perhaps Vothra could shed light on the still-unsolved riddle of his escape from the curse of heskial. "You spoke of the Spirit of the White Flower, once," he ventured. "What exactly *is* it?"

The star-filled eyes blinked. He almost thought Vothra was surprised. *Ah,* said the quiet voice. *That is a question that seeks knowledge, rather than wisdom, and I have said I do not often answer such questions because there would be no end to men's asking. Still,* the voice mused, *it was my words that have led you to ask it. Perhaps I do owe you some explanation.*

There was a little pause, apparently for thought, and then the figure continued.

The Spirit of the White Flower is a healing spirit, one of several such. They are very old— older than I. Each has its realm of influence, and for the White Flower, that realm is the mind. I thought I saw the hand of the Spirit of the White Flower working upon you when first I made your acquaintance. I spoke of it without considering the uncertainty of whether it were true.

Nagaro was alarmed. "Do you mean it *wasn't* the Spirit of the White flower after all?"

Another sigh preceded the response. *Truly I do not know. I thought it possible the Spirit of the White Flower was involved because it is known to use the healing power of forgetfulness.*

Nagaro frowned. "But can't you ask it? If it *was* that spirit, it may have saved my life, and I'd like to give it my thanks."

The silvery figure shook its head. *The Spirit of the White Flower has no conscious awareness— although it has a clear purpose. And it does not dwell in the void, in any case. It is enim, which is spirit, that dwells in onam— in what you would call physical substance. It dwells, specifically, in a plant with white flowers. Hence its name.*

This was unexpected and confusing. "But how can it work if it's in a plant?" Nagaro portested. "How could it take or restore memories, living in a plant?"

Vothra sighed. *The spirit lives through time by dwelling in the plant, in every separate shoot and seedling of it. But freshly gathered leaves, or distilled juices from leaves, can carry it. And when a person partakes of the juice, he comes under its influence. A living person must, of course, pick the leaves and distill the juice. But the magic is not in the person, it is in the spirit that was in the plant.*

Nagaro's mind was racing. "Then there must have been a person who gave me some of this plant," he said eagerly. "And it could have been in the wine after all! I must have had some friend in the palace..." But *who*, he wondered. The princess would have lacked the knowledge, and Dreigen would have lacked the desire... He drew a hopeful breath. "Do you know who it was?" he asked.

But the figure shook its head. *That is not a question that I would answer even if I knew, though in fact I do not. I had scarcely begun to form and was not yet watching you then.* The spirit sighed. *But you leap too far from too little knowledge. It could have been in the wine, which you recall, but it could equally have been in something after the wine, which you do not. And perhaps I am mistaken to invoke the Spirit of the White Flower. This abomination called heskial is new to my experience. I can make no guess as to its effects when mingled with wine, or otherwise. But, do you see?* The musical voice turned suddenly discordant. *If once I begin to answer these questions, there is no end! Already I have answered more than I intended.*

The voice paused ever so briefly, as if to collect itself, then continued more gently. *Try to be content in your deliverance, if you can, without knowing the means, Spirit called Nagaro. Farewell now, and sleep well.*

Nagaro blinked. The Sign of Vothra lingered, still glowing in his vision, but already it was fading, and beyond it lay nothing— only the wall and ceiling of the bedroom he shared with Taru and Pavo.

He was awake, but the sounds of his friends' breathing told him that they both still slumbered. He should have been too wrought up to sleep, but he found his mind awash in a peaceful weariness. He closed his eyes with a sigh, and before he knew it, his thoughts were drifting. Sleep soon overtook him, and this time he slept soundly until morning.

Chapter 14

Preparations

The days that followed were full of activity, leaving Nagaro little time to think about what Vothra had told him concerning the Spirit of the White Flower. Under such circumstances, being content with his deliverance wasn't difficult. He still had the task of cleaning the inn's stable, but the rest of his time could be spent advancing his new plan. Taru and Pavo had run out of work at the kuma mill— at least that they were willing to do— and their time was thus available as well.

The first thing the three friends did was start making practice swords. This they expected to take some time, since they wanted to make at least twenty of the wooden weapons. Tego immediately asked to help, and the next day, Moraga came as well. Both former merchant seamen were good at the task, having a sailor's skill at whittling wood and lashing cord. Moraga surprised Nagaro with his enthusiasm.

"Will he stay with us, d' ye think?" Taru wondered on one of those early days, after Moraga had gone, but while Tego was still there helping them tidy up the wood shavings. "And I don't just mean for the makin' o' these swords. Will he really stay all the way t' the end o' this?"

Tego, who knew Moraga best since he roomed with him, brushed Taru's concern aside. "Ye mustn't think ill o' Moraga," he told them. "It's his way t' see a storm brewin' in every shred o' cloud, and he does speak his first thought without waitin' for his second more often than not. But he's not got a bad heart in him. An' he generally comes 'round t' the right heading in the end."

Since such things as lumber, tar, rope, and canvas were supplies that they would now need, Nagaro paid an early visit to Gedras to make sure the merchant didn't sell anything else from the ship's stores, only to find that Gedras was already aware of his plans.

"You really mean to do this?" the merchant asked. "This freeing of slaves?"

"We mean to try, if we can get enough men," Nagaro told him. "I'd like to have at least forty."

"How many do you have now?"

"Thirty-four."

"That many?" Gedras' eyebrows went up. "What sort are you getting? Reckless young hotheads mostly?"

"I wouldn't say so. I don't take anyone under twenty," Nagaro told him. "And I've only turned two away for that reason." (The second had been Yuli's son, Habu.) "The most recent recruit is another former Fleet warrior, an old shipmate of Timegar's, named Rubo. He's past fifty, knows one end of a sword from the other, and doubles as a ship's cook."

"Well that was good luck," Gedras conceded, "But most of them will have no skill in swordsmanship. How will you remedy that?"

"By training them myself. With the help of the former Fleet warriors."

"Really?" Gedras looked skeptical. "Do you think you can do it by spring?"

Nagaro shrugged. "By late spring, I hope," he said seriously. "It will take a great deal of hard work, and I won't sail until I think they're ready."

"I... see." The merchant adjusted his glasses. "What you have in my warehouse won't be everything you'll need to refurbish the ship, I'm afraid. How will you pay for the rest?"

"We have the money from the iron and leather," Nagaro pointed out. "And the men are all willing to put in their own labor— to careen her and scrape the hull clean. She's a fast ship when she's clean, and we'll need that speed. We can only hope to succeed against single ships after all. We'll have to flee if we encounter any force of numbers."

Gedras was beginning to look impressed in spite of himself, but he had a businessman's penchant for practical details. "What about provisions?"

This caused Nagaro to frown. "That may be difficult," he admitted. "We may have to ask the townsfolk for charity— unless we can sell some of the jewelry before we're ready to sail. There's some hope of that, since I don't expect the men will be ready very early in the season. A ship or two may have called at the island by then."

The merchant considered him for a long moment. "Well," he said at last, "I can't say I'm pleased to see you take this risk, Tor Nagaro. But I see you're determined. If I can be of any help, I hope you'll ask." He smiled fleetingly. "And, if you should come up short of men or money, or simply change your mind, the offer of employment I made still stands."

Nagaro swallowed and managed to convey his appreciation.

As he left Gedras' study and stepped out into the entry hall, he was startled to encounter Berenil. The merchant's eldest daughter appeared to have just come down the stairs, and Nagaro came to a dead stop when he saw her. Recalling her previous reaction, he didn't venture a greeting, but he couldn't help staring. She wore deep blue— a form-fitting gown with simple lines that accentuated the slimness of her figure.

For her part, Berenil gave him a single very direct glance that was serious to the point of severity. Then, pausing, she dropped her eyes to look fixedly at a point on the floor beside the hem of her skirt. Something white fell from her fingers and came to rest in the exact spot marked by her gaze. She then raised her head and swept on, without looking at him again or speaking, to disappear through a doorway on the other side of the hall.

Nagaro stood still, puzzled, for several seconds after she had gone. Then he walked over and picked up the fallen object— for she had clearly meant him to do so. It was a piece of paper, folded in half three times. He unfolded it and read two words, written in a neat, elegant hand:

Ask him.

Nagaro stood frowning at the paper. Did she want him to ask her father if he might sit with her? The notion surprised him since her manner scarcely even seemed friendly. He half expected to hear Gesrin's voice, and Lissel's giggles, again from the upstairs landing. But the room remained silent. Apparently he was alone. He sighed, re-folded the paper, and put it into his pocket. Then he took his cloak from the hook on the wall and left the merchant's house. He certainly was not going to turn around and ask Gedras anything without giving the matter some thought. *And seeking the advice of his friends...*

***

"Well it's obvious, isn't it?" Taru observed after sounding out the words on the paper. "She means ye t' ask for a sitting."

It was evening and the three friends were seated at the small table in the room they shared.

Nagaro hunched his shoulders and frowned. "That's what I thought as well, but I don't see why she'd want me to."

Taru shrugged. "She must have taken a fancy to ye."

"But she'd seen me only once before. I spoke just three words to her, and she didn't seem very pleased about it at the time."

Taru shrugged again. "Well, she must've decided she liked your looks," he said easily.

Nagaro frowned harder. "No. When they were talking about me, it was the second one— Gesrin— who commented on my looks. Berenil just said that her father had said I had a good head on my shoulders."

"What does that mean?" Pavo asked. "Good head on your shoulder?"

Taru waved a hand. "It means he's good at thinking. Has good sense. That sort o' thing." Taru looked at Nagaro a little skeptically as he said this, as if it were not the way he would have described his friend.

Pavo, however, nodded and then turned eagerly to Nagaro. "Maybe her father say good thing about you, and she like what she hear. Then she want to sit with you."

"Well..." Nagaro hesitated. "I suppose it *could* be something like that..."

"Whatever the reason," Taru put in, "Ye're lucky t' have got your boot in that door, as they say. There's three daughters t' choose from under that roof, and none o' them spoken for." He shook his head. "That won't last."

Nagaro sighed. He supposed Taru was right, and if he had to choose one of the three daughters based on what little he'd seen, Berenil seemed marginally the best prospect. He didn't like Gesrin's preoccupation with appearances, and Lissel was simply too young. All she seemed to do was giggle. One bright spot was that the merchant's house didn't have a front porch. They would have to let him sit with Berenil *inside*— probably in the parlor. He'd called a parlor a useless room, but this was just the sort of thing a parlor was good for. He sighed again. He supposed he should ask Gedras about it the next time he had a chance.

Taru's thoughts had apparently already moved on, for he now said, "I thought of a name for the ship today, and I want t' know what ye both think of it."

Nagaro and Pavo were immediately eager to hear. Everyone had agreed, of course, that the ship must be re-christened, but so far there had been no agreement on a new name.

"*Well...*" Taru said, pausing for effect. "She used t' be called the *Fist of Death...* and we're going t' be using her t' give men their *freedom...* so I thought, why not call her the *Sword of Freedom*?"

Nagaro balked. "Don't you think that's a bit overly dramatic?"

But Pavo was nodding vigorously. "It is *exactly* right name," he said with conviction. Sword of Freedom! Yes! When other man all hear it, they will say so too."

Nagaro pushed back his chair, stood up, and stretched. "Well, we'll see, I suppose," he said wearily. "Right now I'd like to get some sleep."

Taru stood up and stretched as well. "I'm sure ye'll like it better after ye've got used to it," he said.

Nagaro doubted that, but he was too tired to argue.

***

As it turned out, it didn't matter what Nagaro thought. Pavo's prediction turned out to be quite accurate. The irony of turning the *Fist of Death* into the *Sword of Freedom* seemed to appeal to everyone.

Nagaro appreciated the irony as well, but the name seemed to him to make a boastful claim in advance of actual accomplishment. Besides that, he was all too aware that many of the men were already referring to the Mahuk sword he had kept as the "sword of freedom," and that they seemed to regard it as a kind of talisman. It didn't help that some of them had heard Nagaro refer to the sword as a gift of Lokundas. The Kelorin among them understood that he only meant it had been a gift of chance. To the Turowans, however, it sounded like an invocation of spirit magic. Although Nagaro continued to insist that the sword was only a sword, his words had made little impression. It was as Vothra had told him in his dream. The men would believe what they needed to believe.

Once the ship's name was decided, some of the precious common supply of money was spent for paint. The Hashti characters on the ship's stern were scraped and sanded away, and the words "Sword of Freedom" were boldly painted in their place, spelled out in the letters of the Kelorin alphabet, the *reivinkor*. Next the blood-red diamonds along the ship's sides were stripped and painted white so that the *Sword of Freedom's* markings were alternately black and white instead of black and crimson.

This last was done following some discussion of the colors under which they should sail. Nagaro had vehemently rejected the suggestion that they sail under Lord Baalkir's colors and flag as a ruse. It was not honorable, and he would have none of it. So the traditional pirate colors had been chosen instead. The related matter of a banner caused further discussion. The flag of Edrovir— a white hawk on a field of blue— was suggested, but again this seemed false colors to Nagaro, since the Crown hadn't sanctioned their intended activities. At the same time, he didn't like the pirate ensign— the traditional white death's head on black. It suggested they meant to deal out death— rather than setting men free. He cast about for some more appropriate emblem and finally yielded to Pavo's suggestion that it should be a sword.

If the truth were told, Nagaro was rather proud of the design he ultimately devised. It depicted a white sword on a black field, the blade lying horizontal with the hilt nearest the mast so that the point might appear to be brandished as the banner whipped in the wind. He bought white and black cloth to make the banner, and drew the shape of the sword, but then came to an impasse because he lacked the skill to do the sewing. Taru surprised everyone by suggesting that the young tavern woman, Tulara, could perform this task.

"She's very handy with a needle," he informed them. "She sews all her own clothes— and she'll likely do this for a few rins."

Upon further questioning, it turned out that Tulara wasn't happy as a tavern woman and had expressed interest in finding other employment. Nagaro considered this something to be encouraged, so he agreed and handed the cloth pieces over to Taru to take to Tulara. "You should tell her to ask for work at the inn," he added. "Yuli's been looking for help in the kitchen."

In the midst of these preparations, the practice swords were finished, and it was time to begin the training in swordsmanship.

***

The day Nagaro chose for the first sword practice dawned cold and drizzly. Everything outside was damp and slick. Despite the weather, the three friends went out to the deserted stable yard before breakfast with their arms full of wooden swords. They found an empty barrel and pressed it into service to store the carefully trimmed and lashed sticks.

Nagaro pulled out two of them and handed one to Taru. "Here," he said. "Let's see how much you remember."

Taru grinned a little uncertainly.

For the next half hour, the quiet of the stable yard was disturbed by the sharp *crack, crack,* of the wooden swords coming together. When at length the two friends stopped to catch their breath, they're shirts were sticking to their backs from the combined effects of the drizzle and the exertion.

Nagaro smiled with satisfaction. "Well done, Taru," he observed between breaths. "You were a bit rusty to start with but you're already almost back to where you were in Wotana."

Taru gave him a rueful look. "Maybe so, Nagaro," he gasped, his chest heaving. "But I've a long way to go... before I'll frighten a Mautep warrior into laying down his sword!"

Nagaro laughed. "We have time to work on it. And we only have to hold them long enough for the slaves to get on deck. Then we can retreat and loose the grapples if we have to."

Pavo had picked up a wooden sword while they were talking, and now he planted himself before Nagaro. "I try now!" he declared, brandishing his stick.

Nagaro nodded. "All right," he said, wiping his brow. "But first we have to work on your stance. Turn your body so your side is towards me, not your chest— like this— so you make a smaller target."

Pavo quickly mastered the proper fighting position, and Nagaro began to walk him through a few basic moves, with Taru offering encouragement. Looking up after a while, Nagaro discovered that they had acquired an audience. Moraga and Tego had come out and were standing at a little distance, watching with keen interest. By the time the three friends stopped for breakfast, several more of the inn's guests had joined the onlookers.

Landros was one of these. He fell in beside Nagaro as they crossed the stable yard, making for the back door of the inn. "Ye're a pretty fair swordmaster, Nagaro," he remarked. "And that's a rare thing in a man o' your talent. Most o' the ones it comes easy to have no idea how to teach. *They* know what t' do almost without thinking, and they've no patience for men who don't."

Nagaro shrugged. "I had to learn like everybody else," he said. "And every man must learn at his own pace. I remember how I was taught, and I try to do it the same way."

Landros gave him a sidelong look. "Ye never told me who your master was."

Nagaro hesitated, trying to think how to answer truthfully without revealing too much. "The man who taught me did it for half his usual price," he said after an uncomfortable pause. "Part of the agreement was that we wouldn't name him."

Landros crooked a conspiratorial eyebrow. "Ah," he said knowingly. "The man didn't want it noised about that he had given charity, so he wouldn't have every poor lad knocking at his door?"

Nagaro didn't meet Landros' eyes. "I expect that was it," he said carefully. Undoubtedly it was part of the truth, but the Lady Marmine had also wanted his training kept secret for reasons of her own.

After breakfast, the three friends went back to the stable yard. The drizzle had stopped by this time, although it seemed to have gotten colder. A light wind had sprung up out of the northwest. In spite of the chill, there were a dozen men who came out with them, all clamoring for a chance to try their hand with a practice sword. Nagaro stood them all in a row and demonstrated the proper stance. Then he took them in pairs, showing them a simple move and the matching defense and directing them to practice with each other. When he had them all working, he stood back to watch, then went around to each pair in turn to give pointers. After he'd been around the whole group once, he called a halt, bade them change partners, and repeated the entire process.

The word must have been getting around the town, for more men kept appearing by ones or twos all morning. By the time Nagaro called a halt for the day, he had worked with more than twenty, including two he hadn't seen before.

Nor did the attendance lighten in the days that followed. In fact, it was rather the reverse. The more experienced former Fleet men, Landros,

Tredhold, Timegar, and Rubo, all lent their assistance. There came days when it rained and with the innkeeper's approval they moved into the common room, pushing the tables and stools aside. As the days went by, Nagaro found he was getting a feel for the strengths and weaknesses of each of his recruits.

And more men kept coming. Three additional men swore themselves to his covenant in the first week of sword practice. By the end of the second week, he'd taken the oath of the decisive fortieth man, and still there were some more after that.

***

It was in the third week that Gedras paid a visit to the stable yard. Nagaro had just stepped back from the melee of whacking sticks when he noticed the merchant working his way around the edge of the yard, moving in his direction. Nagaro was puzzled. He knew better than to think that Gedras had decided to exchange the merchant's trade for any form of piracy. As the merchant drew nearer, Nagaro noted that the man's brow was furrowed in a frown.

"Good morning Tor Gedras," he said. "What brings you here?"

Gedras nodded a greeting, and coughed apologetically. "I'm afraid I'm here on behalf of the Town Council."

Nagaro was startled. "The Town Council? Have they a message for me?"

Gedras shifted his feet uncomfortably. "We, ah, met last night, and I'm afraid there's some... ah... *concern*," he ventured cautiously. "About the training of a force of armed men in our town and on our island."

"Oh." Nagaro was somewhat taken aback. "I hope we're not breaking any law. Tor Dakuro said nothing against it when I spoke to him about making the swords."

"Well, no," Gedras responded hastily. "There's no *law* regarding it. There hasn't needed to be, since it's never been done before. And I don't think Tor Dakuro gave any thought to there being objections, since he favors the undertaking himself. It's just that, well, some folk are nervous about the prospect of having armed men walking about our streets, and some of them have asked the Council to take action."

Nagaro frowned. "As you can see, we're using wooden sticks, not swords."

The merchant sighed. "Yes, I do see that. But the word's gotten out that some of these men have real swords made of steel that they might wear if they chose. And it's known that you've asked Dakuro to make more."

"I... see." Nagaro rubbed his bearded chin thoughtfully. "I suppose that could be worrisome to folk who haven't any means of defending themselves— though I assure you none of us means any harm to anyone on Pakoa..." His voice trailed as his mind worked on the problem. Abruptly, he turned towards his men and raised his voice to carry above the sounds of wood cracking on wood.

"*All halt!*" he cried in a ringing voice.

Every man who was practicing in the stable yard stopped as if frozen in his tracks.

Nagaro addressed them again in a loud, clear voice. "Lower your weapons! I have something to tell you."

All across the yard, sticks were shifted to point at the ground.

Nagaro nodded in satisfaction. "I have just learned," he told them, "that the Town Council has some concern with what we're doing here. To put it simply, they don't care for the idea of men going about armed and possibly frightening honest citizens." He swept his eyes over the ranks of the men. They were all listening attentively. "You all know there's no need for anyone to be wearing a real sword at all right now," he went on. "But we *will* want to do some practice with steel before we sail. So I ask that you not wear your sword— those that have one— anywhere outside of this stable yard for any reason. If you must carry your blade elsewhere, I ask that you carry it sheathed and sling the belt over your shoulder so it can't be easily drawn. Is that clear?"

"Aye, Cap'n!" That was Tego, who was standing closest, and whose training as a merchant seaman tended to assert itself whenever Nagaro used a tone of command.

The words were immediately echoed by a dozen other voices as all present nodded their heads vigorously. Those who were formerly with the Royal Fleet saluted.

Nagaro acknowledged their responses with a raised hand. "Very good," he said. "Change about and carry on." He turned back to Gedras as the practice resumed. "Is that sufficient?" he inquired seriously. "Will it satisfy the concerns of the Council?"

Gedras had been standing with his mouth open. Hastily he closed it. "Ah, yes... yes... I believe they will be quite satisfied when I tell them what I have seen," he said quickly. "You seem to have things well in hand. I, ah, shan't be troubling you further at this time, Tor Nagaro."

The merchant started to turn away, but Nagaro had just remembered something. "Tor Gedras," he said hurriedly. "There's something I wish to ask you."

The merchant turned back. "What is it?"

Nagaro cleared his throat, suddenly abashed. Still, if he didn't ask now, when would he ever? So he said, all in a rush, "I, ah... I wonder if I might sit with your daughter Berenil," then added, "The eldest one, I mean," just in case he hadn't gotten the names right. He could feel the blood in his face.

Gedras studied Nagaro for a moment, amused and trying not to show it. This young man had men twice his age jumping to his word and calling him "Captain," but asking to sit with a young woman got him flustered. Well, it hadn't been easy when *he*'d done it himself years ago, had it? And Berenil was enough to fluster any man, even if Nagaro didn't know that yet. Gedras resisted the urge to smile and said simply, "Of course you may sit with Berenil. Would tomorrow afternoon be convenient?"

Nagaro swallowed. *Tomorrow afternoon!* "Yes," he managed to say. "Yes, it would. Thank you." He made a small bow then, because he'd been taught to show respect in that way, but already he was feeling a knot of apprehension beginning to form in his stomach.

The merchant gravely returned Nagaro's bow before turning to take his leave.

Turning back to the men, Nagaro saw that Landros was gesturing for his attention.

The old sea warrior cupped a hand to his mouth and shouted over the din. "Timegar wants a demonstration, Captain! Will ye stand a bout with him?"

Nagaro smiled with sudden relief. Here was something he knew how to handle. Raising a hand in acknowledgment, he called a halt to the practice and laughingly accepted a wooden sword from one of the men. Timegar stood ready and waiting. Stepping up to face him, Nagaro raised the practice sword in a formal salute and then came on his guard in one fluid motion.

Gedras paused at the gate leading from the stable yard and stood watching the two men begin to circle and spar with one another. Gedras had never been a swordsman, but he knew Timegar had the reputation of being a good one. The veteran sea warrior might be past fifty, but he hadn't lost his edge, and after two weeks' practice, he was in good fighting form.

Gedras was impressed by the older man, but even more by the speed and grace of the younger one. As he watched, Nagaro scored his third hit and stepped back, lowering his sword to signal that the match was over. The one named Landros gave a shout then, and stepped in beside Timegar. There were shouts of encouragement from the men, and soon another bout began, this time two against one.

Gedras had meant to go, but he found himself lingering, fascinated. The two former warriors seemed at first to have the upper hand. Their efforts kept forcing Nagaro to retreat, step by step, to prevent either man from flanking him. Still, as long as Nagaro could keep both men in front of him, it was apparent that they couldn't break through his guard, try as they might. The battle continued until Nagaro came to a halt with his back against the stable wall, and then of course, the other two men had the advantage, and the bout was soon over as they scored their hits. There was a general cheer from the assembled men as Landros and Timegar stepped forward to shake Nagaro's hand.

Gedras, still standing at the gate, shook his head. "The Prince of Pakoa," he murmured aloud to himself. Someone had called Nagaro that, in jest apparently. But there was something about this young man... *Give him five years, if he lives so long*, thought Gedras, *and he* will *be the Prince of Pakoa*. Berenil could do a good deal worse. Gedras wondered if he should speak to her, then frowned, thinking that perhaps he should instead have warned Nagaro about Berenil. In the end, he decided it was probably best not to meddle.

As he turned to leave, he nearly collided with a piebald pony, its bridle held in the strong brown hand of Tira Zomora. She had dismounted and was leading the animal. The sound of her approach must have been masked by the clash of the practice swords.

Gedras knew the medicine woman by her horse and her dress, if not her face. Though he and his wife had never used the woman's services, he knew better than to be disrespectful to one whose standing among her people rivaled that of the Town Chief or the members of the Council. Accordingly, he gave her a small, stiff nod, and said, "Tira Zomora. Good morning."

"Good morning to ye also, Tor Gedras," she responded, her broad face impassive. Turning to look past him into the stable yard, she added, "The kuma-painted one is no prince *here*."

Gedras fidgeted with a shirt cuff. "Nor anywhere else of course," he said hastily. There was no advantage to arguing with the woman. By way of explanation for his overheard remark, he added, "I merely meant that he fights well."

Her dark eyes came back to him, unreadable. "Yes, he does." It was a flat statement of fact. "But this is not his place." She gave Gedras a stiff nod. "Good day, Zirda." And with that terse courtesy, she mounted her pony, ascending to her strange side-saddle with regal dignity.

Gedras frowned as he watched her ride away. He didn't understand the woman. It occurred to him, as he made his own way home, to wonder how Tira Zomora had known that Nagaro wore kuma stain. He'd supplied the ointment himself, and had scrupulously respected the young man's request not to speak of it to anyone.

Chapter 15

The Ways Of Women

Nagaro sat stiffly in Tor Gedras' parlor on the padded window seat in front of the large bay window. The seat cushion was covered in an elegant satin fabric featuring stripes of rust and gold, and the rest of the room was decorated to match. There was nothing soothing about the colors. Outside, rain pelted down into the cobbled street and pounded a drumbeat on the window glass. There was nothing soothing about the sound either.

Berenil sat beside him, scarcely less stiff than he. The merchant's wife had formally introduced them and made her exit, leaving them to their own devices. Berenil had suggested they sit, and so they had sat, and now the seconds were ticking by. Nagaro stole a glance at her. Her features were pleasing enough, although her nose was perhaps a little too aquiline for ideal beauty. Her mouth was rather thin too, but perhaps it was only the way she held her lips pressed together as if annoyed by something. Her hair was black, and she wore it braided and coiled at the back of her head. The effect was rather elegant, though a little severe. He was aware of the scent of lavender sachet.

She must have felt his eyes, because she started to turn, and he hastily looked away. He was certain she was waiting for him to say something. He swallowed. "Well," he said, venturing to look at her again. "As you see, I have asked your father for a sitting. I hope that's what you intended."

Berenil delivered him a piercing glance. "You took your time about it," she observed tartly. "And of course it's what I intended. What are you, *simple?*"

Nagaro's shoulders tightened. The last word cut him far more than she could know. "I'm sure I am not!" he said indignantly. "How was I to imagine there was any urgency from two words on a bit of paper? And I don't think much of this custom that leaves a man to guess whether his attention is wanted or not, and then requires that he ask permission before he can say three words to a woman. If we'd just been allowed to speak to each other when we passed in the hall, it would have saved a great deal of trouble!"

Berenil's answering laugh was short and mirthless. "Well, *that* is certainly true," she said. "It's a perfectly ridiculous custom that leaves me no choice but to drop a paper note when I merely wish to ask a man a few questions."

"Questions?" Nagaro frowned. "What questions?" Was she going to ask him why he wore a beard and tied his hair? At least they shared a dislike for the custom of sitting. That was something.

She arched a slender black brow. "Are you seeking a wife, Tor Nagaro?"

"*What?*" He was so startled by her directness that the word slipped out before he could stop it. "I mean," he said hastily, "if you're asking whether I hope to marry some day, when I find the right woman, then the answer is yes."

Berenil gave a sharp little nod. "Very good," she said. "You are seeking a wife— and I am seeking a husband— a *proper* sort of husband, that is."

Nagaro swallowed. "Ah... proper?" The conversation was not going at all the way he'd expected. He wondered whether all the young women on Pakoa were so direct. Did the custom of sitting make them so?

Berenil was regarding him critically. "Yes, proper," she said. "One that is sensible, steady, responsible, and who has a respectable trade. You don't *really* intend to go through with that plan to sail off in a ship to hunt Mahuk warships, do you?"

Nagaro's stiff posture became noticeably stiffer. "Yes, I do."

And now Berenil's slim black brows came together in a delicate frown. "But Father said you were sensible. Why on earth would a sensible man do such a thing?" She asked with what sounded like genuine perplexity.

Nagaro was frowning now as well. "For one thing, I made a promise," he answered seriously. "I swore to the men that I would be their captain, and I can't very well go back on my word."

Berenil gestured dismissively. "You men and your *honor*," she said. "This is foolishness. Perhaps that's what *they* want of you, but what do *you* want, Tor Nagaro?"

"To free slaves," he said curtly. He didn't care at all for the way she brushed the entire concept of honor aside with a wave of her hand.

"*Free slaves?*" She stared at him in utter incomprehension. "But you can't possibly hope to free more than a handful— out of all the hundreds that there must be. And you're likely to be killed, trying! It makes no sense to risk your life for such a thing."

This time Nagaro's eyes flashed. "I *know* I may be killed," he said sharply. "But it's a risk worth taking to do even a little good in the world! You have no idea what it's like to be a slave. To be without hope—"

But Berenil was shaking her head at him. "I think you are quite mad," she declared. "And I certainly have no intention of marrying a man who would waste his life on such folly. And after Father offered you a respectable position, too!"

This was too much. Nagaro stood up. "In that case," he said coldly, "I think I had best be going. And you needn't worry that I will trouble you again."

Five minutes later, he was outside in the rain, striding up the street with his head bent low under the hood of his cloak. He had managed to observe the polite formalities in taking his leave of Tira Delmanei because it was the way he'd been brought up. Inside, however, his mind was a roiling sea of indignation shot through with bitter disappointment. He had dared to hope he would like Berenil, that she would like him, and that love might have grown between them. It could have been an uncomplicated courtship, too, since Gedras seemed to have a favorable impression of him.

Instead he'd found that he didn't like Berenil at all! The woman was entirely mercenary. *Why*, he wondered, had she bothered to write him that note if she so completely disapproved of what he had chosen to do?

***

When Nagaro put the same question to Taru and Pavo that evening, his friends' responses surprised him.

"But Nagaro," Taru exclaimed. "It's a *good* sign if she doesn't want ye t' risk your neck."

Pavo nodded. "Yes. She maybe do not want you to get hurt because she like you. Tenepti talk to me like that too."

Nagaro stared. "Tenepti *talked* to you, Pavo? When? How did you manage it?"

Pavo smiled broadly. "It have happen only yesterday," he said. "Tenepti sister, Matahi, ask for Tenepti to visit her house. I wait outside gate in garden wall, and Tenepti sit by gate on inside. So we talk with only gate in between!"

Nagaro laughed. "That's wonderful, Pavo! Thank goodness Matahi likes you, even if her father doesn't."

"Oh yes!" Pavo beamed. "Matahi think I am best thing ever happen for Tenepti. She think her father have it all wrong to keep us from see each other."

Nagaro knew that Matahi had started serving as Pavo's go-between, since she had turned out to be acquainted with Yuli's younger daughter, Luweda. A number of messages had been passed back and forth between Tenepti and Pavo by way of Matahi, Luweda, and Yuli— passed by spoken word, since none of those involved could write. The tryst Pavo had just described represented a significant improvement in communication between the sweethearts.

Nagaro was therefore very glad to learn of the meeting, but he frowned at what else Pavo had said. He cast a worried glance at his friend. "Do you mean that Tenepti doesn't want you to sail with us, Pavo?"

Pavo immediately looked very serious. "She say 'Oh no, please do not go, Pavo! I am afraid you will be killed.' But I tell her I want to go, and it is very good thing to do to make slave free. And now she understand."

"Ye see, Nagaro?" put in Taru. "That's the way women are when they care about a man. That's probably all Berenil was on about."

Nagaro shook his head. "I don't think so," he said. "She plainly thinks it makes no sense to do what we plan to do, and she doesn't want to marry a man who isn't sensible. She was quite clear about it."

Taru cast his eyes heavenward. "Nagaro," he said. "When are ye going t' learn that women don't say what they mean?"

Nagaro frowned. "Well some of them don't," he conceded, thinking of Jila. "But some of them surely *do*. Probably most of them. I'm sure my Lady Marmine always meant what *she* said."

Taru brushed this aside. "It's *different* when they're being *mothers.*"

Nagaro's frown deepened. "Well, *I* meant what *I* said—"

"Oh, ye mustn't do *that,*" Taru interrupted. "Ye'll let on too much. Ye mustn't say what ye mean on account o' *she's* not saying what *she* means, ye see."

Nagaro passed a hand over his eyes. "Taru," he said. "Did it ever occur to you that if a woman isn't speaking plainly to you, it might be because she thinks you're not speaking plainly to her? And how are a man and a woman ever to come to an understanding if they don't say what they mean? Pavo and Tenepti are speaking plainly to each other—" He turned to Pavo. "Aren't you?"

"Oh, yes!" Pavo was emphatic.

Taru was obviously unimpressed. "Well that's all right for *them,* I suppose, but I still say Berenil doesn't want ye going after Mahuk ships because she fancies ye."

Nagaro sighed. "Well it seems to *me* that she thinks I'm either a madman or a fool," he declared. "And I'm certainly not going back to ask her if I'm right. I didn't really like her very much anyway."

Taru rolled his eyes, but apparently decided not to continue the argument.

***

There was so much to do, between sword practice and making the ship ready, that Nagaro had little time to dwell on his encounter with Berenil in any case. The oar deck of the *Sword of Freedom* had to be thoroughly cleaned and scrubbed, and a new coat of varnish applied to the rowing benches. The varnish was donated by the ship's chandler who employed Neved's father. The boy's ankle had healed very well, but the father had struggled to complete the payment, and his employer's generosity allowed Tredhold to consider the debt settled. The men were all very grateful for it as well. No one had liked the idea of sitting on those benches very much. The varnish made the benches seem new, and it was much cheaper than replacing them.

So the days passed.

Idrin came and went with a significant snowfall, but no greater misfortune. It was shortly after the turning of the year that Taru presented Nagaro with the black and white sword banner that Tulara had sewn, and informed him that Yuli had hired the young woman as kitchen help and general house-maid.

Nagaro looked forward to meeting the girl who had made the ship's flag, but nearly two weeks went by before he finally got more than a passing glimpse of her.

It was late one afternoon in the middle of the month of Genorel and threatening snow, and he'd just finished cleaning the stable. Being chilled, and thirsty from the work, he decided to go in through the kitchen to get a cup of hot sothiril. As he rounded the corner of the building, he came upon Tulara, drawing water from the cistern in the kitchen garden.

The young Turowa had filled one bucket, which was standing on the ground at her feet, and was ladling water into a second one balanced precariously on the edge of the cistern. She wore no gloves and had only a shawl wrapped around her for warmth. Nagaro approached her. "Here," he said, reaching for the balanced bucket. "Let me help you with that."

She started so violently that the bucket would have tipped over into the cistern if Nagaro hadn't been steadying it with his hand.

"*Mercy!*" she exclaimed. Then she turned and froze, staring at him wide-eyed and apparently tongue-tied.

She was very young, with wide-set brown eyes in a face that had a fragile prettiness. The chill wind was tugging at her loosely-bound dark hair.

"I'm sorry, Zirdyn" he said hastily. "I didn't mean to startle you."

When Tulara continued to stare at him without speaking, he began to feel uncomfortable. He glanced at the bucket. It was only half full. "I can fill this more quickly," he ventured, and taking the bucket with both hands, he scooped it full of water by dipping it into the cistern. He set it down, dripping, beside the other bucket. "There," he said, straightening.

She had stopped staring at him but was now looking at the ground, instead. "Thank ye, Zirda," she murmured with downcast eyes.

He saw that she was shivering. She was unusually slender for a Turowa. She appeared so delicate, in fact, that he doubted she could carry both of the heavy buckets of water at once. She might, he thought, manage one by lifting it with both hands. "Look," he said. "Why don't I just carry them in for you, since I'm going that way."

Tulara's head came up then, her eyes wide with alarm. "Oh no, Tor Nagaro," she cried. "Ye mustn't do that! It's my task, and ye're a guest o' the house."

Nagaro had to laugh. "That's ridiculous," he said easily. "They're very heavy for you, and it's no trouble for me. It's very cold out here, and it would take you much longer to make two trips." He lifted the two buckets by their handles and set off for the kitchen door. "Besides," he added over his shoulder. "Didn't they tell you? I'm the stableman."

Tulara came after him, skipping to keep up, and murmuring, "No, no... Zirda... please..."

The kitchen was warm and bright and filled with the savory aroma of fish stew emanating from a large pot over the fire. Nagaro set the buckets down just inside the kitchen door. "There," he said. And then, in an effort at humor, he added, "Now you can struggle with them as much as you like."

Tulara had come in after him, and now she bobbed him an awkward curtsy. "Thank ye, Zirda," she said in a low voice, with her gaze glued to the floor.

Nagaro frowned, puzzled. "You did a very fine job of sewing the ship's banner," he ventured. "It's quite beautiful."

That earned him a single furtive glance before she dropped her eyes again, murmuring something inaudible. Then, a little louder, she said, "I... I... I'd best get some more wood from the woodshed." And turning without looking at him, she pushed the door open and vanished back into the frigid evening. A gust of wind banged the door shut behind her.

Nagaro stood staring blankly at the closed door for a moment. Then turning, he found Yuli watching him from across the kitchen. "There's hot sothiril in the kettle," she observed nodding towards the open fireplace. "Ye can help yourself." When he continued to hesitate, she added, "There's no sense standing there. She'll not be coming back in as long as she thinks ye might still be in the kitchen. She'll find something needed in the shed, I expect."

"I don't understand, Yuli," Nagaro frowned as he fetched a mug from the cupboard and crossed to the fireplace to fill it. "She acts as if she's afraid of me."

Yuli sighed. "It's not fear. It's guilt."

He looked up from pouring his sothiril. "*Guilt?* But why?"

"It's that business with Jila." Yuli crossed to the fireplace to stir the kettle of stew. "Tulara didn't do what Taru asked her to that night, and things turned out badly— so she feels guilty about it."

Nagaro stood with his hands cupped around the steaming mug. "I made my own mistakes that night," he said. "I'm certainly not angry with Tulara. From what Taru said, she didn't want to trick me, and I can't blame her for that." He went to the table and sat down with his cup.

Yuli was studying the stew pot as she stirred. "There's more," she said quietly. "Tulara knew that Jila had found ye that night, and she could ha' told Taru, but she didn't. That's why he didn't find out 'til morning."

Nagaro frowned. This was something new. "Do you know *why* she didn't tell him what she knew?"

Yuli sighed. "It gets a mite complicated." She looked up at him. "Tulara thinks the world o' Taru, ye see. She near t' worships him. Seems she never had a lot o'... customers... bein' so shy an' all." Yuli sighed. She stirred the stew absently. "She was barely scratching a living, I think, afore she met Taru. And after she met him, she just stopped takin' any others."

"I think I understand." Nagaro studied the cup of sothiril, untouched on the table in front of him.

Yuli nodded. "Aye," she said. "Tulara was afraid ye'd take her interest seriously if she did what Taru asked, and she didn't want ye to. And it hurt her that Taru was so willing to... *share* her with ye. She hoped he had feelings for her."

Nagaro raised a questioning eyebrow. "Does he?"

Yuli sampled the stew, frowned slightly, then crossed the kitchen to get the salt. "The way *I* read it, Taru's quite taken with Tulara, but won't admit it," she said. "It was Taru that came t' see me about hiring Tulara. And he fetched her over t' talk to me about it too. He nearly had t' drag her. She didn't think she *deserved* this kind o' position. And I've noticed how he looks at her— follows her with his eyes, he does."

Nagaro picked up his sothiril and took a long drink while he considered this revelation. He remembered what Taru had said— about not saying what you meant and not letting on too much. He drew a long sigh as he set down his cup. “He hasn’t said anything to Pavo or me, but I’m not sure he would. I’m afraid he probably isn’t ready to settle down yet either. I think he will be in time. At least I know his father did. Tulara may have to wait quite a while though.”

Yuli sighed in her turn. “Well,” she said, with a significant cock of her head, “Taru had better not keep her waiting *too* long. She’ll wake up one day and see that there's other young men in the world.”

Nagaro sat frowning. His normal inclination would have been to try to break through Tulara’s shyness, to reassure her that he wasn’t angry with her. But now it seemed he might risk getting in his friend’s way if he did that. *Best to keep his distance instead...*

Yuli had returned to tending the stew pot while he sat thinking. Now she turned and waggled her stirring spoon at him. “I'd be obliged if ye’d finish your sothiril, Tor Nagaro,” she said with mock severity. “I need my new kitchen help back in here afore it’s time t’ serve this stew.”

Nagaro smiled wryly. He gulped his sothiril, rose, and put his cup in the wash tub. At the doorway leading to the common room he paused and turned back. “Yuli,” he said. “How did Tulara ever come to be a tavern woman in the first place? She doesn’t seem at all the kind to take up that sort of work.”

Yuli eyed him uncomfortably. “It was her mother’s trade... years ago,” she said carefully. “So when her mother died, sudden, last spring, leavin’ her to fend for herself, Tulara naturally turned to it. I guess she didn’t think she was fit for anything else.”

Nagaro frowned. “What about her father?”

Yuli’s mouth set into a hard line. “Tavern women don’t go lookin’ for the father,” she said tersely. “Even supposin’ they knew who it was.” She paused for a moment. Then she said, “Tulara’s mother gave up the trade a few years after Tulara was born— when she got married. Her husband’s still living, but he’s only willing t’ look after his own get. He always let Tulara know he thought she was trash ‘cause o’ how she was gotten, and he’ll have nothing t’ do with her now that her mother’s gone.”

“Oh.” Nagaro looked at the floor. He almost wished he hadn’t asked since there was nothing he could do about any of it. Taru had told him that if one of the tavern women found herself with child, she “just took care of it,” or at least didn’t trouble the man involved. He looked up, meeting Yuli’s gaze. “I’m glad you hired Tulara,” he said. “You’ve done a good thing, Tira Yuli.” He turned, then, and left the kitchen, not waiting for her response.

Chapter 16

News From Lankura

More busy weeks passed for the former slaves and the other men who had chosen to join them. Sword practice continued, more inside than out, interspersed as weather permitted with mending the ship's sails and rigging, which had taken damage in the storm that had covered their Jaamra escape. Nagaro kept what Yuli had told him about Taru and Tulara in his mind, but if Taru had any special interest in the young Turowa, he kept it to himself. Once Pavo asked Taru quite innocently why he no longer went so often to the tavern. Taru simply shrugged. "I was spending my money too fast," was his response.

Dakuro had given Nagaro his price for forging a sword, based on his first experiment. Nagaro made a calculation and ordered five more. That number would use all the money they could spare, and it would be hard enough for the blacksmith to produce so many before the end of the spring. Nagaro had to hope it would be enough.

When the weather warmed and the storms let up near the end of Madrel, the men set about careening the ship. There was a primitive sort of dry dock for this purpose at the shallow southern side of the harbor. It consisted of nothing more than a number of pairs of pilings sunk deep in the sand. The *Sword of Freedom* was carefully guided in between the pilings at high tide and made fast on one side. As the tide ebbed, the ship heeled over, and one side of her barnacle-encrusted hull was exposed for the men to work on with scrapers until the tide came in again. When one side of the hull was clean, the ship could be tied up on the other side so she heeled the other way. Nagaro, Taru, and Pavo all worked along with the rest, and it took many days to finish the task.

It was early in Evrel, and the *Sword of Freedom* was still lying in the dry dock, when the first merchant ship of the season, the *Steady Hand*, sailed into Pakoa Harbor. The captain of the vessel was perhaps surprised to see a war galley of unfamiliar colors in the harbor, but not unduly dismayed.

The *Sword* must be a friendly craft if she was making use of Pakoa's dry dock, and she was quite helpless there besides.

The merchant ship's crew came ashore to avail themselves of the town's amenities, especially the tavern and the inn. So of course they heard the tale of the *Sword of Freedom*, of her remarkable young captain, and the unlikely purpose for which she was being readied. Hearing of the daily sword practice, some of the merchant seamen came to the stable yard to see for themselves. They came to laugh, stayed to watch, and left impressed.

The *Steady Hand* brought goods from the mainland and a pair of merchant's agents, potential buyers for anything Pakoa's folk had to sell. Nagaro made contact with one of them through Gedras and was able to sell a few small gold trinkets, adding substantially to the funds he and his men had at their disposal. The former slaves who had chosen to sail on the *Sword* all agreed to pool their shares for the purpose, and even after he'd distributed shares to Obedo, Kunoa, and Simion, Nagaro calculated there was enough money to buy three or four weeks of provisions for the ship. These could be made to last longer on tight rations, but it wouldn't be enough to last through the summer, and he knew that most of the men who followed him were running low on their personal funds because of the contributions they had made to purchasing swords and re-fitting the ship.

Nagaro concluded that they could make one voyage without having to resort to charity, but the future of the entire undertaking would hinge on whether they had success during that single voyage. He freely shared these concerns with the other men since he disliked deception. Landros, Tredhold, and Mendorel all listened seriously, but most of the others— including even Taru and Pavo— seemed confident that luck or the Spirits were on their side and success would surely come to them. Nagaro was much less sanguine, and the matter preyed heavily on his mind.

Help ultimately came from an unexpected quarter. The *Steady Hand* stayed for more than a week, while the agents aboard her conducted their business. On the evening before the day she was to sail, Nagaro was in his room, having come in to get his cloak, when he heard a knock at the door. It was a light knock, a little hesitant.

Upon opening the door, Nagaro found himself staring into Simion's deep blue eyes. "Oh," he said, surprised. "Good evening, Simion."

The young man's elfin face was set in somber lines. "May I come in?" he asked, and added apologetically, "I swear it will be only for a minute."

"Yes, of course." Nagaro stepped back to allow Simion to enter. As he closed the door behind the young man, he glanced both ways along the hallway, feeling a wash of guilty relief to see that it was quite deserted. But then, Simion would have seen to that.

"I'm leaving," Simion said abruptly. "I've bought passage on the *Steady Hand*. I... I wanted to give you these before I left."

For the first time, Nagaro noticed that the young Kelorin was carrying two objects, which he now held out in offering. One was his Mahuk sword in its scabbard. The other was a leather purse. "I was going to keep the sword," Simion went on, "but I won't have any use for it where I'm going, and you'll need every blade you can get."

Nagaro accepted the offered sword. "Thank you, Simion," he said quite sincerely. Then, rather more hesitantly, he reached for the purse. The coins in it clinked as he grasped it. It was quite heavy. He met the young man's gaze with a questioning look. "Simion, are you sure?"

Simion's nod was quick and emphatic. "I haven't spent much," he said hastily. "I have enough for my journey. This is only what I won't need. It's to help provision the ship."

Nagaro's first impulse was to hand the purse back— to tell Simion he should keep his money in case he needed it, but something in the young man's face stopped him. "Thank you, Simion," he said again instead, and read gratitude in the young man's eyes. He laid both sword and purse on the table. "Where are you going?" he asked as he turned back to the young Kelorin.

A look of pain, mingled with longing, crossed Simion's face. "Home," he said quietly. "Back to Lankura. Back to Brandle, if he'll have me. I know he loved me once... If only he'll forgive me for having left him..."

"Oh." Nagaro felt as if he'd walked into a bedchamber unbidden. "I'm sure your parents will be glad to know you're safe," he added quickly.

The pain in Simion's eyes increased. "My mother will be... but my father..." His voice was bitter and his words trailed off. He looked away.

Nagaro wished he hadn't raised the subject. His stomach twisted in sympathy as he sought for other words that might help, even if only a little. "You fought well, Simion," he said seriously. "You did everything I needed you to do. From what I saw, you have nothing to be ashamed of."

Simion gave him another grateful glance. "But it's true what they all say," he said ruefully. "I wasn't meant to be a warrior. I can't kill a man."

Nagaro shook his head. "That," he said, "is nothing to be ashamed of either, Simion. I wish that I could say the same."

Simion's countenance registered disbelief. He searched Nagaro's face for some trace of dissembling, but found none. "Thank you for your kindness," he murmured, dropping his eyes. "All of it. And I'm sorry to have caused you trouble."

Nagaro shook his head. "I've been no more kind than anyone ought to be. It's only because so many are so unkind that it seems otherwise. And you haven't caused me any trouble."

Simion's head came up. "But I have! There was talk, even if you didn't hear it. And it wasn't your fault at all! You never did anything to give me hope—" Simion checked himself, then blurted, "I've been such a fool!"

Nagaro felt himself blush scarlet at this proof of the feelings Simion still harbored for him. "Well, if you have, you've at least been an inconspicuous one," he offered, through his embarrassment. "*I* made a fool of myself with a woman, and the whole island knows it."

Simion looked stricken. "You wouldn't have had to break the ban if it hadn't been for what I—"

"I didn't *have* to do anything, Simion." Nagaro cut across the young man's words. "I made a mistake. And the main reason had nothing to do with you at all."

Simion searched his face again, and finally shook his head. "You're much too kind," he said in a tone between incredulity and reverence. "And much too good. There's nobody like you." The young Kelorin shook himself then, and before Nagaro could protest, he added, "I know you'll be just as good to Nanu and Chaheel."

"To Nanu and Chaheel...?" It took a moment for Simion's meaning to dawn on him. When it did, Nagaro had trouble believing it. "Nanu? And... and *Chaheel?*" he stammered. "Are you *sure?*"

Simion nodded ruefully. "I found out by accident. They've been very discreet. Please don't tell them I told you."

"No, of course not." Nagaro was still stunned.

Simion shuffled his feet awkwardly, then said, "I'd best be going." Turning, he made for the door.

Nagaro recovered in time to say, "Goodbye, Simion. Good luck. And a safe journey."

Simion hesitated with his hand on the door handle, and turned back one last time. His deep blue eyes were very bright. "Won't you tell me your name?" he asked. "Your real name— the one you had before?"

Nagaro froze.

Simion was looking at him pleadingly. To the young Kelorin it must seem only a small confidence, but Nagaro felt his world begin to tilt. *What should he do?* If he turned down the request, he would seem untrusting or unkind, but if he divulged his secret, he had no idea what might come of it. *Still...* he did at least know that Simion was good at keeping secrets—and was also no stranger to ridicule. For the space of several heartbeats time hung poised while Nagaro teetered on a knife-edge and Simion held him with his intense blue gaze.

At last Nagaro drew a decisive breath. "It's not my name anymore," he said huskily, his mouth as dry as dust. "If I tell you, you must never use it. And you must promise not to tell another living soul."

Simion's eyes widened. "I promise."

Nagaro swallowed. "It was..." he began, and stopped. His throat felt tight, as if he were going to weep. "It was... *Leyel...*" He couldn't bring himself to say the whole of it, but he didn't have to. He watched Simion's face— saw the young man's expression pass from initial puzzlement, to startled realization, to shocked disbelief.

"*That's* why I thought I had seen you somewhere," Simion breathed. "Such a face is not to be forgotten. Or such grace—" He must have read the mounting horror in Nagaro's eyes for he bit off his words. "I thought it such a shame, that you... that *he*... was simple— But... *how?*" Simion's face and voice registered utter bafflement. "How can this be? *What happened to you?*"

Nagaro shook his head, desperately. "No! No more questions— *please!*"

He saw the light of sympathy flare, then, in Simion's eyes— a glow like firelight on a winter's eve.

The young man abruptly pulled himself erect, and his hand snapped up in a Fleet warrior's salute. "Then farewell, Captain Nagaro," he said with fervent formality. "And thank you again— for everything." Then he turned, and was gone. The door swung shut behind him with a soft click of the latch.

For a long moment, Nagaro stood where Simion had left him, waiting for his heart to slow to something like a normal pace. *Why had Simion asked him that, of all things? And why had he answered?*

***

Later, when he came to count the money in the purse, Nagaro was astonished to find that it came almost to Simion's entire share of the *Fist's* bounty. The young Kelorin had paid for his room and board by doing the innkeeper's bookkeeping. He must have lived very frugally otherwise, for the amount not accounted for came to no more than the price of two suits of clothes and the passage to Kel Tierna. Nagaro sincerely hoped that Simion had taken enough with him to see himself safely on his overland journey to Lankura, and that his family would take him in when he got there.

Even Moraga and Gurd didn't have a single harsh word to say about Simion when Nagaro told his followers of the young man's generosity. The money Simion had given to them was enough to provision the ship for another three or four weeks. Their resources that could previously have been made to serve for up to two months now might be stretched to almost four. They could afford to make two voyages now instead of one, and their opportunities to find success had just been doubled.

Nagaro relaxed a little after that. Although Simion's gift didn't solve all of the problems he could foresee, he resolved not to dwell on the rest of them, and threw himself into the continued training of the men. He wanted them to be ready to sail by the end of Medrin. He also turned to Pavo Maat to teach him more words and phrases in Hashti, thinking it would be useful to be able to say something besides "Put down your sword" to the Mautep warriors he would face. He pursued this study with dogged patience, though he knew he would still to have to rely on Pavo as a translator.

***

It was truly spring now. Evrel and Medrin brought other merchant ships to the island, the *Rose of Harmoth* first, and later the *Bountiful* out of Lankura, and others after that. Nagaro failed to sell any more gold jewelry outright, but he did find a merchant's agent on the *Rose of Harmoth* who undertook to carry away several pieces and try to sell them, for a ten percent commission, in the ports where the *Rose* would call.

Ships meant not only trade, but also news, and an opportunity to send letters. Mendorel had bought a pen, ink, and paper, and had sent a missive to his family aboard the *Steady Hand*. He and the few others who were literate found their skills in demand to pen letters for the majority who were not, since all who had kin in the world wished to inform them of their miraculous deliverance— as well as their summer plans. Mendorel's quill pen and bottle of ink were passed from hand to hand, and none of the long-lost men seemed to care how long they might have to wait for a reply.

Landros wrote a letter to his daughters in Lankura, to be carried away on the *Bountiful*, while the *Rose of Harmoth* left carrying two letters from Tredhold. One was addressed to Tredhold's father in Harmoth. The healer declined to say for whom the second letter was intended, but Nagaro couldn't help noticing how long the Leithian sat over it with the pen poised in his hand and an uncharacteristically wistful expression on his face.

When Nagaro learned that the *Bountiful* would be visiting the mainland's coast, north of Lankura, he suggested to Taru that they send a letter to Gama. Taru readily agreed and dictated the contents, marveling at the way Nagaro's hand propelled the pen in quick sure strokes across the paper.

"Ye make it look so easy," he said with a sigh.

Nagaro shrugged. "I've been doing it since I was a boy."

Taru rubbed his chin. "Do ye want t' add anything?"

"I don't think so. You seem to have said everything there is to say." In fact, Taru's description of Nagaro's role in winning their freedom had seemed to him a bit too glowing, and he had surreptitiously made some adjustments to the wording.

Taru scratched his ear and looked uncomfortable. "What about Aramei?" he asked cautiously. "Don't ye want t' know if she's still waiting for ye?"

Nagaro frowned. "It's been more than two years," he said. "And she didn't seem to want to have anything more to do with me."

"All right then." Taru shrugged. He reached for the paper. "I just thought of one more thing, but I can write it myself. It'll be good practice. I can seal it and carry it t' the ship too. Ye go on and take your ride before it get's dark."

Nagaro agreed, glad to see Taru so eager to practice the skill he had taught him.

***

The preparations continued through Medrin's balmy days. With the *Sword of Freedom* out of dry dock and refitted, it was time to test her crew's sea-craft with small maneuvers inside the confines of Pakoa Harbor. Half the men had never been slaves and needed to learn the ways of a warship's oar deck. Many of those who were fishermen also needed instruction in manning the rigging of such a large vessel.

It was a good time for Nagaro. He was busy with something that he cared about, and making good progress with it. The month would have been quite unmarred were it not for a single piece of the news that came from Lankura.

There had been earlier news on Pakoa, beginning with rumors that had reached them the previous autumn, so much of what came on the ships that spring was only elaboration of what they already knew. The aftermath of the plague was still being felt on the mainland. The contagion itself had run its course by the end of the previous summer, but it had carried off so many that there was scarcely a soul on the Main who hadn't lost a family member, a friend, or an acquaintance. Things had been the worst in the south, closest to Jinara whence the plague had come. Harvests had been small the previous summer and fall, and the production of most other goods had been depressed, owing to the loss of skilled labor.

There had been a lull in the war with Jinara, by necessity, since both sides had been short of men and supplies to support the conflict. There seemed little doubt, however, that hostilities would soon resume. All of this information was of only indirect concern to the townspeople, because Pakoa, like most of the islands, had entirely escaped the plague and was not generally called upon to supply men-at-arms. The principal local concern was whether the tax levied by the Crown in the fall would again be heavier than usual, as the king sought to make up for shortfalls from the mainland at the expense of the islands, which the plague had largely spared.

Other news that came on the ships that spring was of more interest, at least to some. Yuli was always more interested in people than in politics. Like Taru's mother, Olomi, she relished hearing about the lives of noble women at the court in Lankura. Many of the seamen who came to eat and drink in the common room of the Bay Tree Inn knew Yuli, and they delighted in bringing her tidbits of gossip from the court, which she in turn delighted in sharing with anyone inclined to listen. While Nagaro didn't share her general interest, there was one lady in Lankura whose welfare did concern him, and Yuli's curiosity now played to his advantage since Princess Nevien was one of her favorites.

By early Medrin, Nagaro had learned that the queen and the princess both had labored in the sick-houses during the plague, tending the poor folk of Lankura who were taken ill. The princess had, herself, been stricken, but had recovered fully. He'd also learned that in the early days of their marriage, the princess's husband, Gillard Marchent, had been away at the battle front in Jinara. With the interruption of the war, however, he'd come home, having avoided contracting the plague himself.

But Nagaro had yet to learn the worst.

It was on an evening in the latter part of Medrin, with the planned departure date for their voyage just two weeks away, and Nagaro, Taru, and Pavo were eating dinner in the common room. Pavo was quizzing Nagaro on his Hashti as the three devoured platefuls of fish fritters, green onions, and fried potatoes. Nagaro had just succeeded in getting through the recital of a particularly challenging phrase.

"You have say that very good, Nagaro," Pavo told him. "I have to think hard what I am go to ask you next."

As Nagaro awaited Pavo's next query, Yuli's raised voice came to his ears from a nearby table.

"Gillard seems like a very wicked man," she was saying. "It's a pity the plague didn't take him."

"Aye, that it is," replied the seaman with whom she was speaking, a gray-haired, bewhiskered Kelorin with a weathered, kuma-stained face. "There'd be no tears wasted in Lankura on Gillard's account, I can tell ye that."

"How has he been treating her?" Yuli inquired. "There haven't been any more bruises, have there?"

Nagaro stiffened. It was the first he had heard of any bruises, and he didn't like what it implied. He was sitting with his back to the other table, which was fortunate since it meant that neither Yuli nor the sailor could possibly have seen his expression. Taru and Pavo were seated across from him, however, and they saw it quite plainly.

"No... At least none that folk have *seen*." The seaman was speaking again. "But there's been talk. She goes about with her neck covered all the time, no matter what the weather— which ain't natural. And of course there's the scar—"

Nagaro had been about to take a drink of sothiril, but froze with his cup in his hand and a feeling like a lump of ice in his stomach.

Across from him, Taru hastily swallowed the mouthful he'd been chewing. "*Just don't listen, Nagaro,*" he hissed.

Pavo looked worriedly from one friend to the other.

"*Scar?*" Yuli asked. She sounded alarmed. "What scar?"

"It's just a small one." The sailor seemed in a hurry to reassure her. "On the side of her face. They say it don't hardly spoil her good looks, but it don't seem likely that she came by it in any natural way, if ye know what I mean."

Nagaro hadn't moved. Anger was filling him up like black bile.

Yuli's tone turned sharp when she spoke next. "And what is the poor child's father doing about this?"

"The king? He don't seem t' see. Or he turns a blind eye."

"But what of her mother? Surely our dear queen must be pleading for her daughter!"

"Ah, well, ye never know if Semrel even knows about it. Elgurn shields his queen from everything..."

By this time, Nagaro had begun to fear that he would choke on his rage if he didn't let it erupt into action— which would, of course, be disastrous.

He shouldn't listen anymore... shouldn't stay in the room...

He set his cup down, harder than he intended, and stood up so quickly that his stool nearly tipped over. Scarcely seeing the alarmed looks on his friends' faces, and completely forgetting his unfinished dinner, he turned and struck off across the common room, making for the doorway at the other end of the room that led to the stairs. He brushed past Yuli, avoiding her eyes and those of the man she was speaking to.

Taru and Pavo exchanged looks, hastily gulped down the last of their food, and went after their friend.

***

Nagaro's feet carried him automatically up the stairs and along the hallway while he held onto a rage that threatened to sweep him away like a western gale.

...bruises... a *scar on the side of her face... Gillard was abusing her— and the king did nothing!*

Once safely in the bedroom with the door securely closed, he eased his iron grip on his temper— only to find himself still severely thwarted. He wanted so very badly to smash something, but every stick of furniture in the room belonged to the inn! He couldn't allow himself to do damage to things that belonged to Yuli and Ramu.

When Taru and Pavo arrived, they found him pacing like a wild beast in a cage, swinging his fists at the air in impotent fury.

It was Taru who entered the room first. "Ah...Nagaro..." he began, with the hesitancy of a man approaching a hissing serpent.

Nagaro spun around to face him, eyes blazing. "*He's hurting her!*" he exploded. "I should have known he would! That *vile, vicious cur!* That *monster!* That *horrible, evil, disgusting brute!* That... that... that—" Nagaro's vocabulary was failing him. His upbringing had been far too gentle for this work.

Pavo had never seen Nagaro so angry before, and he came to a halt just inside the doorway, throwing Taru an agonized look that silently implored his friend to *do something.*

Taru *had* seen something like this before, and he was intensely grateful that this time it wasn't directed at *him.* He took a breath and metaphorically waded in. Physically, he kept his distance. "I'm sorry ye had t' hear that, Nagaro," he said, soothingly. "It's a bloody shame, I know. But there's nothing ye can do about it—"

"*You said that before!*" Nagaro stabbed a forefinger at Taru, causing the young Turo to reflexively back up two paces. "You said it on the ship after the Mautep took us! But I'm not chained to bulkhead anymore! *And I have a sword!*"

Taru re-gathered himself and spread his hands. "Well, aye, that's *true...* but what d' ye think ye're going t' *do* with that sword?" he inquired reasonably.

Nagaro faltered. *Why did Taru have to bring up these awkward details?* "I don't know!" He ran a distracted hand through his hair. "I'll... I'll go to Lankura... I'll fight him. They say he's good, but—"

"Ye'll *fight* him?" Taru checked himself, and lowered his voice. "How d' ye think ye can do that, Nagaro? What would ye say t' him? That she's *your* wife, and ye want her *back?*"

And that stopped Nagaro dead.

"*Bishka!*" He swore. *Because he knew he couldn't do that... couldn't go back there... couldn't let the world know who he was... what he'd been...* His shoulders sagged. "*No*—" He choked on the word. "I can't go back. But I should do *something*.. .something to help her..."

But Taru shook his head. "*Why?*" he asked. "It's not *your* fault what's happening, Nagaro. This isn't your fight. Ye have t' let her father handle it."

Which was unfortunately exactly the wrong thing to say because it brought back Nagaro's anger in a blinding blaze.

"*You heard what that man said, Taru!*" he raged. "*Elgurn isn't doing anything!*"

Taru retreated again, coming up against Pavo's hovering figure, even as he threw up his hands. "By all the Spirits, Nagaro!" he cried in exasperation. "Be *reasonable!* What if ye did kill Lord Gillard? The other lords'd never let ye just walk away! Ye *know* that! Ye know it'd be the death of ye! And besides," he added. "Ye promised the men ye'd be their captain."

Just at that moment, the possibility of dying in such a just cause didn't feel like much of a deterrent, but Taru's final point struck home.

"*Keshaal!*" Nagaro put all of his stifled fury into the word. *He had promised, hadn't he?*

For a moment he stood with his teeth clamped together, his fists clenched, staring at his friends. Then he very deliberately uncurled his fingers and a shudder ran through him.

"*I'm going for a walk!*" he snarled.

Striding past Taru and the gaping Pavo, he yanked his cloak from its hook on the wall and stamped out, slamming the door behind him so hard that it threatened to split the wood.

It was several seconds after Nagaro's abrupt departure before either of his friends moved or spoke.

Then Pavo found his voice. "Nagaro will not go to Lankura?" he asked.

Taru let out a pent-up breath. "Of course not. He's got too much sense for that."

There was a pause before Pavo said hesitantly, "I do not understand why he is so angry. I thought you have tell me he do not love this princess."

"He doesn't." Taru wiped his brow with a hand that shook, went to one of the chairs that stood by the table, and sank down onto it. "It's just the way Nagaro is made," he explained "Whenever he hears about something that's not right, he wants t' stop it. He just needs t' cool down, that's all."

***

Nagaro sat in the deep blue shade of descending evening, cross-legged on the cold rock floor of the stone seat, his cloak wrapped around his shoulders. He didn't really need the cloak. The night wasn't that cold, but the cloak was the same gray as the rock, and he felt invisible shrouded in it, as if he were a part of the place. Below him the town lay spread, a few lights winking in windows as folk moved through the rituals of evening that led to comfortable beds and peaceful slumber. Beyond the town lay the harbor, in the midst of which the ship they had boldly named the *Sword of Freedom* rode at anchor, all black and silver in a swath of moonlight. A merchant ship lay there too, but she was nearer, made fast to the wharf where the warm light from a pair of lanterns gilded her masts and spars.

Nagaro's anger had passed from white-hot fury to the smoldering red of lingering outrage. Taru was right. Taru was generally right, he reflected, when it came to purely practical things— things that had gotten all the nobleness squeezed out of them.

And, at the same time, Taru was wrong. Nagaro *could* go to Lankura. He *could* try to do exactly what Taru had proposed. And if they killed him, well, at least he would have tried to do what was right. He wasn't afraid of death. It was quite possible he might meet it, after all, sailing off in pursuit of Mahuk warships.

Nagaro let out a long, shuddering breath. No, he wouldn't go back to Lankura. He wouldn't sail away on that merchant ship to rescue a princess like some hero in one of the old tales. Instead he would sail with the other ship. He would be "Captain Nagaro", and— if it pleased Lokundas to tweak the arrogant noses of the Mautep— he would be permitted to free slaves. This was surely not a bad choice, he told himself. Freeing slaves was just, and right, and arguably a larger good than trying to save a single woman from her husband's abuse.

He frowned. Why then did he feel so guilty? Was it because he had, in effect, abandoned a woman to whom he had been married— however involuntarily? Or was it because trying to help that woman now would mean revealing his identity— a thing he feared far more than he feared death? It seemed he must be either a cad, or a coward, or both.

Nagaro sighed. He told himself that he should take comfort in keeping the promise he had made to the men. He had made that promise before he'd learned of the princess's plight, after all, and she had her father to protect her. His choice had been made. His path was clear. The sword that had come to him would become the sword of freedom— not the sword of vengeance.

He sat for a long time on the cold stone seat. The lights below him winked out, one by one, and the night grew ever more chill. Naru, the dark moon, ponderously pursued the bright moon Talebra across the sky. Nagaro tried to mark their progress as they rode through a low, thin bank of cloud and mounted serenely toward the zenith. Their movement was so slow as to be all but imperceptible, yet they would reach the western horizon before dawn. It would take many more turnings of the world before Naru would catch Talebra, yet that too would come to pass. The Leithians believed that Kroneg, the god of war, rode on Naru. And that Talebra carried Lissafel, the goddess of love. Tredhold had once said that when Naru passed across Talebra's face, Kroneg and Lissafel would vie for power over the hearts of men and one of them would prove the stronger. Time would bring these things to pass, just as time would reveal the consequences of the choice he'd made.

Nagaro drew in his breath. He stretched his legs stiffly and got to his feet, then stood yet a while, thinking. The Leithians asked their gods for things they wanted in their prayers. What a comfort it must be to believe there were powers in the world that would make things happen the way one wished— if only one wished for good things and asked sincerely. The Kelorin didn't believe in such powers. To them, a prayer was not a request, but a mere expression of hope.

He raised his eyes to Talebra's pale orb.

"Vothra," he said, pitching his words softly upon the evening breeze. "There is no need to answer if you're listening. I know you don't like to meddle in the workings of the world, so I won't ask you to. But if Elgurn has done nothing to end his daughter's suffering because he doesn't know about it, I pray that he may learn of it before she comes to any greater harm."

He lowered his eyes then, feeling a little comforted. Turning, he descended from that lonely place. He passed through the ironwood grove, a shadow among shadows, and made his way back down the curving road and through the slumbering town to the Bay Tree Inn, the company of his friends, and the comfort of his waiting bed.

***

Two weeks later, the fully refitted war galley the *Sword of Freedom* sailed out of Pakoa Harbor with a crew of forty-four men, all trained to the ways of the sword, and the rigging, and the handling of oars. Nagaro stood on her stern castle, his face set, his eyes fixed dead ahead, locked on the point where the sky met the flashing sea.

Chapter 17

Taking On Water

Three months later, Nagaro paced the stern castle deck. It had begun to look as if the whole brave shining venture would come to naught for want of a mahuk warship to prey upon. They were well into their second voyage, the first one having ended without success in the middle of the month of Duleyin when they'd been forced to return to Pakoa to re-provision the ship. That first voyage had carried the *Sword* up and down the whole length of the Lomoas, where they'd hoped to catch some lone Mautep galley making a foray for gold or slaves without themselves having to sail out of friendly waters.

They had sailed up the Inside Passage that ran from south to north in a long zig-zag course between the islands. It was safe water for their less-than-perfect mastery of their craft, being sheltered from the weather blowing in off the open ocean. There were also plenty of safe harbors there, known to Landros, Timegar, and a number of the other men who had been merchant seamen. Nagaro had at last concluded that while it was safer for *them*, the Mautep were far more likely to use the Seaward Passage along the western shores of the outer isles, despite being exposed to more weather. That way was far safer for Mahuk craft trying to get through what for them were the hostile waters of the Lomoas.

Several times, Mendorel or Tego, who alternated as the *Sword*'s lookouts, had glimpsed small fleets of enemy ships out there in the open sea while passing one of the many straits between the isles on the western side of the Inside Passage. Such groups of Mahuk craft were, of course, beyond their ambitions.

At the northern end of the Lomoan archipelago, they had reversed course, without entering the wide strait that separated the Lomoas from the Inner and Outer Faranos. Sailing south again, they had gone more slowly, weaving in and out between the western Lomaon islands and sometimes lying in concealment in some cove, sending men ashore to keep a wider lookout from higher ground. Twice they'd actually sighted lone marauders. The first time they'd lost the Mahuk ship to darkness and an oncoming squall. The second time, their quarry had bolted between two islands, out into the Seaward Passage and straight into the arms of three of her compatriots, forcing the *Sword of Freedom* to turn and flee.

Their only consolation had been that, in both these cases, they had routed enemy ships in the very act of pursuing small fishing boats, and so had prevented hapless fishermen from being taken into bondage. The fishermen had been profusely grateful, declaring that the *Sword of Freedom* had been more use to them that summer than Lord Kuran and all of his fleet. The praise was heartening, but it yielded nothing to help finance their future efforts.

Their second voyage, after re-provisioning, was so far proving no more fruitful than the first. Nagaro had decided to keep to the southern end of the Lomoas this time, thinking that hiding and lying in wait might be a more effective strategy than sailing about at random. Yet everything depended so much on luck...

Nagaro deliberately stopped his pacing, reminding himself that there was no point in dwelling on these frustrations. The *Sword* was at that moment making good headway in easy seas. The sound of her passage was no more than the whisper of water against her hull. The small outer Lomoan isle whose shore had sheltered her through the previous night lay well astern. Directly ahead, their destination was a familiar spot near the northern tip of Pakoa Island where a stream emptied into the sea, a convenient place to refill their waterskins.

There was, of course, not a single Mahuk galley in sight, but it was a gloriously clear day in late Duleyin. The wind was a light, steady breath out of the west with a kiss of salt. The sea was bright, the air like crystal, and the sun was warm on Nagaro's shoulders. It was a day to make a sailor's heart sing.

In an effort to further banish the lingering clouds from his mind, Nagaro replayed the event that had been the high-point of the summer, Tredhold's wedding. The memory, as always, made him smile.

It had been completely unexpected and somewhat precipitous. The healer had come to him in the last days of the *Sword's* first voyage and asked if they might put in briefly at Harmoth so he could go ashore to find out whether a woman was willing to marry him. Apparently the mysterious second letter Tred had sent from Pakoa on the *Rose of Harmoth* had been addressed to a woman named Ilsafeth, whom he had met in the spring before he was taken by the Mautep. She'd been a new "Fleet widow" then, with two young children left fatherless. He'd taken a liking to her, and she to him it seemed, but her grief had been very fresh, and he hadn't pressed his suit. Since some time had passed, however, Tredhold had thought that Ilsafeth might be ready to consider remarriage. Accordingly, he had taken his heart in his hands and made the leap of proposing to her in a letter.

Nagaro had readily agreed to making the stop, and the *Sword* had come to anchor in the Bay of Harmoth— drawing many a curious look— while the healer had been rowed ashore to pay a visit to the object of his affections. An hour later, Tred had returned— looking very excited and more flustered than Nagaro had ever seen him— to ask whether the ship could stay the night so that he and Ilsafeth could be wed the following day.

Ilsafeth, it turned out, had been so taken with Tredhold that she had sought news of the fate of his ship, the *Fairwind*, after the plague summer. When she'd learned that the ship had been lost, she had naturally assumed that Tred had perished along with all of the crew. Finding him alive after all, the woman was taking no chances of losing him again. So Nagaro had found himself a guest at a hasty wedding, along with Landros and the other former Fleet warriors among his crew.

Tredhold had left his new bride to wait for him in Harmoth, pending the outcome of the *Sword's* summer voyages. If they were successful, he would bring Ilsafeth and her children to Pakoa to live with him. If, on the other hand, they failed to take any Mahuk craft, Tredhold planned to go to join her in Harmoth and resume his interrupted plan to practice the healer's trade in the city of his birth.

Nagaro's smile died. *If they failed...* It always came back to that.

The Pakoa shore had grown much closer during his reminiscence. The waters they were entering were more green than blue, revealing their decreasing depth. The little stretch of sand, cut across by the stream's mouth, was clearly visible dead ahead. Beyond it rose a steep hillside, partially clad in pines and cedars. A rocky promontory jutted from the hillside, just to the left of their intended landing spot, and formed the island's northern tip. Nagaro would post lookouts on that headland for a view to the east along the southern shore of the neighboring island of Haru, and southeast across the Great Channel between Pakoa and the mainland. Meanwhile, the ship's crow's seat would continue to provide a wide view of the Inside Passage from almost due north, all the way around to the west and southwest. Though not a sheltered anchorage, it was safe enough from weather on such a calm day, and the openness meant they would have ample warning of the approach of any vessel, Mahuk or otherwise.

Nagaro had no need to take soundings since he knew the location well. He cupped his hands to his mouth and shouted, "Prepare to drop anchor!" He had the immediate satisfaction of hearing Landros, below on the main deck, bellowing for the deck crew to go up the masts to take in sail. The first mate's voice was drowned out an instant later by the pelting of feet as the *Sword*'s oarsmen, who were still top-side, made for the oar deck with all speed. Nagaro's smile returned, fleetingly. If all the sailing about had accomplished nothing else, at least the crew had learned their sea-craft.

He stepped up to the captain's platform. It was a raised area six feet by three feet, by twelve inches high, placed at the center of the stern castle's forward rail where it offered a view of the ship and the sea before her. Mounting it, he put his mouth to the speaking tube that communicated with the oar deck below. "Timegar, we're about to anchor. Oars out and ready. Prepare to break speed."

"Aye, Captain!" Timegar's response came up through the speaking tube, ringing hollow but clear. The second mate's voice continued, more distant and less distinct, as he stepped away from the speaking tube to direct the actions of the men under his command.

Timegar had been a natural choice for the oar deck officer, since he'd served in that capacity in the Royal Fleet. Landros, of course, had always worked with the upper deck crew who managed the sails. The two men had explained to Nagaro that the standard practice in the Fleet was for the officer who commanded the oar deck to be first mate, and the main deck officer the second mate, the logic being that the oar deck officer commanded more men. Nagaro had rearranged this normal Fleet chain of command, making Landros the first mate, and Timegar the second. It had simply made more sense for the *Sword of Freedom*. Landros was known and trusted by the former slaves who made up the core of the crew. They'd seen what he could do at Jaamra. By contrast, these men didn't know Timegar, though they respected the bearded Kelorin's high standing among the Pakoan recruits. Fortunately, Landros had allowed himself to be cajoled into a promotion despite his previous insistence that second mate was all he ever wanted to be.

A short time later, the oars were dipped and held steady in the water, slowing the ship's progress until the *Sword* lay completely still, about twenty yards from shore. The anchor was pitched over the side, and soon one of the ship's two longboats was headed for shore with Nagaro sitting in the stern, facing forward so he could monitor their approach to the beach and direct the rowers, who necessarily had their backs to it. His presence wasn't strictly necessary for such a mundane expedition, but Nagaro was exercising his captain's prerogative. Opportunities to go ashore were rare, and he relished the chance to stretch his legs. Besides, the activity would distract him from more gloomy preoccupations.

The other men he had chosen for the shore party consisted of Taru, Pavo, Moraga, Tego, and a Turowan merchant seaman named Haruda. He had left Mendorel manning the crow's seat atop the mainmast, and both of his officers were still aboard the ship. In the unlikely event that the

Sword needed to be quickly moved, Nagaro had complete confidence in Landros and Timegar.

The five rowers diligently bent their backs, and the longboat's keel soon grated on the sand beside the mouth of the stream. While the men shipped the oars, Nagaro leapt over the side, his boots splashing ankle-deep into the foam. The other men soon followed. The wind wasn't strong enough in the Inside Passage to generate waves of any great size, but they pulled the longboat well up onto the sand as a precaution.

With the boat secure, they set about their duties. Tego and Moraga headed for a trail that led to the top of the headland to keep a lookout, while Nagaro and the other three men each grabbed an empty waterskin from the pile in the bottom of the boat and struck off towards the sloping hillside. They knew better than to try to fill the skins where the stream fanned out across the sand. No one liked sand in his sothiril. Part way up the hill, there was a better place, where the stream emerged from a stand of leaning pines. There the water came cascading over a tumble of stones, pouring through chinks like so many natural spigots.

The other men had done this before, and they quickly made for their favorite spots. Nagaro had to go farther up the slope to find what looked like a good place. It was difficult to fill the waterskin efficiently because of the stream's irregular flow, and he was so focused on the task that he didn't immediately notice a disturbance above him on the hillside. When the sounds did penetrate and he looked up from the filled waterskin, he was surprised to see Moraga working his way down the slope between the trees.

He straightened and raised his voice. "Moraga, is something amiss?"

"Ah... Capt'n... it's—" Moraga broke off as he lost his footing and slid the last bit of way, coming to rest beside Nagaro in a shower of pine needles. He stood up, dusting the seat of his pants. "It's that Tira Zomora, Capt'n! She's up *there*." He gestured towards the top of the slope. "She want's to talk t' ye. Alone."

Nagaro's stomach had dropped at the mere mention of Zomora's name. "What does she want?" he asked, trying to keep his voice even.

Moraga rolled his eyes. "*I* don't know! It's ye that she wants t' talk to, not *me*, Capt'n." The scar-lipped Turo belatedly made something resembling a salute.

Nagaro resisted the urge to swear. *As if he didn't have enough to worry about already...*

Taru and Pavo had set aside their waterskins and come up the slope to see what was going on, and at this point Taru said, "Ye'd best go if Tira Zomora wants t' talk to ye, Nagaro." The young Turo's expression was deadly serious. Behind him, Pavo was impassive as usual, though Nagaro detected a narrowing of the Hashtep's eyes that betrayed his interest.

"Right." Nagaro stoppered the full waterskin he held and thrust it at Moraga. "Take this back to the longboat. Then go back to your post." He knew he had no excuse not to talk to the medicine woman, though it was the last thing he wanted to do. He couldn't explain his reservations in front of Moraga, and even with the former merchant seaman gone, he'd be hard-pressed to say exactly why he felt like he was being summoned before a tribunal.

It helped that Moraga gave him a look of sympathy before starting down the hill with the waterskin on his shoulder.

There was sympathy in Taru's glance as well. "She *is* a medicine woman," he said, a bit lamely. "Ye don't just *not* talk to a medicine woman." He forced a brittle smile. "And be sure ye're polite. I don't *think* she can actually turn ye into anything, but—"

Pavo's shoulders had stiffened. "When is Nagaro not polite?"

Nagaro heaved a sigh. "Carry on with the water," he said, and turned around to begin picking his way up the slope.

It was not easy going. The slope was quite steep, and the pine needles were slippery. And the air was so thick and resinous that it threatened to choke him. Fortunately, there were enough rocks and tree roots to provide secure footing at intervals.

The hillside rose twelve to fifteen yards above Nagaro's starting point, the crest forming a ridge that connected it with the back of the rocky headland where Tego would still be on watch. This doubtless explained how Moraga had become aware of Zomora— or she of him. It didn't really matter which, Nagaro reflected, as he negotiated the last few feet of the climb by means of a pine's massive roots that protruded from the earth like the rungs of a crooked ladder. But he couldn't help wondering whether the medicine woman had happened to come this way by chance and noticed the presence of the *Sword*, or whether she'd come looking for him specifically. He didn't doubt that she could follow the ship's movements when it was close to Pakoa by talking to the island's fishermen.

He emerged, sweating and breathless, at the top of the slope and stepped out of the shadow of the trees onto a rough track that followed the crest of the ridge. He recognized the track. He'd ridden this way more than once on his many explorations.

The piebald pony was what caught his eye first, standing on the path a few yards away to his left. Partially silhouetted against a sapphire sky, its black-and-white markings were in vivid contrast to the dusty green of the island's vegetation. An instant later, he noted that Tira Zomora wass standing at the pony's head, holding its bridle. She was dressed exactly as she had been the first time he'd seen her. The green of her blouse and the yellow of her skirt looked paler here, more washed-out in the brilliant sunlight, but there was nothing the least bit less potent about the challenging glance she leveled at him with her sharp black eyes.

Nagaro drew a breath and approached her, noting that at least there would be no witnesses to whatever passed between them. Under her gaze he was acutely aware that he was dressed for battle: black pants and boots, and the dark red leather vest that had been plundered from the *Fist of Death* and which he wore shirtless, baring his arms and throat.

"Tira Zomora," he said, bending his head in acknowledgment.

Before he could say more, she addressed him in her cool contralto. "So," she said sharply, "Last winter ye were the swordmaster, and now it seems we must call ye 'Captain.'"

Nagaro's shoulders stiffened even as his stomach settled. This wasn't going to be about his past, but rather about his present actions— which was safer ground. "You may call me whatever you please, Zirdyn," he said evenly. "Though I prefer 'Tor Nagaro.' Or 'Zirda.'"

She raised an eyebrow. "Respect for respect?"

He spread his hands. "That seems fair."

This brought the flicker of something to her eyes, gone too quickly for him to identify it. She looked past him and downward, towards the water below. When he turned to follow her gaze, he discovered that he could just glimpse the *Sword of Freedom* through the screen of trees.

"Ye've got some of our island lads on that ship," she said accusingly. "How can I be sure ye're not leading them to their deaths?"

Nagaro sighed. "You can't," he said. "Though I pray I am not." Then he added with more than a touch of irony, "So far there seems little danger of it."

Tira Zomora released her pony's bridle to step closer. Her eyes still challenged him. "Do they believe ye will lead them to glory?"

This struck a nerve, although Nagaro did his best to hold her gaze without flinching. "Some of them do," he said earnestly. "Because some of them think I'm something that I'm not— even though I keep telling them that I'm only a man, and that what we mean to do has nothing to do with glory. It has to do with freeing slaves."

Something in what he had just said seemed to have surprised the medicine woman. Her eyes narrowed. "Ye say ye're just a man?"

"Of course." Nagaro was mystified. "What else would I be?"

"Why do ye flaunt that mark?" Her glance stabbed at the slave brand that stood out, pale and livid, on his bare kuma-stained shoulder.

Nagaro frowned at her tone. But there *was* a reason. "Those of us who were slaves show our brands to let the slaves we intend to set free know that we were slaves like them. And we dress for battle all the time," he added. "Because we never know when we might encounter a Mahuk ship."

This time it was Tira Zomora who frowned. Her pony had begun to stray, foraging for edible greenery along the edge of the dirt track, and she stepped two paces away from Nagaro to retrieve the animal. When she returned, the glance she leveled at him held more speculation than challenge. "Your ship causes much hopeful talk," she conceded. "Some of the fishermen are pleased to have such a ship sailing about these waters carrying men with swords."

Nagaro's own frown deepened. "We've made no use of our swords so far," he said bitterly. In point of fact, he wasn't wearing his. It would only have been in the way while filling waterskins. "And we've only a few more weeks to find a chance to do so," he added, "or there will be an early end to our sailing about."

"So? Ye can't find your enemy?" The medicine woman arched a fine black brow.

He studied the woman's face for signs of mockery, but found none. Apparently it had been a serious question. "We need to find a single ship. One that will face us rather than flee," he told her. "Or one that's caught in such a place that she can't flee. But the sea is wide, and there are a great many islands. And the Mautep are wary, besides."

Zomora acknowledged the point with nod and a small shrug of her shoulders, but her fierce dark gaze slid past him to the trees behind him, and the beach and ship beyond. Her expression had turned thoughtful. After a moment, she said, "Have ye tried to catch one that's doing what ye're doing down there?"

"One that's taking on fresh water?" *It wasn't a bad thought.* He rubbed his chin. "That could work, Zirdyn. But not *here*. We have lookouts posted who can see in every direction, except due south where the island both shields us and blocks our view. No ship can approach us by sea without our seeing it. And if any tried, we could flee in any direction. A Mahuk ship could do the same."

"Ah." She nodded, as her gaze came back to him. Still, she was very clearly thinking now. "So ye need a place where ye can lie in wait... and where they have a reason t' come..." Her dark eyes grew distant.

"Ye-es..." Nagaro was also thinking. *They were hunting in Tira Zomora's territory.* "Do you know of such a place, Zirdyn?" he asked.

Her eyes came back to him, hard and sharp. "Perhaps," she said. "The best would be Chitaopa."

"Chitaopa?" He stared at her. *The island where they had weathered the plague?* How could she know of Chitoapa? It lay a good fifty miles to the south, and west. "I spent... several weeks there," he said cautiously. "It's a common watering place for the Mautep, with a small enclosed cove that could trap a ship. But there's nowhere to *hide*, no accessible vantage point to keep watch. Except for the cove and the bit of land around it, the whole island is just one great rock with cliffs going straight up out of the sea."

"Ye're so sure o' that?" And now her black eyes glittered. "Did ye never go around to the seaward side?"

"The *seaward* side?" Nagaro's mouth dropped open. He wanted to protest that he had been a slave, his ankles hobbled by a chain... but that wasn't the point. *He'd never seen anyone go around to the seaward side.*

She must have read the dawning in his eyes. "Ye'll not have seen the needle's eye," she said, a trifle smugly. "I've not seen it with my own eyes either, but the old tales tell of it. A narrow way in, but deep. Dangerous to pass, but with a safe anchorage inside and a trail that goes t' the top o' the rock, where a man can see the sea all around."

Vothra's eyes and ears!

Nagaro drew an excited breath. His mind was racing. "*Dangerous...*" he murmured. "*Narrow, but deep...*" His eyes came to a focus on her face. "*How* narrow, Zirdyn?" he asked sharply. "Narrow but passable for a fishing boat, could be *too* narrow for a war galley."

She shrugged. "I've never seen it," she reminded him. "But there's a tale that tells of two small boats going in, side by side, without the oars touching."

Nagaro pictured this, comparing it in his mind to the breadth of the *Sword of Freedom*. Like all war galleys, she was a narrow craft, built to slice through the water, not to carry cargo.

"Thank you, Tira Zomora!" He felt a surge of generosity toward the medicine woman, and he made her a bow. In his excitement, he started to turn away then, but caught himself and turned back. "Your pardon, Zirdyn. It was you who wished to speak to me," he said. "Have you said what you wished to say? Have I answered you?"

She stood, holding her pony's bridle. Her face had gone very still. Somewhere, a wild bird called, sounding too loud in the waiting silence—a silence that lasted for several seconds before Tira Zomora lifted her chin, holding him with her eyes. "Yes," she said decisively. "For now."

***

Nagaro careened down the slope beneath the trees, leaping from rock to rock and ending in a long slide that raised a choking, resin-scented dust cloud around him. Ducking out of it to draw breath beside the stream, he whistled a signal for Tego and Moraga to call them down from the headland. The other men had finished filling the waterskins and were in the act of loading them into the longboat. They looked up, startled.

"What's wrong, Nagaro?" Taru called, sounding alarmed.

Nagaro closed the distance to the boat with long strides. "Nothing," he said. "But we need to take council when we get back to the ship. With all hands. I want to know everything anyone can tell me about Chitaopa."

***

Nagaro ordered the ship out into deeper water, farther from shore, before calling the men to a council on the main deck. They gathered between the two masts, some sitting cross-legged, some standing or leaning on the rail. Mendorel remained at his post aloft in the crow's seat, being needed there and having nothing to offer regarding Turowan fishermen's tales.

Nagaro recounted only enough of his conversation with Tira Zomora to provide context for her revelation about Chitaopa. "Do any of you know these tales?" he asked. "What do the stories say? And do you think they're true?"

Most of the men looked around to see if anyone else would speak. A number of the Turo rolled their eyes, or looked uncomfortable. Rubo, the ship's cook, and Tego— who were the two oldest Turo present—exchanged glances. "*We-ell*," Rubo ventured when it was clear that no one else was going to volunteer anything, "There surely are tales that mention an island called Chitaopa."

"Aye," put in Tego. "And havin' *seen* the island the Mautep call by that name, I'd say it *looks* likely t' be the same place."

Moraga spat. "Would ye listen t' these two old men?" he growled. "Dancin' like scalded cats." He looked Nagaro straight in the eye. "I'll take no wagers against a medicine woman," he said flatly. "If Tira Zomora believes the tales, then so do I."

Nagaro saw Torowan heads nodding on every side. Rubo and Tego looked relieved, as if Moraga had spoken their minds as well. Nagaro sighed. "All right," he said. "The Turo here all trust Tira Zomora that this 'needle's eye' exists on the seaward side of Chitaopa. So what do the tales say about it? What is it like?"

And at that, they all started talking at once.

The picture that emerged was fairly consistent. The existence of a safe anchorage, after passing through the eye, was a common feature in the tales, and there was also general agreement about there being a way to get up onto the top of the island's massive central bastion from that anchorage. The needle's eye was variously described as "small" or "narrow." It was either a "crack," or an "opening," or a "passage." There were either "rocks" on both sides, or "cliffs." And all of the remembered versions of the tales agreed that threading the needle's eye was dangerous.

When it came to the matter of two boats passing through the eye side by side, it turned out that only Tego and Rubo had heard the tale containing this particular incident, but the detail about the boats' oars not touching was something both of those men agreed on.

Finally Nagaro raised both hands for everyone's attention. "This is how I see it," he said. "And let any man speak if he can say that I'm wrong. We've been offered an ideal place to spring a trap, supposing only that the *Sword* can pass through the needle's eye. And the only way to know if she can is to go there and take a look. But Chitaopa lies a long way south and west. It will take two or three days to get there, depending on the weather, and as many to sail back again if we find it's all for naught. And it means sailing into Jinari waters."

"Aye. Don't forget that we're at war with Jinara." Timegar spoke for the first time.

Landros put up his hand. "*Edrovir* is at war with Jinara," he said pointedly. "We're not flyin' the white hawk on blue. And Jinara's got no fleet. No warships."

Timegar inclined his head to Landros. "Points well taken," he said.

Nagaro gave a nod to his officers. "What's more to the point," he said, "is that there will quite possibly be Mahuk war galleys crossing those same waters, and they may not be sailing alone. It's open sea all the way, with no islands to hide behind. Which is why I would propose to set a course as far to seaward as we dare. That will shorten our route, since the island is almost as much west of us as south. It will take a greater risk with the weather, but the Mautep know that too. They tend to stay close to the coast— unless, of course, they're planning a make a stop at Chitaopa."

Nagaro paused, surveying the men's faces, noting a number of frowns and doubtful looks. "I know it will be dangerous," he continued. "Coming, and going, and being there as well, and we might find that the only safe harbor on Chitaopa for our ship is the one we mean to use for a trap. All of that is true. *But*, we've all seen how hard it is to catch a lone warship here in the Lomoas. And we're running out of summer." Again he scanned their faces, reading excitement in some, doubt lingering in others. "Chitaopa seems worth the risk to me," he continued. "It looks like the best chance we have to secure the future of our plan. But I'll not lead an unwilling crew on such an uncertain venture. I know you've all pledged to follow me, but it seems only right to give you the choice in this. So, how many are in favor? Stand forward and be counted."

Landros and Timegar, who were already standing, stepped forward together. Landros spoke for both of them when he said, "It's a damn sight better 'n skulking about these islands waitin' for Lokundas to throw us a fish!"

Tredhold followed the example of the other two former Fleet officers, as did most of the remaining Kelorin crewmen. Taru and Pavo had sprung to their feet as soon as Nagaro had finished speaking and stepped forward as well, to be followed by Tego, Rubo, and most of the Turo.

A dozen men still lingered after that. Moraga was among them, still lounging against the rail. Seeing this, Nagaro had a moment's qualm, but the former merchant seaman abruptly straightened and stepped away from the railing. "I'm for it," he announced to the world. "They say the Spirits find ways o' speakin' to us, and as I've said, I'm makin' no wagers against a medicine woman's word."

That did it. The rest of the men stood up, some of them shrugging a bit sheepishly, and stepped into line.

Nagaro breathed a sigh of relief, though he'd rather Moraga hadn't invoked the Turowan World Spirits. "All right then," he said. "We'll put back into Pakoa Harbor for tonight, and leave tomorrow morning as soon after dawn as we can. Now, all hands to your posts!"

The crew quickly dispersed, talking excitedly.

Taru gave Nagaro a broad grin as he passed him on the way to the oar deck. "Finally!" he said. "Maybe we'll see some action!"

Pavo met Nagaro's eyes with a nod, and said, "This is go to be good story!"

Nagaro winced as he turned and headed in the direction of the stern castle ladder. Before he had gone half a dozen steps, Landros caught him with a hand on the shoulder and spoke low into his ear.

"I'm not sure ye should ha' given the lads so much time in Pakoa Town," the first mate confided. "We might see some desertions. Give a man too much time t' think, and he'll think himself out of the plan and right home to bed."

Nagaro sighed. "Actually, I'd rather give them that chance," he said seriously. "I'd rather be a few hands short than have men among us who only came because they didn't want to look bad in front of their mates."

Landros rolled his eyes, but said no more.

Chapter 18

Looking For The Needle

As it turned out, there were no desertions. The *Sword* weighed anchor half an hour after sunrise the next morning with all hands aboard. Nagaro set a course west-by-southwest, and they kept to that heading until the mainland coast was reduced to a long, low ribbon, away to port. Then they bore due south. The day was fair with a stiff wind out of the northwest. All through the morning and into the afternoon, they made good time with the sails. As the day waned, Nagaro, Landros, and Timegar gathered at the starboard rail of the stern castle deck, gazing at the long golden trail blazed across the sea by the sinking sun. The western sky was taking on a tinge of pink.

"Not a sail in sight all day," Timegar remarked with obvious relish. "Our luck is holding. They do say Lokundas favors the bold."

Squinting at the expanse of empty sea, Landros responded. "Aye, but they also say the Turner of Worlds delights in setting traps for the cocksure."

Nagaro frowned. Rather than "bold" and "cocksure", he preferred to think they were being hopeful and decisive. "It will be getting dark soon," he observed, "and when it does, we'll lose our sighting on the mainland coast. Talebra will be only half full when she rises, and she won't give enough light to see that far."

Landros nodded. "Aye, ye're right, lad. We'll lose the wind too. It drops at sunset this time o' year in these waters. We should furl the sails when that happens, and leave 'em furled 'til we take stock o' things in the morning. No sense risking getting blown off course during the night."

Nagaro had to agree. Being blown in closer to shore would increase their risk of being sighted, while being blown out to sea posed a danger of getting lost. They could always find the coast again by sailing east, but they might waste valuable time in reestablishing their position relative to Chitaopa. And there was a chance of missing the island in the dark, though he doubted they were close enough for that to happen on this first night.

When the sun finally slipped below the horizon and the wind died, Nagaro ordered the oars out for a time and they rowed on into the gathering twilight. Eventually, however, he had to order the oars shipped and the watches posted. Soon after that, he sought his own bed in the ship's great cabin.

The room was in the stern castle and boasted two broad officer's bunks, a small table with stools, and a pair of windows looking out over the ship's stern. The cabin had been Urchak's domain when the ship had been the *Fist of Death*, and Nagaro hadn't originally wanted to use it. But the men had insisted, and the truth was that there weren't any bunks to spare on the ship. So Nagaro had resigned himself to his quarters. If Nanu and Chaheel could sleep in the cabin just aft of the oar deck that had housed Baruk, Raak, and the slave tenders, he supposed he could sleep in Urchak's cabin. Whichever of the two bunks he chose to use, he could always pretend that Urchak had slept in the other one.

Their good luck must have lulled him that night, for he found sleep easily. He awoke with the dawn to a frantic cry of "*sails!*"

He rolled out of bed, blinking sleep from his eyes, and dressed hurriedly, grabbing his spyglass from its hook by the door on the way out. On the main deck, he joined a small knot of men at the port rail. Landros was already there, taking a report from Tego who had just relinquished the crow's seat to Mendorel with the changing of the watch.

Tego was breathless and apologetic. "I *swear* they weren't there five minutes ago," he was saying. "I turned 'round to scan ahead of us, an' when I turned back, there they were!"

"It's because of the off-shore breeze that just sprung up," Landros opined. "They probably just let their sails down. And it's a good thing we left ours furled, or they'd ha' spotted us as easy as we've spotted them."

Nagaro's stomach clenched. *Had they been seen in spite of their furled sails?* "How many ships?" he asked sharply. "Where are they, and what's their heading?"

"There's three ships, Capt'n! Over *there!*" Tego flung out his arm, pointing astern and to port. "They're headed south, near as I can tell."

Nagaro found that he could just see the white specks without the spyglass. With it, he could still make out few details, but he didn't need to. The ships had to be Mahuk war galleys. The Mautep made no trade with Jinara, ruling out merchant craft from the Baar. And with the border war always threatening, there was no trade between Edrovir and Jinara either, and therefore no reason for merchant ships from either of those countries to be in these waters. Nor was it likely that Kuran Kel would be sending Edrovirin warships south so late in the season.

A tense few minutes of tracking the sails by eye was enough to reassure him that the ships were still south-bound, running parallel to the *Sword*'s course, though much closer to shore.

"What are your orders, Captain?" This came from Timegar, who had made his appearance on deck in the meantime.

Nagaro was chewing his lip, his eyes still on the three sets of sails. "We'll have to depend on the oars as long as we can still see those sails," he said. "Rouse your crew as quickly as you can, Timegar, and give me word when they're at their benches. I'll be on the captain's platform."

On the platform, and having Timegar's word via the speaking tube that the men were ready, Nagaro gave the order to row. He called to Moraga, who was manning the tiller, to bring the bow around to the southwest. It was a heading that would simultaneously take them closer to their destination and farther out to sea.

They held the southwest course until the Mahuk sails were tiny specks, with the glass, and the mainland coast scarcely more than a gray thread on the horizon. Nagaro then changed course again, to due south, and soon after that, he ordered the rowers to rest and told Landros to unfurl the sails, though no more than halfway. When the men were rested, he had them row again for a time with the canvas still spread.

And so it went. Nagaro left the stern castle deck only long enough to eat a hurried breakfast. He returned to the captain's platform to continue either sweeping the sea ahead with his glass, seeking any sign of the island of Chitoapa, or studying the progress of the tiny distant sails off their port stern.

On one occasion when he lowered the spyglass, he found Landros at his side. He handed the glass to his first mate. "They're still sailing south," he observed. "If they keep that course, they'll be out of sight and of no concern to us by the time we reach Chitaopa. If they plan to *stop* at Chitaopa, on the other hand, they'll have to turn, and their course will converge with ours."

Landros made an affirmative grunt as he squinted through the glass. "It'll depend on whether they filled their waterskins in the southern Lomoas," he said. "If they mean to stop at Chitaopa, their captains'll be looking for some landmark on shore. Some rock or bluff that marks the place for a course change to west-by-southwest— or maybe due west— to bring 'em in sight o' the island."

Nagaro nodded, recalling their earlier visit to Chitaopa after fleeing the battle of Jaamra. Approaching from the south and using the Mautep charts in the great cabin, they'd set a course west-by-northwest from the tip of the northernmost Jinari isle of Judaba. Of course they'd had Chitaopa in sight within an hour on that occasion. On a clear day, Judaba and Chitaopa were within sight of each other. Coming from the north as they were now, there was no island in similar proximity to the far-flung isle of Chitaopa.

"I wish I knew how near we were to sighting it," he said. "We could be half a day from the island, or a day and a half. Tell your deck crew to raise a cry if any man sees a sign that those ships are changing course. And I'll want the sails bound tight to the yardarms if that happens."

Landros saluted smartly. "Aye, Zirda!" He handed the spyglass back to Nagaro and made for the ladder to the main deck.

Noon came without any change in their situation, except that the Mahuk ships were nearly abeam of the *Sword*, rather than being clearly to stern. The wind had swung around to the north and stiffened, and the Mautep were making good time, probably by the combined use of oars and a full spread of canvas.

Half an hour later it was the lookout, Mendorel, who shouted, "They're turning!" and every man who could be spared from his task rushed to the port rail to look. Nagaro brought his glass to bear and soon confirmed the observation. The three sets of sails were distinctly larger and had moved farther from shore. The *Sword*'s sails were immediately furled, and he ordered the oars dragged to stop the ship.

In due course, the *Sword of Freedom* came to a halt, bobbing, dead in the water, while the deck crew anxiously followed the progress of the three enemy ships. Nagaro watched intently, alternately by naked eye and through the spyglass.

Landros came bounding up the ladder to join him at the captain's platform. "Even without the sails, this wind 'll catch our hull and push us south," he panted.

Nagaro nodded and gnawed his lip. "Can you judge their heading, Landros?"

The former Fleet warrior answered him without any hesitation. "West-by-southwest."

"And you believe that course will be aiming them straight towards Chitaopa?"

Landros shrugged. "It's what I'd do in their place: Make straight for it. It's a pebble o' land and a great wide ocean."

"Good." Nagaro lowered the glass. "They're going to show us the way. But we have to keep a safe distance, and right now they're closing." He put his mouth to the speaking tube. "Timegar, can the men back-paddle for any distance?"

There was a pause, then, "Reverse way, ye mean, Captain? Aye, they can. Ye can't steer with the rudder, and we can't give ye speed, but we can make way."

"Set to it then. Reverse way."

Nagaro heard the order given, the drum begin to beat. He felt a gentle backward surge with each slow swing of the oars and watched with satisfaction as the distant sails off their port beam gradually began to shrink.

Beside him, Landros' hands tightened on the rail. "Even without the sails, they might spy us, Nagaro. They'll likely be scanning for other Mahuk craft making for the same landfall, and it's not impossible that some Mautep captain would be sailing out this far."

Nagaro's mouth tightened to a grim line. *He'd deal with that in a minute.* He watched the Mahuk sails receding for a little longer, then bent to the speaking tube and said, "Drag the starboard oars, Timegar. Port oars, maintain reverse way."

"Aye, Zirda."

Timegar's voice had held a note of puzzlement, but Nagaro heard the orders repeated to the men, and presently observed their effect. The *Sword* began to turn, pivoting on the starboard oars until her bow came into line with the Mahuk sails. He put his mouth again to the speaking tube. "Lift starboard oars. All oars reverse way."

"Aye, Zirda." Timegar gave the order before asking, "What are ye about, Captain?"

Landros laughed aloud. "He's showin' them our bow, ye lumbering landsman!"

Nagaro's teeth flashed in a quick smile. "It's like a sword-bout, Timegar. I've made us a smaller target."

There was a pause, and then Timegar's voice rang through the speaking tube. "Nagaro, ye're bloody brilliant!"

Nagaro's smile died. He shook his head, though he knew his second mate couldn't see it. "It's only brilliant if it works."

The next hour was an alternating series of backings and turnings, with rests interspersed, under a bright, cloudless sky with the north wind sweeping the deck. The Mahuk ships held to their course, passing by to the south, while the *Sword* tracked them with her bow and kept a nearly constant distance. Eventually Landros wearied of watching this dance and headed for the galley to get something for their mid-day meal.

Nagaro continued to stand and watch and give orders. At last he let out a pent breath and called for one more rest, this one with the oars half-shipped. The enemy warships had passed the half-way point, where a line drawn from the *Sword*'s prow to the Mahuk craft would intersect, exactly at right angles, the line described by the three ships' course. *It was time to stop backing.* He shifted his weight from one foot to the other as he waited out the rest period and the Mahuk ships' sails began to recede. Finally he addressed the speaking tube. "Oars out, Temegar. Prepare for forward way."

"It's a chase then?" Timegar's voice came back to him.

"Not quite. We'll run parallel to their course. As long as we keep those ships in sight, we can't miss the island."

It was more easily said than done. Taking a parallel course, Nagaro couldn't keep the *Sword*'s bow turned to the other craft. To reduce the risk of being spotted, he therefore let the *Sword* drop back, only to find it difficult to keep up with the Mautep when he decided he'd given up enough way. The enemy ships had the wind while the *Sword* still didn't dare use her sails, and her oarsmen had already done a fair amount of rowing and were tired. As the day lengthened, the Mahuk sails dwindled alarmingly.

And they still hadn't sighted Chitaopa.

Landros re-joined him on the stern castle, bringing Nagaro a chunk of flat bread and a strip of dried meat, as well as a cup of sothiril. Nagaro chewed and swallowed, smiling grimly to himself. The food was little different from galley-slave fare. He took a gulp of the hot sothiril and winced as he burned his mouth.

Landros had the spyglass to his eye. "I'd swear they just turned," he said. "About a quarter point t' the south."

Nagaro frowned sharply as he belatedly blew on his sothiril. "Why would they—?" He stopped. "Could they have just sighted the island and corrected their course?"

Landros whistled through his teeth. "Not a bad guess, lad," he said. "Of course, they *could* just think they're too far north. Or maybe they've spotted something else that's making 'em turn. Us, maybe?"

Nagaro sipped gingerly, still frowning. "Three ships running away from one? They were losing us even before they turned. And if Chitaopa was anywhere to the north of them, we'd have seen it."

Landros nodded. "That's sound reasoning. Ye've got an old head on young shoulders."

Nagaro smiled crookedly and gently probed the scalded roof of his mouth with his tongue. "Now if I could just learn not to burn myself on hot sothiril. We'll hold our course for a quarter hour, then bear another quarter point to south."

A quarter of an hour later when he gave the order to change course, he was having misgivings. The tracklessness of the open ocean had never before struck him with such force. The mainland, somewhere to the east, had long since disappeared astern. There was nothing to be seen to the north, all the way to where the sea met the sky. To the southwest, the Mahuk sails— the only features Nagaro's glass could find— had become reduced to the merest specks, a long way ahead and just to port of their new heading. Beyond those sails, the sea stretched, disturbingly empty. The sun, an hour past its zenith, struck blinding highlights from the wave crests across a blue-gray expanse of sea that ran all the way to the encircling horizon in every direction, under the cloudless arch of the sky.

Where was Chitaopa?

The Mautep *must* be making for it, but it was impossible to gage the heading of those distant ships.

Behind Nagaro, Moraga raised his voice from where he was manning the tiller. "Looks t' me like ye're sailin' us into the Great Empty, Capt'n."

Nagaro resisted the impulse to agree with the former merchant seaman. "Those ships have to be close to the island by now," he said, keeping his voice firm, praying it was the truth. "We should see it soon."

At last, a quarter of an hour later, Mendorel's voice cut across the wind. "Land! There! Dead ahead!"

A cheer rose from the men on the main deck, and was echoed a moment later by the voices of the rowers carried to Nagaro's ears through the speaking tube. He brought the spyglass to his eye and found the island, a small blue-gray smudge against a darker sea and a lighter sky.

***

Their approach to the island of Chitaop was a cautious one. Nagaro steered a course that swung well to the west and kept the sails furled to reduce the risk of being seen. Since the rowers had to be rested at intervals, the *Sword*'s progress was slow, and it was nearly sunset by the time they drew near enough to see the white flashes of foam made by waves breaking against the island's cliffs. Well before then, Nagaro had the satisfaction of seeing the three sets of Mahuk sails converge with the island's silhouette and disappear one by one as they did so. Either the Mautep captains had furled their canvas as they approached their anchorage, or else the headland at the northern border of the island's little cove had obscured the ships from his view.

They made their final approach to the island from the northwest, coming in very carefully indeed because of the breaking waves. Nagaro had no intention of anchoring close to the island's western shore, even if the water there were shallow enough, but he was determined to see if they could find the Needle's Eye before nightfall. They couldn't attempt to pass through it until daylight, but he wanted some evidence that they hadn't come all that way in vain.

Chitaopa was no more than three miles across in any direction, but it was singularly impressive, especially at sunset. The bulk of the island consisted of a flat-topped mass of upthrust basalt, rising a hundred feet or more straight out of the sea. The setting sun was kindling the normally silver-gray rock to golden fire, and occasional vertical streaks of purple shadow interrupted the gilding where weather had cut channels or facets in the stone. From their initial angle of approach, however, none of these channels looked wide enough or deep enough to be the promised Needle's Eye.

When the *Sword* reached a distance of a hundred feet from the cliff, Nagaro directed Moraga to turn southward and steer a course running parallel to the rock wall. Great ocean swells heaved against the cliff face with a rhythmic rush and hiss, intermittently breaking into snow-white foam with a muffled roar. The glowing edifice towered above their little craft, its lofty crest etched sharply against the deepening blue of the sky. Snow-white gulls circled up there, crying mournfully as they sought perches for the night.

Nagaro tore his gaze away from that dizzying height and trained his eyes ahead as the *Sword* followed the curve of the cliff under the power of her oars. The ship's slow, steady progress continuously brought new stretches of the rock wall into view. Each new vertical swath of shadow brought a new hope, and one after another those hopes were dashed.

Until...

It was the appearance of a widening gap in the line of breaking foam that made Nagaro sure of what he was seeing. "There!" he shouted, pointing.

Other excited shouts rose from the main deck.

The gap in the cliff face, once the *Sword* drew abreast of it, turned out to be sixty or seventy feet wide, between vertical walls of stone with the sea swirling around their bases. The golden sunset light struck some twenty yards into the passage beyond, but the cleft angled away from the sun's rays, and its farther recesses were lost in deepening shadow. Everyone agreed there could be no doubt that they had found the Needle's Eye of the old Turowan tales. And the majority of those who had experience with larger ships also agreed that it was at least possible for the *Sword of Freedom* to pass through it— provided the passage didn't grow much narrower than the part of it that they could see.

"And always supposin' that it's deep enough," Moraga pointed out. "And there ain't no hidden rocks."

Landros counseled spending the night with the ship well off-shore, and admonished those on watch to keep both eyes and ears open. Their anchor could find no bottom at that distance and the sound of the crashing waves might be their best warning of danger if they drifted too near the rocks in the darkness.

Nagaro saw the wisdom of this advice and gave the order to make it so.

***

Shortly after daybreak the following morning, they brought the ship in close to the cliffs again, only to discover that they still couldn't see more than a hundred feet into the cleft that formed the Needle's Eye because the passage curved enough to pass out of their line of view. Nagaro promptly dispatched a crew of volunteers in one of the longboats to explore the Eye and whatever lay beyond it.

The longboat disappeared into the cleft, and there followed a tense wait that seemed unbearably long, until the boat reappeared and the scouting party returned. They reported that the passage was narrowest at its entrance and opened out within two hundred feet into a narrow valley that formed a long harbor. The harbor ran about half a mile into the interior of the island. While the sides of the valley were steeply sloping, they appeared climbable, and there was a bit of shingle beach at the far end of the valley where a stream flowed into the sea.

Before he was willing to try taking the *Sword* through the Needle's Eye, Nagaro took the further precaution of waiting through a cycle of tides, during which Tego and Moraga employed the longboat to take soundings within the narrow passage and the wider harbor. When the two merchant seamen found the water amply deep and free of obvious rocks, even at low tide, all the way to within a dozen yards of the pebble beach, Nagaro decided it was time to thread the eye of the needle.

He conferred with Landros on the stern castle deck before making the attempt.

"We'll have no canvas on her," Landros was saying. "So I'll be free to stand in the bow on the forecastle deck and signal to ye which way t' steer." He demonstrated with his arms, port and starboard.

They were joined by Timegar. "I've left Taru manning my post," the second mate informed them in answer to Nagaro's questioning look. "When I asked for a volunteer to learn the task, that saucy young buck said he could do it without any teaching. So I've put him t' work. Since we're going nowhere at the moment, the young fool can't do us any harm."

"I assume ye'll be taking it slow with the oars through the passage," Landros put in, drawing the discussion back to the matter at hand.

"Aye," Timegar affirmed. "But not *too* slow. She'll not answer the tiller if her rudder's not cutting water."

Nagaro nodded. He was familiar with the concept. "A slow, even stroke then," he said. "And be prepared to immediately fold the oars as flat as you can against the hull if I tell you to. Even going at a slow pace, there may not be time to ship them."

"Aye, Captain," Timegar agreed. He saluted, before making for the ladder.

Within minutes, the word came from below that the men were ready. Nagaro gave the order, and the *Sword* was underway.

During that first running of the Needle's Eye there were many tense faces, with the sea-swells serging against the cliffs a scant dozen feet from the oar tips. But it took only a half dozen oar-strokes to pass the Eye's narrowest point, and the rest of the way was much less harrowing. Thanks to Landros' signals and Moraga's quick responses with the tiller, they had no need to fold the oars.

Eventually the *Sword of Freedom* came to rest, peacefully at anchor at the end of the long valley-harbor, about fifty feet from the beach. Since they were at the bottom of a steep-sided narrow valley, the sun hadn't yet reached the water there— it wouldn't for hours yet— and the bay lay deep in shadow. It was a sheltered haven, quite invisible from the open sea. The sharply sloping valley sides were broken by outcrops of bare rock, their lower reaches dotted with cedar trees, the higher slopes dominated by juniper. All that Nagaro could see lay serenely silent, mirrored in the still water of the bay.

Landros joined him on the stern castle, flushed and grinning, a more sober-faced Pavo close behind him. "That was some sweet sailin', if I do say so," Landros declared. "Not a nick or a scratch on her!"

Nagaro allowed himself a smile. "Yes. We did well." He sobered. "But I'm thinking we could be very effectively trapped here. Do you think it's possible the Mautep don't know about this harbor?"

Landros' grin also died. "They might not," he said. "Or then again, they might."

Nagaro looked at Pavo. "Do your people know anything about this place?"

Pavo lifted his broad shoulders. "I have not hear any story in Saar Tipaal," he said. "Not like all those story of Turowan fisherman."

Landros blew air through pursed lips. "Even if they know," he said, "they've no reason to come around if they don't know we're here. Not when the cove on the other side fits their needs like an oar in an oarlock."

Nagaro nodded. "You're right, Landros, but I don't think we can safely use this place the way we intend to more than once or twice. The word will get about." He frowned as his eyes followed the stream's course from a stand of bush-willow near the beach up to the valley's lip. "We'll have to see what we find up there." He gestured towards the heights. "Whether there's a good vantage point— or if the old stories have led us astray.

We're a long way, over here, from that cove where the Mautep are taking on water."

***

The windswept crown of Chitaopa Island turned out to be anything but smooth and level. It was instead an undulating landscape of miniature peaks and mountain ranges formed of lichen-crusted basaltic rock, with numerous small valleys in the form of gullies cut by rivulets, and little plains where pockets of soil supported a profusion of grasses, brambles, and small herbaceous plants. There was nothing there that could be called a real tree, though there were copses of stunted juniper that occasionally reached heights of five or six feet, rooted in cracks in the weathered rock.

They quicky found the highest point in that domain, a flat-topped block of wind-blasted basalt lying about half a mile south of the headwaters of the stream that emptied into the bay where the *Sword* lay anchored. The climb to the top of this rock was facilitated by an almost step-like formation on the rock's western side. Once atop it, a man could sit or lie at relative ease in the shelter of several wind-blasted juniper bushes.

The view from that vantage was spectacular, encompassing the broad expanse of the sea in all directions, out to the distant horizon. The island of Judaba could be seen quite clearly, and even the low, gray line that was the mainland shore. One could not, however, see Chitaopa's own shore, including the cove where the Mahuk ships presumably waited, because the island's bulk blocked the view of anything within a few hundred yards of the base of her cliffs. On that first afternoon, Nagaro led a small party past the stair-step rock to try to get a view down into the cove from the eastern cliff-edge, only to find the way was blocked by large numbers of sea-birds that made their nests all along the edge of the cliff top.

Standing at a safe distance, he shook his head ruefully as he squinted at the birds. "We can't get close enough," he said. "We'd send the whole flock of them screaming into the air, and anyone down below would know something was amiss up here."

"Ye're right." Taru ducked his head against the wind and kicked at a tuft of grass. "We'll have t' make do with that 'stair-step' rock back there."

Landros shrugged. "That's not so bad. The rock gives a better view to the east than where we're standing right now. And in all the other directions, besides. From there we'll see anything coming, long afore it gets close to the cove."

Since this was clearly true, Nagaro decided to set a two-man watch on Stair-Step Rock every day from dawn to dusk. He reasoned that no sensible captain was likely to try to approach Chitaopa in darkness. About mid-morning of the following day, the lookouts witnessed the departure of the three Mautep ships they had followed to the island. The craft sailed away, heading east by southeast, apparently making for Judaba.

***

In the days that followed, the *Sword*'s crew explored the harbor valley and found it well supplied with ground-squirrels, rabbits, yaba root, and onions. Nagaro drilled them with daily sword practice, and in making tight turns with the ship in the confines of the narrow bay, not to mention making a number of practice runs out and back in through the Needle's Eye.

There was nothing else to do but keep on watching and drilling and waiting for the coming of a lone Mahuk war galley. In this way, the days flowed from one to another and became weeks.

When the ship wasn't on maneuvers, Nagaro went often to sit for an hour or two with the lookouts. During those watches, he saw several groups of Mahuk ships come to Chitaopa's cove and sail away again, always going south. Twice the men watched in frustration as a single ship passed in the distance without stopping at the island, sailing far to the east on a course paralleling the mainland coast. The summer was waning and Nagaro couldn't help wondering how many more Mautep raiders could possibly be left who still needed to return to Mahuk waters.

Chapter 19

The Trap

It was on a day in mid Oteyin that Nagaro approached the Stair-Step Rock to find Pavo in the act of coming down to meet him. The young Hashtep was moving with haste, his usually impassive face alight with excitement.

"It is ship," Pavo explained breathlessly as they met at the foot of the rock. "One ship only. It look like she have turn to come this way!"

Nagaro'a heart jumped at the words. He sprang up the rough steps to the rock's flat top with Pavo at his heels and flung himself down under the low-hanging branches of the juniper, next to the other member of the day's lookout team. "Let me have a look, Landros," he said.

The grizzled sea warrior handed him the spyglass, and pointed. "There," was all he said, but there was a note of triumph in his voice.

The sail was a bright speck against the strip of blue-violet haze that was the mainland coast. Nagaro studied it critically. "Are you sure it's coming this way?"

"As sure as I *can* be at such a distance," Landros responded. "But we'll know soon enough. She came out o' the north— from the direction of Edrovir. And she's just changed course to take her away from shore."

For the next hour they watched, passing the glass back and forth, as the sail steadily increased in size, until it became a blazing rectangle, lit by the late summer sun. From their position atop Chitaopa's towering height, the ship certainly did seem to be heading directly towards the island.

Landros allowed himself to gloat as he peered through the glass. "She's a galley, all right. I can see her oars. And Kuran would never send one o' his warships alone into these waters, so she *must* be Mahuk, on her way back from plundering our coast. This is our chance!"

Pavo was actually grinning. "Making trap here is very good plan!" he said.

"It comes barely in time for our purpose." Nagaro squinted at the sail. "The summer's almost gone. In less than two weeks we'll have to return to Pakoa— with or without freeing any slaves."

"Almost ain't the same as quite." Landros gave the rock a satisfied slap and held out the glass to Pavo. "See if ye can make out her colors, lad. Ye know the Mahuk houses better 'n we do."

Pavo stretched out on the rock and peered through the spyglass. After a long moment, he lowered the glass, and said, "I think is ship of Lord Angkat. Color look like brown and gold."

Nagaro laughed shortly. "Well," he said. "That's only fair, I suppose. We took a ship-full of slaves from Lord Baalkir at Jaamra. Now we'll try to do the same to his chief rival."

The battle they'd escaped from at the Straits of Jaamra, between the powerful warlords Baalkir and Angkat, had apparently been indecisive. Continuing Mautep depredations along the Edroviran coast showed clearly that the rival Mautep warlords still needed gold and slaves to support their struggle for dominance, meaning that the Mahuk Baar still lacked an emperor.

"Aye, but if we want to be really fair about it, we ought t' take the ship, too," Landros observed pointedly.

Nagaro shrugged. "We'll see about that." He didn't like to admit that he had thought about it, and not for the sake of fairness. But truly, if they could just manage to get away with the slaves this time, it would be enough. "How long do you judge it will be before she makes the cove?"

Landros turned back to study the approaching ship. "Maybe another three hours, if the wind holds. Less if they row."

"Right." Nagaro stood up. "Landros, I want you to stay and watch her until the island blocks your view. That should put her within a half hour of entering the cove. Come back then as fast as you can. Pavo and I will go now to alert the foraging party and start making the ship ready to sail."

"Aye, Zirda." Landros grinned as he raised his hand in a casual salute before turning back to his observation of the approaching vessel.

Nagaro shook his head. He couldn't quite understand why Landros seemed to positively enjoy being told what to do. He was quite sure the veteran Fleet warrior could just as well have been giving the orders himself. "Come on," he said to Pavo, and the two younger men headed for the rough stairs.

From the bottom of the rock, they made for the stream and the ravine leading down into the valley where the *Sword* was anchored. Within half an hour, they stood, breathless, on the shingle of the little beach beside the two longboats.

Nagaro turned to Pavo. "Find Taru and his party and tell them to come back immediately."

Pavo acknowledged this with a silent nod and moved to obey.

Nagaro pushed off one of the longboats, climbed in, and vigorously plied the oars. Soon he was mounting the rope ladder that swung from the *Sword*'s rail.

On the deck, his news brought cheers and excited cries from the men.

"Hakura!"

"Praise the Spirits!"

"It's about time Lokundas showed us some favor."

Nagaro smiled faintly. The men were understandably eager after their three months of futile searching in the Lomoas and weeks of lying in wait on Chitaopa with nothing to do but rehearse battle strategies, practice their swordsmanship, and put the ship through her paces. By now they could do all these things in their sleep. All Nagaro had to do was watch in satisfaction from the stern castle as the men moved to stow gear and make everything secure.

His gratified thoughts were interrupted by Tredhold. The Leithian came up the ladder from the deck below, wearing a serious expression, and stepped up to the rail beside him. The healer cocked his head. "Are ye ready for this, Nagaro?"

Nagaro gave the other man a sidelong glance, having noted the use of his name, rather than the title "captain." As ship's doctor, it was Tred's duty to look after the mental as well as the physical well-being of the men under his care. Nagaro wasn't offended. He knew he'd given the healer cause for concern when doubt had overtaken him after he had slain five men at Jaamra.

"I think so," he answered earnestly. "At least I don't think I'm ever going to be any more ready." Then, on an impulse, he added, "What about you, Tred? Is it harder to face the prospect of battle now that you're a married man?"

Tredhold responded with a wry look. "Aye," he admitted. "I'd be lying if I said it wasn't." He turned to stare out across the ship's main deck. "Every voyage I've ever been on, I've *meant* to come back," he said. "But this time I feel I *have* to— because there's someone will suffer if I don't. But don't ye worry about me, lad," he added quickly, turning his bright blue gaze back to Nagaro. "I can take care of myself. Don't think ye have to be looking out for me."

It was Nagaro's turn to look away. "I know," he said quietly. "But part of me will be looking out for every member of this crew."

Tredhold frowned. "They chose to be here. And ye can't protect them all, Nagaro."

"I know that too." Nagaro turned back to meet the other man's eyes. "Vothra told me the same."

Tredhold's gaze slid away, across the water. To him, Vothra was alien territory.

Nagaro went on: "I mean to see this through, whatever happens, Tred, because I made the men a promise. After what I did at Jaamra, I believe I can do that much. But if it goes badly... if we lose any of them... well... you may have to help pick up the pieces." He gave the healer a brittle smile.

This time Tred nodded and there was understanding in his eyes. "All right, lad," was all he said.

Nagaro looked out over the main deck for a time, watching the men still making the ship ready. At last he sighed. "I suppose I'd best make myself ready for battle," he said, and made for the ladder.

In the captain's cabin, he exchanged the shirt he'd been wearing for the dark red leather vest that would display the slave brand on his left shoulder. The other former slaves among the crew would be in vests or bare-chested to show their brands as well. Hopefully, the slaves on the Mahuk oar deck would understand quickly that the strange men invading their prison with knives in their hands were friends. The leather vest fit too snugly for Nagaro to comfortably wear his ring underneath it. Since he didn't like leaving his precious keepsake in the cabin, he solved the problem by tying the leather string with the ring on it about his waist and tucking it inside the waistband of his pants, much as he'd done while he was a slave. Finally he took down his sword belt from a hook on the wall and buckled it about his waist.

He straightened and squared his shoulders, drew a long breath, and let it out slowly. Then he turned and stepped out of the cabin, dressed for battle. He emerged onto the main deck just as Pavo, Taru, and the rest of the foraging party were coming up the rope ladder and over the rail.

Taru's eyes were alight. "So! There's finally a ship in the cove?"

"There should be by the time we get there."

"Well it's about time!" Taru dropped a bag of freshly-dug onions unceremoniously on the deck. "Our snares took half a dozen rabbits," he went on breathlessly. "We'll have a nice rabbit stew to celebrate our victory."

Nagaro was just about to say he would be glad enough of a victory, with or without stewed rabbit, when Mendorel's cry rang from aloft in the crow's seat.

"It's Landros! Comin' down the trail!"

Nagaro immediately ordered one of the longboats out with two rowers to fetch the first mate.

By the time the boat had returned with Landros, and all three men were aboard, the ship was fully ready to sail. The oarsmen were below on the oar deck, and the anchor had already been weighed.

Nagaro mounted to the captain's platform and gave the order to execute a tight turn-about to port. The verbal responses from Moraga at the tiller and Timegar on the oar deck came, prompt and sure. He smiled with satisfaction as the *Sword* gracefully completed the turn. The crew could make the turn with equal facility in either direction. The shape of the hull resisted actually turning the ship on its own axis, but an arc of remarkably small radius could be accomplished by putting the rudder hard over and dragging the oars on one side of the ship while plying them on the other. It was an elegant demonstration of one of the advantages of having free men at the oars. The necessary precision would be difficult to achieve with slave oarsmen, many of whom didn't even speak their masters' language.

As the *Sword's* bow came into line with the bay's exit, Nagaro raised his voice. "Tiller to center! Steady ahead!" The ship surged forward, traversing the length of the bay and slipping between the buttresses of rock that guarded the narrow passage at the end of it. With guidance from Landros at the forecastle rail and Mendorel in the crow's seat, it wasn't long before the *Sword of Freedom* glided safely out into the heavy swells of the open sea.

Nagaro laughed aloud for sheer joy when he felt the wind in his face. As soon as they were safely clear of the cliffs, he called into the speaking tube:. "Ship oars, Timegar! Let the men rest a while." Then he raised his voice to shout across the deck: "Landros, get some canvas on her!" To Moraga at the tiller, he gave instructions to steer along the base of the cliff at about fifty yards distance.

In less than a minute, Landros had men aloft shaking out the sails, while many of the rowers had emerged to tread the deck or lean on the rail, resting their muscles from rowing and savoring the feel, the sight, and the sound of wind, and sun, and sea.

Resting the rowers now made sense. There was no point in tiring them when the ship had a favorable wind, and Nagaro was not in a great hurry in any case. He wanted to give the Mautep plenty of time once they reached the cove to put some of their men ashore in quest of water and forage. The fewer men there were aboard the Mahuk warship when the *Sword* came around the headland, the better.

Nagaro frowned. The greatest weakness in his battle plan lay in the fact that all but a handful of his men were newly trained and untested in battle, together with the fact that they had only seventeen swords among them. The Mautep crew would be fully armed and at least moderately experienced sea warriors. Nagaro had a good sense of who the most able fighters were among his untried recruits, but it was harder to guess who might falter in the face of a real enemy and who would stand firm. The men who had faced battle before must now be counted on to carry the day. *And he of course was one of them.* He tried to shrug off his tension. He'd been over all of this before.

Leaving the captain's platform, he went to lean on the stern castle's starboard rail where he could watch Chitaopa's west-facing cliffs slide by as he braced himself to the surging motion of the deck. He could trust Moraga to steer and Landros to manage the ship's sails, so there was no need at the moment for him to stay at his post.

The island's massive walls of basalt gleamed silver where the sun touched them. The crevices and cracks were etched in charcoal shadow. The *Sword* was making her course as close as she dared to the cliff's base, and at this distance the sound of the waves breaking against the rocks was a cacophonous roar. The air all about them was damp with salt spray as the ship swung slowly around to follow the north shore of the island.

Landros came up the ladder to stand beside him. "The sails are set for now," the first mate informed him. "And Pavo's keepin' a sharp eye on 'em."

Nagaro smiled fleetingly. Pavo was well on his way to becoming Landros' right-hand man. The young Hashtep seemed determined to learn how Landros read the wind and made decisions about trimming the sails. Oddly enough, Taru was coming to serve Timegar in a similar fashion on the oar deck. Nagaro found it amusing that his friends were both gravitating to the kinds of apprentice, or back-up, officer roles played by third mates in the Royal Fleet, without coming into direct competition with each other.

After a moment's silence, Landros cleared his throat and spoke again. "Are ye ready for battle then, Capt'n?" he asked, raising his voice so the wind wouldn't carry his words away.

Nagaro hid a second smile. Landros couldn't know that Tredhold had asked him the same question. "Yes," he said over the wind. "I'm ready." Then, because he'd recently been thinking about it, he asked, "Are we counting too much on my skill, Landros?"

The grizzled warrior shook his head and moved closer so he could lower his voice. "Ye have t' trust me on that, mate," he said seriously. "There's always a lot riding on the front line. I might be worried if ours was weak, but we've a good solid one. Me and Timegar, and Tred an' Rubo could carry the first line even without ye. And *with* ye... well... seeing the way ye move kind o' has an effect on folk." Landros paused, reading Nagaro's discomfort. "I know ye don't like that kind o' talk, lad, but it's true. And I don't want ye to fret about it. Ye just wade in like ye did before. We'll keep 'em off your back just like we did at Jaamra."

"All right." Nagaro tried to sound confident. At Jaamra he hadn't even been aware of what the other men were doing to protect him. He would just have to trust them, as Landros said.

For a long moment, both men stood watching the cliff slide past. Then Landros spoke again, almost idly. "I wonder what Vothra would think o' what we mean to do."

Without thinking, Nagaro answered. "The Spirit called it a noble venture. Worthy of the effort."

Landros turned to stare at him. "Ye've *talked* to Vothra?"

Nagaro felt himself floundering. "Well, yes," he said awkwardly. "I mean, I don't do it *often*. I'm sorry," he added weakly. "I thought Tredhold would have told you about it after Jaamra."

Landros eyed him narrowly. "We-ell..." he began. "The truth is, he did. The morning after we won our freedom. And he had me believing it, *then*, but when I thought about it afterwards, I wasn't so sure."

"Oh." Nagaro ran a nervous hand through his hair. "Anyone can talk to Vothra," he said. He read the other man's doubt. "I mean, I don't suppose, it's *common*— yet," he added quickly. "Vothra only re-gathered two years ago. And the Spirit wouldn't be paying so much attention to me if my Lady Guardian's spirit hadn't became part of it." He stopped speaking, suspecting he had only made matters worse.

Landros was studying him warily. "What's it like then?" he asked cautiously. "This talking to Vothra."

Nagaro frowned. "It's like talking to someone who is very wise, and very kind— and very, very forgiving."

Landros frowned in his turn. "What's it *sound* like, I mean? Can ye *see* Vothra?" He gestured vaguely at the air in front of him.

Nagaro shrugged. "Vothra usually comes in a dream," he said. "But regardless, it's all inside your head. The Spirit doesn't have a real body or a voice, so it can look or sound like anything it wishes. *I* see a figure that's all silver and black, and the voice I hear is... well, musical."

"Ah... I see." Landros' eyes were uncertain and he shifted his feet. "And ye ask the Spirit for advice?"

"Well, yes... Or comfort. After the men all pledged to follow me, I was afraid of what would happen if this venture went badly, and—"

"And Vothra told ye it would go all right?"

Landros sounded hopeful, but Nagaro shook his head. "Vothra can't see the future. The Spirit only said it was a noble venture—"

"—and worthy o' the effort," Landros finished, resignedly. "That sounds like something the Spirit would say." He sighed. "Can't say I'd be comfortable with voices talking inside *my* head. If there's any talkin' to Vothra to be done, I'm happy to let ye do it."

Nagaro was about to say that it really was not alarming, but Landros' attention had turned elsewhere, and he followed the older man's gaze to find that they were approaching the base of the low headland that formed the northern side of the cove where their prey awaited. "This may not go so well if the Mautep have a lookout posted on that headland," he muttered.

"Oh, aye," Landros conceded. "But our old friend Urchak never did that."

Nagaro grimaced at the reference to the captain of the former *Fist of Death*, a man who had cruelly slain Taru's parents but whom Nagaro had chosen to spare. "Urchak was only one captain, and not the wisest of the lot, I think," he said. "We don't know what any other Mautep captains may do."

"No, we don't. But the headland's a fair walk from the best landing in the cove. And why trouble to put a lookout there when ye think ye can see everything ye need to without it? Maybe ye can't see all the way t' the main from the beach the way we can from up top, but there's still a good long view from northeast all the way to due south. And no reason to expect a ship to be coming 'round the island the way we're doing."

Nagaro accepted his first mate's assessment with a nod. He'd been through the same reasoning in his own mind, but it was reassuring to hear it from the seasoned veteran. He finished the argument by saying, "And even if there *were* a lookout on the headland, it would take him time to get back to the cove with the news, and the captain wouldn't be sure if we were friend or foe." He glanced at the top of the mainmast where the black-and-white sword banner snapped in the wind. *Pirate colors, but not a traditional pirate flag...*

"Aye." Landros' nod was decisive. "There ye have it."

A quarter of an hour later, the *Sword's* bow was coming abreast of the tip of the headland. Landros squinted appraisingly at the ship's sails, then back at the low rocky point. "Time t' be trimming the sails for the turn," he said.

Nagaro nodded. "Give me word when you're ready for the tiller."

"Aye, Zirda!" The older man was away and down the ladder with a spryness that belied his years.

Nagaro returned to the captain's platform. He scanned the headland for any sign of a human figure, but saw none. If a man was there, he was making himself quite invisible. *Which was what a good lookout should do...* Nagaro cut the thought short. He tightened and relaxed his shoulders, trying to work out some of the tension in them. He let out a long breath.

Minutes later, the sails had been adjusted and Landros gave his signal that all was ready. Nagaro shouted to Moraga. "Put her over two points to starboard!"

"Aye, Capt'n!"

As the *Sword* began her swing around the headland, Nagaro called for battle positions and watched the men quickly move to their places. For most of them, that meant descending to the oar deck. Those left above were the most that could be spared from rowing. They had, of course, been trained to work the rigging as needed, but every one of them was also a member of the *Sword*'s front line— with the exception of Mendorel in the crow's seat who would stay on lookout or descend to fight as the situation warranted.

The core of the *Sword's* front line was made up of the best fighters: Landros, Tred, and Rubo the warrior-cook, together with Nagaro, and Timegar from the oar deck. But they'd needed more than that. Nagaro had agonized long over the choice of the other four, settling on Gurd, Moraga, Pavo, and Taru.

Gurd was young, but bold, and he had Fleet experience, and his swordsmanship had improved significantly under Nagaro's instruction. Moraga had turned out to have an impressive talent for the sword, which he combined with a natural ferocity that could be quite intimidating. Pavo could be intimidating as well— based on size and strength alone, but also on the steady, cool intensity with which he wielded his blade. And finally there was Taru, who was quick, and whose devious streak gave him a propensity for doing unexpected things— often enabling the young Turo to get the better of men with greater skill.

There were other reasons for choosing Pavo and Taru for the front line of course. Nagaro needed Pavo close at hand as a translator. Besides that, neither of his friends would have accepted being anywhere else.

These nine men would lead the fight when the crew boarded the other ship— or provide the first defense of the *Sword*'s deck in case the Mautep managed to board her instead. Nagaro's stomach tightened. He hoped for the advantage of surprise when they made their appearance, and he would know very soon whether he had it. With luck, their quarry would be anchored in the cove with her longboats either on the beach or in transit.

And if not?

He tried not to think about that possibility. It was impossible to plan for all contingencies. He would have to respond to whatever he found. To reinforce his resolve, he reminded himself of how good it had felt that day at Jaamra, when he and his fellow slaves had won their freedom. *If he could now just do the same for other men...*

***

Nagaro's heart was in his mouth and the spyglass to his eye when the *Sword* cleared the headland's tip and gave him his first view of the cove. The expanse of turquoise water was embraced by a pair of sand spits, one extending from the rocky headland they had just rounded, the other from the main mass of the island on the other side. A narrow gap of darker water between the tips of the spits marked the harbor's entrance. A part of Nagaro's mind took in the broader scene, including the tranquil cove, the pale sand of the beach, and the deep green foliage that skirted the cliffs beyond it. But the main focus of his attention was on the Mahuk ship.

It was there. Anchored in the still water near the center of the cove. He breathed a sigh of relief. The first hurdle had been cleared.

But the *Sword* had still to traverse the length of the nearer sand spit, then make a sharp turn to starboard to enter the cove. The bow of the enemy craft was facing the cove's outlet. It was an orientation well-chosen for flight, but the ship couldn't flee if any of her crew were ashore. Nagaro's fingers tightened on the spyglass as he scanned for Mautep crewmen and longboats.

What he saw told him that their luck was holding.

"One of her boats is beached," he reported, his voice raised to reach both Landros on the main deck and Timegar below, by means of the speaking tube. "The other's along-side of her. I see a few men on shore and a dozen on deck—" He sucked in his breath. The men on the ship had started dashing about. "They've seen us!"

"Your orders, Captain?" Timegar's voice rang hollow through the speaking tube.

"Hold the oars in. Let them wonder a little longer what we're about." Nagaro turned around to call, "Moraga! Make ready to turn."

"Aye Zirda!" came Moraga's prompt acknowledgment.

The *Sword of Freedom* was approaching the mouth of the cove under the power of her sails, her fighting readiness not immediately apparent to an external observer. There were only nine men above deck, counting Nagaro at the captain's post, Moraga at the tiller, and Mendorel in the crow's seat. The other six were lounging about like sailors waiting for orders. In fact, they were ready to cast the grapples and man the ropes until the other members of the crew could get up the ladders. Only the swords they wore suggested they belonged to the *Sword's* front line.

The other crewmen were on the oar deck, waiting with oars poised just inside the open oar ports. They would row during the final approach to the quarry and join the fray on deck as quickly as possible when the order came to ship oars. Both the fore and aft hatches were open and furnished with ladders. Each man knew his exit, and the shortest route to reach it. When Nagaro had expressed concern about Timegar being at his post below as battle approached, the Fleet veteran had smiled grimly and said, "I'm quick up a ladder." He'd proven the truth of it during practice.

Nagaro lowered his spyglass for a moment and met the eyes of Landros, standing directly below the stern castle. The seasoned sea warrior grinned wickedly up at him, then sobered and asked, "Do ye suppose Vothra's watching right now?"

"I wouldn't be surprised." Nagaro answered seriously. "The Spirit was watching me at Jaamra." He had to smile as Landros cast a glance over his shoulder. In fact, Nagaro suspected that Vothra watched him quite a lot. It was something else he tried not to think about.

"The boat! Look!"

The warning shout came from Mendorel, and Nagaro's attention snapped back to the Mahuk ship and her two longboats. He no longer needed the glass to see that the nearer longboat had left the ship's side and was being rapidly rowed toward the beach by a pair of men. His stomach knotted. The Mautep officer in command had clearly decided to recall the landing party. Everything now depended on speed. The *Sword* must close with her prey and seize her before the Mautep crew could be restored to full numbers.

"Oars out, Timegar!" Nagaro cried. "Ahead, all speed!" Through the speaking tube he heard Timegar's orders to the rowers. An instant later he heard the drum begin to throb and felt the ship surge under his feet as the oars bit the water. He glanced at the rigging. In close quarters a shifting or unsteady wind could be more hindrance than help. Cupping his hands, he called across the deck, "Furl the sails!"

Landros saluted and turned, shouting. "Ye heard the captain, lads! *Step lively!*"

Five men went up the masts like monkeys, and Mendorel left his place in the crow's seat to help with the main sail. In less than a minute, the canvas was being gathered up for binding to the yardarms.

The *Sword* came abreast of the cove's entrance, and Nagaro shouted, "Moraga! Hard to starboard!"

Moraga barked an acknowledgment, putting the tiller hard over, and the ship swung into a turn. Nagaro stood on the platform, trying to simultaneously assess the *Sword's* movement, the Mahuk longboat's approach to the shore, and the progress of his crew in the rigging.

By the time the *Sword*'s crew had finished aloft and begun to descend, the Mahuk longboat had reached the beach where its sister lay. And Mautep on shore were coming from all directions, converging on the two small craft. As the men in the *Sword*'s rigging reached the deck, they ran to the ship's port rail, each taking up a grappling hook with a heavy coil of rope attached. By the time the first of them were in position, the *Sword* had completed her turn, slipping cleanly between the tips of the sandbars and making straight for her target.

Nagaro's task now was to bring the *Sword* in along-side the Mahuk craft— not too fast, and as close as possible— so that his men could engage her with the grapples. Watching both ship and shore, he thought he could achieve this before the Mahuk longboats could return, *but how long before?* How widely scattered was the landing party? If those warriors returned too soon, the entire enterprise would fail... and what then would befall the men who had given him their trust?

The *Sword* was less than a hundred yards from her intended victim, and closing, by the time the two Mautep rowers had dragged their longboat onto the sand. The Mautep commander on the ship must have realized his danger, for the war galley's oars suddenly sprouted from their ports and dipped raggedly into the water.

After that, things happened so fast that Nagaro had no attention to spare for the Mautep landing party.

The Mahuk vessel began to make forward way, trying to move out of the *Sword's* path. Whoever commanded her clearly hoped to bypass the *Sword* wide enough on the port side to be out of grapple range. Nagaro smiled grimly. He had used every opportunity since taking command of the *Sword of Freedom* to study how the ship moved in response to oars and rudder. He'd always been quick to master new skills, and he could now feel the ship like an extension of his body. He didn't hesitate.

"Half a point to port, Moraga! Timegar, oars steady ahead!"

The *Sword* veered left, aiming now for a point twenty yards in front of the other moving ship. If their relative speeds remained unchanged, the *Sword of Freedom*'s iron-clad ram would meet the Mautep's bow at an angle that couldn't fail to find purchase. The Mautep commander couldn't know that Nagaro had no intention of sinking his prey— that he would, in fact, go to great lengths to avoid it. All the man could see was that his adversary was on a ramming course and that increasing his own speed would only result in the *Sword* striking his ship farther aft. There was only one thing the Mautep could do to save his ship: He gave the order to brake, to back-paddle.

Nagaro saw the other ship's oars pause, waver, and dip back down, spray pluming around the blades as the slaves struggled to slow the craft. But Nagaro had anticipated this. He waited, feeling the *Sword's* speed, gaging her momentum and the distance between the two ships. He watched as the Mahuk craft became dead in the water and then slowly, ponderously, began to make reverse way. *But rowing backward wasn't as efficient as rowing forward, and the rudder didn't work properly, besides.*

"Steady ahead!" he cried.

The ships were only forty yards apart... thirty-five yards... thirty yards...

Now!

Nagaro saw his moment. "Moraga!" he barked. "Quarter point starboard! "Timegar! Starboard pivot!"

The Second Mate's answering orders to his men came up through the speaking tube. The rowers on the *Sword*'s starboard side dipped their oars and held them in the water, leaning on them hard, while those on the port side held their oars high, clear of the water but ready. The *Sword* swung sharply back to the right, onto a course that would bring her in parallel to the Mahuk craft— with the port rails much closer together than they had been before the two course changes. This was, of course, the entire purpose of Nagaro's maneuver.

The Mahuk ship was twenty yards distant, still moving backward, but if she moved very far in that direction she would beach herself in the shallows, and her commander knew it.

"Starboard oars, clear!" Nagaro cried.

Below, Timegar echoed the order, and it was instantly obeyed.

For a moment then, the *Sword* was coasting, all oars clear of the water. Though slowed by her turn, she was still gaining on her quarry. Half a dozen of her crewmen stood poised at the rail, grapples ready.

For Nagaro, it was now a matter of slowing just enough— and of getting the oars shipped in time to avoid injury to the rowers on both ships. "Tiller dead ahead! Oars, all slow!"

He felt the *Sword* shudder under his feet as the oar blades bit the water on both sides, throwing up showers of spray as the rowers braced their backs. The ship began inexorably to lose way.

And watch... and wait...

Twelve yards... ten yards...

"Ship oars! Now!" Nagaro gave the order when the two ship's bows were just yards apart. He felt a forward surge as the *Sword's* oars left the water even as he cupped his hands to his mouth and bellowed, "*Slaves! Ship oars! For your lives!*"

Pavo on the main deck echoed the cry in Hashti, repeating it three times, and Nagaro saw the other ship's oars lift unevenly from the water and begin to swiftly disappear through the ports. He heaved a sigh of relief at another hurdle safely passed.

The two ships' bows slid past each other, their port rails within feet of one another. Nagaro had judged well and his first mate was ready. When the *Sword's* bow was nearly level with the Mahuk craft's foremast, Landros shouted, "*Grapples away!*"

The iron hooks with their tails of rope snaked out, catching the other ship's rail as the men yanked on the ropes to make the tines bite the wood.

With the grapples set, the *Sword's* crew braced their feet against the inside of their own rail and began to haul the ropes in, hand-over-hand, drawing the two craft together for boarding. At the same time, Mautep warriors rushed forward to take up fending pikes, thrusting the heavy steel points into the *Sword's* rail from the outside, trying desperately to keep the two ships apart.

The men who were hauling on the ropes had no hands free to deal with the fending pikes, and just beyond the pikemen stood grim-faced Mautep warriors waiting with drawn swords.

Even before the grapples had taken hold, Nagaro had heard the trample of feet as the *Sword's* oarsmen made for the hatches: The call for the grapples was the cue that all hands were needed on deck. Now Moraga sprinted past him, heading for the ladder. Seeking a faster route, Nagaro vaulted to the top of the stern castle rail and dropped to the main deck below. Landing in a crouch like a cat, he sprang up and dashed for the port rail.

There were two ways to deal with a fending pike. One was to grab the pikeshaft and push as hard as you could to knock the man holding it backward off his feet. Nagaro chose the other way. Darting between Landros and Tredhold in the middle of the row of men, he leaned over the rail and seized the nearest pike. Gripping it by the hook, he twisted it free of the wood, then yanked it up— clear of the rail— and *pulled* with all his might. The Mautep wielding the pike, who had been putting all his weight on it, stumbled forward and let go in a reflexive effort to keep from falling. As soon as Nagaro felt the pike come free in his hands, he hauled it aboard and flung it away, bouncing and clattering across the deck.

Turning then, he took stock. The rowers were arriving all around him, pouring from the doors of the fore- and stern castles as well as from both hatches. Some went for the pikes. Others moved to help with the grapple ropes.

Nagaro looked to Mendorel in the crow's seat and shouted, "Where are the longboats?"

"One just left the beach, Capt'n, full o' men! The other'll soon follow!"

Bishka! Nagaro turned back to deal with a second pike. Seconds later, wood ground against wood as the Mautep pikemen lost their fight and the *Sword*'s crew manning the ropes closed the gap. The ropes were promptly made fast to cleats spaced along the rail, lashing the ships together from forecastle to amidships, overlapping along half their lengths.

Nagaro stood facing the rail. On the deck of the other ship there bristled a row of Mautep swords. He drew his own blade. All along the *Sword*'s port rail, other blades flashed in the sun as his men followed his example.

The two opposing forces stood face to face, taking each other's measure.

Chapter 20

Kiraam Shaku-Tal

Nagaro counted twenty Mautep warriors, all armed. These men could see they were outnumbered two to one. What they couldn't see was that fewer than half of the men facing them had swords. Those who had none kept to the back. He easily picked out the Mautep commanding officer, standing directly across from him in the center of the front rank. The man was tall and hard-eyed with an air of command. By the insignia on his tunic, Nagaro knew he was not the ship's captain, but the first mate. Nagaro passed his sword into his left hand and raised his right hand, palm outward, in sign of parley. Then he spoke, in a ringing voice, the first words he had learned in Hashti.

"*Kia kaar hanuk-tak.*"

It meant, "Put down your swords," and he added a phrase that he had learned more recently. "*Sho naneef lashir-aan,*" meaning that the Mautep would not be harmed if they did so.

Most of the Mautep warriors stared at him. Some of them muttered under their breaths, but the tall hard-faced man with the officer's stars on his collar laughed derisively.

"*Droviri chateef!*" He spat the words, then strode forward and lunged over the rail, his sword leveled at Nagaro's chest.

Nagaro's sword was back in his right hand in the blink of an eye as he stepped in to meet the blade. His arm shot out and his blade seemed to wrap itself around the other man's in a movement too swift to follow.

"*Keshal!*" The man swore as his sword was torn from his grasp and sent flying through the air, up and away to Nagaro's right.

Landros took two steps back and deftly caught the arcing blade by the hilt. A cheer went up from the crew of the *Sword of Freedom* as Landros passed the captured weapon back to one of the unarmed men behind him.

The Mautep officer took two steps back, in his turn, scowling and rubbing his wrist. The rest of his crew stepped back as well, which opened more space between them and the rail.

Seeing this, Nagaro immediately gave the signal to board, vaulting over the rail to land in the space the Mautep officer had vacated. Simultaneously, the fighting crew of the *Sword* poured over the rail to his left and right, coming to stand with swords ready.

The Mautep warriors fell back again before this advance, drawing together, looking uncertainly to their disarmed leader. Nagaro motioned for his own men to hold. For a moment the only sounds were the wind in the rigging, the cries of circling gulls, and the waves breaking on the beach.

Abruptly, Mendorel's cry cut the air. "The boats are coming!"

Nagaro risked a quick glance in the direction of the shore and noticed the top of a rope ladder hooked over the port rail near the stern castle.

"Pull up that ladder, Nanu," he cried, addressing the man nearest to it. "Don't let them come aboard!"

"Aye Zirda!" Nanu sprang to obey.

The Mautep officer had followed Nagaro's glance. He could also see what Mendorel had seen. Knowing that help might be at hand seemed to embolden him, for he grabbed a sword from one of his crewmen and faced Nagaro defiantly.

Reading the Mautep's face and stance, Nagaro tried his offer in Hashti again, without much hope.

"*Nan!*" The Mautep's rejection was immediate and emphatic. It was followed by a stream of angry Hashti that Nagaro couldn't understand, although he caught again the word "chateef" and also "shaku raal."

Pavo Maat spoke from Nagaro's left. "He say we are *chateef*— that is pirate. Also he call you slave-dog."

Before Nagaro could decide how to respond, the Mautep officer made his move. Dodging quickly to his right, the man gestured to his men to attack even as he threw himself at Nagaro.

Nagaro instantly gave his own signal to attack. As he parried the Mautep's thrust with a ringing stroke, he cried: "Push them back, but don't kill unless you have to!"

Swords clashed together all along the line.

Trusting his men to do their part, Nagaro focused on his adversary. He knew the man would not be disarmed so easily again. Indeed, the Mautep was fighting now with all his skill— which was considerable. Despite that skill, Nagaro managed to consistently turn his assailant's attacks and advance across the deck, driving the Mautep officer before him inch by inch.

The *Sword*'s crew needed to force the Mautep warriors back far enough to allow their own rear rank— led by Tego and armed only with knives— to get to the forecastle door. That goal was in the back of Nagaro's mind as he gave most of his attention to keeping pressure on his opponent without driving the Mautep commander to do something that would force him to kill the man. He was aware that Taru and Pavo, flanking him to right and left, were holding their own. Between parries, he glimpsed Landros, Tredhold, and Gurd, farther to his right, pressing to wrap around the end of the Mautep line and force them closer together, cutting them off from the stern castle. A flick of his eye to the other side showed Timegar, Rubo, and Moraga trying to do the same on their side, to push the other end of the Mautep line away from the forecastle.

The Mautep commander was beginning to look worried. His attacks were becoming more reckless. Nagaro continued his methodical assault, relaxing none of his guard. A desperate man, he knew, would only fight the harder.

"The boats are closing, Capt'n!" Mendorel's shout rang from above.

And the next instant, Tego's voice cried, "*Now!*" The weathered merchant seaman must have seen a clear path to the forecastle door.

Bad news, and good, Nagaro thought as he heard the trample of booted feet behind him. It was time to finish this. He looked into his adversary's eyes. The man had stepped back to breathe. He appeared heartened, presumably by the progress of the longboats. Nagaro gave the Mautep his best pirate smile. Then he attacked with blinding speed. The Mautep parried wildly, his expression turning from hope to dismay as he realized that Nagaro had been holding back. The Mautep officer retreated desperately, dodging and parrying, his face contorted in concentration. He seemed determined not to yield.

Nagaro had seen the man take a new blade once when disarmed. He needed something more effective. *But first, one last chance...*

"*Kia kaar hanuk-tak,*" Nagaro grated through his teeth.

"*Nan!*" the man gasped.

So be it. Two strokes, and Nagaro slipped past the Mautep's guard, deliberately slicing deeply into the flesh of the man's sword arm, just below the shoulder.

The Mautep cried out in shock. His sword clattered to the deck as he staggered back, clutching his wounded arm with his left hand and barking words at the two men on either side of him. They looked shaken, but closed ranks in front of their leader, advancing on Nagaro with simultaneous attacks.

Nagaro stepped over the officer's fallen sword, knowing one of the men behind him would retrieve it. Once more smiling his pirate smile, he engaged both blades, moving like a whirlwind. "*Kia kaar hanuk-tak!*" Three strokes, and the sword on the left went flying from its owner's grasp. Two more strokes, and the sword on the right skidded across the deck. Both blades were pounced upon by members of the *Sword's* crew.

The two disarmed sea warriors turned pale and threw up their hands. "*Judili!*" they cried, nearly in unison.

Nagaro turned on the next Mautep to his right, but the man backed away, eyes full of fear, dropping his sword on the deck before Nagaro could begin his assault. Nagaro kicked the sword behind him and swung back to his left, but the next Mautep on that side was standing frozen, his sword dangling loosely in his hand. The man's lips moved. "*Judili hanuktar,*" he whispered hoarsely.

Instantly Nagaro halted. He would not fight men who made no effort to defend themselves. He turned, seeking Pavo Maat's translation of the man's words— and discovered that all fighting on the deck had ceased.

In the sudden silence, a hailing shout from one of the Mahuk longboats was heard quite clearly.

No one answered it.

The Mautep crewmen on the deck were standing bunched together, surrounded on three sides by Nagaro's men, their backs to the starboard rail. Some eyed Nagaro fearfully, others glanced at their wounded leader as if hoping he wouldn't ask them to continue. The *Sword's* crew were standing or crouching in menacing attitudes, making it clear they would be glad to carry on the fight.

Nagaro saw men bleeding on both sides. Taru had a nasty-looking cut on his temple. Moraga had a gash on his forearm but a look in his eye like a hunting cat that has tasted blood. The young Mautep he'd been fighting had several wounds and the look in *his* eyes said he was beaten.

Pavo was watching Nagaro. "They call you 'demon swordman,'" he explained in answer to his friend's questioning look.

Nagaro frowned and gestured with his head at the Mautep officer. "Tell him no one else will be harmed if his men lay down their swords. Tell him I swear it on my honor."

Pavo immediately addressed the Mautep commander in rapid Hashti. The disarmed man stood his ground, eyes flicking back and forth between Pavo and Nagaro. Blood was soaking through his shirt and oozing between the fingers of his left hand where he clutched his wounded arm. He appeared unsure how far he could trust the honor of a Droviri pirate.

It was at this moment that the first slaves stumbled out of the forecastle, blinking in the brilliant afternoon sun. One after another they stepped through the door, shuffling onto the deck and crowding together warily.

Prepared though he was, Nagaro was shocked by the condition of the freed men. They were all half naked, unkempt, and unshaven— and above all, unspeakably filthy. Tego and the others who had cut the slaves free came forth after them, covering their mouths and noses. Worse than the condition of the slaves' bodies was the state of their minds. No more than a third held up their heads and walked as free men should. Others moved timidly, cowering as if they expected punishment to fall at any second. And then there were the ones that looked either half mad or else dull-eyed, too sunk in misery to comprehend that they were free.

Nagaro felt his anger rising. Knowing he must maintain his control, he turned quickly away, back to the Mautep officer. The man was staring at the slaves, frowning darkly.

Mendorel's voice cut into the waiting silence. "The boats are here, Capt'n! Ten men in each. They've gone for the starboard rail!"

Nagaro tensed, keeping his eyes on the Mautep officer. The men in the boats had understandably decided to try to board on the side opposite the one where the *Sword* was lashed.

"Landros," he said, without turning. "See to the starboard rail. Don't let them aboard."

Landros moved promptly to obey, beckoning a contingent of men to follow. Although the Mautep on the deck responded by raising their swords, they were pressed back by those under Landros' command. The crew of the *Sword of Freedom* quickly secured control of both rails, port and starboard.

Nagaro immediately turned to Pavo. indicating the wounded Mautep commander, he said, "Tell him the landing party will not be allowed to board unless they give up their swords."

The Mautep officer needed no explanation. The situation was plain enough. The longboats carried rope ladders but they were awkward things that could only be climbed by one man at a time— and the pirates would not allow them to be deployed. There would be no help from the landing party after all. The Mautep first mate scarcely waited for Pavo to finish speaking before he turned to his men and spat out his order.

"*Karash hanuk!*"

Nagaro saw Pavo relax. The Mautep warriors lowered their swords and laid them on the deck. Some were glowering, but most looked relieved. The surrendered weapons were quickly collected by crewmen from the *Sword of Freedom*.

Nagaro let out a pent breath and sheathed his own blade.

The Mautep officer glumly watched as the swords taken from his men were distributed among Nagaro's followers. Then he spoke, addressing Nagaro in Hashti.

Pavo promptly translated. "He ask what do you want."

Nagaro made a small bow to the man. "Tell him we will keep the swords, because we can use them. Tell him also that these men will go free." Here he gestured at the rag-tag crowd of slaves. "And," he added,

"Tell him that we will take anything of value that we find on board this ship, because we need to live so that we may set more men free."

As Pavo rendered this speech into Hashti, it was evident that portions of it surprised the Mautep commander. He turned startled eyes from Nagaro to the slaves and back again, and when Pavo had finished he said something.

Pavo turned back to Nagaro, frowning. "He wonder what will happen to slave that are Hashtep," he explained. "He ask will you make them be slave in Edrovir?"

Nagaro stiffened. "Tell him we do not keep slaves!" he said, eyeing the Mautep coldly. "What the free Hashtep decide to do is up to them."

He turned away then, leaving Pavo to translate, and directed the gathering of the Mautep warriors beside the wall of the forecastle, where they could be held under guard. He then told Tredhold to see to the wounded. "All of them," he said. "Deal with the worst wounds first, wherever you find them."

One of the slaves, a short stocky Turowan clad in the remains of a pair of seaman's pants, stepped forward as Tred was saluting in acknowledgment. "That there's the slave driver," the Turo declared grimly, pointing at one of the men being led away towards the forecastle. "Give me th' whip and I'll give him a stripe for every one he gave me! And then ye can pass the whip around t' the other lads so they can all have a go."

This drew some appreciative murmurs from among the other slaves. The Mautep warrior in question must have seen the man pointing at him. Judging by his sudden look of apprehension, the man could guess the meaning of the slave's words.

Nagaro considered the Turo who had spoken. "What is your name?" he asked.

"Bouno," the man responded.

Nagaro inclined his head. "Well met, friend Bouno," he said. "What you suggest is just, but I've given my word that no harm would come to these men if they laid down their swords. I would not be foresworn."

Bouno frowned. "Ye're the one they call Capt'n Nagaro, that was a slave yerself?"

"Yes I am. And I was."

Buono's frown continued unchanged. "They said ye *killed* yer own slave driver," he ventured pointedly.

It was Nagaro's turn to frown. "It was in battle," he said. "He came at me with his sword, to kill me. The other Mautep crewmen surrendered and were spared."

Bouno's brow relaxed a little. "Well if ye can stay yer hand, I s'pose I can do the same," he growled. "But it burns me t' let him walk away, an' that's a fact!"

At this point, a young Hashtep slave stumbled forward and dropped to his knees at Nagaro's feet. Words poured from his lips in rapid Hashti.

Nagaro stared for a moment in dismay. "Please get up," he said, reaching down to put his hand under the young Hashtep's arm and raise him to his feet. "There's no need for this."

Pavo quickly translated Nagaro's words for the Hashtep slaves, then explained to Nagaro. "He call you 'lord,' and say he will row for you all that is left of his life, because you have save him from Lord Angkat."

Nagaro shook his head. "Ask him his name."

The young slave answered Pavo's question promptly, saying, "Seftep."

Nagaro looked directly into the young man's eyes. "Friend Seftep," he said earnestly. "I am no one's lord. If you decide to join us, we will be glad to have you. But you are a free man this day, and you can go wherever you choose."

When the young Hashtep heard Pavo's rendering of this, he stared at Nagaro in pure astonishment. "*Daashu...*" he murmured. "*Daashu!*"

Nagaro understood the Hashti word for thanks. He smiled. "*Inan pash*," he said, giving the appropriate response.

This exchange caused some murmuring among the other Hashtep slaves and drew surprised looks from the Droviri among them. Before anyone else could speak, however, there was a commotion at the starboard side of the ship, and Nagaro had to turn his attention to the handling of the Mautep shore party.

Beckoning Pavo to follow him, he strode to the starboard rail and surveyed the occupants of the longboats. He quickly identified the Mautep captain by the markings of rank on the man's tunic. The man was standing in the middle of one of the boats, balancing easily to the gentle swells. He was a quick, sharp-eyed man, neither as tall nor as broad as his first mate, the man who had fought Nagaro. He was gesticulating at Landros and speaking angrily in Hashti.

Landros turned, grinning. "They tossed up a pair o' lines with grappling hooks," he explained. "We threw 'em right back!"

Nagaro tried not to smile. Instead he instructed Pavo to explain to the irate Mautep captain that his ship was in the hands of the "Droviri chateef," and if he wished to keep his sword, he must stay where he was until the Droviri had departed with the slaves and whatever valuable cargo they could carry.

The captain was plainly not pleased by this news.

There followed a rapid exchange between Pavo and the captain that became increasingly heated on both sides. Nagaro had to intervene, requesting a translation, to learn what had gotten the usually unflappable Pavo so worked up.

"He have call me traitor!" Pavo's eyes blazed. "Because I help Droviri chateef attack Mautep on ship. But I have answer him," he added with a flash of teeth. "I tell him I do not follow man who burn my skin with iron and make me slave for stealing two rabbit. I follow man who set me free and call me friend!"

Landros laughed outright at this, and exclaimed, "Good for ye, lad!"

Nagaro had to smile. "Did he say what he intends to do?"

Pavo shrugged. "He say all his man will keep their sword and stay in boat— only he want to talk to first mate."

Nagaro could not immediately think why he shouldn't allow this, and Landros only shrugged. So the Mautep first mate was brought over at sword point, presumably to give his captain an accounting of what had passed.

The first mate answered his captain's questions in a firm voice, with no hint of apology. Nagaro understood enough to gather that the man didn't feel he'd done badly under the circumstances, since he'd put up a good fight and been wounded into the bargain. The word *kajadeem* was uttered more than once, as was the phrase *judili hanuktar*, and the man indicated his arm, freshly bandaged with a piece of his own torn-off shirt sleeve. There was a convincing red stain on the white fabric.

Stepping close to Nagaro and speaking low, Pavo said, "First mate say you have show honor, and you are very good with sword. So it is not dishonor for him to have surrender."

The Mautep captain didn't seem impressed however. He asked his questions in short clipped sentences and listened, glowering. At length he grunted and turned back to Nagaro and Pavo. He spoke at some length, ending with a questioning inflection. Nagaro looked his own question at Pavo, who translated.

"He say he is Captain Ilaam jir-Taak, and he ask who are you that rob ship of Lord Angkat and steal his slave."

Nagaro turned to the Mautep and answered in Hashti, identifying himself as Captain Nagaro. "*Il sep Heeruk Nagaro.*"

Pavo promptly added, "*Haya sep Kiraam Shaku-Tal!*" And then said something else in which Nagaro was able to pick out the name of Roheed jir-Akaan.

The Mautep captain reacted with a start, and the first mate gave his commander a look that said plainly, what did I tell you?

Nagaro turned on his friend. "Why did you tell him I am Kiraam Shaku-Tal?" he demanded. "I don't want to be called that!"

Pavo's face was impassive. "I know," he said. "But is better—you will see. I think he have hear that story!"

It seemed so indeed, for the Mautep captain was looking Nagaro up and down with renewed interest. Presently his gaze fell on the hilt of Nagaro's sword. Immediately the man uttered something that could only have been an oath. Pointing at the sword, the Mautep captain launched into a torrent of angry words.

Nagaro could understand none of it. Helplessly, he turned to Pavo. The young Hashtep's forehead creased with a frown, and he spoke with evident care when he translated.

"Captain say he know that sword. It have belong to chief of House of Shofeer. It have pass from father to son, but last Chief of Shofeer die at Jaamra. Captain Ilaam ask how you get it."

Nagaro felt a chill. "You were there, Pavo," he said. "You know how it was." He turned to look down directly into the face of Captain Ilaam. "The man died from falling through the hatch into the oar deck," he said evenly. "He had no more use for the sword. I took it because I had need."

The Mautep had been eyeing Nagaro keenly. Now he turned his demanding gaze upon Pavo Maat.

Pavo appeared uneasy, but he launched into his translation. He was rewarded with another torrent of angry Hashti. He turned back immediately to Nagaro, distress and anger warring on his countenance. "This is not good," he said, shaking his head. "This I do not like at all!"

"Why? What did he say?" Nagaro glanced from Pavo to the scowling Mautep and back again. "Come on, Pavo. Out with it!" he added, when the young Hashtep hesitated.

Pavo licked his lips, his brows knitting. When he spoke it was with obvious reluctance. "He say... you are thief. You have no honor. That you... should not have sword of Shofeer. Because you do not win it in battle."

"I see." Nagaro swallowed. An uneasy knot in his stomach was added to the cold prickling down his spine. He'd never been entirely comfortable about keeping the sword. A thing that was finder's gold might be used to serve your own need or the need of another. He had tried to look at it that way. But if an owner appeared, it made a difference.

"Now see here!" Landros had been listening with keen interest to all that had passed, and he now flung his words at the uncomprehending Mautep captain. "Nagaro fought a dozen men that day! He killed five o' them fair and clean. No one can say he hasn't won that sword!"

But Nagaro shook his head. "I've used it honorably, Landros," he said quietly. "But that's not the same thing."

Captain Ilaam's face betrayed nothing as he looked from Landros to Nagaro. Then, emboldened perhaps by Nagaro's apparent hesitation, he spoke again in strident tones.

Pavo reacted to the man's words as if struck. He turned to Nagaro in dismay. "He say if you have honor like you say, you must give sword to him! He say he have blood of House of Shofeer from mother of his father. But this is not right, Nagaro!" Pavo was nearly beside himself. "Sheptuum have give this sword to you! I know it! I saw how that man fall. Sword point right at *you!*"

In the boat below them, Captain Ilaam thrust up his hand, and said words that Nagaro knew meant "give me the sword!"

For several seconds Nagaro stood irresolute. He didn't believe in miracles from Sheptuum, and he couldn't in honor simply disregard the captain's claim. At the same time, he didn't wish to give up the sword. The work he meant to do with it was surely much better than the work it would do in Mautep hands.

Captain Ilaam still stood with his hand raised demandingly. The Mautep repeated his strident request.

Nagaro looked down, straight into the man's eyes. "*Nan,*" he said in a firm voice. "*Il hataaf sho ja hanuk.*" The simple phrase stretched the limits of his Hashti.

The captain stared back him, his expression turning gloatingly triumphant. "*Il vatah!*" was all he said.

"What did he say? Landros demanded of Pavo. "What did Nagaro say to him?"

Pavo's face had gone still, but his eyes shown when he looked at the older man. "Nagaro have say he will not give sword," he answered quietly. "He say he will fight Captain Ilaam jir-Taak for it. And Captain Ilaam have accepted."

Chapter 21

The Challenge

It was nearly an hour later by the time the two captains at last stood facing each other in the middle of the main deck of the Mahuk ship. Each held his sword in his hand, tip pointed at the planking. It had taken some time to work out the arrangements for this affair of honor to the satisfaction of both sides, and a number of the members of the *Sword's* crew were manifestly still not happy with some of the details— or the lateness of the hour. The sun was already slipping westward and the shadow of Chitaopa's cliffs stretched far over the waters of the cove.

Behind Captain Ilaam stood the Mautep first mate, who had given his name simply as Hatheer. His sword had been restored to him for the duration of the challenge match. He held it gingerly, unsheathed because it was acknowledged that his wound would hamper his movements. Behind Nagaro stood Landros, also armed but with his sword in its scabbard. The task of the two first mates was to witness the fairness of the fight, call the hits, and declare the victor— and to intervene in the event of treachery.

Behind the two first mates were arrayed the crewmen from their respective ships. The Droviri crew and the freed slaves stood on the port side, to which the *Sword of Freedom* was still lashed. The Mautep who had surrendered stood to starboard. Those who hadn't surrendered still waited in the longboats, having been relieved of their grapples and rope ladders to ensure that they couldn't try to sneak aboard during the fight. As a precaution, Nanu was stationed atop the stern castle to keep an eye on them.

Pavo Maat, as translator, stood near the combatants, to aft. Tredhold, as ship's doctor, stood similarly near at hand on the forward side, his healer's bag in his hand. This was not to be a fight to the death, but with real swords rather than blunted practice blades it was to be expected that a hit could draw blood.

Aside from the four officers, the other men were all unarmed, the remaining swords having been laid in a pile by the wall of the forecastle some distance from where anyone was standing. It was this last detail that had raised the most protest among the *Sword's* crew. Timegar had expressed the opinion that it was going too far. Moraga had sworn a number of choice oaths, and still wore a face like thunder.

Taru, who'd been incensed at the very idea that Nagaro should have to fight for the sword, had been put even further out of temper at having to give up his own weapon. "I don't trust that lot," he'd growled, eyeing the Mautep warriors. "Not as far as I can spit! Didn't we already win this fight?"

Nagaro had pointed out that both sides were equally positioned to recover the blades if things went sour, and the *Sword's* crew outnumbered the Mautep warriors more than two to one. The Mautep, he reasoned, would be foolish to attempt treachery under conditions where they would likely be overwhelmed. Taru had shot back that the numbers could be quickly evened if the men in the longboats got aboard. It was this observation that had resulted in Nanu's assignment.

Landros had kept his own misgivings to himself throughout the negotiations. But now, as he took up his position behind Nagaro, he moved close enough to mutter, "By the Eyes of Vothra, man, I hope ye know what ye're doing! That captain and his mate have had their heads together out o' Pavo's hearing, and I don't trust them any more 'n Taru does."

Nagaro inclined his head slightly. "I'm sure that Vothra's eyes *are* watching me, Landros," he said quietly. "I don't intend to die today, but if I do, at least it will be with honor."

"The man'll be very good, Nagaro. He wouldn't have taken this challenge if he weren't— not after what his mate must ha' told him."

Nagaro nodded again. "I know," he said. "If I am slain, Landros, it will fall to you to keep my covenant. To bring the men safely home."

Landros didn't hesitate. "Ye can count on me, Captain," he said. "I'll do whatever needs doing. But I'd rather ye made sure it wasn't necessary." Then, seeing that all was ready and everyone waiting, the old sea warrior stepped back into position.

Nagaro studied the two Mautep officers. Captain Ilaam stood silent and ready, his expression unreadable, his eyes narrowly fixed on his opponent. Hatheer stood stiffly behind his captain. The first mate's face was also scrupulously blank, but something about his eyes and the tension in his stance suggested apprehension.

Pavo raised one hand. "You are ready? *Sho abtaak?*"

Nagaro and Ilaam both nodded.

Pavo brought his hand down in a chopping motion. "*Yaah!* Begin!" he cried in a clear voice.

Nagaro raised his sword in a salute, bowed with a flourish, and came on his guard.

Captain Ilaam's salute was perfunctory by comparison, and was followed immediately by a lightning-quick attack, requiring a parry from Nagaro that turned the Mautep's blade aside inches from his chest. There was a collective gasp from the onlookers, and as the two men leaped apart, Nagaro caught a flicker of disappointment in Ilaam's eyes.

Landros stepped forward. "Here, now!" he said angrily. "We agreed this ain't for blood!"

Ilaam smiled a quick, brittle smile and said something in Hashti.

"He say was only test— and maybe he get a little too close." Pavo sounded skeptical.

The Mautep captain's next several moves were of a very different kind, almost clumsy compared to the first. Nagaro parried them easily, his brows knitting.

The first move had been no accident. The man was better than this. He didn't like men who played such a game, but there was a way to put an end to it. He attacked fast and low, coming in under the other man's guard, forcing the Mautep to use his skill.

Quick as a snake, Ilaam turned Nagaro's blade. Nagaro stepped right, as if to catch his balance, but even as his foot struck the deck, he made a fresh attack— and scored a hit, drawing blood from his opponent's thigh.

First blood!

There was a groan from the Mautep ranks, a cheer from the Droviri.

Again the two men leaped apart, circling, wary and watchful. Anger now glinted in Ilaam's eyes.

Nagaro didn't smile. He knew he had both skill and speed, but Ilaam was also skilled and faster than most. Nagaro took his swordmaster's advice very seriously to never underestimate an opponent. *No matter how good you are, the other man can beat you— if you let yourself be overconfident, if you become careless...*

Nagaro's ploy had at least forced Ilaam to abandon pretense. The Mautep launched a sudden swift assault. Nagaro parried. He side-stepped nimbly out of his parry, but the other man spun to follow him and struck again. Again Nagaro parried and again he shifted position. Ilaam tried move after move after that in swift succession, only to be thwarted time and again by Nagaro's blade. The increasing speed and intensity of the fight was drawing gasps from the onlookers.

Captain Ilaam was beginning to sweat. Hatheer had warned him that the Droviri was good, but he knew he was a significantly better swordsman than his first mate. As he failed over and over to break through his opponent's guard, but still hadn't taken another hit, he began to suspect that the Droviri captain was playing with him. Since the man had cut him, this pirate who called himself Captain Nagaro— this Kiraam Shaku-Tal— seemed to be fighting defensively. Much as Ilaam would have liked to think he had the Droviri too much off-balance to mount an attack, the flawless precision of his opponent's movements belied the notion. Besides that, maddeningly, the Droviri's face showed no sign of stress. There was only cool intensity in the gray eyes. Watching those eyes, the phrase "demon swordsman" began to tug at the Mautep captain's mind. Annoyed, he told himself that he didn't believe in such things. It was true that he had yet to draw blood from this man, but he hadn't used his best attacks either, nor his best speed. *Perhaps it was time for both...*

Nagaro had been studying his opponent's repertoire of moves. The man was indeed very skilled. A couple of Ilaam's ploys had been novel, and Nagaro welcomed the opportunity to learn, but he was now beginning to think of pressing for a conclusion. He had just decided it was time to go on the offensive when, without warning, Ilaam came at him with renewed speed in a series of moves he hadn't seen the man use before, forcing him to defend with all his skill.

For half a minute the two men's swords whirled and clashed with redoubled ferocity. Their movements were too quick for the observers to follow, and it was only when at last the two captains stepped apart again to breathe that it was clear that both had taken hits. Nagaro was bleeding from a small cut on his right shoulder. The Mautep captain's shirt was slit along the ribs on the left side, the edges of the rent stained scarlet.

Elaam was crouching now, his sword extended before him, his chest heaving as much with fear as with exertion. His thoughts were racing. This Kiraam Shaku-Tal was mortal. He could bleed. *But he was too good! Too fast. Too clever.* First Ilaam's attempt at a preemptive strike had failed. Then his effort to lull his opponent into a false sense of security had been thwarted. He'd just put everything he had into the last series of attacks and had managed only a draw! And while he'd barely managed to nick the Droviri's shoulder, he suspected the other man could have run him through instead of sliding his blade along his opponent's ribs.

Nagaro was standing on his guard, getting his breath back. He looked into Ilaam's eyes and saw the seeds of the man's defeat. Sighting along the length of his blade and fixing his gaze on the other man, he smiled his best pirate smile, white teeth flashing in his black beard. It was a smile that said, "*I have been enjoying this, but I think you have not.*"

Then he attacked.

Captain Ilaam retreated, taking one step after another, desperately defending himself from Nagaro's onslaught. At length the Mautep took another cut along the ribs, this time on the other side.

Nagaro stepped back, still on his guard. "Three hits," he said. "Ask him if he yields, Pavo."

Ilaam was crouching, glowering. He spat out something in response to Pavo's question.

"He say in Mahuk Baar it take four—"

Ilaam lunged before Pavo had finished speaking.

Nagaro sidestepped like a dancer and caught the other man's blade, hilt to hilt. As he disengaged, he saw an opportunity to get past the other man's guard. Ilaam had expected to strike home and his failure had left him off balance. Lightning-quick, the tip of Nagaro's blade flicked the Mautep's forearm, drawing blood once more. "Four," he said as he stepped back. He held up four fingers with his left hand to make his meaning clear.

A groan went up from the Mautep warriors. They knew the score.

"*Basirah!*" It was Hatheer who spoke. Nagaro recognized the word that meant "enough".

"*Nan!*" Captain Ilaam cast a furious glance at his first mate.

But Hatheer was insistent. He frowned at his captain. "*Haat!*" he said, "basirah!" and then more words that Nagaro didn't understand.

Pavo stepped closer to the combatants. "Hatheer say fight is over, Nagaro. He say it was fair fight and you make four hit."

Nagaro bowed to the first mate. Then he considered Captain Ilaam, who stood, mute, still with his sword in his hand, shaking with anger. Nagaro bowed to Ilaam as well. "You fought well," he said. "There is no dishonor." He turned to Pavo Maat. "Tell him that, Pavo. And tell him that he may keep his sword, but he must go back to the longboat—"

"*Nagaro, look out!*"

The warning came from Landros. The grizzled sea warrior's blade flashed as he drew it.

Captain Ilaam had lunged while Nagaro was speaking to Pavo, but Nagaro had caught the movement from the corner of his eye. Even before he heard Landros' warning, he was already turning, whipping his sword around, quick as thought. Steel clashed on steel and Ilaam's blade was struck from his hand and sent tumbling across the deck.

The Mautep captain came to a halt, horror etched on his face.

The disarmed man stood, breathing heavily, waiting to feel Nagaro's steel. By the rules of Mautep honor, Captain Ilaam's failed attempt at treachery had given his opponent the right to kill him. Although he hadn't considered this fight with a Droviri pirate to be a proper challenge bout, it was apparent that Captain Nagaro had, for the Droviri captain's icy stare was boring into him, pinning him with its furious intensity as the pirate stood with sword raised and ready to do the deed.

Behind his captain, Hatheer was visibly sweating, his knuckles white where they gripped the hilt of his sword.

At last Nagaro moved. He lowered his sword. "No," he said, speaking evenly. "I do not wish to slay you, but I *will* now take your sword. And having won it, I will bestow it where I choose."

Pavo translated as Nagaro walked calmly to where his opponent's sword lay on the deck. Captain Ilaam could only stare, stunned. Hatheer released a pent-up breath and relaxed his grip on his sword hilt.

Nagaro stooped to pick up the fallen weapon. Turning, he strode back to where Pavo stood and presented the hilt of the sword to the young Hashtep. The muscles of Pavo's face betrayed no emotion but his eyes were alight as he accepted the sword of Ilaam jir-Taak with an awkward bow. He held the blade aloft. "This now will be my sword," he said. And he slid the new blade into the empty sheath at his hip.

Nagaro turned back to the Mautep captain and his first mate. Hatheer was watching him curiously, but Ilaam's eyes were elsewhere. The Mautep captain was gazing out to sea, out through the cove's entrance. Nagaro followed the man's gaze, frowning, but he saw nothing there except deep green sea and pale blue sky. *Perhaps the captain's eyes were turned inward?*

Nagaro turned his attention back to the rest of the assembled men. He held his sword up for all to see and spoke loudly for all to hear.

"Is it agreed that I have today won the right to bear this sword— the sword of the House of Shofeer— by victory in a fair match against Captain Ilaam jir-Taak?"

The Mautep captain's attention was apparently pulled back to events on the deck by the mention of his name. He scowled as he listened to Pavo's translation. "Haat." He pronounced the affirmative grudgingly. Hatheer answered at greater length. Some of the words were familiar.

"He say Captain Nagaro, that is called Kiraam Shaku-Tal, have fought with honor and have won sword of Shofeer." Pavo translated with obvious relish. A cheer went up from the crew of the *Sword of Freedom*, and was echoed from among the newly-freed slaves.

Nagaro lowered the sword and sheathed it. He bowed to Hatheer. "Tell him, Pavo, that if he will now go into one of the longboats he may keep his sword."

Hatheer nodded in response to Pavo's translation. Then he bowed to Nagaro and sheathed his own weapon.

Nagaro turned about to address his crew. "Go take up your swords," he said. "We are finished with this."

The men moved to obey.

"Captain! I see sails!"

Mendorel's cry halted the men in their tracks. Atop the *Sword's* mainmast, the former shopkeeper was pointing out to sea. All eyes turned in the direction indicated. Far out over the water was a cluster of white dots— dots that hadn't been there just minutes before.

Captain Ilaam's laughter cut across the startled silence. The Mautep captain raised both arms in a gesture of victory. He turned to Nagaro, his face exultant, and spoke triumphantly in Hashti. A cheer went up from the Mautep warriors in answer to his words.

Pavo's usually impassive face became a picture of dismay. "He say it is fleet of Lord Angkat! He say now we must flee or we be taken!"

Nagaro's brows drew sharply together. "How many ships do you see, Mendorel?"

The shopkeeper had the spyglass to his eye. "At least five."

"Can you make out their colors?"

"Not clearly, but it could be Angkat's brown and gold— just as he said."

Nagaro's thoughts spun. The Mautep captain was right of course. They would have to flee at once, which meant no time to transfer the Mautep ship's cargo!

"*Bishka!*" The slaves were free, but if they couldn't reap the reward of the ship's goods, this first ship-full of rescued slaves would likely be the last. He glanced at the approaching sails, already noticeably nearer, and then at the western sky. The sun was about to dip behind the island's crest. The shadow of Chitaopa's cliffs had already engulfed the stern castle of the ship on which they stood, and he bitterly regretted having taken time to fight the challenge. They could have been long gone, had he not decided to fight for the sake of his honor!

He looked into the face of Ilaam jir-Taak and saw mockery.

"*Keshaal!*" He lunged across the deck, his sword taking fire from the westering sun as he whipped it from its sheath. He stopped his thrust with the tip of the blade a bare inch from the Mautep captain's naked throat and had the satisfaction of seeing the man blanch. Behind the captain, Hatheer had his hand on his sword's hilt, the blade half drawn, his eyes full of alarm.

Nagaro spoke in a voice tight with anger. "Will you swear that you truly bear the blood of the House of Shofeer? That this was no false claim? No ruse to hold us here?"

Pavo's own anger was unmistakable as he translated Nagaro's words.

Captain Ilaam could manage no better than a weak shake of his head, but Hatheer answered hurriedly, and at length.

"Hatheer say is true that captain want to make you wait too long— if he could not beat you. But also he say Captain Ilaam have true claim to blood of Shofeer." Pavo sounded relieved. "This he swear by Sheptuum."

Nagaro stepped back and lowered his sword. Pointedly ignoring the captain, he looked Hatheer in the eye. The obvious solution had occurred to him.

"Pavo," he said. "Tell the first mate I am sorry for this, because he has acted honorably, but Ilaam's treachery has made it necessary for us to take his ship."

Without waiting to hear Pavo translate the words, he turned around and began shouting orders. He had to act quickly. The defeated Mautep had to be put ashore, and a crew had to be chosen for the newly captured ship.

Hatheer raised a protest on understanding Nagaro's pronouncement. The first mate made it clear he couldn't freely consent to what Nagaro proposed. Nagaro obligingly ordered the *Sword's* crew to force the Mautep warriors over the side at sword point, thus allowing Angkat's sea warriors to claim duress. Captain Ilaam went surprisingly quietly, either because he'd run out of will to resist, or because he was hatching other plans. The looks he was giving Hatheer suggested the captain was thinking of trying to blame the whole fiasco on his first mate. Nagaro hoped Ilaam wouldn't succeed in that. Altogether, he was glad he wouldn't have to hear the words that passed between the two men once they were out of earshot.

After ridding the captured craft of Mautep, Nagaro instructed the newly-freed slaves to return to their benches. "Now you must row," he told them. "But this time you will row without chains, and you will row for your freedom." The words drew a ragged cheer from the bedraggled ranks. Even those whose minds were most ravaged seemed to understand that something good was happening.

Nagaro chose Moraga to captain the captured ship, and the former merchant seaman immediately asked if he could call it the *Tiger*, thinking perhaps of the beast that had so terrorized Roheed and his father in Sar Tipaal— a symbol of Sheptuum's retribution. Nagaro readily agreed.

Nagaro picked Rubo, who had Fleet experience, to direct the *Tiger's* oar deck, with Nanu and Chaheel as his lieutenants. The two huge lone men, he reasoned, could help row, and also explain things to the former slaves. Chaheel's mastery of the Common Speech was improving, and he and Nanu always seemed able to understand each other. A young Turowan slave who was a fisherman from Pakoa was sent aloft as lookout, and Bouno, a former merchant seamen, was put in charge of a minimal main deck crew made up of newly-freed slaves who could handle sails and tiller.

Nagaro gave Moraga strict instructions to follow the *Sword's* lead. "If the Mautep come after us," he said, "Let the *Sword* do any fighting that must be done. With only four swordsmen, you're in no position to help. Just make for Pakoa. We'll meet you there when we can."

Moraga nodded soberly, apparently already feeling the burden of command. "Aye, Capt'n," he said. "I'll do me best."

All told, it took a quarter of an hour to get both ships underway, out of the cove, and bound on a course around the headland under the combined power of oars and sail. Behind them, the two longboats floundered towards the beach, laden to capacity with Mautep warriors. Other Mautep were in the water, some clinging to the boats' gunnels, others swimming for the shore.

Once around the headland's tip, the *Sword* and the *Tiger* headed due north in the fading light of the fast-waning afternoon. The course Nagaro chose lay far out to sea, beyond sight of land, and they made good time with free men pulling at the oars – free men who wished to remain free.

The lookouts kept their eyes pinned on the sails astern. At first they reported that the flock of white dots was converging on Chitapa's hulking mass, but then Mendorel announced that the ships of Lord Angkat's fleet had split into two groups and that three ships were coming after them.

For the better part of the next hour, as the sun set and night began to fall, every eye that could be spared was turned aft, watching the progress of their pursuers. The sails at first appeared to grow nearer, but as the light began to fail, the little squares of white dwindled. By the time night lowered its shroud, it appeared that Angkat's ships had turned back, unwilling perhaps to risk themselves at night out on the trackless sea so far from land. The Droviri pirates and former slaves breathed a collective sigh of relief.

Nagaro ordered a change of course, turning east, making for the mainland coast for their own safety. They continued in darkness at a reduced speed, under power of the sails until the wind slackened. By that time, the men were weary from having rowed for several hours with only short breaks. Food and water were passed around, and Nagaro ordered watches posted and directed that the rowers sleep in shifts. Too tense to sleep himself, he first paced the deck, then sat on the edge of the captain's platform in a pool of lantern light while Tredhold tended to the cut on his shoulder.

Tred worked quickly. "Well," the Leithian observed, as he tied the bandage, "The battle's over. We've proved we can do it, and we're all still alive."

Nagaro nodded. "Yes, Tred, I'm glad for all of that. And that we didn't have to kill any of the Mautep."

"Mmm." Tred considered him. "We won't always be so lucky."

Nagaro looked off across the main deck. The planking shone dimly by starlight, like tarnished silver. "I know," he said seriously. "If we do enough of this, someone will die. And I will have to kill." He turned his face towards the healer. "But I *do* want to keep doing it, Tred. When I saw those men come up out of the oar deck into the light..." He paused and looked away to hide his emotion. After a moment he said, "That's worth anything, Tred."

Tredhold nodded. "Aye," he said. "It is."

There was a little silence. Then the healer said, "The other first mate expected ye to kill Ilaam. And Elaam tried to kill ye twice, if I'm not mistaken."

Nagaro sighed. "Yes, I think so," he said wearily. "Even though his men were so outnumbered. And I don't think Landros was surprised."

"There's some who think that if they cut down the captain, the crew'll go to pieces," the healer explained. "That Mautep captain would ha' found he'd misjudged our lot, though, I think. If he'd cut ye down, our men would ha' been fighting each other for the chance to avenge ye. There wouldn't have been enough of Ilaam jir-Taak to go around. Though I think Landros would've beat them all to it," he added. "That old salt-fish loves ye like the son he never had."

"Oh." Nagaro looked down, embarrassed. "I hope he would have remembered his promise to get the men safely home."

"He'd have done that, too," Tredhold said quietly. "It just would ha' come second, that's all."

Nagaro wanted to say that it *should* come first. That vengeance wasn't a reason to take unnecessary risks, but he held his peace. Once he had slain a Mautep for dishonorably killing two men under his command, and he'd killed Raak the slave driver in part for having beaten a man to death. It seemed that honor had its demands.

"Why did ye spare that Mautep captain?" Tredhold spoke lightly, as if it were a mere matter of curiosity. "Pavo said he thinks it was so the man would have to live with his shame."

"That sounds like Pavo." Nagaro sighed and rubbed his forehead. "Pavo knows how to tell a good story— even if he has to make up a few details." *Pavo knows how to craft a legend— the legend of Kiraam Shaku-Tal...* He sighed again. *He* knew he was just a man, not a legend, and those who knew him must surely know it too. "I just don't like to kill a man if it isn't necessary, that's all," he murmured. "I'll have to set Pavo straight."

Tredhold laughed. "Everyone's been asking," he said. "Several of them asked *me*— as if I'd know. So now I do."

Nagaro stood up. "I have to ask the Hashtep we just freed what they want to do," he said. "Before they all go to sleep. If we're going to double back to the Baar to set them ashore, we need to do it soon." He glanced down at the healer. "Thank you, Tred," he added. "For the bandage, and for the words."

Tredhold smiled, and raised a hand in acknowledgment. "As soon as possible, ye should get some sleep," he said. "We'll wake ye if there's need."

"I'll try," Nagaro told him. "As soon as I have their answer."

***

Most of the freed Hashtep wished to return to the Mahuk Baar rather than try to learn how to live on Pakoa, so Nagaro ordered another change of course, this time to southeast.

As he was returning across the main deck, he encountered Timegar under the light of a lantern hanging from the main mast. The bearded Kelorin raised a hand to detain him. "I want to tell ye that ye did good work today," he said in a tone not to be overheard by the other men of the first watch who were standing at their posts. "Ye handled the ship like a master. If I hadn't known, I'd have never believed it was your first time taking a ship into battle."

"It's because you direct the rowers so well," Nagaro told him quite sincerely. "Whatever I ask you for is done in an instant."

Timegar smiled broadly. "Aye, we do our best for ye," he said with a touch of pride. "But fighting that Mautep for the sword was nothing short o' brilliant. I thought it a bit daft at first, mind ye," he added. "And it would ha' been a right ruddy mess if ye'd lost."

Nagaro was taken aback. "It's only a sword, Timegar," he protested. "I could fight just as well with a different one."

Timegar gave him a conspiratorial wink and lowered his voice a further notch. "*I* know that. And *you* know that. But we both know most o' the lads set a lot of store by the 'Sword of Freedom,' as they call it. Well, now it's the 'Sword of Shofeer' too, won in a fair fight with Captain Ilaam jir-Taak! Ye were beautiful to watch. It was brilliant, I tell ye!"

Nagaro face darkened. "I did it to honorably secure my right to carry that sword, Timegar. It's a beautiful weapon, and it pleased me to keep it, but it came to me quite by chance, and that's always bothered me."

Timegar studied Nagaro's face in the glow of the lantern. "By the Eyes!" he exclaimed. "Ye mean that. Ye did it for honor."

"Yes." Nagaro spoke bitterly. "And pursuing my honor almost cost us dearly. We could have been caught there by Angkat. And Captain Ilaam was a good fighter. He could have killed me with just a little luck. If I had just given him the sword—"

"How can ye say that?" Timegar was aghast. "For my money, ye played it exactly right. And ye got honor from that Mautep first mate too, just as ye said. They *do* have honor— some more than others." He paused. "What was that Hashti thing they kept calling ye, anyway?"

"Kiraam Shaku-Tal." Nagaro sighed. "It means 'One who steals slaves.' Lord Baalkir's nephew, Roheed, called me that, and I wish he hadn't. I didn't *steal* them, and I couldn't have done it alone either. We *all* won our freedom at Jaamra, and today it was the whole crew that freed those men."

Timegar laughed. "Well, I wouldn't be so shy about it if it helps those sea-wolves remember who ye are. Ye just carry on, Captain. Wherever ye choose to lead, I'll follow. And now," he added with a grin, "I'm for my bunk and a wink o' sleep before second watch."

With that, Timegar saluted and sauntered off across the deck.

Nagaro watched the older man go with a sigh, and went to seek Landros who was commanding the first watch. He found his first mate on the forecastle deck watching the dark expanse of the sea.

"I want to set the Hashtep ashore just south of the Jinari border, at Alam Shufa," he explained. "As soon as we sight the coast, we'll turn south, and once it's daylight we can use the Jinari islands for cover as we pass through their waters."

Landros nodded. "That's a good plan. Angkat's lot won't expect it. They'll assume we kept sailing north, so they'll not be looking for us in these waters. The lookout'll have to stay sharp, though. Talebra's going to be just a crescent when she rises."

"All right." Nagaro nodded. "I'll leave her in your hands, Landros. I'm going to try to sleep. Wake me if there's any change."

Landros delivered a crisp salute. "Aye, Capt'n!" Then he glanced surreptitiously about to make sure no one was listening before leaning closer. "It was well done, lad," he said, with a note of pride. "Never seen better, and I've seen a lot. Vothra must be pleased tonight."

Nagaro winced. "It turned out better than it might have. Forty men freed, and we're safely away. And I've proven my right to carry this sword." He touched the elegant hilt at his hip.

"Aye." Landros grinned. "O' course the next challenge will be harder, 'cause the man'll know who ye bested."

Nagaro's stomach instantly tightened. "What do you mean, the *next* challenge?"

Landros looked hard at him. "Ye don't think ye're done fighting challenges, do ye?"

This time Nagaro felt a chill. "But not for the *sword*," he said with some alarm. "I've just fought a man for the sword!"

"Oh, aye. And ye won it fair and clean. That bloody captain might try to tell a different tale, but he'll have a hard go of it. There was two score o' Mautep witnesses. No, lad, ye won the sword, but that don't mean ye're done defending it. When this tale gets about, ye'll have every Mautep on the Baar that fancies himself good with a blade itching t' see if he can out-fight Kiraam Shaku-Tal to win back the Sword of Shofeer!"

Nagaro stared in dismay. "Are you saying I shouldn't have challenged him?"

"Bodjer it, *no!*" Landros shook his head emphatically. "But a talent like yours can't be hid, Nagaro. Not if ye're going to use it. This makes twice ye've gone up against Mautep sea warriors and got the best o' them— and that Captain Ilaam was no mean swordsman. If ye went back t' Pakoa right now and set yourself to being a fisherman, ye might just manage not to fight another challenge for the rest o' your life— but I wouldn't wager money on it. At least by fighting a formal challenge ye've set the tone, so to speak. A proper duel is safer than having a challenger come at ye in a melee."

Nagaro stared past the older man, out across the dark water. "I see," he said quietly.

"At least I won't fret myself so much the next time, Landros said easily. "Now that I've seen ye can take care o' yourself."

Nagaro gave him a sharp glance. "I hope you'll still warn me if a man makes a treacherous move," he said seriously. "I don't have eyes in the back of my head."

"No?" Landros chuckled. "I thought ye might." Then, seeing Nagaro's puzzled look, he sobered. "Vothra didn't, ah... warn ye, then?" he asked cautiously.

"I don't think Vothra does that sort of thing. I saw the man move— this time."

Landros nodded. "Well, don't worry. I may fret less, but I'll not be taking any chances."

Feeling somewhat reassured, Nagaro left Landros and went to his cabin. Once there, he unbuckled his sword belt and hung it on the hook above his bed where it would be ready to hand in the event of any trouble. Then he replaced the leather vest with a cloth shirt, pulled off his boots, and lay down on his bunk to try to sleep.

Memories of the day just past jostled together in his head, beside imaginings of what the future might hold. He had meant what he'd said to Tredhold— that he wanted to continue what he'd begun— but Timegar's words troubled him, and those of Landros even more. He wasn't at all sure that following his personal honor had been the best course. He considered calling on Vothra, but decided against it. The Benevolent Spirit wouldn't tell him outright what to do, and he suspected he already knew. It just appeared that it would be more difficult in ways he hadn't expected.

In the end he must have fallen asleep, and somewhere amid his chaotic dreams, Vothra came to him anyway.

The silver figure, robed in a nebulous gray garment, stepped easily through the fading lines of the circle-within-a-circle-joined and stood gazing down at him. Nagaro sat up, finding himself apparently in a place of shifting shadows. The Spirit didn't wait for him to speak.

You wished to show the Mautep that men of other peoples could have honor, Spirit called Nagaro. Today you have made a good beginning.

Nagaro frowned. "And that is good. But it seems I'm to be Kiraam Shaku-Tal, whether I like it or not! And that I must expect to be fighting challenges for the rest of my life. If that's to be the price, I don't like it at all!"

Ah, well. The Spirit seemed to shrug. *Treating you with honor requires that these Mautep see you as an equal. This title— Kiraam Shaku-Tal— helps them do so. Your friend Pavo understands, though he could not perhaps have explained it so simply.*

This assessment did seem plausible, based on what Nagaro knew of the thinking of Roheed jir-Akaan, the man who had first called him Kiraam Shaku-Tal. He was not, however, inclined to be so dispassionate. "They ought to see that *all* men are their equals!"

The silver figure sighed its musical sigh. *True. But that is not likely to occur in this generation. For the little child who cannot leap, a small step is an accomplishment. And if you stride ahead too fast, you will only have to stop and wait for him to catch up.*

"Then you would council me to lead the Mautep with small steps? Is this what you came to tell me?"

No. The Spirit spoke with mock severity. *You have led my thoughts astray, as usual. I came to say that you had made a good beginning— something you seemed to doubt, despite the praise of the ones called Timegar and Landros. You should not discount their words.*

Nagaro frowned. "They've told me I can captain a ship, lead a battle, and fight a challenge," he said wearily. "I don't discount any of that. But I chose to do the last thing for the sake of my personal honor— and because I wished to keep the sword— and it could easily have turned out much worse."

Vothra spread ethereal arms. *Do you think those two veteran sea warriors do not know this? These men are wise in the ways of war. They know one cannot lead without the risk of leading awry. That one cannot chance anything without chancing misfortune. It is a foolish man indeed who demands a guarantee that his leader must make no mistakes, or that every enterprise must come to a happy conclusion. The ones called Timegar and Landros know these things, and this day they have praised your deeds, and saluted you, and called you Captain. Can you not accept that they are as satisfied with your choices as with the outcome?*

Nagaro hesitated. *If Vothra thought so...* "Well... maybe," he said at last. "Though I still wish the men didn't think the sword was so important."

The soft musical sigh came again. *It isn't, of course, and then again it is. It is only a thing of metal, finely wrought. And it is also a thing that chance has handed you, with which you can do good work. Follow your honor and do not let the sword become more than it is, in your own mind...* The spirit stopped abruptly, and stood for several seconds as if listening. *I have said what I came to say and now I must go, for I am needed more urgently elsewhere. Fare well, spirit called Nagaro. Sleep peacefully.*

The dream faded, the image of the Sign of Vothra glowing softly amid the night's shadows.

When Nagaro awoke some hours later at the bell for the second watch, it was from dreams of his idyllic childhood, and to a steadier sense of purpose.

Chapter 22

Stopping At Harmoth

They reached Judaba, the northernmost of Jinara's islands, just as the sun was rising, while Talebra's slim crescent was beginning to descend the western sky with Naru's pale sliver close behind. As the morning waxed towards noon, the two ships dodged their way among the Jinari isles. Fishing boats fled from them, and once they sighted a Jinari merchant ship, which also abruptly altered course to avoid crossing their path. Since Jinara had no warships to defend herself, there was no threat to the *Sword* or the *Tiger* from the local powers. Nagaro wished he might reassure the local folk that he meant them no harm, but there was no easy way to do it.

It was early afternoon when they anchored at Alam Shufa, a place the *Sword* had visited before her re-christening, where a headland sheltered a short stretch of beach that offered a safe landing for a longboat.

Nagaro, Pavo, Taru, and several others rowed across to the *Tiger* to bid farewell to some twenty of the newly-freed Hashtep who had chosen to take their chances on the Baar. The former slaves who were departing stood huddled a little uncertainly by the rail, freshly shaven and shorn, and wearing a motley assortment of rags and scavenged Mautep clothing. Moraga presented each with a quantity of money in coinage of the Mahuk Baar. The *Tiger* had proven a rich prize. Besides assorted marketable goods, Moraga's men had found gold, in the form of Edroviran dokan coins and also a chest-full of small gold bars stamped with the royal hawk crest of Edrovir. A sizable trove of Mahuk coins had also been found. Since they could not be spent in Edrovir, they were divided among men who could actually use them.

Pavo quietly informed Nagaro that each man was receiving "very good amount of money," and the Hashtep certainly seemed grateful for the gift. They bowed awkwardly to Moraga and to Nagaro and Pavo, and said "daashu"— in some cases several times. Moraga and Nagaro were both called "*heeruk*," which meant "captain," and Nagaro was several times called "*saatif*,' which he understood to mean "lord."

Pavo waved this aside. "It is only how they show they have very much respect for you," he explained. Reluctantly Nagaro let it pass.

Eventually, the departing Hashtep descended the rope ladder to the longboats and were rowed ashore. Three of the newly-freed Hashtep stayed behind, one of them being Seftep, the youth who had said he would serve Nagaro for the rest of his life for being freed from Lord Angkat. Nagaro sincerely hoped the young man wasn't coming to Pakoa out of such a sense of obligation.

They worked their way north again after that, retracing their course among the Jinari isles, spending the night anchored in the lee of one of them. As they were getting underway the following morning, the *Tiger*'s lookout caught a glimpse between two islands of Angkat's fleet, six war galleys flying brown-and-gold banners, passing to seaward on their way south. The alarm was instantly given, and the *Sword* and the *Tiger* moved hastily into the shelter of the island of Ororu. There they huddled tensely on the island's landward side, marking time while waiting for Angkat's ships to pass.

"They must have taken their time at Chitaopa," Nagaro observed.

"Well, aye." Landros' teeth showed in a feral grin. "I dare say it would ha' taken them a bit o' time to figure out how to parcel out forty extra men among those half dozen ships. Not to mention having to figure out who t' blame for it."

Timegar's smile was positively gleeful. "One perfectly good ship and a whole crew o' slaves lost to them! I'll warrant Angkat's none too happy."

Nagaro found himself hoping once again that it wouldn't be Hatheer who bore the brunt of the warlord's wrath.

After an hour, they deemed it safe to pass through the narrow strait between Ororu and Atadalba, and they headed north once more with the bulk of Ororu between them and the dwindling Mahuk fleet. By sunset, Nagaro judged it safe to bear more to the west, to skirt the seaward shore of the isle of Janidi. Nearing that island's northern tip, they struck out on a north-westerly course into more open water as night was falling.

Dawn found them well out from shore in an empty sea. As they continued north, they stayed well to westward at first to avoid any last, late Mahuk craft that might still be sailing south out of Edroviran waters. Once they entered those waters, however, they turned eastward to strike the mainland coast some distance south of Harmoth. Twice they stopped along that coast to put freed Edroviran slaves ashore at places requested. These men were Turowan fishermen returning home, against all hope, after absences of more than two years in some cases, and their homecomings were joyous indeed.

On the second stop, there were two men set ashore as a pair, the first being one who wasn't right in the head. The second man thought he knew how to find the poor man's family. The *Sword* waited at anchor until the second man came back to report success. Not only had he found folk who recognized the other former slave, but the confused man had seemed to recognize several relatives and had begun to seem more coherent in familiar surroundings. So there was hope that the man might recover in time. This relieved Nagaro's mind a great deal, for the man's case had been one of the worst.

***

When the two ships came to Harmoth, they anchored in the bay there while Tredhold went ashore to meet his wife. There seemed no reason why Ilsafeth and her two children shouldn't travel to Pakoa aboard the *Sword*, and so the successful pirates stayed the night in that safe harbor while Tredhold's new family packed their belongings.

The following morning found Nagaro, Taru, and Pavo leaning on the *Sword's* rail, admiring the view of the city across the bay while they awaited breakfast. The two ships had been roped together side by side the previous evening to allow their crews to pass easily from one to the other, and Rubo was in the process of cooking up enough pancakes in the *Tiger's* galley to feed both crews. It was a brilliant morning. The deep green water of the bay sparkled with diamond highlights. Beyond the busy wharfs that lined the water's edge, the city of Harmoth mounted the flanks of three low hills, the clean white walls of her buildings gleaming in the early sunlight.

There were nine or ten merchant ships in the harbor that morning, and literally dozens of smaller craft. Most of the latter were fishing boats, and one by one their sails blossomed and unfurled to the wind as they made their way out to sea with the day's work ahead of them. The three friends couldn't help noticing that quite a number of these small craft contrived to pass close to where the two warships lay at anchor. The *Sword of Freedom*, with her unusual banner and colors, was known in this port, having stopped here before. Under her escort, the *Tiger* had caused no alarm, but both ships continued to draw considerable interest. The fact that Nagaro and Mendorel had been ashore the previous day to exchange a gold bar for currency so that they could purchase supplies had undoubtedly contributed to that interest.

"Just look at them! They've all got t' come see for themselves!" Taru observed, laughing. "The word's got about that we were after Mahuk warships— to free slaves— and I'll wager nobody thought we could do it! Now they're all comin' around t' see the proof."

Nagaro smiled fleetingly. It was little more than three years since the day he had stood in Jomo's little fishing boat, awestruck at the sight of a merchant ship sailing by. He had wondered then what it would be like to stand on the deck of such a craft. Now he was captain of a war galley. *Strange were the workings of Lokundas.* "Do you remember, Taru, when we were fishing with your father, and we wanted to follow those two Fleet ships that were chasing a Mahuk galley?" he asked. "Your father thought us a pair of fools."

Taru grinned. "Aye," he said, the light of memory in his eyes. "We wanted to see a sea battle!" Then he sobered. "My father was right, o' course. Hakura knows we'd ha' been bloody fools to risk it, and— Hoy now!" he cried suddenly, cupping his hands to his mouth. "Turn aside, mates! Or we'll be at ye with the fending pikes!"

This last was directed at a fishing boat, with two men aboard, that was bearing down upon the *Sword* on a collision course. At the last moment, the man in the stern put the tiller hard over while at the same time the other man swung the boom so that the sail went slack. The little craft turned sharply, swinging in parallel to the *Sword's* hull and losing way so that it glided to a halt immediately below where the three friends were standing. They found themselves looking down into the weathered faces of two bearded Turowan men.

The younger of the two, who was handling the lines, looked to be in his forties. The other was much older, with hair and beard quite gray. "Here, now," said the older man, who was at the tiller. "Naught t' worry! We've only come so's me mate can put his hand on 'er. He'd like to be able t' say he's touched a real pirate ship."

The younger man grinned up at them sheepishly as he reached out and put his palm against the *Sword's* sleek hull.

"There now, ye see? No harm done." The gray-haired man nodded indulgently at his mate, then turned to look up again at the men leaning on the rail. Nagaro couldn't help noticing that the older fisherman surreptitiously put out his own hand and brushed the ship's side with his fingertips.

Pavo addressed the older man with classic Hashtep deadpan. "You have handle your boat well, Zirda."

The fisherman seemed to really notice Pavo for the first time. "*Hamanei mata noa!*" he exclaimed. "It's a Mahuk! An' he's talkin' the Common Speech!" He glanced at his silent comrade, who was staring open-mouthed.

Pavo's face remained impassive. "I am Hashtep, not 'Mahuk'," he explained calmly. "Hashtep is common man of Mahuk Baar. Mautep is word for warlord, and Mahuk is not word to use for people. And," he added with a slight inclination of his head, "I was fisherman like you before Captain Nagaro teach me to fight with sword."

"*Hakura!* And is that a fact?" The gray-bearded man blinked up at Pavo. The darker-haired fisherman continued to stare.

Nagaro was trying not to smile. He was also carefully holding his tongue, hoping to get through this conversation without it being mentioned that *he* was Captain Nagaro.

Taru, on the other hand, was grinning hugely. "It *is* a fact," The young Turo observed smugly. "And if he fishes as well as he wields a blade, the fish should be glad he gave it up! Now make yourselves useful, mates, and tell us the news. Have they started up the war again with Jinara?"

"The war?" The older man spat emphatically over the gunnel. "*That's* for yer war!"

The younger man scowled. "Aye, it's started again," he said angrily, speaking for the first time. "Back in Duleyin. An' three weeks ago they come and took the best o' the young men t' be soldiers. They took my sister's son!"

At this, Nagaro felt a need to speak. "I'm sorry to hear that. There ought to be some better way than bloodshed to settle where a border is to lie."

The two men nodded emphatically, muttering, "Aye," and "That's what *I* say."

"Is there any other news?" Nagaro asked as casually as he could. "Anything from... Lankura?"

"We-ell, no," the older man drawled "There's not been much news from Lankura since we heard about Lord Gillard bein' dead."

Nagaro started as if he had been struck. "Lord... Gillard...?" he stammered. "Gillard Marchent? *Dead?*"

The fisherman looked surprised. "Aye," he said. "Dead as a squashed bug. Hadn't ye heard? I thought the whole world knew about it."

Taru had given Nagaro a warning glance, and now stepped in. "We've been in southern waters chasin' Mahuk warships, mate, and we've had no news in weeks. When did it happen? And how?"

The gray-bearded fisherman scratched his chin. "It were about a month ago. Just after the war started up again. As for *how*... well, there's two tails t' *that* dog."

"Two stories, ye mean?" Taru was frowning.

Nagaro had recovered his composure but was glad to let Taru do the talking. Apprehension was churning in his gut. *The man he had thought about confronting— even killing— was dead.*

"Aye, well... ye see... there's the *official* tale what comes from the king's ministers," the old man explained. "And then there's the tale the common folk are tellin' in the street."

"Will ye just give us both, then?" Taru put in impatiently. Such discrepancies were common with respect to news of the doings of lords, ladies, and the inhabitants of the royal palace.

"Hold yer hawsers, mate, and I will." The fisherman was plainly enjoying himself. "The thing *everybody* agrees on is that he died from fallin' three floors off a balcony." The man paused to spit. "An' the *official* tale is that it were an *accident*. But the *other* tale is that he went mad, and jumped. And they're sayin' the madness warn't natural!"

"*Not natural?*" Nagaro forgot himself in his shock. "How can anyone possibly know—?" He caught himself as Taru jabbed him in the ribs.

"How can they know how it happened?" The fisherman raised a conspiratorial eyebrow. "There's *guards* on the third floor o' the palace. And *servants* too. An' they've all got eyes an' ears. So when they goes home t' their families, the tale o' what they's seen an' heard gets about. An' us common folk can add up two and two as well as any lord, can't we?"

"Course we can," Taru put in quickly. "So what did the guards see? And hear?"

"They saw an' heard plenty," the old man asserted grimly. "I ain't told ye the half of it. It's like this, ye see. It started one night with a bloody great row 'tween Gillard and the king. It were all about the princess— how Lord Gillard warn't treatin' her right. Seems King Elgurn lost his temper an' ordered Gillard out o' the palace. An' Gillard swore he wouldn't stay another night under th' same roof as Elgurn. So off he goes in the middle o' the night— out o' the gates of Lankura. There was some what saw him go, and plenty what said good riddance, I can tell ye!"

"But he must have come back," Taru pressed, frowning. "If he died falling off a palace balcony."

"Oh, he came back all right— the very next day! 'Cause ye see..." the fisherman went on, "King Elgurn was all set to go off t' the war in the morning. There was a troop o' men all mustered and waitin', an' he couldn't very well change his plans on account o' some tiff with his son-in-law. So the king rides *out* o' gates at noon. An' Lord Gillard rides *in* at sunset— with a troop of armed men at his back!"

"*Hamanei!*" Taru exclaimed. "Then what?"

The fisherman adjusted his position on his plank seat. "There was another great row, o' course. But *this* time it was 'tween Gillard and the princess. *He* tells her t' pack her trunk 'cause he's takin' her back to his Hold with him. An' *she* tells him she ain't goin'!"

"*Good for her!*" Nagaro muttered the words under his breath, and hastily shut his mouth. He was aware of Pavo studying him with his narrow eyes.

The old fisherman had apparently heard Nagaro, but fortunately merely agreed with the sentiment. "That's what *I* say, mate." He bobbed his head. "Good fer her! But Lord Gillard warn't in no mood t' take no for an answer. He would ha' dragged her away with him if the queen hadn't stepped in—"

"The *queen?*" This time Nagaro and Taru spoke in astonished unison.

Queen Semorel was much beloved and widely respected throughout Edrovir. Her natural kindness and generosity led to her doing much charitable work in Lankura and the surrounding countryside— work in which the princess often joined her. The queen was widely believed to be incapable of thinking ill of anyone, and Nagaro had seen for himself how thoroughly the king shielded her from all unpleasantness. *If the queen had witnessed this, it could not have failed to get back to Elgurn.*

"Aye, the queen." The old man repeated, nodding smugly. "She comes out o' her room an' tells 'em please not to quarrel, and says no one has t' leave, what with night comin' on and all. So Gillard and the princess each goes to bed in their own bedrooms." The fisherman paused to shake his head in bafflement. "Funny thing, that," he said. "Them havin' their own bedrooms. No wonder the princess ain't gotten an heir, I say. But I guess it ain't fer us ordinary folk t' judge."

Nagaro, who was quite aware of the palace sleeping arrangements, managed a convincing expression of amusement by picturing the queen gently berating her daughter and son-in-law for raising their voices and then sending both of them off to separate beds like naughty children.

"And *then* what?" Taru asked eagerly. "Tell us about the part where Gillard goes mad."

"I was just *comin'* t' that." The gray-haired fisherman looked slightly hurt. "It happened twice, it seems, and the first time was that very night. All the servants was gone home or gone t' bed. An' maybe the guards was dozing, 'cause all at once, there was Lord Gillard, runnin' up and down the hall screamin' that he was bein' attacked by demons! They caught him the first time, an' but him back t' bed, an' he came to himself by morning— far as his head was concerned. But he was sick, they say, an' out o' sorts, and he spent most o' the day in his room. Everyone thought it was over, but the next night it happened again the same way, 'cept the second time they couldn't catch him. He ran out onto the balcony, screamin' all th' way, and over he went! That was the end of him, and good riddance to bad meat!"

The old fisherman sat in his boat and regarded his stunned audience with obvious satisfaction. "Now don't that seem kind o' *unnatural?*" he inquired. "It happenin' just *then*— and just that way?"

"Aye, it does." Taru was frowning. "I wonder what got into him."

Despite the morning sun on his back, Nagaro shivered. "Dreigen," he said quietly. And then he shut his mouth again before he could utter any more of his thought. But all eyes had turned to him.

"Well, o' course that's what a lot o' folks is saying," the fisherman said quickly, as if put out that Nagaro had stolen his thunder. "They're sayin' more'n that, too. They're sayin' the king must ha' *told* Dreigen t' do it. Left orders, that is, in case Gillard came back. The king warn't there, after all, when it happened."

Taru nodded. "Ye-es," he said. "That... makes sense. But how could Dreigen make a man go mad?"

"Who knows?" The fisherman shrugged. "How'd he kill Lord Berinar, years ago, that was twenty miles away?"

For a moment, no one spoke.

Nagaro was staring unseeing across the sparkling bay as his thoughts went running down dark corridors. He was remembering what the Jinari merchant's agent, Utabala, had said about the contents of the scrolls they had found aboard the *Fist of Death*. Scrolls that had been part of a secret cargo from a Jinari merchant ship. *Poisons and medicines that could be misused. A cure for palsy that could make a man see things that weren't there...* The *how* didn't matter. He had no doubt that Dreigen could have done the deed. And he also knew— as those around him did not— that the king's Lore Master had harbored no love for Gillard Marchent. Gillard's quarrel with Elgurn could have provided just the excuse that Dreigen needed to pursue his own vendetta.

"Anyway," the old man was saying, "ye wanted news, an' there it is."

"But ye left out the other bit." The younger fisherman spoke up suddenly. "About that *other* lord what died two weeks later. What was that man's name?"

"Lord Kale," the older man supplied. "And that were suspicious, too— happenin' so soon afterwards, an' him bein' a friend o' King Elgurn's since they was boys."

Kale Fendred dead?

The sun seemed to dim a little, and Nagaro drew a sharp breath. He felt as if he'd been hit in the stomach. *No! Not Kale!* The words shot blindingly across his brain and it was only with an effort that he stopped himself from shouting them aloud.

No, no, no! Not Kale!

Taru was asking how it had happened... whether Kale had gone mad as well...

And the gray-haired fisherman answered.

"No, it were different. His coach turned over on the road— killed him and his wife, together. Sad, that was. They was decent folk by all accounts. They left a son an' a daughter not quite out o' their teens."

"Aye," put in the younger man, with obvious relish. "It were *supposed* t' have been an accident too. But there's some is sayin' it was murder! Revenge for Gillard—"

"*We-ell*, now..." The older man turned suddenly cautious. "Maybe it were, an' maybe it weren't. Kale an' the king *was* this close." He held up two fingers twined together. "But, ye know how 'tis. Folk love a good tale, an' they'll say almost anything—"

There was some more, but it wasn't important. Nagaro scarcely heard it. As soon as the fishermen's boat pushed off from the *Sword's* side, he spun away from the rail and struck off across the deck.

Taru came running after him. "Nagaro? Where are ye going?" His friend's voice was tense with worry.

"I'll be in my cabin." Nagaro answered woodenly, without turning.

"What about breakfast? I just heard the bell."

Nagaro barely paused. "You and Pavo go," he said bleakly. "You can bring me something if you like, but I don't want to sit with the men right now."

What he wanted was to be alone.

Taru hesitated as if torn, but apparently his stomach won. "All right then," he said as he beckoned to Pavo to follow and headed for the galley.

***

The captain's cabin was the only private place Nagaro had on the ship, and he was lucky to have it. He sat down on his bunk, tucking his legs up and wrapping his arms around them the way he used to do on his rock ledge, his "high seat", when he was a boy. Wearily, he rested his forehead on his knees, letting pain wash over him.

Not Kale! Not Kale Fendred... and his wife, too...

He was still sitting there when Taru and Pavo knocked on the door nearly an hour later.

"Nagaro?" Taru's voice came cautiously through the closed door. "Are ye all right?"

Nagaro sighed and lifted his head. "Come in."

His friends had brought him a plate of pancakes with honey, and a mug of sothiril. They sat on the bunk across from him and waited in awkward silence while he ate and drank. He hadn't much appetite, but he knew he should eat something, if for no other reason than that he'd asked Taru to bring the food. He ate mechanically, not meeting his friends' eyes.

It wasn't until he had more or less cleaned the plate and was finishing the sothiril that Pavo said in genuine puzzlement, "I do not understand why you are not happy, Nagaro. Taru say these two man who die are man that have hurt you."

Nagaro studied his empty cup. He would rather not have talked about it, but he couldn't deny Pavo's sincere request for information. He cleared his throat.

"Kale was a decent man. He never meant to hurt me," he said quietly. "When I tried to get away— to... to die— he would stop me, because Leithians believe suicide is a sin. But he never meant me harm."

There was more to it than that. Sitting there on his bunk, he'd come to realize that he had secretly imagined he might find a way to repay the red-haired Leithian one day. At least thank him. *And now the man was dead.* There would be no such chance.

"But ye must be glad about Gillard, at least!" Taru exclaimed. "Ye called him a monster!"

Nagaro leaned back against the planking of the cabin wall and closed his eyes. "I'm glad the princess is free of him," he said carefully. "But it wasn't necessary for him to die. And not like *that*..." He opened his eyes to find Taru staring at him.

"Are ye *daft?*" the young Turo demanded. "Ye were ready t' go to Lankura and kill him yourself!"

Nagaro regarded his friend somberly. "Yes," he admitted. "And as I recall, you talked me out of it."

"Because it was a daft idea that would ha' got ye killed!" Taru was exasperated.

Nagaro sighed. He looked down at his hands. "Do you know what I did the night you talked me out of it? After I left you?" He looked up to find them both staring at him, so he answered his own question. "I went and sat in the dark, and thought about a lot of things. And then I prayed to Vothra. If Elgurn didn't know what Gillard was doing, *I prayed he would find out*. Well apparently Elgurn *did* find out. And *this* is the consequence. Gillard is dead. Did you know that Leithians think madness is a curse from their gods?"

Pavo was nodding. "Gurd have told us that," he observed knowingly. "Do you think this have happen because you pray?"

"No!" Nagaro's answer came too quickly. "I mean," he added, "Vothra doesn't do things like that." *But they say Lokundas hears wishes, and prayers especially. And Lokundas delights in twisting things...* He wearily massaged his temples. "It would have been enough to dissolve the marriage," he said dully. "Gillard didn't need to die like that. And if Kale's death— and his wife's— were *connected* to it, then the price is far too high."

He stopped speaking.

Taru and Pavo were looking at him, and from their faces he knew they believed that *something* had answered his prayer— whether it was Vothra... or one of the World Spirits... or Sheptuum... Nagaro wished he could dissuade them, but before he could offer any counter-argument, cheers and whistles sounded from the deck outside.

"Hoy! What's that about?" Taru jumped up with grateful haste and ducked out of the cabin door to see what was afoot.

He returned quickly. "It's Tred and Ilsafeth and her children," he explained excitedly. "They're about to come aboard! "Come on," he added, turning to Nagaro. "Ye have t' come out and welcome them!"

Nagaro felt something let go inside of him, and he managed to laugh. "Well I should say so!" he said with relief. "Especially since I told Tred they could use this cabin for the passage to Pakoa."

He followed Taru and Pavo out onto the deck.

Ilsafeth was a good Fleet wife who came up the rope ladder with no more than a hitch in her skirts. The crew were delighted and made a great show out of bringing her belongings aboard. Ilsafeth had arranged for many of her possessions to be sold, with the proceeds to be sent after her. She brought only four small pieces of cherished furniture and such clothing and crockery and other items as would fit into two trunks.

Nagaro found he quite liked Tredhold's new wife. She was a cheerful woman, a little plump, with golden hair and bright blue eyes in a face that seemed meant for smiling. Her older child, a girl of six, was thin and sad and clung to her mother. "Still missing her father, poor dear," Ilsafeth explained, giving her daughter a gentle hug. The younger child, a boy of three, was a grinning flaxen-haired cherub, too young to understand death or long hold onto grief. Indeed, the little boy was a bundle of curiosity whose antics delighted everyone.

They were all watching Tredhold's attempt to transfer the younger child's attention from a tar bucket to a bit of rope, when Pavo turned to Nagaro and quietly asked, "What will happen to princess now?"

Nagaro's laughter died. He didn't want to think about it, but he thought he knew the answer. "I expect she'll marry again after nine months. There will be three months of mourning, and then the courting will begin. This time, though, I expect that Elgurn will choose more carefully."

"I see." Pavo regarded him closely for a moment before he nodded, apparently satisfied. "Then that is good," he declared flatly.

An hour after that, the two ships were ready to set sail. Ilsafeth's possessions had been safely stowed, and the ropes binding the *Sword* and the *Tiger* together had been loosed. The anchors were weighed, and the sails unfurled to the stiffening breeze.

Nagaro stood on the captain's platform, leaning on the rail. He was determined not to waste further thought on things that might have been. They were bound for Pakoa now, after all, and they would be returning in triumph with nearly a score of newly freed slaves and their first prize ship to prove the validity of his covenant and the value of his risky venture.

Chapter 23

Narei

Nagaro frowned at the folded piece of paper with its stiff, labored writing. It was just after breakfast, on a morning about a week after their return to Pakoa, and the three friends were sitting together in the Bay Tree's otherwise deserted common room. The *Bountiful* had just arrived on what would be her last stop of the season, bringing a letter from Gama in response to the one Nagaro had written for Taru. Yuli had handed it to Taru at breakfast and Nagaro was about to read it aloud.

"Dear Taru," he began. "I am holding your letter in my hands again, and even after all these days, I still can hardly believe it is real. Tor Goran the trader brought it to me on his way north, and Tor Boronin the blacksmith was good enough to read it to me. Now Goran has come back on his way south, and he is waiting while Boronin writes my words as I tell them to him."

Nagaro paused as Tulara approached the table with a teapot and shyly refilled their cups with sothiril. Nagaro couldn't help noticing how the young woman's glance kept furtively coming back to Taru. He thought Pavo's quick eyes noticed it too. Only Taru seemed determined not to look at her.

As she moved away, Nagaro spoke as casually as he could. "Tulara is looking better, don't you think? She doesn't seem as thin."

Pavo nodded, and added with his accustomed directness, "Why you do not smile at her, Taru? Do you want that Nagaro and I should go away first?"

Taru shot the young Hashtep a sharp look. "Why should I want ye t' go away?"

Pavo's brow furrowed. "So you can talk and we will not hear," he explained patiently. "I think Tulara like you very much. And she do not have father to ask for sitting."

Taru suddenly seemed to find something of great interest outside the Bay Tree's front window. "Tulara only wants to find someone who'll marry her," he said flatly. "To make her respectable so folk won't think of her as a tavern woman anymore."

Pavo looked as if he wanted to respond, but Nagaro caught his eye from across the table and gave a tiny shake of his head. He felt that pushing Taru in this matter would be a mistake. He cleared his throat and made a show of finding his place in the text of the letter he still held in his hands. He began to read again:

"It is the most wonderful news that you and Nagaro are safe. I thank the Spirits every day for this miracle. When they came to tell me they had found your poor father and mother dead, and you gone, my heart almost died. I thought I had lost all of you forever. How wonderful it was that a sword fell where Nagaro could reach it, and everyone got free, and that there was a storm so the Mahuk couldn't catch you. Every morning and every night I thank the Spirits for this. I have told everyone, and all of Wotana is buzzing about it. No one ever heard of such a thing before. I have sent word to your mother's sister in Galenor—"

"*What*?" Taru's gaze had returned from the window. "Is that all she has to say about our escape? I know I said more than that about what ye did, Nagaro."

Nagaro shifted uncomfortably under his friend's eyes. "I, ah, didn't feel right— writing some of that," he admitted. "So I changed a few words."

"And ye didn't tell me so?" Taru's tone was somewhere between amusement and rebuke. "Blast it, Nagaro!" He shook his head, then laughed. "Ye're supposed t' be the honest one. I swear I'll never trust ye again!"

Nagaro ducked his head sheepishly and gave his attention back to the letter.

"We buried your father and mother together at the edge of the forest where the sea will never come. There are always flowers there in spring." Nagaro swallowed past a lump in his throat and read on. "I had to sell your father's house to young Gudo. You remember him, Taru? You used to play together when you were boys. Since he married Lanei, he needed a place, especially with the baby coming."

"Gudo's married t' Lanei?" Taru broke in again. "And they've a baby coming?" He frowned. "*Hamanei*," he muttered, shaking his head. "I think I know how *that* happened. Poor old Gudo. I heard Lanei never could cook anything without burning it—" He broke off. "Go on Nagaro."

Nagaro hid his smile. "Gudo is paying me a little bit at a time," he read. "He misses sometimes, of course, but I forgive him because I know how the fishing goes. I am getting by with the neighbors' help, so don't fret. This last winter was hard, but I am as well as can be expected for an old woman. I hope you will come visit your old Gama one day in your ship. I know you must be busy, though, making other slaves free. That is a wonderful thing to do, and I am so proud of you, and it is wonderful that Nagaro is the captain. I know you will make many men free and many poor mothers very glad, because the Spirits surely are watching over you both. I send all my love to both of you. Your Gama."

Nagaro put the letter down. "We should go there in the spring, Taru," he said. "We can take her some money so she won't have to turn to the neighbors if the fishing is bad and Gudo can't pay her."

Taru nodded. "Aye, of course," he said. "It's the least we can do." Then he frowned again. "At least ye left in the bit about being captain."

Nagaro grinned. "Next time you'll have to write it, Taru. Then you can say what you want." He glanced back at the letter. "There's a little note still," he added. "At the bottom. It's signed by Boronin." He began to read to himself, and his face darkened. "It says that Aramei married a tanner's son last spring, and they moved to Galenor. It's funny he should happen to mention that." He looked up and caught Taru's guilty look. "You asked about her, didn't you, Taru?" he said accusingly. "After I said I didn't care to. You wrote that last bit by yourself, and you asked about her."

Taru shrugged. "Well, I don't see that it hurts to know," he said defensively.

Nagaro regarded his friend darkly. "I hope you didn't say it was because *I* wanted to know!"

This time Taru ducked his head. "How was I t' know Boronin would be doing the reading and writing for her?" he mumbled.

Nagaro groaned. He'd been congratulating himself just that morning on not having dreamed about either the princess or Aramei in many weeks.

Pavo's glance had been darting from one of his friends to the other, and now he innocently inquired, "Who is Aramei?"

Nagaro said, "Tor Boronin's daughter," at the same time that Taru said, "A girl Nagaro was courting."

"I wasn't courting her!" Nagaro was indignant. "I was talking to her, to see if I *wanted* to court her. But she didn't want to talk to me anymore, and that was the end of it. And you *really* didn't have to ask about her, Taru!"

"All *right!*" Taru waved a hand. "I'm *sorry*. Are ye satisfied? And if we're done with the letter, can we go on up to the house? There's quite a bit o' work t' be done if we mean to move in at the end o' the week."

Nagaro heaved a sigh. He wasn't likely to get a more gracious apology from Taru, and actually it *was* a relief to know that Aramei was married and no longer available. He could more easily stop thinking of her as something he'd left unfinished.

He stood up. "All right," he said. "Let's go then. We have some errands to do besides."

"Do we need to go upstair for money?" Pavo asked. "If some thing are ready, we need to pay."

"I still have quite a lot of what I got from Gedras yesterday," Nagaro told him. "I was going to count it as my 'captain's share,' but if there's anything to pay for, I can do it, and you and Taru can settle with me later."

As the three young men headed for the outer door of the common room, Taru suddenly paused. "Ye two go on," he said. "I'll meet ye at the house." In response to Nagaro's raised eyebrow, and Pavo's questioning look, he added hurriedly, "I'm just going to the kitchen to get something for our lunch."

Nagaro nodded and pulled the puzzled Pavo after him and out the door.

"Why do we not all go to kitchen?" Pavo asked.

Nagaro gave him a significant look. "If Taru had wanted us to *all* go to the kitchen, he wouldn't have told the two of us to go on ahead."

"Oh." Pavo's eyes narrowed. "You think he is maybe go to talk to Tulara?"

Nagaro sighed. "Maybe," he said. "But knowing Taru, it's more likely he's going to ask Yuli whether Tulara can cook things without burning them."

***

Nagaro had mentioned his interest in the Fendorin house to his two friends soon after their return to Pakoa, thinking that the bounty of the *Tiger's* stock of gold would make the purchase possible.

Taru had listened to the description of the house, and exclaimed, "Five rooms! Why d' ye want to be rattling about in a place like that all by yourself? If we each put in one gold dokan, we can share it! There's a bedroom for each of us, if one of us takes the parlor." When Nagaro had pointed out that Pavo still had hopes of marrying Tenepti in a year or two, Taru had shrugged. "If any of us wants t' leave, the others'll just buy out his share," had been his sensible answer.

Since Pavo had liked the idea just as much as Taru, they had all gone to see Gedras about it. The gold had been laid down and the deed of sale duly drawn up and signed by all parties on the spot. They'd been working at fixing up the house ever since, and were finally close to moving in. But as Taru had said, there was still work to do. Some of that work was of a kind that the three friends couldn't do themselves, which was why Nagaro and Pavo set out first to go to the seamstress to check on the progress with several sets of bed-linens.

A gusty northwest wind was shepherding cottony puffs of cloud across a cobalt sky as the two men made their way up Front Street. The air was bracingly chill, and sharp with the smell of brine. They passed the *Bountiful* where she lay tied up at the wharf. The ship that had brought Gama's letter would carry Mendorel home to his wife and family in Kel Tierna when she sailed in two day's time. Without even waiting to total up their takings, Nagaro had given the candlemaker enough gold to buy back his shop with some to spare. "I'm sure there'll be plenty for everything we need," he'd told the once-and-future shopkeeper. "And I want to be sure you get your house back— even if that villain raises the price."

He smiled at the memory. There had been a tear in Mendorel's eye as the older man gratefully accepted the money. "Ye'll stop by and visit sometimes, won't ye?" he'd asked. "My shop's in Kettle Street, four blocks from the water. Don't ye forget. Ye're welcome there any time."

There were numerous townspeople abroad that morning, and many of them greeted Nagaro by name, calling him either "Tor Nagaro" or "Captain Nagaro." Since the *Sword of Freedom's* dramatic return, he was even more widely recognized than before, if that were possible. And also more admired. Nagaro was reluctantly becoming resigned to this. He returned every greeting and managed not to flinch at hearing the word "captain" so frequently attached to his name.

The seamstress' shop was several blocks past the wharf. Halfway there, they encountered Gedras coming in the opposite direction. The merchant hailed them, stopping under a shop awning to steady his hat against a gust of wind. "I've a message for you from the Town Council, Tor Nagaro," the bespectacled Kelorin informed him. "We've approved your plan to build a barracks and a practice field on the tract of land behind the Inn. I'm happy to say the decision was unanimous."

"Unanimous?" Nagaro was frankly surprised. "I expected there to be some opposition— since it will mean more men with swords going about the town."

Gedras waved this aside. "Everyone is quite satisfied that you keep good discipline," he said. "And they couldn't very well deny you anything after you made up the tax shortfall for the entire island."

Nagaro frowned. "I hope no one thought I was trying to buy their good will," he said seriously. "I put it to the men, and they agreed it was only right that we should pay some extra tax. Last year we paid none, though Pakoa sheltered us through the winter. And we couldn't have taken the prize we did this summer without having this safe haven for our preparations."

Gedras coughed delicately. "The Council appreciates the *justness* of you're paying some of the extra tax," he said carefully. "It was the *magnitude* of your contribution that surprised them."

"Oh." Nagaro frowned. "I couldn't see the sense of asking the poor folk of the island to give up any more of what they've saved for the winter, when we had more than enough to cover the need."

"Ah, yes. Quite so," Gedras said quickly. "Still, it was generous. And you must understand," he added, "that the Council expects Pakoa to benefit from the future results of your activities for as long as the island continues to facilitate them."

"Of course we'll contribute as we're able," Nagaro assured him. "It's only fitting."

Gedras looked at him appraisingly. "Yes. Right," he said. "I was further instructed to tell you to come to the Council Hall on First Day next week at the second hour past noon to present the details of your plan for the barracks." Then he smiled broadly. "I must say I'm impressed with your success, myself. And I look forward to continuing to serve your business needs as you continue your... shall we say... *work?*"

"Ah. Of Course." Nagaro nodded awkwardly. He then thanked the merchant and bade him good day.

As he and Pavo continued along the street, the young Hashtep turned to him and said, "Why you do not complain about tax, Nagaro, like everyone else?"

Nagaro sighed. "Folk complain because they can't see what becomes of the money, I expect. There's a portion taken out of what's collected that stays on Pakoa for public works, like paving the streets, mending the wharfs, and building public buildings, but most folk take those things for granted. Pakoa gets a share of the protection provided by the Royal Fleet, but folk aren't very impressed with that as long as they still suffer anything at the hands of the Mautep. And of course, most of the tax goes to maintaining things in Lankura and on the mainland— places the folk here have never even seen."

"And you do not mind that our gold have go to pay tax for other people? Here or on mainland?"

Nagaro shrugged. "Not when we have plenty to spare. It pleases me that the Pakoa folk will have more for the winter, and I don't mind helping people on the mainland who suffered more from the plague than the island folk did, since that surely wasn't their fault." He paused, then said. "I confess I am a little worried about what they'll think in Lankura when they see a part of Pakoa's tax paid in gold bars bearing the king's mark. I'm afraid they'll wonder how gold that was on its way to the state coffers in Lankura came to be *here*."

This time Pavo frowned. “Captain Ilaam surely steal it from Droviri ship,” he said. “If we did not steal it back, your king in Lankura would have never see it at all.”

“I know.” Nagaro sighed. “But the king may think such gold belongs to the Crown and should be returned. And we still have more of it.”

“You do not think it belong to king?”

Nagaro shook his head. “I think wealth that lies buried in the earth belongs to all the people. It should be used for the benefit of the people of Edrovir. Besides that, I think of it as ‘finder’s gold’— to be used to serve our needs or the needs of others. That’s why I paid the tax with it, and why I’ll use some of it to help the freed slaves rebuild their lives, or to help other folk here on Pakoa.”

Pavo regarded him seriously. “What if king send man to Pakoa to look for this gold?”

Nagaro had come to a halt outside the door of the seamstress’ shop. “I’d do my best to explain it to him,” he said. “And I would give it up, if I were commanded to. It’s only gold, after all.”

Pavo’s teeth flashed. “I think you are very honest man, Nagaro.”

Nagaro sighed as he swung the shop door open. “I try to be. But I’ll be more comfortable when we’ve used all that gold to do good work that can’t be undone.”

***

When they entered the seamstress’ shop, the woman, Tira Jilena, told them that the three sets of sheets and pillowcases they’d ordered would be ready the following day. Nagaro inquired also about the cost of a set of curtains for the front window. He was told that he needed to take the measurements, and the seamstress gave him instructions for doing so.

From the woman’s shop, the two friends went to find the caretaker, Ulapa, at the house where he boarded on an alley just off the bottom of Hill Road.

The gnarled old sailor met them at the door, grinning from ear to ear. “Got yer paint, I did,” he told them. “Just this mornin’. The money ye give me was enough. And the brushes is in me bag with me hammer an’ nails. I’ll fix up them loose boards in two winks, an’ we can give ‘er a good sloshin’, inside ‘n out!”

Nagaro grinned back. “That’s good,” he said. “Have you any word about mending the broken window?

"Aye, well, the glazier says he's got the four little panes all cut, but he needs t' re-do the leading that holds 'em in. It'll take two or three days an' cost ye another trokin."

Nagaro nodded his acceptance. "We can pay that."

He and Pavo each picked up one of the buckets of white paint, Ulapa shouldered his bag, and the three of them set off up the hill.

At the house, they found Taru waiting for them. The young Turo was sitting on the front porch with a bulging sack beside him. He seemed preoccupied, for he didn't notice them until they had gotten quite close. Then he jumped up, grinning, however, and showed them the contents of the sack. "There's a whole loaf o' bread, and a sausage, and apples," he pointed out. "Ulapa can join us. I made sure there's enough."

So they went to work. Ulapa set about nailing the loose boards while Taru and Pavo began painting the outside of the house, starting at the front.

Nagaro had a task of his own. He had seen that the path running from the front porch around to the walled garden became a sea of mud when it rained, and he'd decided to do something about it by laying paving stones. The stones were large irregular slabs of the local cream-colored shale that he'd arranged to have carted up and stacked beside the house, along with three buckets of sand. He had finished the first four feet of path near the garden gate the previous day, with several times that distance left to go, and he was soon busy with sand and stones and trowel. It was exacting work, fitting the shapes of the stones together and making sure that each one lay flat and level. The task required a lot of patience, and the other three men had been quite happy to leave it in Nagaro's hands.

He was kneeling beside the path, completely absorbed in what he was doing— digging away a little more dirt, sifting in a little more sand, and trying and retrying a close-fitting stone. He hadn't heard anyone approach, and so he nearly dropped the stone he was holding when a voice suddenly spoke to him from very close at hand.

"Good morning, *Captain* Nagaro."

The voice was low and throaty, and unmistakably female. And the timbre was uncomfortably familiar as well. He looked up and stared in dismay at the figure standing only a few feet away on the other side of the path.

"Jila!"

The name slipped from his lips even as his stomach turned over. Deliberately, he put down the stone he was holding and stood up.

Jila wore a plain brown cloak. She was holding the front of it bundled about her with one hand so it concealed the shapeliness of her form, but she'd thrown the hood back, and the lustrous cascade of her dark hair framed her heart-shaped face with those wide brown eyes and the cherry lips that he remembered all too well. The lips now curved into a little smile as the eyes measured him.

"Ah, ye *do* remember me," she said. "That's *good*."

Nagaro had not thought about Jila during all of the summer's voyaging, nor in the days since his return to Pakoa. But here she was, in the flesh, watching him with that secret, knowing smile.

"Better for me than for you, I think," he said levelly, finding his voice. A quick glance around revealed that the other three men were nowhere in sight. Their work must have taken them around to the other side of the house.

Jila pouted. "Now what kind of talk is that? When I've come all this way to bring ye something."

Nagaro's brows knit. "There's nothing I want from you, Jila," he said coldly. "Unless it's my five hundred and thirty rins."

Jila raised a perfect eyebrow. "What makes you think *I* took your money?" she asked archly. "Can ye say ye saw me do it?"

Nagaro's frown deepened. Obviously he couldn't, because he hadn't. "Who else then?" he demanded."

Jila shrugged. "It could have been *anyone*," she said coyly. "You were sound asleep when I left, and I couldn't very well lock the door from the *outside*, could I?"

Nagaro regarded her narrowly. He was in no way convinced of her innocence, but there was an unfortunate lack of evidence. "All right," he conceded. "I'll not press the matter of the theft, since I can't prove it."

"Ye're *very* kind," she purred. "Though it comes a little *late*— after the tale's been all over the island. I've been quite afraid to show my face." Her eyes narrowed catishly. "Why didn't ye tell me ye were famous?"

This was an awkward question, because Nagaro had deliberately not mentioned how well known he was. He'd actually been glad that she seemed to know nothing about him. "I don't like being famous," he said defensively. "Folk treat you differently, for one thing. And, if it comes to that, you didn't tell me *you* were famous, either— or just exactly what you're famous *for*."

She shook her shoulders then and clucked her tongue. "Ye mustn't believe everything ye hear," she chided. "Being famous, *you* should know that." Suddenly she stepped right up to him, still holding her cloak tight about her. Her lashes half veiled her eyes as she tilted her face up to his. "It was *good* lying with you," she said, her voice low and breathy. "Ye've a gentle way with you even when ye're drunk. I'd not at all mind trying you sober."

Nagaro stiffened. Jila was so close he could smell the scent of her body, and the memory evoked by that scent was maddeningly potent. For a moment there flashed through his mind an image of days stretching into the future, all ending in nights spent in this woman's arms. In that moment he understood how those merchant captains had fallen.

The siren was calling... but he didn't have to answer.

He stood his ground, resisting conflicting urges to either move closer or back away. "If you think I'd ever listen to your lies again, Jila," he said, "You're a greater fool than you must think me."

If Jila was disappointed, she didn't show it. "*What lies?*" she crooned. "That ye're *strong?* That ye're *handsome?*"

"That you ever really wanted to get to know me at all," he said, and anger gave an edge to his voice.

Something flickered in her eyes, then— uncertainty, perhaps. She stepped back a pace, but then she rallied. "But I must show you what I've brought you," she said sweetly, and with that, she put aside her cloak to reveal a bundle she was carrying underneath it, wrapped in gray homespun. She held the bundle out to him. "This is your daughter that I made for you," she said with an ingratiating smile. "Isn't she *beautiful?*" With her last word, Jila flicked aside part of the soft cloth to reveal the face of a tiny infant.

Nagaro stared in horrified dismay. A pair of large brown eyes stared innocently back at him from a little round face under a tuft of raven hair. The child's skin was the color of mingled cream and honey— a shade darker than his own natural color, but lighter than Jila's.

Now *he* backed away, almost missing a step, as the ground seemed to shift under his feet. For a moment the world seemed to turn around him. "*Oh Vothra...*" he murmured.

It was at that moment that the other three men came around the corner of the house.

"Who are ye talking to, Nagaro?" Taru asked, then stopped dead as the answer to his question became glaringly apparent.

Nagaro gave him a stricken look. He felt as if he were suffocating. "It's... Jila," he said weakly. "She... she says the baby's mine..."

Oh Vothra...

Ulapa eyed Jila askance. "Bloody bad luck, I'd say that is, fer one night's work," he opined, and spat expertly onto one of Nagaro's carefully laid paving stones.

Jila drew herself up. "One night's work is all it takes for a *young* man," she said tartly. "Maybe it's been so long that ye've forgotten that— *if* ye ever knew it!"

Before Ulapa could make a retort, Taru stepped forward. "Now see here!" He leveled an angry finger. "Ye can just be off, an' take your bastard get with ye! Haven't ye caused Nagaro enough trouble?"

Jila turned on the young Turo and her glance flashed fire. "Oh that's *fine*— coming from *you!*" she said, all but spitting the last word. "What he and I did together could have been *our* secret— but *you* had to spread it all over town! And ye call yourself his friend!"

The scathing rejoinder left Taru momentarily speechless.

For Nagaro, Jila's words seemed to be coming from a great distance, scarcely penetrating the maelstrom of his thoughts: *How could he have had such bad luck? Or was the bad luck perhaps deserved? He had strayed from Vothra's Path... from the path of wisdom... and the Writings said that ill choices begot ill consequences...*

But Vothra didn't punish...

No, not Vothra, but Lokundas did. Lokundas delighted in humbling the proud, in bringing down the mighty... Nagaro closed his eyes. He wanted no part of Jila, nor any child of hers. He wished he hadn't lain with her... had never laid eyes on her. He wished he'd never even *thought* about breaking the ban... But as Chula, the old Turowan gardener at Averwin, would have said, "*Wishes don't water the lilies.*"

He opened his eyes. Jila still stood before him, though her attention was on Taru. She was radiating outrage, and Taru was red in the face. Pavo and Ulapa were hanging back, looking extremely uncomfortable, and the baby in Jila's arms was puckering her little forehead in a miniature frown, responding instinctively to the angry voices.

Nagaro knew he had to end this. He forced himself to speak. "What do you want of me, Jila?"

The words fell like lead.

Taru spun on him. "Don't ye give her anything, Nagaro! Ye don't know that child is yours! She could ha' lain with a dozen other men!"

Jila's eyes flung daggers at Taru. "*I never did!* I had no chance—" Abruptly she bit off her words.

Hope had flickered, but Nagaro frowned afresh. The child was clearly of mixed blood. And he knew what he had done. "Why didn't you come to me before?" he asked her. "When you first found you were with child? If you thought it was mine?"

Jila contrived to look aggrieved. "How could I dare to show my face? With all the lies folk were telling?"

"Lies? *Ha!*" Taru shook his finger at her again. "If ye didn't dare t' show your face *then*, how d' ye dare t' show it *now?* I'll wager that baby was got by your merchant captain— only ye found he didn't want it. So ye're trying t' fob it off on Nagaro!"

The look Jila gave Taru this time would have etched steel. She was uncommonly tall for a Turowan woman, and quite able to look Taru in the eye without tilting her head. "If ye're so sure of *that*— little Turo," she said in a voice that was smooth as silk and cold as ice, "Why did ye pay the tavern women to hush up the other tale?"

Nagaro caught Taru's guilty flinch, and his heart sank. "*What* other tale?" he asked, with dread in his heart.

Jila looked smug. Taru stood frozen, shock and anger warring on his countenance.

When neither of them answered, Nagaro's frown grew darker. "What is she talking about, Taru?" he asked sharply. "You didn't pay the tavern women to keep silent about something ...*did you?*"

"*Well,* Taru?" Jila demanded with obvious relish, "Are ye going to tell him the truth this time? Or will it be more lies?"

Taru shot her a venomous look before turning to Nagaro. "Well, I didn't..." he began, then stopped. He squared his shoulders and started again, this time speaking fast and low as if to get it over with. "One o' the tavern women had heard Jila tell someone she was looking for a Kelorin man t' get a child with," he explained. He licked his lips, swallowed, and went on. "Tulara told me about it the next day— afore I knew ye'd been with Jila. After ye told me about lying with her, I... well... I went back and gave the women some money t' keep quiet about it, that's all."

Nagaro suppressed a groan. Certain things he remembered from that night were beginning to make altogether too much sense. "And you didn't tell me *because...?*"

Taru met his eyes pleadingly. "Just 'cause those women were *saying* it, didn't make it *true!*, And I was afraid ye'd think ye had to marry her!"

Nagaro put a hand to his forehead. He felt sick. *Once again he had been someone's stud horse, and this time just because he was Kelorin.* "Taru," he said quietly, "She asked if I was Kelorin or Turo— because my skin was brown. And when I told her it was kuma stain, she said I was *perfect...* And afterwards she said my task was done."

His words drew an anguished groan from Taru, and a small, startled movement from Jila.

Glancing sharply at Jila, Nagaro surprised a look of annoyance, and realized that the woman hadn't expected him to remember those details. She'd brought up the tavern women's story to discredit Taru, possibly planning to deny it, herself, if pressed.

Nagaro had some choice words for Taru, but now wasn't the time for that— not with Jila waiting to pounce on any rift between them. Instead, he turned the full intensity of his gaze upon the Turowa. "Tell me what you want of me," he said coldly. "But understand that I will not marry you, Jila. You *deceived* me, you *used* me, and I'm far too angry with you for marriage to be a healthy thing for either one of us— or for your child."

Beside him he heard Taru murmur, "*Praise the Spirits!*"

Jila lifted her chin defiantly, clutching the baby to her so tightly that the little thing began to whimper. "Who says I ever wanted to marry you?" she sneered. "And ye needn't be so sour about it, either. I gave ye what ye wanted! I always give men what they want— a night to remember. You came to me willingly enough."

"I don't deny it." Nagaro spoke evenly, and his glance didn't waver. "That, and the fact that I was drunk, will always be my shame. But *your* shame is that you knew I was more than 'just a little drunk,' and you never said a word about wanting to get a child. Even drunk as I was, I would still have said 'no' to that if you'd asked. If you don't already know you did wrong, I hope you do before you die. And now, *what do you want of me?*"

Jila stood, eyes smouldering, yet she held her peace for the space of several heartbeats. Then her expression become more calculating. "The baby needs a wet nurse," she said on a wheedling note. "I have no milk, and the girl my sister found won't keep coming without pay."

Nagaro swallowed. "How much do you need?"

Jila's eyes narrowed speculatively. "Two hundred rins."

"*Two hundred rins!*" Taru burst out. "Nagaro, ye don't owe her *anything!* She already took more than that from you—"

Nagaro motioned his friend to silence. "She and I have spoken of that already, Taru," he said wearily. "I can't prove she took it. And if she did, I expect she's spent it."

Taru groaned, and Jila shot the young Turo a gloating glance.

Nagaro put his hand to his purse, then paused, frowning. "There's something I want to know first, Jila," he said. "Why did you do it? Did you want a child so badly? Or did you mean to trick the merchant captain into marrying you?"

At this, Jila burst into mirthless laughter. "Is that all ye can think of?" she cried. "Is that all you men ever think a woman wants? *Marriage.* And *children.*" She spoke the two words with loathing. "Do any of you ever imagine that a woman might want what every man takes for granted? To go wherever ye choose? To leave all of *this!*" Jila held the baby in the crook of one arm and with the other made a sweeping gesture that included— and dismissed— hill, harbor, and town. "What do *I* want, Captain Nagaro? Only to be *free.* To sail to Harmoth. Or Kel Tierna. To *travel,* and *see* things, and *do* things, before I die! But I can't expect ye to understand that."

Nagaro stood still in the face of Jila's vehemence. Her answer wasn't what he'd expected. Yet he *did* understand it— part of it at least— he who had been a slave, and worse, and who had so recently felt imprisoned by Pakoa's shores.

Pavo spoke for the first time, into the hanging pause. "Why you do not save your rin to buy passage on ship?" he wondered.

"Aye," Taru put in. "Ye took enough from Nagaro for that."

Jila bristled. "What good are *rins,* when a woman can't travel on a ship alone?" she demanded. "No captain will take me without a father or a husband or a brother *to look after me!* As if I needed looking after!"

Next to Taru, Ulapa nodded reluctantly. "She's got a point, lads. A woman on a ship without a man is bad luck. An' one what looks like *her* is worse."

Nagaro could read the truth of Jila's claim in the fierceness of her frustration. "So, you thought your captain would marry you for the baby's sake," he said, thinking aloud. "And take you off of this island. Only he didn't want the child, is that it? So you came to me?"

Jila didn't answer. Her chest was heaving with emotion, and she looked as if she had said more than she'd meant to. Nagaro considered her for a long moment. When he spoke again, his voice was deceptively gentle, for there was steel in his glance.

"Who is the father of your baby, Jila?" he asked. "Tell me truthfully— if you know."

Jila seemed to shrink a little under his eyes. She licked her lips. "*You* are," she said. "*He* sailed before it was my time that month, and there was no one else but you. I swear it by all the Spirits!"

Taru shifted his feet and his hand jerked as if he thought of striking the woman. "Don't believe her, Nagaro!"

Nagaro ignored his friend. He thought he understood this woman. She had no desire for marriage or children, but had been prepared to embrace both to get what she really wanted— which was nothing more than a little freedom. He felt sympathy for her, even though he knew she was a desperate, misguided creature, and not at all to be trusted. What, he wondered, would have become of the child and the marriage once she'd gotten free of Pakoa?

He unlaced his purse and drew out a coin, which he held out to her. "Take it," he said, when she didn't immediately move.

She put out her hand then, hesitantly, and he placed a golden half dokan coin into her open palm.

Beside him, Taru drew in his breath. "*Aye, Nagaro!*" he murmured under his breath.

Jila's eyes widened when she saw the yellow glint of the gold and felt the weight of it in her hand.

"That's for the child," Nagaro told her. "To see that she has whatever she needs." Then he put his hand again into his purse, drew out a second half dokan, and placed it in Jila's palm on top of the first. This time there was a general gasp from the other men.

"*Nagaro—*" Taru began, but stopped when Nagaro motioned him to silence.

"And that one is for *you,* Jila," Nagaro continued. "To buy passage on the *Bountiful* when she sails in two days' time for Kel Tierna. There's a man named Mendorel, staying at the Bay Tree, who'll be sailing on her. He'll escort you for my sake, I'm sure, if I ask him."

Jila's glance went from the coins to Nagaro's face and back again, her perfect eyebrows knit into a frown. Abruptly she closed her hand around the two gold pieces and slipped them into the drawstring neck of the plain white blouse she was wearing. When she raised her eyes to look at him again, they were half-veiled by her dark lashes, and her cherry lips were beginning to curl into a sly smile.

Nagaro frowned in his turn. "You're to use none of your wiles, Jila," he told her sternly. "Mendorel has a wife and children in Kel Teirna. And his oldest is a boy just coming to manhood. If I hear that you've caused any trouble, I'll come after you myself and bring you back to Pakoa, and that will be the end of your adventure."

Jila's eyes flashed. "That's hardly fair," she said petulantly. "When it can be the *man* that makes the trouble!"

Nagaro's brow didn't relax. "*That* is surely true. But I think you know how to say *no,* Jila— and make it clear you mean it."

Jila tilted her chin and the veil of her lashes descended a little further. "Men don't always take no for an answer..."

At that, Nagaro's frown grew thunderous. "If you are innocent, and any man tries to take you by force," he said coldly, "he'll answer to me!"

Jila's lashes were raised for an instant, but then she let them fall again. She stepped up to him, smiling invitingly, and raised her free hand to touch his cheek. "Oh, Captain Nagaro," she said in a voice that dripped honey. "And here I thought ye didn't care—"

And then she must have read the warning in his eyes, for she broke off and withdrew her hand as if she'd burned her fingers. Nagaro had neither flinched nor responded to her touch.

"*Why are ye doing this?*" she cried in genuine bewilderment.

It was a fair question. He'd asked *her* why, after all.

"There are two reasons," he said. "First: Everyone deserves a chance for happiness." He paused and when he continued there was an edge of anger to his words. "And second: I wish never to lay eyes on you again! *And now you had better go!*"

Jila backed away from him several steps, then stopped and held the baby up. "Won't ye give her a name?" she asked. "Before I go. It's your right."

Nagaro paused uncertainly. He had no desire to name her child, but he knew it was the Turowan way for the father to choose the name, the opposite of the Kelorin custom.

Taru had stepped up beside Nagaro as soon as Jila moved. *"Don't do it!"* he hissed in Nagaro's ear. "Jila's a born liar. Ye'll never know if that baby's *really* yours, and if ye give it a name it'll be yours forever!"

Nagaro was looking at the baby's tiny face, the little rosebud mouth and wide brown eyes that returned his glance with innocent incomprehension. *Could he let this child be fatherless?* It wasn't *her* fault that her mother had used him. He swallowed, his mouth dry.

"Call her *Narei*," he said. It meant "sea," and it was the first Turowan word that came into his head. *"Now go!"*

Jila's face briefly registered something that was either relief or satisfaction. "Then *Narei* she shall be," she declared, and without another word, she tucked the baby against her breast and wrapped her cloak about them both. Then she turned, and went— without a backward glance— moving away through the pale gold autumn grass in the direction of the grove of ironwood trees.

Nagaro knew there was a path beyond the grove that led down into the town. Jila must have come up that way. It explained how she'd managed to approach unnoticed. He watched her go. She went, not like a beaten dog, but with her head up and her back straight and a distinctly unapologetic swing to her hips.

Taru exploded as soon as he thought Jila was out of earshot. "Now what'd ye go and do *that* for?"

Nagaro let his breath out in a long sigh. "Every child deserves a father," he said quietly.

Taru sputtered. "But what if that baby isn't *yours?*"

Nagaro gave his friend a pained glance. "She *could* be," he said. "I did what I did. And for all I know, my own father turned his back and walked away. I can't do that."

Taru looked at the ground. "I can't believe I wasted a hundred rins," he muttered. "Ye didn't ever need to have known."

Nagaro sighed. *A hundred rins.* That was why Taru had said he was spending his money too fast, and why he'd been looking so hard to find work. "You would have had me possibly go through life with a child in the world that I didn't know about?" he asked carefully. "What Jila did wasn't right, but *that* wouldn't have been right either. I'm sorry about your money, and I know you meant well. You always *mean* well. I just wish you'd start letting me handle my own affairs. And now," he continued without waiting for a response, "I'm going for a walk."

With that, he turned and strode off in the direction of the ravine and the fenced pasture.

The three other men watched his retreating figure in silence for a long moment. Jila had already disappeared among the trees.

At last Ulapa spread his hands to the sky. "Well I'll be a blisterin' barnacle!" he exclaimed. "If that woman ain't a blast o' wind from leeward! I'd swear he warn't buyin' half o' what she was sellin,' and she still walked away with a thousand rins and a name for the baby! Yer capt'n's a strange one, an' no mistake."

Pavo spoke for just the second time. "Nagaro always do what he think is right," he explained. "Even if it is not good thing for *him*."

Taru shook his head. "A thousand rins and a name for the baby," he repeated. "Why not just marry her, then, and have done with it? Ye don't suppose she'll go, do ye? On the ship, I mean?"

"Oh, she'll go, all right," Ulapa opined. "There ain't nothin' left for her here on Pakoa. Ye've seen t' that. But she'll leave the baby. Ye can mark my words."

There was a length of silence. Then Pavo said, "Jila is very beautiful woman, but she have too much fire in belly. How do Turowan man do, if Turowan woman be like that?"

Ulapa gave the young Hashtep a sidelong glance. "How do we *do?*" he growled. "There's not a married man *I* know what's master under his own roof— though every man o' them'd swear that he was. Best ye can say o' Turowan women is they lets their men *think* they're holdin' the tiller. *Hah!*" He spat. "That's why I never hitched meself t' one." Then he sighed. "'Course, I *have* missed havin' a warm squeeze of a cold night," he added thoughtfully. "And wouldn't I like to be one o' them two gold pieces he give her— goin' where she put 'em! *Hakura Kili*, what a view!"

***

Nagaro settled himself onto the cold stone. He had come to his stone seat by a round-about way, wishing to avoid any appearance of following Jila. By the time he arrived at his perch and looked down, he was relieved to see no sign of the woman. She must have already rounded the first turning where the path disappeared around the curve of the hill.

The day was unforgivingly bright— clear, crisp, and crystalline— but Nagaro felt as if he were under a dark cloud. He breathed the fresh, tingling air, but did not feel refreshed. A weight had come to rest upon his shoulders. With a groan, he drew up his legs and wrapped his arms around them, bending his head down to rest his forehead on his knees.

How... how... how could this be? Everything had been going so well— and now this!

It was a position he had never expected to find himself in— having to take responsibility for a child he didn't want. It should be an easy enough thing to avoid, after all. *If* one followed the Path. He knew he had stumbled, badly, and fallen. *But it had been only once!*

Of course, once was all it took. As Jila had pointed out...

With an effort he wrenched back his thoughts, refusing to ride the horse any further down that road. What was done could not be undone. There was no use in complaining that the consequences were unfair.

He forced himself instead to review the actions he'd just taken, and concluded that, all in all, he had done the best he could. It was true that he might never know if he was really the child's father, but the evidence pointed uncomfortably in that direction. He didn't doubt that a woman like Jila, well versed in the art of *avoiding* conception, would know how to go about *getting* a child if she wanted one.

Still, he felt fully justified in refusing to offer her marriage. Guilty though he knew he was, he judged the greater balance of the blame to be Jila's. She had deceived him about her feelings and her intentions. She'd manipulated him. She'd taken cynical advantage of his condition— although his condition had been his own fault. Yes, that last was true, but the thing he could not countenance was that Jila had set out to purposefully get a child by him without telling him so. It was a completely unacceptable violation of the trust that he felt should exist between a man and a woman in such matters. He could understand her desire to leave the island, but her methods ran counter to everything he'd been taught.

And yet... *understanding begets compassion, the chief of all virtues. And from compassion are born charity, mercy, and forgiveness.* So the Writings said. Well, he had given the woman charity. Mercy, thankfully, was not required in this case. And forgiveness? Perhaps it would come in time. For now, he was still too angry.

Nagaro never liked to feel angry. It made him acutely uncomfortable, and the discomfort persisted until he could find a way to put the anger aside— which was difficult to do when he felt justified in being angry. And that was really why it was best for Jila to leave Pakoa, since *he* had no intension of doing so. That she wished to go, made it easy. He could only pray that he wasn't turning a she-wolf loose to hunt among a larger flock. If that proved to be the case, he would have to go after her and bring her back as he had threatened to do. At least he didn't doubt that Jila would go. She wanted her freedom too badly. Perhaps she would abandon her old ways in Kel Tierna because she no longer needed them? He could hope.

And what of the child?

He had no illusions that Jila would take the child with her. A woman who wanted freedom that much would see a baby only as an encumbrance. She would probably leave the child with her sister and the wet nurse. Nagaro sighed, and raised his head to confront the unrelenting cheerfulness of the view. Brilliant sunlight glittered on the waters of the harbor, where two warships now lay at anchor instead of one. *That* was one thing done well...

...but now this...

Again he jerked on the reins of his thoughts.

Had he done enough for the child?

Well, he'd given her a name, which would give her the right to call him "father." He wasn't sure how he felt about that. She was a little piece of Jila. Still, he felt that naming her had been the right thing to do. There was probably no other man on the island who would name this particular baby, and he knew what it was like to be a fatherless bastard. If he couldn't give more of himself, he could at least give her the name and the gold to pay for her needs. The money he had given Jila should last for some time. He knew he would carry this burden for years to come, but there should be some respite, at least for now, before he had to deal again with the child he had named Narei.

For a while longer he sat there, gathering himself, until at last he heaved a long sigh and got to his feet. The air of gloom that had settled on him hadn't dissipated, but there was still work to be done.

As he descended from the rocky outcrop, a thought struck him that drew a small, bitter smile to his lips. How ironic that a bottle of wine and one devious woman had sufficed to get from him in a single night the very thing that an honest princess and the wily Dreigen had failed to obtain in nine long months! Then he frowned. *No*, he thought, *not quite the very thing*. The king had surely hoped for a man-child. It would have served Elgurn right if Leyel had gotten the princess with child and she had borne a daughter. Jila had likely hoped for a boy as well, if it came to that. And her merchant captain might have been more pleased if she'd presented him with a son. Nagaro's bitter smile returned. Jila had hatched her plan, found herself the "perfect" man to prey upon, and then had gotten herself a *girl*-child. If Lokundas loved a joke, that one, at least, was on Jila.

Chapter 24

An Unwelcome Summons

"Is the *Bountiful* finally gone?"

Nagaro sat hunched over his cup of sothiril in the nearly deserted common room. His question was addressed to Taru and Pavo who had just come in by the front door.

"Aye," Taru responded. "We watched her 'til she was clear o' the harbor mouth."

"With Jila and Mendorel both on board?"

Taru nodded. "Jila came, with her sister. That's who they said she was anyway. I just saw two women wrapped in cloaks. They said a few words t' Mendorel on the wharf, and Jila walked up the landing plank as meek as a kitten."

"There was big crowd of people that came to watch, Nagaro," Pavo added as he sat down. "Many, many people who say it is good that you make Jila go away. They make big cheer when she walk onto ship."

Nagaro grimaced. "I heard it from here." The crowd was no surprise, only embarrassing and inconvenient. The tale of his second encounter with Jila had run up and down the island even more quickly than the tale of the first. While he would have liked to see Mendorel off, the idea of being on public display at this time hadn't appealed to him. He shook his head. "Just what I need. Being famous again."

Pavo regarded him. "You have never stop being famous," he observed sagely.

Taru saw the look on Nagaro's face. "It's not my fault this time! Ye can blame Ulapa. That man's worse than any old woman when it comes t' gossip!"

"Now what have ye got against old women, Taru?" Yuli had emerged from the kitchen with a pair of mugs in one hand and a teapot in the other. "Seems t' me we all like to repeat a good tale if we hear one." She dangled the mugs in front of Taru and Pavo. "Will ye two be having some sothiril and seed cakes?"

Pavo smiled broadly. "Oh yes, Tira Yuli."

Taru shrugged and nodded.

Yuli set the mugs down and leaned over to fill them with the fragrant, steaming golden liquid. As she straightened she met Nagaro's eyes. "Now why are ye lookin' like the boat just sunk?" she demanded. "Surely not just 'cause ye're famous again!"

He gave her a dismal glance. "It's what I'm famous *for*."

"Nonsense!" Yuli flourished the teapot. "Ye did a good thing, Tor Nagaro— a good thing for that little girl child, and for this island." She turned towards the open doorway that led to the kitchen and called, "Tulara, will ye bring out that plate o' seed cakes now, please?"

"Coming, Tira Yuli!" Tulara's voice answered from the kitchen.

Nagaro ducked his head and took a gulp of tea. "I don't suppose Jila took the baby." He looked up to meet Taru's eyes.

Taru shook his head. "I'm sorry, Nagaro. She had all her things bundled up in two baskets. There was no sign o' the baby."

Tulara sailed in, bearing a large plate piled high with round, flat golden-brown cakes. With her came wafting a mouth-watering aroma of honey, butter, and spices. She set the plate down in the middle of the table and turned to Nagaro, her dark eyes sparkling. "Here's your seed cakes, Zirda." She beamed. "I hope ye like them. We just baked 'em fresh this morning, and I mixed the batter!"

Nagaro stared in astonishment. *Was this the same Tulara?* "Ah... thank you," he managed. "They smell... wonderful."

Beyond Tulara's shoulder he could see Taru with his mouth agape and a frown gathering.

Yuli looked as if she were having trouble containing her laughter.

Tulara was still standing there. Still looking right at Nagaro. Still smiling.

He swallowed. "You seem to be very happy this morning, Tulara," he ventured,

"Oh, I am, Tor Nagaro!" Tulara blushed prettily, but didn't drop her eyes. "It's such a beautiful day!" She managed something like a curtsy. "I'll be in the kitchen, Zirda, if there's anything else ye're wanting. Ye've only t' call." She gave him another glowing smile, then finally turned and all but skipped out of the room.

"Now what's got into *her?*" Taru demanded as soon as she had disappeared through the kitchen door. "Nagaro might ha' been the only one in the room! She didn't even look at me or Pavo."

Nagaro shook his head, mystified. "*I* certainly don't know! That's more words than she's said to me in the last six months. A week ago she'd barely stay in the same room with me."

Pavo reached for a seed cake, took an experimental bite, and nodded appreciatively. "These are good cake," he said around a mouthful, then added, "I think she have heard some very good news."

Nagaro scowled. "Well if she did, I've no idea what it was!"

Yuli's shoulders had been shaking, and now she laughed aloud. "Then ye're not very quick, Tor Nagaro." Her eyes were dancing with mirth as she met his wounded glance. "It's because ye named the baby! Ye named that little girl child that was got in a tavern by the likes o' Jila. Ye made that child respectable, and as far as Tulara's concerned, that puts ye on the right side o' the road."

"Oh, is that it." Nagaro's glance slid away and he sought refuge in his cup of sothiril. He lifted it to his lips and took a long swallow. Then he studied the table top. He wished he could say that he'd been glad to name the baby. It had been the right thing to do, but he had felt more enthusiasm for paying the island's taxes.

"And don't ye worry about Jila leaving the baby with her sister," Yuli went on, coming around the end of the table to top off his mug of sothiril. "Any mother that 'd leave her child so easy like that isn't fit to be one. The poor little thing'll be much better off with Animara."

She sighed then, and to Nagaro's relief, she turned the subject. "Are ye lads really moving out o' here in two days' time?"

Nagaro pounced on the question. "Yes. We plan to. The house will be ready tomorrow, and it will take us a day to move our things."

"Well, I knew it had to come, soon or late. But I have t' say the Bay Tree won't seem the same without ye lads." She paused, eyes moist. "Maybe I'll see ye here for meals? Unless ye've found someone t' cook for ye?"

"Nagaro can cook." Taru spoke around a mouthful of his second seed cake.

Yuli turned to Nagaro. "Can ye, now?" she inquired archly.

"A little. Pavo actually has more experience."

Yuli turned to Pavo. He smiled broadly. "It is true. After my mother have died, all of us— my father, my two brother, and me— we learn to cook or else we starve."

"Well, fancy that." Yuli looked a little deflated.

"I'm sure we'll come here for meals fairly often, Yuli," Nagaro said hastily. "We all really like your cooking, and just because Pavo and I can cook doesn't mean we're eager to do it all the time."

"Now that's better!" Yuli smiled and waggled the teapot. "There's a bit more in here if anyone wants it."

Taru raised his cup and Yuli topped it off before returning to the kitchen.

"If ye want any seed cake, Nagaro, ye'd best take one," Taru observed. "Before Pavo eats them all."

Indeed there were only two cakes left on the plate.

Pavo didn't even blink. "Oh, yes, Nagaro," he said brightly. "Tulara will be very sad if you do not eat seed cake that she bring for you. And it is waste if I eat them, because Tulara know my eye is only for Tenepti."

Nagaro winced as he dutifully reached for one of the remaining cakes.

Taru gave Pavo a sharp glance. Pavo pointedly ignored it. Then they both simultaneously made a grab for the last cake. Taru won, and grinned smugly at Pavo as he devoured it.

Nagaro ate his cake more slowly, savoring it. It was really very good.

And it was good to have Jila gone, he reflected. And to have Tulara talking to him at last. He really should try to look on the brighter side of the storm cloud.

"So when are ye going to teach us to ride?" Taru asked, reopening a subject that had been in contention for several days.

Nagaro looked away. "Not this week," he said. "There's still the rest of the furniture to get and the curtains to hang..."

Pavo eyed him closely. "Do not forget you have promise to give riding lesson," he said.

"That's right," Taru agreed. "The way ye keep putting it off, I'm beginning t' think ye don't want to part with your secrets."

Nagaro sighed. "That's because I don't *have* any secrets. Everything I do with horses just comes naturally."

But he *had* promised, and he knew he was eventually going to have to deliver.

***

Four days later he was trying to do exactly that.

It was a sunny morning and the three friends were in the stable yard with the sorrel mare, Cinnamon, saddled and ready. Nagaro had just finished demonstrating how to mount and dismount, and Taru was in the process of trying to duplicate the first maneuver while Nagaro held the mare's bridle.

The young Turo's efforts were not going well however. Cinnamon managed to move away every time he approached her.

"Can't ye make the beast stand still?" Taru demanded in frustration as Cinnamon side-stepped again.

Nagaro frowned. "I'm think you're making her nervous."

"*I'm* making *her* nervous?" Taru threw up his hands, and Cinnamon immediately flung up her head and rolled her eyes. "Ye see!" Taru added accusingly. "She's giving me that *look* again!"

Nagaro sighed. "Well I guess I should say you're both making each other nervous," he amended. "Maybe it would be better to try Sugar. She's a bit more sedate."

Taru scowled. "Sugar is a fat old lump," he grumbled. "And if *ye* can ride this one, I don't see why *I* can't. I just want t' know what ye do that's different, that's all."

This was exactly why Nagaro hadn't leaped at the idea of teaching his friends horsemanship. It had been far too long since he'd learned to ride. He'd been a small child at the time. Unlike his more recent study of swordsmanship, he couldn't remember much about the learning process.

"Well," he said thoughtfully, "I don't make sudden movements, for one thing. I'm firm but gentle when I touch the animal. And," he added, "I talk to them."

"Ye *what?*" Taru stared at him.

Nagaro nodded, speaking half to himself. "I always talk to them. Especially if they're skittish, or if they don't know me." He refocused on Taru, who was still staring. "Yes," he said decisively. "I think it would help if you tried talking to her."

Taru opened his mouth, then closed it again, seeing that Nagaro was completely serious. "What am I supposed to say to a *horse?*" he inquired plaintively.

Nagaro considered. "Tell her how beautiful she is. Or how strong, or how swift. Tell her you won't hurt her... That you just want to go for a run with her."

Taru licked his lips. "Ah... Nagaro..." He stopped, clearly embarrassed by the whole idea.

Pavo spoke into the pause. "Do you think that horse understand?" he asked earnestly.

Nagaro turned to his other friend. "No," he said, frowning a little as he tried to think how to explain something that was clear to him but apparently not to them. "Not the *words,*" he continued. "But the *tone*. You want her to know that you like her. That you want to be friends. That you want the same thing she wants— which is to run— and you won't ask her to do anything too hard, or too dangerous. You want her to trust you."

Pavo's expression had turned speculative. "Maybe it is like talking to woman," he suggested.

Taru made an annoyed gesture. "That's daft!"

But Nagaro didn't dismiss the idea. "It *could* be like talking to a woman, I suppose," he said. "Except that if you want a woman to trust you, I think you had better really mean what you say. But when you talk to a horse, it doesn't matter so much *what* you say as *how* you say it. I just find it easier to sound sincere if I am sincere." He found himself blushing as he remembered the young woman he'd encountered beside the stream at the other end of the island— the rather forward young woman who'd overheard him talking to Cinnamon and had thought he was imagining talking to a woman. Perhaps there really was something in Pavo's notion.

Pavo turned to Taru. "You will be good at talking to horse," he said encouragingly. "Because you have talk to so many woman."

Taru looked uncomfortable. "Actually it was only one or two at first, and then it was all just Tulara," he confessed in a low voice.

Pavo grinned. "Then pretend you are talk to Tulara," he said brightly.

Taru flinched. "I, ah, don't think so," he said. "We didn't do that much talking anyway."

Pavo turned back to Nagaro. "I think maybe I like to try," he said.

Nagaro was trying hard not to smile. "Of course, Pavo," he said. "Go ahead."

Taru shrugged and moved away from Cinnamon, and Pavo stepped up to stand beside her head. Cautiously Pavo put out a hand and patted the mare's neck. At the same time, he spoke words in Hashti in a gentle, coaxing tone.

The mare's ears swivelled around towards Pavo and her large dark eye regarded him. Then she turned her head towards him, lightly nuzzled his shoulder, and blew wetly against his shirt. Pavo's broad countenance registered surprise and delight.

"Go ahead and rub her nose, Pavo," Nagaro suggested. "She likes that."

Pavo grinned, and gently rubbed the mare's muzzle with his strong brown fingers. "Oh," he exclaimed in surprise. "It is very soft!"

Nagaro nodded. "That's right. Now talk to her some more."

Pavo spoke more Hashti, almost crooning as he rubbed the velvety muzzle. Cinnamon blew into his hand. Pavo laughed. "Now she make my hand wet!" he complained, but without rancor.

Nagaro smiled. "I think you should try to mount now," he said. "Give her another pat on the neck, down near the pommel of the saddle, and then tell her what you're going to do."

Pavo did as instructed, and the mare remained quietly standing. "That's good, Pavo," Nagaro told him. "Now put your hands on the pommel and your left foot in the stirrup, and swing your right leg up and over, the way I showed you."

Pavo complied, and succeeded somewhat awkwardly in mounting into the saddle. He was so big that he quite dwarfed the little sorrel mare. "Look!" he exclaimed as he settled himself astride her. "I am sitting on horse!"

Taru had watched the progress of events with an incredulous frown. "I don't believe it," he said, shaking his head. "What did ye say t' her, Pavo?"

Pavo's face suddenly became wooden. "I do not think I am go to tell you."

"That's not fair!" Taru protested. "Just because ye know how to speak Hashti—"

Pavo gave him a challenging look. "Can you not speak Turowan?"

"Well, yes," Taru admitted. "Some. But the Turo don't really *use* Turowan much any more."

Cinnamon's ears had been flicking back and forth, and now she shifted her weight uneasily from hoof to hoof. Nagaro reached up to rub the mare's neck. "Steady, my lady," he murmured. "These are my friends." He addressed himself to Pavo. "I think you had better stop arguing. Why don't we try walking her in a circle?"

Pavo agreed, and so Nagaro took the mare by the bridle and began to walk her around the stable yard. Pavo grimaced and clutched at the pommel of the saddle at the first swaying lurch of movement. "Are you sure she is not go to fall down?" he asked apprehensively.

Nagaro laughed. "*She* won't, though *you* might. When Pavo looked alarmed, he quickly added, "No, don't worry. You're not going to fall off when she's just walking. Now relax and try to get the feel of the motion."

After once around the stable yard, Pavo was persuaded to let go of the pommel, and after another circuit, Nagaro released the bridle and told his pupil to pick up the reins. "Now squeeze her a little with your legs to tell her to go forward," he instructed. "*Gently!* Use the reins to turn her head the way you want her to go, and draw them in both at once when you want her to stop." Several minutes later, Pavo had successfully executed a circle and a number of figure eights. He pulled the mare gently to stop. "This is easy," he said, grinning from ear to ear.

"Is it my turn again now?" Taru had been watching with frustrated impatience.

Nagaro suppressed a smile. "Yes, I think you might try again now, Taru."

Pavo gave the young Turo a deliberately deadpan look. "What you are go to say?" he inquired innocently. "Have you figure it out?"

"Yes, I have," Taru retorted, "But I'm certainly not going t' tell *you!*"

Pavo inexpertly swung down from the saddle and extricated his foot from the stirrup, while Nagaro held Cinnamon's bridle. The big Hashtep gave the mare a final pat on the neck. "Thank you, lady," he said with evident sincerity. He stepped away then, turned, and came to a sudden halt facing the inn. "Oh," he said. "Here come Tulara."

Startled, Nagaro turned around.

Tulara had evidently emerged from the back door of the inn, which exited the kitchen, and was approaching them. He glanced hurriedly at Taru and found that his friend had struck a pose of studied unconcern.

Turning back, Nagaro found that Tulara's attention was not on Taru, but entirely on *him.* Since she had continued to behave more freely in his presence ever since Jila's departure, he wasn't greatly surprised when she now came straight up to him and addressed him with barely a trace of shyness.

"I've a message for ye, Tor Nagaro."

He gave her an encouraging smile. "Yes? What is it?"

"It's from Tira Animara," she said a little breathlessly, and when he looked blank, she added, "Jila's sister. She want's ye t' come to her house this afternoon. She wants to talk to ye."

Nagaro's heart dropped like a stone. He tried not to let it show in his face, however, not wanting Tulara to know how little he wanted anything to do with Jila's child. He swallowed. "Did she say why?"

Tulara brushed a strand of dark hair from her eyes. "She didn't come herself. She sent her daughter, Bahiri. I think Jila took all the money ye meant for the little one."

Bishka!

Nagaro looked at the ground, disappointed if not entirely surprised. "Oh," he said aloud. "I see." He raised his eyes. "Is, ah... Bahiri... still here? Perhaps I could speak to her?" He was thinking he might simply give the girl some money to take back to her mother.

But Tulara shook her head. "She couldn't wait, and I didn't know ye were back here 'til Yuli told me. I thought we'd have to send someone up t' your house, so I told Bahiri I'd give ye the message. I told her ye'd surely come. It's all right, Zirda, isn't it? I didn't think ye'd mind."

Nagaro carefully kept his expression neutral, though he was writhing inside. "Of course it's all right." He hoped the lie sounded convincing. "It will have to be after I meet with the builder though," he added. "We're going to pace out the site for the new barracks right after lunch. But there should be time after that."

Tulara looked relieved. "Oh good," she said, and then she stood there, twisting her fingers together while the silence lengthened. "Ah... Tor Nagaro? Could I ask ye a favor?" she blurted at last.

He did his best to smile. "Of course, Tulara."

"Do ye think ye could teach me how t' work sums? So... so I could help Tor Ramu with the books?"

Nagaro's mouth dropped open in surprise, but he recovered quickly. "Yes, of course," he said. "I'd be glad to." And then he mentally kicked himself for not stopping to think whether this was wise. From the corner of his eye he'd seen Taru stiffen.

"Oh thank ye, Zirda!" Tulara's eyes were alight with gratitude. "Yuli says we could work at the table in the kitchen, and she'll watch so there won't be any talk."

Nagaro saw Taru relax a little at that. "That's a good idea," he managed.

"Could we start tomorrow?" Tulara was nearly bouncing now with eagerness. "After lunch? Ye *were* planning t' come down for lunch, weren't ye?"

"Well, yes, I suppose we could do that."

"Oh thank ye, Zirda! Thank ye so much!" She bobbed him a curtsy and bolted for the kitchen door. She hadn't so much as glanced at Taru.

Nagaro stared after her, then mentally shook himself. He considered saying something to Taru, but thought better of it. Tulara's request appeared to be entirely innocent and it was best just to treat it that way. *Besides, he had to worry about Jila's sister...*

The sense of doom engendered by Animara's summons had been temporarily displaced by the shock of Tulara's request, but it now descended again like a lead mantle. Nagaro ran a hand through his hair. "Bishka!" he muttered. "That Jila—"

"Aye! That thieving Jila!" There was relief plainly audible under Taru's indignation. "How many times are ye going to have t' pay?"

Nagaro gave his friend a dark look. "I expect I'll be paying for the rest of my life," he said tightly. Then, to turn the subject, he asked, "Are you going to try to ride Cinnamon this morning, or should I unsaddle her and put her back in her stall?"

Taru's face darkened. "Since Pavo's gone and done it," he said. "I'm going t' ride that mare if it kills me."

"Well, let's hope it doesn't come to that." Nagaro forced levity into his voice. "And let's get on with it." He reached for the mare's bridle.

He tried to focus on the riding lesson— with moderate success. Taru seemed not nearly as comfortable as Pavo about talking to the horse, but he eventually managed to mount, and rode Cinnamon around the stable yard as Pavo had done. So at least the lesson ended on an encouraging note.

After that, they all went to the inn's common room for lunch, though Nagaro found he had no appetite. He was too preoccupied with what he had to do.

The meeting with the house-builder helped take his mind off the summons because it made him think about something that really interested him. Pavo accompanied him for this activity— Taru having begged off— and the two of them walked around the site with the builder, pacing out distances and debating just where the barracks should be situated, and how many rooms they should have, of what size, and so forth. The builder was a middle-aged Turowan, and a true craftsman. He had things to say about the limitations imposed by the site. He offered a number of viable options and was able to provide general cost estimates for each of the plans they discussed. The whole process took nearly two hours, during which time Nagaro nearly forgot about the promised visit to Animara.

It quickly came back to him as he and Pavo started up the hill to their house.

"There's nothing else for it," he said gloomily. "I have to go talk to the woman."

Pavo was sympathetic. "Maybe you should not go to our house," he suggested. "Just go right away to talk. Then it will be over, and you will not have to think about it any more."

Nagaro sighed heavily. "I need to refill my purse," he confessed. "She's sure to ask for more money, and I don't want to have to go back a second time."

The morning had been clear and breezy, but clouds had begun to gather during lunch, and the afternoon looked likely to be rather dreary. The gathering gloom matched Nagaro's mood as he walked up the hill. At the house, he went to his new room. It was furnished with just a narrow bed, a chest of drawers, and a washstand. Aside from the white curtains on the window— and the fact that it was about half the size— it didn't look very different from the room he had been sharing with Taru and Pavo at the inn. It wasn't much bigger than the room he'd shared with Taru in the little house on Wotana Bay, but it was his.

He sat down on the bed and reached under it to pull out his cash box. The box had found a new place there, along with his sword and the three suspicious Jinari scrolls. He frowned as he replenished his supply of silver. His mistake was costing him dearly. Not that he was in any danger of running short of money, thanks to the "captain's share". The men had insisted that he take it, despite his protest. Those who were merchant seamen were accustomed to the captain of the ship being more highly paid than the common sailors. He had intended to use the extra money to help others when he saw some need. Paying for the support of Jila's child wasn't exactly what he'd had in mind, but he was determined to pay for his mistake out of his own money rather than claiming hardship and drawing on the stock of money set aside for unusual needs.

With his purse full, he had no excuse to wait any longer.

He left the house, taking his cloak this time because the day was looking more and more like rain, and went back down the hill. As he reached the bottom of the Hill Road, he stopped short with a muttered oath when he realized he had only the vaguest idea of where Animara lived. He would have to go back to the inn to ask Yuli for directions.

He found her kneading bread in the kitchen amid a strong aroma of yeast and a faint miasma of flour.

"I've never been there myself," Yuli told him in answer to his question. "But I can tell ye the way. Ye take the Front Road around to the south end o' town and turn right into the cross-road just as ye come t' the kuma mills. When that road ends, ye turn left into the track that leads up over the headland. There's only the one path, so ye can't miss it. Animara and her husband have a kuma farm in the little valley on the other side o' the ridge. Ye should be able t' see the house from the ridge-top."

Nagaro found Yuli's matter-of-fact response reassuring. He'd always found the innkeeper's wife easy to talk to, and he was in no great hurry to be on his way, so he asked, "What can you tell me about her?"

Yuli mopped her brow with the back of her hand, leaving a smudge of flour. "Well, she's an honest woman," she said. "If she says Jila took the baby's money, ye can be sure it's true. I'm sure she's tried t' look after her sister too, but she's not more 'n a half dozen years older, and Jila always had her own mind. Folks all say Animara and her husband are decent folk. They've got three children o' their own, too, so that says something."

Hearing this was comforting, or it would have been if it weren't for the *reason* why this honest, decent woman had summoned him.

Being out of excuses again, Nagaro thanked Yuli for the information. He left the inn, setting out on foot. He would much rather have ridden, but he knew the path over the ridge that Yuli had described. He'd tried riding it just once on Cinnamon and had ended up dismounting to lead the mare, having found the path too steep and narrow to be comfortable going for a horse and rider.

The afternoon was beginning to become quite chill, which gave him an excuse to keep his head down and his hood up as he walked through the town, making it less likely he'd be recognized. Since his return to Pakoa, he seemed to have suddenly become the most eligible bachelor on the island. The same mothers who had once called their daughters in whenever he passed now called them out to smile and wave. Nagaro found it embarrassing and a little unnerving besides.

Passing along Front Street, he remembered that the seamstress had been delayed in finishing Pavo's curtains, and he decided to stop at the shop— since his way led right past it— on the odd chance that they were ready. A fine rain had begun to fall by the time he reached the shop. The bell tinkled as he pushed the door open and stepped into the warm, dim interior. As he threw back his hood, he immediately noticed two things. The first was that Tira Jilena was not at her work table behind the counter. The second was that he wasn't alone. There were three young women in the shop, two seated on the bench provided for waiting customers and the third standing not two paces in front of him. As he froze in surprise, the standing woman turned, and he had another shock when he discovered that it was Berenil. A quick glance in the direction of the bench confirmed that the other two young women were Gesrin and Lissel.

"I... I'm sorry." He began backing towards the door. "I can come back another time."

"Don't be silly," snapped Berenil. "Since you're here, you might as well finish your business. We're having gowns fitted," she added. "Mother's in the back with Tira Jilena and should be done any minute. Besides, she says I'm old enough to serve as chaperon for my sisters."

Nagaro halted his retreat. It *was* silly to leave if no one minded him staying, and leaving sooner would only bring him that much sooner to Animara's door. So he gave Berenil a shrug and a nod.

"*Old* enough, or *cold* enough," Gesrin muttered under her breath.

When Nagaro glanced at the second sister, he found she was looking him up and down with such a frankly appraising glance that it made him blush. Berenil gave no sign that she'd heard her sister, though she could scarcely have failed to do so, the room being so small.

Gesrin raised her voice then, addressing herself to Nagaro. "What *is* your business, anyway, Tor Nagaro?" She managed to make the question sound faintly suggestive.

Berenil raised an eyebrow, but offered no reprimand.

"Curtains," Nagaro said, hastily. "Tira Jilena is making curtains for our front window."

Lissel giggled at that, and Gesrin gave Nagaro a devouring look. "If you had a *wife*," she said sweetly, "It would be *her* task to see about curtains.

Nagaro frowned. "I suppose it might."

This earned him a smirk from Gesrin and another giggle from Lissel. Nagaro's frown deepened.

"*And* a wife would cook for you," Gesrin added pointedly. "Who does your cooking now, Tor Nagaro?"

Nagaro chose not to answer. He thought Gesrin was being rather rude, and he didn't subscribe to the view that things like cooking and dealing with curtains were women's work.

Getting new curtains had become Nagaro's task simply because it had been his idea. He had felt that the curtains were needed because the parlor had become Pavo's bedroom and the existing curtains were lacy and rather transparent. Pavo had been unconcerned, since the nearest dwelling was a quarter mile away, but Taru had decided the matter by declaring that it wasn't right for a man to have lace on his windows.

Silence grew in the room until at length Berenil broke it. "Well, Tor Nagaro," she said briskly, "Are you ready to settle down now that you've managed to free some slaves and come safely back?"

Nagaro stared. *Didn't her father tell her anything?* "Actually," he said, "we're building a barracks and a practice grounds so we can train more men. Next spring I mean to sail with two ships."

"*Oh.*" Berenil looked as if she were tasting something unpleasant. "Do you intend to keep doing this, then, until someone kills you?"

Nagaro shrugged. "That, or until something else happens to change my course. It's the work I have chosen."

Berenil appeared to have no answer to this. Lissel, for once, didn't giggle. She was staring at him open-mouthed from her seat on the bench.

Gesrin leaned forward eagerly. "You don't know *anything*, Berenil," she said. "He's much too good with a sword for anyone to ever possibly kill him!"

At this, Nagaro felt his face grow hot. "Its entirely possible for someone to kill me, I assure you," he said stiffly.

Berenil looked askance at him. "And *still* you choose to do it?"

"Yes. I just explained that."

Again there was an uncomfortable silence while Berenil appeared to study an embroidered sampler hanging on the wall above the counter. Gesrin whispered something to Lissel, who exclaimed, "Oh my!" and immediately clapped a hand over her mouth.

Nagaro was wishing fervently that Tira Delmanei and the seamstress would finish the fitting session in the back room.

Berenil abruptly spoke to him again. "Do you know that I'm likely to be married in the spring?" she asked in a conversational tone.

"You are?" Nagaro was more startled than surprised. It was nearly a year since their sitting, and he supposed there could have been several other young men during the interval.

"Oh yes," she said. "My father has been in correspondence with a merchant in Kel Tierna who has a son of appropriate age."

"Correspondence?" Nagaro frowned. "Will this merchant's son come to Pakoa so you can meet each other? Or will you go there?"

Berenil shrugged her shoulders. "I shouldn't think it necessary," she said lightly. "Father has told me all about him, and I can't see any objections."

It was Nagaro's turn to gape at her. "What if you find you don't *like* him?" he blurted.

"I don't see why I shouldn't," she said. "He's steady and responsible. And entirely dedicated to the trade."

Nagaro didn't personally find this particularly persuasive. "Well," he said diplomatically, "I suppose that's fine, if it's what you want."

It was at this moment that the door from the back room finally opened and Berenil's mother emerged— not a hair out of place— with Tira Jilena right behind her. Delmanei arched an eyebrow as her glance traveled from Nagaro to Berenil, but she then nodded to Nagaro and said nothing. Gesrin was trying unsuccessfully to look demure, while Lissel still sat wide-eyed, apparently too dismayed to giggle.

With enormous relief, Nagaro nodded an acknowledgment to Tira Delmanei and hastily asked his question of Tira Jilena. The seamstress told him the curtains would be ready the next day, and he promptly thanked her and made a bow that included all the occupants of the room. "Good day to you, Zirdyns," he said, and made his grateful escape out onto the street.

Once there, he shivered with a chill that had nothing to do with the wind that was blowing drizzle into his face, and strode off in the direction of the south end of town. He was quite certain he would never understand Berenil. Under almost any other circumstances, he would probably have spent time puzzling over how a single family could produce three such different personalities as Berenil, Gesrin, and Lissel. As it was, however, all thoughts of the young women evaporated once he remembered Animara's request.

His mood instantly turned as dark and dismal as the weather.

"*Keshaal!*" he muttered under his breath. "*Why couldn't Jila have left the money?*" He had so hoped he wouldn't have to do anything more about the baby for at least a year, and he could feel his anger starting to rise. He reminded himself that Jila was at least *gone*.

After that, he tried to focus on keeping his feet moving in the right direction.

Chapter 25

Animara

Trudging through the drizzle, he followed Front Street as it bent southward around the curve of the harbor. When one of the two kuma mills reared out of the mist, he turned right onto a road with a sign that appropriately proclaimed it to be Kuma Mill Road. Pressing on through the dreary damp, he soon left the bay behind and came to where the road ended in a gravel-paved turn-around beside a stand of weathered cedar trees. The gravel was slick with rain, and the trees loomed as dark gray silhouettes in the misty air. Beside the trees, a single path struck off towards the looming ridge, and he turned into it.

Two baskets, he thought. It wasn't much to take with her to begin a new life in a strange city. A thousand rins would obviously help her to make her way... but what kind of mother would steal from her own child?

The track climbed sharply as it worked its way up a steep, rocky hillside set with scattered wind-twisted pines. By this time, everything was dripping water. Nagaro angrily kicked a stone that lay in the path and heard it bounce and rattle its way down towards the town below him. Then he mentally kicked himself. *That stone could have hurt someone.* It had been a rather *small* stone, but he had no idea what was down there at the bottom of the misty slope.

As he continued up the trail, he heaved a sigh and tried to pick apart the knot of his anger. Was it just that things had finally been going well? What with training the men, the successful voyage, and their return with gold, another ship, and nearly twenty newly-freed slaves... Most of those men had already decided to follow him. His future course seemed clear, at last, unclouded by any doubt as to the worthiness or feasibility of the task. He'd thought the matter of Jila was behind him. Everyone made mistakes, sometimes. He'd thought there had been no real harm done, had felt justified in setting the mistake aside... *and then Jila had presented him with the baby.*

He could find no way to feel good about the child he had named Narei. She was Jila's get, the result of Jila's ill-conceived plan. He was thoroughly ashamed of the part he had played in that plan, and he was angry—angry at Jila for spinning her web, and at himself for falling into it. And because of that fall, he now had to bear responsibility for a child he didn't want. He could feel the weight of that responsibility almost physically on his shoulders. Every time he thought about any of it, he felt the twin burdens of anger and responsibility. The only relief he'd felt since learning of Narei's existence had been when he'd managed to put her out of his mind. Which had been working pretty well that morning... *until he'd gotten the summons from Animara.*

Focused inward as he was, Nagaro wasn't watching where he put his feet and one of them suddenly slipped on a wet stone. He sucked in his breath as he caught his balance, then started on again, forward and upward, taking greater care. The trail varied here between slick stones and mud that was scarcely any less slick. He brushed a drop of rainwater from the tip of his nose with the back of his hand. He had considered trying to talk to Vothra about the whole thing, but had discarded the idea because he knew what Vothra would say. Vothra was the very soul of forgiveness. Among Vothra's memories of hundreds of lives, there must be things as bad as, or worse than, what he'd done. He already *knew* that, and it didn't make him feel the least bit better.

Such was the state of his thoughts when he reached the top of the rise and found himself on the narrow crest of a ridge of rock that ran to right and left. The drizzle was slackening, but the air still smelled of rain. A wind off of the sea whistled around his ears. It was a damp, cold wind that bit through his cloak with icy teeth.

For a moment he stood in that exposed place, catching his breath after the exertion of the climb. Despite the wind and the wet, he shook off his hood, the better to look about him. To his left, the ridge ran on to thrust itself like a blade out into the ocean, forming the southernmost tip of the island. The sea stretched coldly gray and flecked with foam, merging in the misty distance with a cloud-shrouded sky. Directly before him, the ground dropped steeply away, being one side of a wide ravine that cut southwestward to meet the sea, where it formed a sheltered cove. Both sides of the ravine had been shaped by human labor into narrow terraces, planted with kuma bushes. He realized that this must be the kuma farm belonging to Animara and her husband. Part of the floor of the ravine, the narrow end to his right, was also planted with kuma bushes. The part directly below him, however, was occupied by a dense stand of trees, a mixture of cedars, pines, and junipers.

Beyond the trees, close to the pebble beach and tucked up against the farther side of the ravine, was a house. It was squat and solid, built of gray fieldstones and topped with a shingle roof. Bigger than many fishermen's huts that Nagaro had seen, it looked as if it had started small and been enlarged with additions at both sides. Even so, it was by no means imposing. Next to it, Nagaro made out what appeared to be a vegetable garden.

The path he was standing on took a sharp bend to the right as it crossed over the ridge-top and ran up the ravine— high along the nearer side— to a point near the ravine's head. There, Nagaro knew the path crossed a stream on a little stone bridge. He could just make out the pale flash of cascading water. The path angled up after that, over the ridge on the farther side of the ravine to disappear from view. Nagaro's eyes followed that path longingly, knowing that it led eventually to Jade Cove and places beyond.

Looking that way, his eyes caught a sudden flicker of white, and a smudge of pale yellow.

It couldn't be... He looked harder.

It was the unmistakable black-and-white spotted pony, standing just below where the path crested the farther ridge. And beside it, a figure that could only be Tira Zomora in her yellow skirt.

"Bishka..."

She was just standing. Not going anywhere. And he was almost certain that her face was turned in his direction. What on earth could she be doing there? Unbidden, the thought came creeping that she was watching him. *That she'd been waiting for him to come this way... to make sure he went where he was supposed to go... that he didn't take the other path, the one that led to Jade Cove.*

But no, he told himself. She was surely only resting, catching her breath from having climbed that other ridge. On that path she would have had to dismount and walk the pony. It wasn't safe to ride. And she surely couldn't tell who he was at such a distance. He shook off the crawling sense of dread, tore his eyes from the distant figure, and sought the path that would take him down to the house below. There was a fork very near to where he stood, and the side branch ran steeply down through the kuma bushes, cutting across the terraces in a series of switchbacks until it plunged into the grove of trees at the bottom of the ravine.

Nagaro hurriedly started down the descending path. He had never traveled it before because it clearly could lead nowhere but to that waiting house. After a few paces, he slowed his steps and proceeded more cautiously. The way was steep, and a bit precarious. Besides this, once out of sight of the woman on the farther ridge, he found himself feeling in less and less of a hurry the closer he came to his destination. As he was rounding the bend at the bottom of the ravine, about to step under the trees, a new thought came to him, and his feet slowed even more.

He suddenly realized that, as angry as he was at Jila, Animara and her husband might be just as angry at *him*.

Yuli had told him they had three children of their own already. Well, now they had a fourth to care for, one they hadn't asked for. They might be angry at him for having refused to marry Jila. While Nagaro might consider Jila primarily responsible for the child's existence, he couldn't deny having lain with the woman. There was no telling what Jila had told her sister. And being Jila's sister, Animara might be more kindly disposed towards Jila than towards him. There was also no telling how she felt about her sister having left the island.

He was moving along the path under the trees, with dragging steps, dreading what sort of welcome might await him at the house, when the dismal train of his thoughts was interrupted by the sound of voices coming from among the trees ahead of him. They were children's voices, and they were interspersed with what sounded for all the world like sticks striking against one another. Nagaro frowned as he moved closer, turning off of the path to follow the sounds. Then he smiled as the words came clearly to his ears in the quiet under the trees where the wind didn't penetrate.

"I hit ye that time!"

"No ye didn't!"

"Did too!"

"Did not!"

He pushed his way past the boughs of a cedar tree and stepped into a space where the ground was clear of undergrowth. Here a number of trees made an overarching canopy that opened to the sky on its opposite side. The farther wall of the ravine and the fieldstone house were visible through the opening, beyond the vegetable garden. Nagaro's attention wasn't on the house, however, but on the occupants of the little natural pavilion. They were two Turowan boys who looked to be about six and eight years old, and so much alike in everything but stature that it was easy to conclude they must be brothers. They stood a few feet apart, sticks in their hands, radiating indignation at each other.

Nagaro's smile grew broader. "Whoa, now," he said. "You can't have a proper practice bout if you won't admit when you've been hit, or accept the other man's word when he says you missed. That's what it means to be 'on your honor'."

The two boys both started and turned towards him when he spoke. They stood gaping. The older one found his voice first. "*Hakura!*" he exclaimed. "Are ye Captain Nagaro?"

Nagaro laughed. "I am," he said, crossing his arms. "And *you* are..?"

"I'm Tavo!" the boy responded, proudly.

"And I'm Pilo!" cried the younger one, thrusting out his chest.

"Well met." Nagaro wiped the smile from his face and assumed an air of gravity. "Tavo... and Pilo..." He bowed to each in turn. "Now then, *on your honor*, what have you each to say? You speak first, Pilo."

Pilo knit his brows in a very serious frown. "I think I hit him," he said.

"All right." Nagaro turned sternly to Tavo. "Did you feel a hit? Maybe just a light one?"

"We-ell... maybe he grazed me, just a *little*," the older boy conceded. "But it wasn't enough t' make me bleed! It wouldn't ha' counted if it didn't make me bleed, would it?" he added a little petulantly.

Nagaro sighed. "In a real fight," he said, "only blood counts, of course. And a serious wound counts for a lot more than a little scratch. The point is, though, that there's no arguing over the truth in a real fight. If a man is hurt, it's plain for all to see. But in a practice bout," he continued seriously, "any hit counts, and you're on your honor to report it. The only way either one of you can learn what you did right is if the other one tells you truthfully when he feels a hit."

"Oh." Tavo frowned thoughtfully. "I never knew all that before."

Nagaro smiled at both boys. "Why don't you show me some of your moves? On your honor, of course."

The boys grinned back at him and turned to face each other again. They advanced, sticks raised and ready.

"Tavo! Pilo! What are ye doing?"

It was the high, sweet voice of a girl, and it made Nagaro jump almost as much as it did the two boys. He looked up to find that the speaker was a slender Turowan girl, about eleven years old, who had suddenly appeared at the opening in the trees. She had her chin out and her fists on her hips. "Ye *know* ye're supposed to be gathering firewood! And Mama said no more fighting today, remember?"

"*But 'Hiri!*" Tavo protested. "This is *Captain Nagaro!* An' he *asked* us t' show him our moves!" He still clutched his stick as he pointed defiantly at Nagaro with his free hand.

The girl followed her brother's gesture to where Nagaro stood in the deeper gloom, farther under the trees. Apparently she hadn't noticed him at first, for she immediately dropped her challenging stance, and her hand flew to her mouth. "*Hamanei mata noa!*" she murmured. Then she raised her voice to say, "Your pardon, Zirda! Are ye really Captain Nagaro?"

Nagaro shrugged. "Yes," he said. "And I suppose you must be Bahiri."

She nodded shyly.

Nagaro turned back to the girl's brothers. "You'd best finish your wood-gathering right now," he told them. "That's an important task. It's going to be cold tonight. You can show me your moves later."

"Aye, Zirda!" Tavo saluted him and Pilo nodded eagerly. Both boys then scurried off under the trees.

Bahiri looked after them and sighed. “I suppose I’ll have t’ help them,” she said. “Or they’ll forget, and be at it with the sticks again.” She looked at Nagaro, a little more boldly this time. “Ye’d best go on, Zirda. Mother’s expecting ye.”

It was Nagaro’s turn to sigh. He’d completely forgotten his errand while talking to the boys. Reminded of it now, he hesitated, and a frown darkened his brow.

Bahiri eyed him. “Ye’re not going t’ shout and curse, are ye?” she asked warily.

Nagaro gave her a startled glance. “Of course not!” he said. “Why do you ask that?”

“Because the other one did,” she answered earnestly.

“What... *other one?*” He had a sinking feeling.

“Aunt Jila’s other captain,” she replied matter-of-factly. “The one that came in the summer. He came in the middle o’ the night and started shouting at Aunt Jila. And it woke me up— ‘cause Aunt Jila was staying in my room. Mama told me t’ go and sleep in *her* bed, and I tried to, but I couldn’t sleep because he was so loud. Papa was angry too, but he left, and the man was still shouting. I was scared ‘cause I didn’t know what the captain was going t’ do.”

“Oh. I... see.” Nagaro was frankly shocked to hear this recital. He had surmised that there had probably been a confrontation, but it disturbed him to know that it had happened in the house he was about to enter. “I’m sorry you had to hear all that,” he added after a moment. “And don’t worry. I don’t intend to do anything of the kind.”

“Oh. That’s good.” She was suddenly shy again.

“Is your father at home?” he asked.

She shook her head. “He’s gone t’ help Uncle Ato put up a new shed.”

“Ah, I see.”

It would be just Animara then. The knowledge relieved his mind only fractionally.

Bahiri glanced after her brothers, whose voices and crunching footsteps could be heard some distance off among the trees. “I’d better be after them,” she said. “Afore they get up t’ mischief. Good day ‘t ye, Zirda.” She hurried off, following the sound of her brothers’ voices.

“Look where the trees grow thickest,” Nagaro called after her. “The wood will be drier there.” *But of course she would know that.* He heaved another sigh. Once again there weres no more excuses. Turning, he made his way out from under the trees and approached the house, following a narrow path between disheveled rows of carrots, beans, and potatoes.

The front door of the house was ajar, and it swung open when he knocked on it, revealing a dimly lit interior. He made out a long table with an assortment of chairs and stools. Beyond that, at the other end of the room, there was a woman bending over the fire in the fireplace.

He cleared his throat. "Tira Animara?"

The woman straightened and turned, and Nagaro saw that she was even taller than Jila. Clad in a plain dark skirt and simple white blouse, her figure was a bit fuller than her sister's, but still very well-proportioned. Her hair hung in a single long braid down her back after the custom of married Turowan women. She gave him a brief glance up and down before returning her attention to a large kettle hung over the fire.

"Aye," she said briskly. "And ye must be Nagaro." Her voice was low, and it reminded him of Jila's, except that it contained no hint of sultry insinuation. "Come in and sit ye down," she added. "There's a peg by the door for your cloak. And do be closing the door after ye. Bahiri's gone and left it half open again, and the wind's perishing cold."

Nagaro wasn't sure exactly what he had expected, but the woman's manner surprised him. *Just 'Nagaro'. Not 'Captain Nagaro', or even 'Tor Nagaro'.* Normally he preferred familiarity, but in this case, formality would have provided a reassuring sense of distance. Aware that the open door was indeed letting in a chilling draft, he stepped inside and closed it behind him. This shut out part of the light, since the room was otherwise illuminated only by two windows covered with oiled skin, and an oil lamp on the table. The lamp was already lit even though it was still daylight outside.

Nagaro hesitated, standing just inside the door. "Tira Animara," he tried again, "I've come about the baby's money."

This time the woman turned right around to face him with her back to the fire and a spoon in her hand. "'Course ye have," she said. "And I'd like ye to call me Ani— everyone that knows me calls me that. Now hang up your cloak, and sit ye down. The bread 'll be done in a minute, and I'll have ye some stew in about an hour."

Fresh bread and savory fish stew... Now that the door was closed and the wind no longer gusting in, he could smell both of the enticing aromas. But this was still too much, too soon.

"I... no... I couldn't possibly..." he stammered.

"Now see here, *Tor* Nagaro." She brandished the spoon. "Ye're the father of my sister's child, and that makes ye part o' the family. I know neither one of us planned it this way, but that's how it is— and it means there'll always be room for ye under my roof, and a place for ye at my table. Now will ye make yourself at home or not? Because I can't make myself any plainer!"

Nagaro stood still for a second with his mouth open. The bread and the stew smelled wonderful. He'd eaten almost nothing for lunch, and the long walk in the cold air had given him an appetite. Besides, he was finding that he rather liked this woman's no-nonsense approach to hospitality. He had also liked Tavo, Pilo, and Bahiri.

Nagaro made a decision. He closed his mouth, hung up his cloak, and crossed to the table in two strides. Once there, he pulled out a chair and sat down.

Animara smiled then, a warm, wide, welcoming smile. "And would ye like a cup o' hot sothiril with your bread?" she asked.

He smiled back, hesitantly. "Yes, please... Ani," he managed.

And while she moved about fetching the teapot, pouring hot water into it from a kettle hung over the fire, and adding a handful of dried sothiril berries, he studied his surroundings. The room was kitchen, dining room, and living room all in one, and somewhat larger than the equivalent room in Taru's house in Wotana. Its two windows were placed one in the front wall, next to the door, and the other in the rear wall, opposite. Doorways in the other two walls presumably led to the added rooms he had seen from the outside.

One of these walls had the fireplace built into it, as well as a large oven where the bread was presumably baking. The other wall, behind him, had a narrow sleeping loft running across its entire width that was reached by a ladder at one end. Besides the large dining table, with its miscellaneous collection of seats, the room's furnishings consisted of a rustic window seat under the front window, a large chest of drawers, and a second small table under the rear window. A diverse array of laden shelves occupied available spaces on various walls.

Animara had fetched two large earthenware cups which she set on the table beside the teapot. "Would ye like t' see the baby?" she asked. "She's with Lata in the room behind ye. They're both asleep, but I think ye might take a peek."

"*No.*" Nagaro shook his head. It was almost a shudder.

A flicker in Animara's eyes showed she had noticed, but all she said was, "I guess I'd best fetch that bread out o' the oven afore it burns."

While she went about that task, using a large wooden paddle, Nagaro uncomfortably studied his clasped hands. The bread was soon set to cool on the small table under the window, and Animara came back to the larger table where he sat, bringing a long-handled spoon. She stirred the sothiril in the teapot with it, and poured out two cup-fulls. Then she went to one of the shelves and brought back two plates.

Nagaro raised his eyes. "Ani," he said in a low voice, "Do you really believe the baby is mine?"

Animara studied his face for a second. "Ah," she said quietly. "So that's it." She pulled out one of the stools and sat down. "It must be hard, bein' a man and never really knowin' for sure."

Nagaro frowned. "I'd know as much as I needed to," he said, "if only I could trust the mother. I asked Jila straight out who the father was, and she swore it was me 'by all the Spirits', but... I... I'm afraid I don't trust her." He stopped. "I'm sorry," he added weakly, painfully aware that he was speaking to Jila's sister. For Animara looked like Jila's sister, now that he could see her face clearly by the light of the oil lamp. She was not so exquisitely beautiful as Jila, but she had a subdued beauty of her own. She was older, with a broader face, and a squarer jaw, and little lines at the corners of her eyes from smiling. The eyes themselves were the same as Jila's— large, dark, and luminous. Only their expression as she studied him now was serious, not sultry.

Animara looked down at her hands, cupped around her mug. "I can't blame ye for that," she said, and she sighed. "Not the way Jila is. Hakura knows she's lied t' *me* often enough, though I don't think she'd *swear* on a lie by the Spirits like that." She paused, seeming to consider the steaming sothiril in her cup. "But ye asked me if *I* believe ye're the father," she continued. "And I do. And I'll tell ye why." She looked up then, directly into his eyes. "I was there at the birthing" she said quietly. "It was a hard birthing. And when the worst of it came, it was *your* name she cursed and no other."

Nagaro drew back as if struck. "She *cursed* me?"

Animara made a dismissive motion in the air with her hand, and gave him a small sympathetic smile. "I do beg your pardon, Nagaro," she said. "I don't suppose ye'd know it's a common thing— even with women who love their men dearly— to curse them at the birthing when the pain comes on 'em hard. Times like that, my mother used t' say, the Spirits know better 'n to listen."

Nagaro's mouth had gone dry. He hastily picked up his cup, took a swallow, and winced when he scalded himself. "No," he managed to say. "I didn't know." His awareness of childbirth was solely as a bastion of female secrecy from which men were rigidly excluded. Like the town's healer, Tor Pedril, the men he'd known had been more than glad to keep it that way.

Animara nodded knowingly and favored him with a sympathetic smile. "I think I'd best tell ye the whole tale," she said. "Some of it's not very pretty, but it seems ye've a right t' know." She put down her cup and pushed back her stool. "But first," she added, "I want to stir the stew and cut us both some o' that bread."

By the time she'd cut the loaf, Nagaro had regained his composure. He was relieved that Animara wasn't angry with him, and reassured that she seemed to have few illusions about her sister's devotion to the truth. And although the subject was repellant, he couldn't help being curious about the story he was about to hear. The bread smelled wonderful, and he watched in anticipation as Animara laid generous slices of the warm, fresh loaf on the plates, then took down a pot of honey from a shelf and spread some on each slice. Presently, she settled on her stool again. She let him eat several bites of honeyed bread before clearing her throat and beginning her tale.

"It's like this," she said at last. "On the day that she met ye, Jila came here on her way to town. She did that sometimes— 'cause it was on her way from Jade Cove, I suppose. *That* day, I remember she was all dressed up fine, and she said she had a plan. It was going t' get her off the island at last, she said. But she wouldn't say what it was. She only stayed a little while that afternoon, to rest and drink a little water, and then she was off. I don't know just when she came back the next morning. It must ha' barely been light, 'cause she was here when I got out o' bed. She was sittin' at this table, lookin' like the cat that caught the bird, and I had a feeling that meant trouble for somebody."

Nagaro looked down at his plate, his face hot.

"She said her plan was going perfectly," Animara went on.

Nagaro winced at that last word.

"But still she wouldn't say what it was." Animara shifted on her stool. "So I gave her breakfast, and she went her way." She sighed. "When the men came lookin' for her later— sayin' she'd robbed ye— she wasn't here, and I told 'em the truth when I said I didn't know where she'd gone. By the time she came back t' me, weeks later, they'd given up lookin' for her."

Nagaro ran a finger along the rim of his cup without looking up. "That wasn't any of my doing," he said in a low voice. "I didn't ask them to look for her."

"Didn't ye?" Animara asked. "Well, it doesn't matter now, I suppose, but I want ye t' know that I would ha' told 'em where she was when they came, if I'd known. I don't hold with thieving, and if she'd had your money, I'd ha' seen she gave it back." She paused, and when she continued, it seemed she was less comfortable with what she had to say next. "That's what I would ha' done *then*, before I knew she'd got herself with child. Afterwards— when she came *back*— it was different."

He looked up, questioningly, uncertain how to read her change of tone. Animara met his eyes without flinching. "Jila had some secret place all made ready where she meant t' stay 'til the baby came," She told him. "She had it all planned, like she said, but what she didn't plan on was bein' so sick with the baby—"

Nagaro frowned. "Sick?" he said, bewildered. "Sick— *with the baby?*"

Animara put her palm to her brow. "Oh, but o' course ye wouldn't know about that either, now, would ye?" She waved her hand as if to brush away the old words so she could start afresh. "It's a common thing for a woman t' be a bit sick with carryin' a child— at the beginning," she explained. "Most o' the time it passes pretty early. But some women are sicker than others, and there's some are sick for longer— even all the way 'til their time comes. That's how it was with Jila."

Animara paused again, but still she held him with her eyes. Nagaro said nothing. This was all quite new to him and he hardly knew what to think, much less what to say.

"So," she continued. "Jila stayed in her secret place 'til she began t' be sick and it didn't pass. When it didn't pass for five or six weeks, she got scared, I think, and that's when she came creepin' back here t' *me*. Well, not actually *creeping*. Tira Zomora brought her. Ridin' on that little horse o' hers—"

"Tira Zomora?" Nagaro stiffened. "How did *she* know—" The image of that figure standing at the crest of the ridge leaped to his mind.

Animara gave him a sharp look. "Ye've met her, then?"

Weakly, he nodded.

She sighed. "There's not much happens on Pakoa Island that Zomora doesn't get wind of," she told him. "Especially if it has t' do with birthing babies. My guess is Jila made an arrangement with one o' the midwives t' tend her when her time came, and the woman went to Zomora when Jila's sickness didn't pass."

Nagaro winced and swallowed. "What did... Tira Zomora... have to say?"

Animara shrugged. "That I should send for her if I wanted help with the birthing." Her mouth tightened. "I didn't. I've done birthings before, and I didn't figure we needed Zomora's eyes and ears. 'Course she found out, somehow, when the baby came. She came 'round the very next day, t' see how Jila and the child were gettin' on."

Nagaro's stomach had gone cold. He dropped his eyes. His honeyed bread still lay on his plate. He poked at it. "When did that happen?" he asked. "The birth. What was the date?"

"The seventh day o' Duleyin."

Bishka!

Tira Zomora had already known about Jila's baby when she'd found him and his crewmen filling the water skins! *And she'd asked for him to speak with her*. Had she meant to confront him with his probable paternity, and changed her mind for some reason? Or had she really come about the pirating, as she'd said, and meant to keep him in the dark about the baby? In the end, she had given him information that had sent him away on a dangerous voyage from which he had returned with gold and silver. Had the medicine woman gambled his life and those of the other men to secure a baby's future? He looked back up to meet Animara's eyes. "Did she say anything about... *me?*"

She was watching his face closely. "Not by name," she said carefully. "But we both knew who she meant. She said I should 'send to the father' if I needed anything. That's how she put it. 'I don't think he'll give ye any trouble', she said, 'But if he does, I'll speak to him'."

Nagaro's mouth was dry again, his sothiril forgotten. Obviously it was no coincidence at all that Tira Zomora had been watching the path to Animara's house on *this* day of all days. And Zomora had judged him accurately too. He had come just on the strength of Animara's asking, but if he *had* started down that other path, it would have taken no more than a word from the medicine woman to bring him to heel— no more than a *look* from those cold, dark eyes... He was intensely glad that neither word nor look had been necessary.

"Of course I'd ha' sent for ye anyway, soon or late," Ani was saying. "No matter what Zomora said. It's just easier, now that Jila's gone." She gave him a probing look. "I didn't send any word t' ye while Jila was here because she had enough trouble— bein' with child, and bein' sick, and bein' so weak afterwards. She *is* my sister. Ye understand?"

Nagaro nodded. "Yes," he said. "She's part of your family." *There will always be room under my roof...*

Animara smiled wanly. "Thank ye for that," she said. "I was afraid ye'd take it amiss. Hakura knows, Sudano— that's my husband— didn't like havin' her here one bit. But we couldn't very well turn her out, could we?"

She still seemed to be seeking his approval, so he shook his head. "Of course not."

She sighed, then, with apparent relief, and returned to her story. "I never saw any woman as sick with a baby as Jila was with carryin' Narei," she told him. "She wanted t' have an end to it— wanted that baby out of her—"

Nagaro jerked in his chair. "You can *do* that?"

Animara looked startled. "Oh, aye," she said. "Though I shouldn't be tellin' a man these things. It's one o' the secrets women keep, so we're not just at a man's mercy. But it has t' be done afore the bud grows too big and the spirit grows in it. By the time Jila asked for it, she'd waited too long. It likely would ha' killed her. 'Course she kept sayin' she was like t' die anyway... that it would be better..."

Nagaro's shock turned to horror. *Jila had wanted to die from carrying his child. He knew about wanting to die...*

Animara saw his expression. "Now don't ye pay that any mind," she said quickly. "Women say those kinds o' things sometimes. It's something else the spirits know better 'n to listen to." She gave him a crooked smile, but the smile died when the look on his face didn't change. "Ai, now!" she exclaimed. "I don't want ye t' be afraid to lie with the woman ye love, when ye find her. It's not that bad most o' the time. And women 'll gladly face the risk for the sake o' love. Jila took it worse 'n she needed to 'cause she had no love for what she was doing."

Nagaro swallowed hard. Ani's words helped. "What story did she tell you about... how she got the baby?" He needed to know, now more than ever, what part he had played in all of this.

Animara studied him over her cup of sothiril. "Oh, she told me all manner o' tales. First she said it was her captain's child she was carryin' and that she'd never been in the Red Cask. That those things your friend Taru was sayin' about her were lies. When she saw I didn't believe *that*, she said ye fell asleep and she never lay with ye, but o' course that tale wouldn't wash, either. So then she said she only lay with ye so there'd be another man in case her captain didn't want the baby. Well, that *might* ha' been true. But there were other things she let slip— woman things— that told a different story. And in the end she came 'round to saying it was *your* child, but she meant her captain t' think it was *his*. She said it would ha' been easy, too, if it hadn't been for Taru spoilin' everything. I thought that tale was likely the truth, even afore hearin' what came out of her mouth on the birthing bed. And she stood by it after the baby came too. 'Course, by that time, she knew her captain wanted none of it."

Animara paused for a sip of sothiril. "I told ye Jila's birthing was hard," she went on after a moment. "She couldn't get out o' bed for weeks. To be fair, she did try t' nurse the baby, but she was very weak, an' her heart wasn't in it. So o' course her milk dried up. Luckily I found Lata." She heaved a sigh, and took another sip of her sothiril. "And then, a week ago, Jila told Lata she was takin' the baby t' town to meet her father. And ye know how *that* went," she finished.

Nagaro shifted in his chair, not meeting her eyes. "Bahiri said the other captain came *here*."

Animara coughed and put a hand briefly to her mouth. "Bahiri heard more that night than any child should." She paused to study her sothiril.

Reminded of his own cup, Nagaro drank some to fill the silence, then ventured, "She said he was very angry."

Animara winced, and her eyes came back to his face. "This is the part that really isn't pretty," she said. "But I said ye'd a right t' hear it." She took a long sip of sothiril, then set down her cup. "It was just before the start o' Duleyin, and Jila was getting very near her time. Her captain must ha' come an' anchored his ship at Jade Cove, where he kept that house for her. And o' course, he found her gone. Someone must ha' told him about her bein' with another man too, and where t' find her, 'cause he walked straight here, all the way from that place, even with the night comin' on. He got here after sunset, and he was already angry when he knocked on the door. But when he set eyes on Jila— all big with child... Well, *that* made him madder'n a hornet in a bottle. He cursed her for bein' false— for lyin' with another man— and for tryin' to trick him with another man's child. He called her a liar and a witch and a whore, and I don't know what else. And then he cursed himself for ever having been so weak as t' take up with her."

Animara drew in a long breath and let it out. "It was bad," she said, shaking her head. "Jila was on her knees on the floor... weepin' and cryin' and begging him t' forgive her. She said it was all lies they'd told him. She told him the baby was his. She swore she loved him— and for a minute, it looked like he was goin' t' hit her. That's when she cried for my husband to throw the man out. But Sudano told her she'd made this pot o' stew, and she was going t' have to eat it if it choked her— and it was *him* that went out the door. 'Course he just stood outside listening the whole time. He'd ha' never left me all alone t' deal with that man."

Nagaro felt almost physically sick. "The captain didn't... hurt Jila... did he?"

Animara shook her head. "No," she said. "Except as words can hurt. He went all cold after Sudano left. He said he could see Jila had never loved him, and that she was a fool to think he'd ever leave his wife for her and her bastard get. He said he was done with her once and for all. And then he walked out. I suppose he must ha' found his way back t' Jade Cove by moonlight. I don't think he was the kind o' man that could ever have forgiven himself for hittin' a woman. But he was very, *very* angry. At her. And at himself."

Nagaro stared at the table. His half-eaten slice of bread still lay on his plate beside his cup of sothiril. "I can understand that," he said. These things had happened in this house because of what *he* had done. *And where had he been while it was all happening? Sailing around the islands... looking for Mahuk warships...*

"I'm sorry..." he murmured.

"*Ye're* sorry?" Animara's voice registered astonishment. "For *what*? Sudano was right. It *was* Jila's pot o' stew. Ye were just one o' her fish, and that merchant captain was another— and there were enough others afore either one o' ye t' fill a barrel!"

Nagaro shut his eyes. His hands, resting on the table, curled into fists. Animara's words were well meant, he knew, but they didn't help. "I didn't have to drink too much wine," he said in a low voice. "And I didn't have to lie with her. If I hadn't done those things, none of this would have happened. There wouldn't have been a baby... and there wouldn't have been such a row..."

"And Jila would still be on this island, hatchin' plans t' get off of it."

Animara's hand came down one of his clenched fists and gave it a quick squeeze. His head came up with a jerk at her unexpected gesture.

"Do ye think Jila hasn't had rows afore this, Nagaro?" she asked, searching his face. "It must ha' happened plenty with her other captains. And this man would ha' wearied of her soon or late, like all the rest. Do ye know," she added, "that ye're the first man that's ever thought t' ask her what *she* wanted? Much less give it to her."

Nagaro let out his breath. He felt a little less ill. He and Jila had *both* made mistakes that had contributed to this mess. He unclenched his hands, then looked up to meet her gaze. "But there didn't have to be a baby," he said. "That needn't have happened, if I hadn't... been there..."

Animara sighed. "If Jila hadn't found ye, she'd ha' found some other man, that night or some other. I know ye're not pleased about bein' the father, but for Narei's sake *I'm* glad it was you."

Nagaro looked away towards the back window, without seeing it. *How else could he expect her to feel? He'd given the baby five hundred rins and a name.*

The silence stretched, and from the room behind him came a baby's fretful cry. A woman's voice spoke then, murmuring sleepily. There were rustling and creaking sounds, and the baby was quiet again.

He drew a breath and met Ani's eyes. "Did Jila take the baby's money?"

She nodded. "It seems so. At least the gold's disappeared from that pot up there." She gestured at a shelf on the wall beside the window, where a small brown clay pot stood amongst the other dishes. "And there's only a piece o' paper with writing in its place."

Nagaro heaved a sigh. He reached for his purse and began to count out ten silver half trokin coins. "I've no more gold right now," he said. "But silver is better anyway, I expect. It's easier to spend since it's not all in one piece."

Animara put out her hand to stop him. "It needn't be so much," she said hurriedly. "A hundred rins'll more than pay Lata for her work."

Nagaro frowned at her. "Jila said two hundred."

"And ye believed her?" Animara shook her head at him. Then she sighed. "No, ye didn't more 'n half believe her, did ye?" she said. "And yet ye more'n doubled it. Ye're a generous man."

Nagaro shook his head, and went back to his counting. "It's easy to be generous when you have money," he said. "By this time next year, I may be poor again. Or perhaps some Mautep warrior will have slain me. I meant for the baby to have five hundred rins, and here they are." He pushed the coins across the table to lie beside Animara's plate and cup. "I can at least make sure that she doesn't want for anything— for a time. If you need more when this is gone, you've only to ask and I'll give you what I can."

Animara studied him for a long moment. "I see that ye mean it," she said at last. "And there's sense in what ye say, besides, about the future being uncertain. So I *will* take these." Carefully she picked up the silver coins. "But I want ye t' know that this much money'll go a long way." She rose and went to the shelf, reaching for the little clay pot.

Nagaro remembered what she had said. "Is the paper a letter?"

"I think so. I haven't taken it t' town to have it read." Animara got the pot down and pulled out a tightly folded piece of paper, then dropped in the coins.

"May I see it?"

"I suppose so—" she began, with a puzzled frown. Then the light dawned. "But, o' course," she said. "Ye'd be able t' read it, wouldn't ye?"

She handed the folded paper to him as she sat down. He unfolded it and spread it out on the table. It was indeed a letter, addressed to "Ani" and signed "Jila" at the bottom. It was written in a fine, elegant hand. "It's to you, from Jila," he said. "The writing is quite beautiful. I wonder who wrote it."

Animara shrugged. "Jila did," she said. "I can't read the words, but I know her writin' well enough."

Nagaro was surprised. "How is it she can read and write— if you can't?"

Ani waved a hand. "One o' her captains taught her, years ago. Jila was always tryin' to make herself better 'n what she was born— wearin' fancy clothes, and trying t' talk like a merchant's wife." Animara sighed. "She's very proud o' knowin' her letters."

Nagaro looked at the perfectly formed letters with their precisely curving strokes. "Well, she should be proud of this," he said. He was thinking of Taru's crude, labored characters. "It must have taken a lot of practice to learn to write so beautifully. Would you like me to read it to you?"

"I suppose ye could," she said. "It'll save me walkin' into town. But first let me move the stew pot a little farther off the fire. I don't want our dinner t' burn."

When she'd settled herself again, Nagaro began, bending close over the paper to read by the light of the single lamp.

"Dear Ani," he read. "I do not think I will see you again, because I do not mean to come back to Pakoa. Captain Nagaro said he wants never to see me again, and I mean to see he doesn't."

Nagaro paused to glance guiltily at Animara. "I did say something like that," he confessed.

"It's all right," she said. "That wasn't all ye said, if I've heard the tale aright. Besides, she's always wanted t' go, ever since she was a child, and I don't think she ever meant t' come back if she could manage it."

Relieved, he returned his eyes to the page, picking up the text where he'd left off. "I had to take the money he gave me for the baby. I am sorry for that, but I will need it more where I am going. I would have left some, but I cannot cut gold into pieces. Besides, I know he will give you more if you say the baby needs it. He is a hard man, but it seems he is free with his money."

Nagaro stopped, frowning at the paper. What did she mean by "a hard man?" Had he seemed so?

"Ye don't have t' read it—" Animara began.

"No, it's all right," he said quickly. "I can't expect her to like me." He focused on the page again, but the words came from his lips more and more slowly, the further he read, because Jila had a good deal more to say about him.

"It is only right that I should take his money," he read, "since he has ruined me. I could not possibly stay in Pakoa after what he has done. I cannot think about lying with a man now without thinking of how it all went wrong with him, and being afraid. He is very unkind, Ani, and very unfair. I gave him the love of my body, but he thinks himself so far above me that it shamed him to do it. When we were together, he liked me well enough. I gave him a beautiful baby, but he does not want her. I took a boy and made a man of him, and the man has slapped me in the face."

Nagaro stopped reading abruptly. "I never did!" he exclaimed. "And I don't think I'm better than she is. It's *my* shame that I made myself drunk and lay with her for pleasure instead of love. I'd feel the same about it if she were a princess!"

"Ai, Nagaro!" Animara leaned across the table to put her hand on his once more. "I know all that! This is Jila's pride talking. Her trouble is all of her own making, but she won't admit it— so she blames anyone she can. Besides," she added, "She surely never meant for ye t' read that letter. It was meant for me."

Nagaro was starring blindly at the paper, dimly aware of Animara's words through the tumult of his thoughts. He hadn't expected gratitude from Jila, but her scathing condemnation left him stunned. The anger that leaped at him from the page felt raw and hot.

"Vothra," he murmured, "She's more angry with me than I am with her—" *But how could she see him as such a villain?* He turned the sentences he had just read this way and that in his mind, trying to find a kernel of truth that would give some sense to them. Did Jila truly believe she hadn't harmed him? That lying with him had been a gift? Did she think that taking his seed to mingle with her own, without telling him she meant to do it, was a fair exchange for a night of pleasure? It seemed to him just possibly that she did. She had said, "*I give them a night to remember.*" Well, he did remember. *He would always remember...*

He was aware that many folk thought a man wasn't a man until he'd lain with a woman— though he didn't think much of the idea, himself.

Having lain with Jila *had* shown him that he was capable of completing the act... something his experience with the princess had left unproven. And that *was* reassuring, as far as it went. But the other men had followed him at Jaamra without stopping to ask whether he'd ever been with a woman.

Nagaro shook himself. Animara's eyes were on him. He ignored her questioning look. "There's only a little more," he said, frowning down at the page, and he read the last brief paragraph:

"I know you will take care of Narei much better than I. Perhaps I will see her one day when she is grown. Goodbye now, Ani. May the Spirits keep you. Jila."

He pushed the paper aside. "I don't hate her," he said quietly. "I'm angry about what she did, but that's not the same thing."

"I'm sorry ye had t' read all that spiteful talk," Animara said into the silence that followed his words.

Nagaro toyed with his cup. "What will Jila do in Kel Tierna?" he asked.

"I don't know." There was a sigh and a shrug in the words. "She'll have a plan. She's always got one, at least."

The sound of children's voices came to them from somewhere outside, drawing nearer. Then the voices became mixed with muffled thumping sounds. Finally the thumping ceased, and the voices receded again.

Animara smiled faintly. "The children finally put some wood in the woodshed," she observed. "And I expect they've gone off t' get some more."

Nagaro studied her. Animara seemed so content with her life— the exact opposite of Jila. He frowned. "How can two sisters be so different?" he wondered aloud.

Animara sighed. "That's easy," she said. "I'm more like our Mama, while Jila takes after Papa." She frowned a little. "Perhaps I should tell ye a little bit about Mama and Papa. It might help ye understand."

Nagaro's frown deepened. He had not come here wanting to understand Jila. Still, Vothra said that understanding was good. "All right," he said. "Tell me."

Chapter 26

Ties Of Blood

Animara paused to collect her thoughts. Outside, the afternoon seemed to have grown a little brighter. The oiled skin of the windows glowed, warming the red-brown earthenware of the little honeypot that Ani had left on the table. The sweet scent of the honey finally reminded Nagaro of the honeyed bread on his plate. He picked it up and took a bite to cover the awkwardness of the silence.

Animara's eyes had grown misty with reminiscence. "Papa was a rover," she began. "Ye couldn't tie him down with a rope. That's what Mama used t' say. He was a merchant seaman from somewhere up in the northern isles. At least that's the tale he told most often. Papa liked tales, ye see, and he had a pack o' them, so ye couldn't always tell where the truth left off and the tale began. The ship he was servin' on sailed into Pakoa Harbor one autumn, I've been told, and that's when Papa met Mama. When the ship sailed away again, Papa stayed behind. He and Mama were married that spring, and I was born at the end o' the summer."

Nagaro made a startled movement. Animara caught his look and laughed, a low, musical sound. "Oh, aye," she said. "They lay together afore they were wed. It's the way o' nature, and Papa did what everyone said was the right thing by marrying Mama. It just wasn't the right thing for *him*." Her smile died. "I've never doubted that he loved Mama," she went on. "Ye wouldn't doubt it either, if ye'd ever seen them together. He even tried t' be a kuma farmer for a while, but he didn't take to it. So afore long, it was off he went with a merchant ship again." She shook her head.

"After that, he was gone much more 'n he was here. That's what I remember. Him bein' gone months and months at a time, then here for a few weeks or a few days, and then gone again. It was hard for Mama 'cause she loved him so. She used t' be so happy when he came. He'd hug her and kiss her, and he'd always bring money for her, and a present for me— or for both me and Jila, after she came." Animara sighed. "He wasn't here when Jila was born. I remember that well, though I was only six. And he came less and less as the years went by, so Jila saw much less o' him than I did."

Animara stopped speaking and moved to refill their cups with sothiril.

Nagaro sat still, waiting for her to go on, already caught up in her narrative. "How old were you when he died," he asked.

Animara gave him a quick sharp glance over the rim of her cup as she took a sip. "The last time I *saw* him," she said carefully, "I was twelve. I'd rather believe he's dead, o' course, than think that he just wearied of us, but I don't expect I'll ever know. There was folk that said he had other women... other wives, even... in other ports. No one ever dared t' say that in Mama's hearing, 'cause they knew it would ha' broke her heart. But *I* heard it, and I'm sure Jila heard it too— especially after Mama died."

Animara sighed again and took a long drink of sothiril. When she put her cup down, she turned her eyes to look full into his. "I don't think Jila ever forgave Papa for never coming back," she said. "It's a funny thing, ye know. Jila's so much like him. She always wanted t' go places, an' see things just the way he did. But still she was angry with him for bein' the way he was. 'Course she didn't see that much o' Papa. Mostly what she saw was Mama pining away 'til she sickened and died, waitin' for him." Ani heaved another sigh.

Nagaro took a gulp of his sothiril. "How old were you when that happened?"

Animara eyes seemed to be looking far away. "I was seventeen, and Jila was eleven," she said softly. "Mama lived not quite six years after the last time we saw Papa, and she never stopped hopin' he'd come back. I think she was still lookin' for him t' come through that door the day she died." Animara shook her head sadly. "Jila always thought Mama was a fool for loving Papa that way. She's told me so more 'n once. I think we both knew we wanted our lives t' be different from Mama's. It's just that we found different ways o' doing it. I married a kuma farmer's son— a good, steady man that comes home t' me every night. But Jila... well... Jila always had t' do things different... her *own* way... I guess she's decided she isn't ever going to love a man, and that way she'll never take hurt from one."

Ani shook her head again. "I couldn't keep Jila here after Mama died. Ye couldn't tie *her* down with ropes either. She'd run off whenever she chose, an' go into town— other places too. I've no idea all the places she went. About a year after I married Sudano and he came here t' live with me, Jila moved out. She was sixteen years old, an' she'd found a way to make a living o' sorts in town..." Animara saw Nagaro's frown. "Oh, I *knew* what she was doing," she continued. "Jila made no secret of it. She left because she was angry that I'd gone and brought another man into Mama's house. Said she wouldn't stay longer under the same roof with a man."

Animara took a sip from her cup. "It *was* Mama's house too," she added. "It'd belonged to Mama's father, and *his* father afore him, an' so on. It seemed t' me another man in the house was a good thing. But Jila didn't think so. And we've never seen eye to eye much since."

Nagaro sat frowning after Animara stopped speaking. "Once she saw that Sudano was a good man, and was good to you, why didn't she change her mind?" he asked. He didn't doubt that Sudano *was* a good man, knowing what he knew of Animara and her children

"I think she was determined not t' see it." Animara frowned sadly. "Jila was never anything but spiteful to Sudano. So o' course, Sudano never took much liking t' *her* either, and I can't blame him." She looked down at her plate, then back up at Nagaro. "Well," she said. "Now ye know all there is t' know about this family ye've come t' be a part of. Some of it's not a pretty tale. Still, maybe ye understand us a little better."

Nagaro glanced down. "I think I do," he said.

"What about *your* family," she asked. "Have ye any that ye know of?"

He looked up. "No," he said. "I was a foundling, and the lady who raised me is dead. Taru's like a brother to me— and Pavo Maat is coming to be so— because of what we've been through together." He thought a moment. "Taru's parents made me almost part of their family. But *they're* dead. He has a grandmother in Wotana, and an aunt somewhere, that I've never met. That's all."

"And your parents?" she asked cautiously. Ye've no idea who they were?"

He shook his head. "I prefer to think that they're dead— just as you do with your father— rather than think that they never cared to come looking for me." He paused, then added, "And of course it's likely I was gotten out of wedlock. But I doubt if I'll ever know."

Ani was regarding him with sympathetic eyes. "That must be hard," she said. "Having no one... nothing..."

Nagaro hesitated. Something about Ani's gentle openness invited confidence. "*Almost* nothing," he said on an impulse. "They did leave me this." He reached into the neck of his shirt and drew forth his ring on its leather cord.

Animara regarded the small object with interest. "May I see it?" she asked.

He hesitated only fractionally before lifting the string over his head and handing it to her. The ring could identify him to certain people in Lankura— the few who had seen it. But Ani had surely never been there, and was never likely to go. "It's something of a secret," he said awkwardly. "I usually don't show it to folk."

Animara gave him an understanding glance. "Then I won't speak of it to anyone," she said. "If that's how ye want it." She leaned forward to examine the ring by the light of the oil lamp. "It's a pretty thing," she said, "in a man-ish sort o' way. A picture of a setting sun—"

"Or rising," Nagaro pointed out. "It could be either one."

"Aye. I suppose it could," she mused. "And the flowers look like what we call *farusia*."

"Farusia?" He frowned. "Yes, I guess they could be. Farusia flowers open and close with the coming and going of the sun too, don't they? So that fits."

She nodded. "We have some of them growing here on Pakoa," she said. "Kelorin folk brought them, they say, and planted them 'round their houses years ago. Now they've run wild." She handed the ring back to him. "Was it your father's d'ye think?" she asked.

Nagaro sighed. "If it was my father's, his hands must have been much bigger than mine. It's always been too big for my finger. See?" He demonstrated. Even with the cord running through it, the ring slid on and off far too easily. "It might almost stay on my thumb," he added. "But it's much safer under my shirt, in any case." He slipped the cord back over his head and thrust the ring back into its hiding place.

There came at that moment sounds of movement from the room behind him. The rustling of cloth and creaking of a bed were followed by the soft scuffing sound of footsteps on the earthen floor. The door-skin was swung aside and a short, plump young woman emerged, smiling sleepily and carrying a baby cradled in her arms. "Little Flower wants t' play now," she remarked to no one in particular.

Animara cleared her throat. "Lata," she said, "This is Tor Nagaro. He's *Narei's* father." The emphasis on the baby's name was subtle, but unmistakable.

"Oh my!" The girl's eyes went wide. "Are ye *really* Captain Nagaro?"

He smiled wryly. "I'm afraid so."

"Ye're not at all what I expected. Ye're so *young!*"

Nagaro regarded her. "I'm sorry," he said solemnly, "I'm trying every day to grow older so folk will stop saying that, but I'm afraid the work goes very slowly."

Lata's eyes grew even wider, and her mouth dropped open. Then she burst out laughing. "Oh!" she said, turning to Animara. "I *like* him, Ani. He's funny!" She moved around the table to Animara's side. "Will ye take the baby for a little while? I need t' stretch."

Ani accepted Narei with an indulgent smile, folding the wriggling infant into her strong arms. "Get yourself a plate and cup, Lata, and cut yourself some bread," she suggested. Then, to Nagaro, she said, "How old *are* ye, anyway?"

"Twenty-one," he answered with a shrug.

"Hamanei!" she exclaimed. "I would ha' guessed twenty-four or twenty-five. Jila will be twenty-seven come the turning o' the year," she added after a moment. "Most folk'd say she's a bit old for ye— if ye'd taken to one another."

Nagaro felt his face grow warm, and he gave his full attention to his bread and sothiril. His hunger was reasserting itself, and it gave him something to do so he didn't have to look at the baby in Ani's arms.

When Lata returned to the table, he tried to make conversation with her. "You're younger than I expected too," he ventured.

She rolled her eyes. "I know," she said. "Most folk don't think I'm old enough t' be married, but I am. I lost my own little one," she added, turning suddenly sad. "But at least I'll have Little Flower for a few more months." There was a movement from Animara. Lata glanced over and caught her eye. "I beg your pardon, Zirda," she said, hastily, turning back to Nagaro. "I should ha' said 'Narei', but I've got so used t' calling her Little Flower, and Narei seems a strange name for a girl child—" She broke off, glancing again at Animara, who was making signs at her.

Nagaro felt the blood in his face once more. He looked at the table. The name had quite literally been the first thing that had come into his head.

Animara spoke up. "There's nothing wrong with 'Narei,'" she said firmly. "The sea is wild and strong and beautiful. And it gives livelihood t' so many on this island. Narei's a fine name, and she's likely t' be a strong child— and grow into a strong woman, too— with a name like that."

Nagaro didn't raise his eyes. Ani's description of the sea had sounded like a pretty fair description of Jila. Would Narei grow up to be like her mother? And if so, in how many ways?

The silence grew: No one seemed to know what to say.

Except Narei. She gurgled happily in Ani's arms.

Into the gaping silence, the sound of children's voices came again from outside— from the direction of the woodshed, followed by a thumping and clattering of wood being stacked. When this stopped, the voices became louder and nearer instead of receding. The front door of the house abruptly burst open, and the three children tumbled in, along with a gust of damp, salt-scented air. The children were laughing, their faces aglow from cold and exertion.

Bahiri was in the lead. "Is the sothiril still warm?" she demanded, when she saw the adults all seated at the table. "I want honey in mine!"

"I want *extra* honey on my bread!" put in Tavo.

"Me too!" cried Pilo.

A moment later the children were all sitting on stools around the table while Lata cut bread for them and doled out the precious honey. Nagaro found himself between Tavo and Pilo. Bahiri, seated at the end of the table, set her cup down to address her mother. "Mama," she said excitedly. "I have t' tell ye how good Tava and Pilo were. They worked so hard that they've filled up the woodshed! Because Captain Nagaro told them it was so important."

The two boys were beaming, basking in this rare praise from their sister. Animara looked at Nagaro and crooked an eyebrow.

"Well, it *is* important," he said defensively.

Little Pilo abruptly slid off of his stool and stood facing Nagaro, arms akimbo and chin thrust out. "Aye!" he said belligerently. "And ye promised ye'd watch our sword-fight when we were done! Have ye forgotten, Uncle Nagaro?"

Nagaro started, the word *uncle* reverberating in his brain. He hadn't even thought of the fact that being Narei's father would make him uncle to Ani's children.

"Pilo!" Animara addressed her son sternly. "That's not the way t' speak to a guest!"

The little boy turned on his mother. "But ye said he was one o' the family!" he blurted.

"Aye, Mama, ye did!" Tavo came to his brother's defense.

Nagaro had to smile at the look on their mother's face

Animara coughed. "Well, it's not the way to speak t' your *elders*," she amended.

Nagaro turned to Pilo. "I said you'd have to show me your moves *later*, Pilo," he pointed out. "I didn't say it would be right after you finished with the wood. Besides, I have to ask your mother if it's all right."

Pilo's pouting frown suggested he was no stranger to such adult betrayal. "It's *always* later," he grumbled.

Animara laughed. "Oh, go on," she said, feigning exasperation. "All three of ye! Go and have your bit o' sword-play. The stew can wait a bit longer."

So Nagaro went outside again with Tavo and Pilo. As he was closing the door, he heard Bahiri's voice raised in eager pleading: "Can I hold the baby now, Mama? Can I please? Just 'til dinner?"

Tavo and Pilo had left their stick-swords leaning against the wall just outside the door. They snatched them up and immediately set about energetically whacking and jabbing at each other while Nagaro offered such pointers as he thought they could actually use. The wind was still very cold, though the sky was clearing. A wide gap in the clouds to westward let the late afternoon sun shine through, leaving the house in shadow, but lighting up the ridge crest on the far side of the ravine. Before long, all three of them found their hands and noses chilled and felt their stomachs calling them to dinner, so they went back inside.

Nagaro had scarcely sat down again in his chair when he found Bahiri planted in front of him. The girl held Narei cradled in her arms, and her face was alight with a glowing smile. "It's your turn now, Uncle Nagaro," she said breathlessly. "Hold out your arms."

Nagaro stiffened.

On the other side of the table, Ani turned hastily, her glance taking in his expression. "I don't think he's used t' holding babies, Bahiri," she said quickly. "And perhaps this isn't the best time—"

Bahiri's face instantly registered disappointment and chagrin. "I... I'm... sorry—" she began in a small, uncertain voice.

Seeing the girl so crestfallen, Nagaro was suddenly ashamed of himself. Not wishing Bahiri to know how little he wanted anything to do with her infant cousin, he stiffly put out his arms. "It's all right," he managed to say. "I'll try."

Bahiri beamed at him. "Here then," she said, lowering the baby into his arms. "No, not like that! She can't hold herself up. Put your arm under her. And put your other hand *there!*" She showed him how to position his arms and hands to make a cradle for the child.

So Nagaro found himself holding Narei.

He was amazed at how light the baby was. Perhaps the fact that he'd thought of her as such a burden had led him to expect her to be heavier. He held her stiffly in the curve of his left arm, with his right hand reaching across in front to steady her. She wasn't bundled against the cold now as she'd been when first he'd seen her; but was wearing a little nightdress. Her tiny feet peeked out at the bottom of it, while her little hands were outstretched, trying to reach him. Her wide, dark eyes were fixed on his face with an expression of focused concentration.

The miniature perfection of the child astonished him, from her button of a nose, to her tiny fingers and toes.

Bahiri was watching with rapt attention. "She want's to touch your face," she offered, "But she'll grab anything. Try giving her your finger t' hold, an' ye'll see."

Curious, Nagaro shifted the position of his left hand until he was sure that it held the child securely. With his right hand thus freed, he brought the tip of his forefinger into range of Narei's small hands. For a second, the little arms waved ineffectually, but then the fingers of the baby's right hand caught and closed around his fingertip.

"Oh!" He exclaimed in surprise. "She holds so tight!"

Bahiri nodded, grinning.

Animara was laying the food on the table, which was already set with earthenware dishes. Nagaro turned to her. "Ani," he said. "I never thought a baby could be so strong."

Animara smiled at him. "Aye," she answered calmly. "All babies have a strong grip— so's they can hold onto their mothers, I suppose."

Nagaro tugged gently, experimentally, at his finger, but Narei wouldn't let go. Her little brow furrowed in what looked for all the world like a frown of determination, and her tiny rose-bud mouth formed into a little round "O". The expression was so comical that Nagaro smiled— and the baby smiled, in miniature mimicry of his expression.

In that instant, somehow, everything changed. Nagaro laughed out loud. It seemed as if something that had been frozen inside of him had suddenly melted: Narei was his, and he was hers. And it couldn't possibly have been any other way.

"She smiled at me!" he cried. "Did you see, Bahiri?"

"Oh yes!" Bahiri replied enthusiastically. "She likes her papa! I'm so glad ye're her papa, too," she added. "And not that other man."

"So am I," he said. And he didn't say it only for Bahiri's ears, or for the sake of the baby.

***

The rest of the afternoon fled swiftly. Nagaro insisted on holding Narei all through dinner, managing her with his left arm and hand— with newfound expertise— while he ate with his right. He laughed afresh each time she tried to catch hold of his spoon. By the time Sudano arrived, halfway through the meal, one would have thought that Nagaro had been holding babies all his life.

Sudano was a small, wiry man, shorter than his wife and seemingly quite unconcerned by the fact. He had an easygoing disposition and a ready smile. When he clapped Nagaro on the back and declared himself glad to make his acquaintance, Nagaro saw no reason to doubt the man's sincerity. Indeed, Sudano went on to thank Nagaro, both for having paid the extra tax and for having "got rid o' Jila."

The last comment was made surreptitiously when Animara got up to refill the teapot.

"Folk have been askin' me for years if I couldn't *do* something about Jila," Sudano confided, leaning across the table. "They'd never say a word t' Ani, o' course, but they'd say it to *me*. And what could *I* do? Her bein' Ani's sister?"

Nagaro winced. "I was nervous about coming here," he confessed. "I was afraid you'd be angry about being left to raise the baby. That you'd think I should have married Jila— which I really didn't want to do."

Sudano made a face. "No man deserves that," he said emphatically. "And as for us raisin' the baby, it's a small price to pay." He winked and then put a finger to his lips because Animara was approaching with the steaming pot.

It was only when the meal was done and the dishes were cleared away that Narei began to fuss. Nagaro relinquished her reluctantly to Lata. The girl smiled at him in her drowsy, languid way. "The little dear want's to nurse again," she told him. "An' she'll be needin' a fresh nappy."

By this time, evening was coming on, and Animara expressed concern that Nagaro would be traveling the rocky path over the headland in the dark if he didn't leave soon. Seeing the sense of this, he rose to go. He put on his cloak and thanked Ani very sincerely for her kindness and for the stew. As he was about to open the door, a thought struck him, and he turned back to her.

"There'll be a celebration of the Harvest Festival next week at the inn," he told her. "I'd be very glad to see you there with your family, and Lata and the baby— if you think they'd all want to come."

Ani smiled at him. "Thank you for telling me," she said. "I'd like that, and Lata and the children would love it."

He opened the door then, and chill air swirled in. Suddenly Tavo and Pilo were on either side of him. "Ye'll come back soon, won't ye, Uncle Nagaro?" they chorused.

"Don't worry," he told them. "I will." Then he bade everyone farewell, and set off through the gathering twilight, striding away in the direction of the trees, where he knew he would find the path.

***

Sudano stepped up beside Animara where she stood in the doorway looking after Nagaro. "There goes a good man," he said.

His wife sighed. "I've always said that Jila just needed t' find one," she said, shaking her head, "but—"

Sudano laughed shortly. "And I've always said she wouldn't know what to do with one if she did."

Ani smiled sadly. "Aye, that ye have," she answered. "And ye were right. But he *has* got t' her somehow," she added. "That letter she wrote me was more about *him* than anything else— even if it was all spite. I've never known her t' waste so many words on a man before. And she said she's afraid t' lie with other men now because it all went wrong with him. That's not the same as havin' got a conscience, but if she at least thinks twice, it's a start."

Sudano laughed again. "If ye'll take my advice, ye won't waste your hope," he said. "Now let's close this door before we let all the winter in."

He slipped an arm around Ani's waist and drew her back into the warmth of the house, pulling the door closed behind them.

***

Nagaro set a quick pace through the gloom under the trees in the bottom of the ravine, and didn't slacken it as he climbed the path to the top of the ridge. When he paused to catch his breath at the top, he never even thought to look for Tira Zomora. Instead, he turned to look back down into the darkening ravine. Away at the bottom he could make out the glow of a warm yellow rectangle that was the oiled skin window of the house he had just left. He stood for a moment, wrapped in his cloak and his thoughts. The wind had quite blown the clouds away, and the sky above was a perfect arch of deepening blue.

What a difference a few hours had made! He had come to this place, troubled of heart and fearful of what he might find. What he'd found, against all expectation, was something he'd never had before and never even known he wanted: *ties of blood,* the kind of ties one didn't have to earn. They just *were.* And they couldn't be unmade— or broken— by any thought or word or deed. Ani and Sudano and their children were good people, and they had accepted him completely despite his own uncertain origins.

Nagaro turned to face the path that descended the other side of the ridge. The first stars were pricking through the deepening ultramarine of the eastern sky. They were mirrored by the first lights being lit in the town beside the harbor below— the harbor where there rode two former Mahuk ships of war. He smiled. Everything was going to be all right after all. He had found a way to use his gift to do good in the world— a way to keep the promise he had made to himself so long ago when he'd lain, a slave in chains, in the dark bilge of a war galley.

And he realized he was hardly angry at Jila anymore. Having heard her story had done something to soften his feelings. Understanding had indeed sown the seeds of forgiveness, and those seeds had somehow blossomed and borne fruit in that moment when he had embraced Narei in his heart and accepted the fact that she wasn't only Jila's child, but was his as well. His smile grew broader as he thought of Narei. *He had a daughter... a tiny, precious, perfect, little girl-child.* And he would see that she had everything she needed to be happy. He would be a father who returned— or at least if he didn't return, it would be because his death was certain. And if Narei wished to rove, he would give her the means to do so.

There was a song in his heart, if not on his lips, as he started down the path that led to the town, and to the house where Taru and Pavo would be expecting him— one of two houses on this Island of Pakoa that he could now, in some sense, call home.

Glossary of Names and Terms

Alam Shufa (ah-lahm SHOO-fah): A Location on the northern coast of the Mahuk Baar, convenient for putting men ashore unobtrusively.

Angkat (AHNG-kaht): A Mautep warlord, chief rival of Baalkir.

anim (AH-nihm): In Vothrin teaching, that of which spirit is composed. Spirit energy.

Animara (ah-nih-MAR-ah): A Turowan woman, sister of Jila. Called "Ani" for short.

Aramei (AR-ah-may): A Kelorin girl, living in the town of Wotana. Daughter of Boronin the blacksmith.

Atadalba (ah-tah-DAHL-bah): One of the Jinari islands.

Ato (AH-toe): A Torowan man, uncle of Bahiri, Tavo and Pilo. Brother of Animara's husband, Sudano.

Averwin (AV-er-wihn): The small country estate that was Nagaro's boyhood home.

Baalkir jir-Akaan (BAHL-keer jeer-ah-KAHN): A Mautep warlord to whom the *Fist of Death* belonged. Uncle of Roheed.

Bahiri (bah-HEER-ee): A young Turowan girl, daughter of Animara and Sudano.

Baruk (bahr-OOK): A Mautep sea-warrior, slave-master on the *Fist of Death.*

basirah (bah-SEER-ah): Hashti word for "enough."

batari (bah-TAH-ree): Batari root is a remedy for pain.

Berenil (BEHR-ehn-ihl): A young Kelorin woman, eldest daughter of the merchant Gedras.

bishka (BIHSH-kah): A relatively mild but expressive Hashti expletive.

bodjer (BAH-jer): An epithet derived from a Leithian expression that was originally much cruder, 'bodjer' means roughly to 'do an injury to' as commonly used in the Common Speech.

Boronin (bor-O-nihn): A Kelorin blacksmith in the town of Wotana, father of Aramei.

Bouno (bo-OO-noe): A Turowan slave freed from Lord Angkat's ship. Formerly a merchant seaman.

Brandle (BRAND-l): A young Liethian man, a lord's son, and Simeon's lover.

Bron Sobring (brahn SO-bring): A Leithian man, lord of Sobring Hold and one of Leyel Virden's "keepers."

Chaheel (chah-HEEL): A Hashtep former galley slave freed from the *Fist of Death*. Inseparable friend of Nanu.

chateef (CHAH-teef): Hashti word meaning "pirate".

Chitaopa (chih-TAOW-pah): A small uninhabited island off the northern coast of Jinara.

Chula (CHOO-lah): An old Turowan man, the gardener at Averwin.

crossy (CRAW-see): Derived from "crossed", a colloquial term for homosexual.

daashu (DAH-shoo): Hashti for "thank you".

Dakuro (dah-KOOR-o): A Turowan blacksmith in Pakoa Town. Also the Town Chief, head of the Town Council.

Darion Loros (Dehr-ee-ahn LOR-ose): lord of Loros Wared and first King of Edrovir, called Darion the Great.

dedrel (DEHD-rehl): A soporific drug, used to manage pain by causing unconsciousness.

Delmanei (dehl-MAH-nay): A Kelorin woman, wife of the merchant Gedras.

dokan (do-KAHN): An Edrovirin gold coin. Equivalent to ten trokins or to one thousand rins.

Dreigen (DREHY-gehn) (The "g" is hard as in "get"): A half-Jinari, half-Kelorin man. The king's Lore Master and an expert on poisins.)

Droviri (dro-VEER-ee): Among non-Edrovirans, a word used for the Edroviran language (called the Common Speech by its speakers). Also used as for the Edroviran people or as an adjective meaning pertaining to Edrovir.

Duleyin (doo-LAY-ihn): Seventh month of the Edroviran calendar, equivalent to July.

Dunrel (DOON-rehl): Sixth month of the Edroviran calendar, equivalent to June.

Edro (EHD-ro): The River Edro, longest river in Edrovir, flowing roughly northeast to southwest and emptying into the sea at Lankura.

Edrovir (EHD-ro-veer): Kingdom inhabited by the Kelorin, Leithian, and Turowan peoples, stretching from the Gorietha mountains on the east to the western sea, and from the Kor Vaskol mountains in the north to the borders of Hran and Jinara in the south..

Elgurn Harlind (EHL-gurn HAR-lihnd): A Leithian man, third king of Edrovir, husband of Queen Semorel, and father of Princess Nevien.

Emril (EHM-rihl): A Kelorin woman who raised Roheed jir-Akaan. She was captured and kept as a slave by Baalkir's brother Notep.

Evrel (EHV-rehl): Fourth month of the Edroviran calendar, equivalent to April.

faasha (FAH-shah): The Hashtep custom of "proving" a young man by taking him to lie with and experienced woman. (Faasha women are paid for their services.)

Faranos (FAR-ah-noes): The Farano Islands, inner and outer chains, lie off the northern coast of Edrovir, north of the River Edro.

farusia (fah-ROO-see-ah): A small shrub bearing large white trumpet-shaped flower, also the flowers of this plant.

Fendar (FEHN-dar): Nagaro's swordmaster, a Kelorin man.

Fendorin (FEHN-dor-ihn): A Kelorin merchant, owner of a vacant house on Pakoa Island.

Finorel (FIHN-or-ehl): Twelfth month of the Edroviran calendar, equivalent to December.

Galenor (GAL-eh-nor): A coastal city in Edrovir, north of Lankura.

Gama (GAH-mah): Taru's grandmother. Also the Turowan word for "grandmother."

Gedras (Gehd-rahs) (The "G" is hard): A Kelorin merchant living in Pakoa Town.

Genorel (GEHN-or-ehl) (The "G" is hard): First month of the Edrovirin calendar, equivalent to January.

Gesrin (GEHS-rihn) (The "G" is hard.): A young Kelorin woman, second daughter of Gedras.

Gillard Marchent (GIHL-ard MAR-chehnt) (The "G" is hard as in "give"): A Leithian lord, also called 'Gill". One of Leyel Virden's "keepers" and second husband of Princess Nevien.

givadi (gih-VAH-dee) (The "g" is hard): A small variety of goat kept for meat, milk, and its fine soft hair, which is spun into thread and woven into cloth.

Goran (GOR-ahn): A Kelorin trader working along the coast of Edrovir who stops at Wotana.

Gudo (GOO-doe): A Turowan youth from Wotana, a childhood friend of Taru.

Gurd (gurd): A young Leithian sea warrior formerly with the Royal Fleet of Edrovir and a freed slave from the *Fist of Death*.

haat (haht): Hashti word for "yes."

Habu (HAH-boo): A young Turowan, son of Yuli and Ramu, keepers of the Bay Tree Inn on Pakoa.

Hakura Kili (hah-KOOR-ah KEE-lee): Guiding Spirit of the Turowan people. The exclamation "Hakura!" generally expresses awe or excitement.

hamanei mata noa (hah-MAH-nay MAH-tah NO-wah): Turowan words to ward off evil or misfortune (roughly translated "Spirits protect us".) Sometimes shortened to "hamanei!", meaning "spirits!", which can be used in any distressing situation.

hanuk (HAH-nook): Hashti word for "sword."

Hanuroa (HAH-noo-RO-ah): The spirit world in the Turowan belief system, where the spirits of the dead are believed to dwell.

Harmoth (HAR-mahth): Southern-most major port city in Edrovir. Tredhold's home town.

Haruda (hah-ROO-dah): A Turowan merchant seaman.

Hasaad (hah-SAHD): A Hashtep slave on the *Fist of Death*, killed at Jaamra in the battle to take the ship.

Hashtep (HAHSH-tehp): Name the common people of the Mahuk Baar use for their own race. Also used as an adjective to describe anything pertaining to that race (except the language, which is Hashti)

Hashti (HAHSH-tee): The language of the people of the Mahuk Baar (spoken by Hashtep and Mautep).

Hatheer (HAH-theer): A Mautep sea warrior, first mate to Captain Ilaam jir-Taak.

heeruk (HEER-uhk): Hashti word for "captain," as of a ship or war galley.

Hel (hehl): In Leithian belief, a place of punishment after death for the spirits of those who have transgressed. Roughly equivalent to the Christian concept of Hell.

heskial (hehs-kee-AHL): A will-controlling "spirit magic" drug distilled from the flowers of a variety of the heskia vine grown in Jinara.

Hinda (HIHN-dah): A Kelorin woman, former cook and housekeeper on the estate of Averwin.

Hran (HRAHN): Inland country south of Edrovir and east of Jinara, often involved in a border dispute with Edrovir.

Hranji (HRAHN-jee): Edroviran name for the inhabitants of Hran.

Idrin (IHD-rihn): Thirteenth and final month of the Edroviran calendar, a seven-day period surrounding the winter solstice. Considered an ill-omened time.

Ilaam jir-Taak (EE-lahm jeer-TAHK): A Mautep sea warrior captain under Lord Angkat.

Ilsafeth (IHL-sah-fehth): A Leithian woman, a "Fleet widow" with two children, courted and wedded by Tredhold.

inan pash (EE-nahn pash): Hasthi phrase meaning "you are welcome". Literally, "not (an) obligation."

Jaamra (JAHM-rah): Strait of Jaamra. A passage between two islands on the Mahuk Baar, site of the sea battle during which Nagaro and his fellow slaves took the *Fist of Death* and won their freedom.

Janidi (jah-NEE-dee): One of the Jinari islands.

Jila (JEE-lah): A beautiful and notorious Torowan woman of Pakoa Island.

Jilena (Jihl-AY-nah): Tira Jilena. A Kelorin woman, a seamstress in Pakoa Town.

Jinara (jih-NAR-ah): A coastal country between Edrovir and the Mahuk Baar, involved in a long-running border dispute with Edrovir.

Jinari (jih-NAR-ee): edroviran name for the inhabitants of Jinara. Also their language and an adjective meaning "pertaining to Jinara."

Jomo Nareyo (JO-mo nar-AY-o): A Turowan fisherman of Wotana, father of Taru.

Judaba (joo-DAH-bah): Northernmost of the Jinari islands and closest island to Chitaopa.

judili hanuktar (joo-DEE-lee HAHN-ook-tahr): Hashti for "demon swordsman."

kajadeem (kah-jah-DEEM): Hashti word for "honor."

Kadi (KAH-dee): A six-year-old Turowan girl living in Pakoa Town. Sister of Tobei and daughter of Lunani.

Kale Fendred (kayl FEHN-drehd): A Leithian lord, boyhood friend of King Elgurn, and one of Leyel Virden's "keepers."

kajadeem (kah-jah-DEEM): Hashti word for "honor."

karash hanuk (KAR-ahsh HAHN-ook): Hasti phrase meaning "lower (your) sword(s)."

Kasadrin (KAH-sah-drihn): A board game of Kelorin origin also called "King's Men" but literally translating as "lord's people."

Kel Tierna (kel tee-EHR-nah): A coastal city in Edrovir, south of Lankura. Mendorel's home town.

Kelorin (KEL-or-in): The fair-skinned, dark-haired people originally from the isles of Kelor (the land of Kelornas) in the far western sea. Also their language or an adjective meaning "pertaining to the Kelorin people."

Keros (KEHR-ose): Elder Kelorin healer in Pakoa Town.p, recently deceased.

keshaal (keh-SHAHL): A Hashti expletive, stronger than "bishka."

kia kaar hanuk-tak (KEE-ah kahr HAHN-ook-tahk): Hashti phrase meaning "Put down (the) sword belonging (to you)."

Kiraam Shaku-Tal (KEER-ahm SHAH-koo-TAHL): Name given to Nagaro by Roheed. In Hashti, it means literally "taker of slaves., generally translated as "Thief of Slaves."

komforei (KOHM-for-ay): An herbal remedy for stings and rashes. Possibly comfrey.

Kroneg (KRO-nehg): The Leithian god of war, arbiter of the outcome of armed conflict and ruler of the dark moon Naru.

kuma (KOO-mah): Kuma stain. A brown stain for fair skin used for sun-protection. Kuma ointment is made from the meat of the nuts of the kuma plant as a carrier for the stain that is derived from their shells.

Kunoa (Koo-NO-wah): A Turowan youth from Pakoa, a former slave freed from the *Fist of Death*.

Kuran Kel (KOOR-ahn kehl): Lord of the Royal Fleet of Edrovir, a man of mixed Kelorin and Turowan blood.

Laash (LAHSH): A Hashtep slave on the *Fist of Death* who died of plague on Chitaopa.

Landros Torenin (LAN-drose tor-EHN- ihn): An older Kelorin sea warrior formerly in the Royal Fleet of Edrovir as second mate of the *Fairwind*. Also a slave freed from the *Fist of Death*.

Lanei (LAH-nay): A young Turowan woman of dubious virtue who Taru knew in Wotana.

Lankura (LAHN-koor-ah): The capital city of Edrovir, located at the mouth of the River Edro.

Lata (LAH-tah): A young Turowan woman serving as a wet nurse on Pakoa Island.

Leina (LAY-nah): An older Kelorin woman in Pakoa Town, a friend of Neved's family.

Leithian (LAY-thee-en): Member of a fair-skinned, blond or red-haired people originally from a land called Leith that lies far to the east beyond Arlinas. Also their original language, largely lost in Edrovir, or an adjective for anything pertaining to Leithian people.

Leyel Virden (LAY-ehl VER-dehn): Name given to Nagaro by the Lady Maramine. Also known as the "idiot prince." First husband of Princess Nevien.

Lissafel (LIHS-ah-fehl): "The Lady." The maiden goddess of the Leithians. Ruler of the hearts of men and women, and of the pale moon Talebra.

Lissel (lih-SEHL): A Kelorin girl. Youngest daughter of the merchant Gedras.

Lokundas (lo-KOON-dahs): The "Turner of Worlds", Kelorin personification of fate. One of the old gods of the Cloud Mountain People in Kelor, before the coming of Vothra.

Lomoas (lo-MO-ahs): The Lomoas, a group of islands off the coast of southern Edrovir. The Lomoa Islands lie south of the River Edro and are separated from the Inner and Outer Faranos by the broad straight known as "Farano's Mouth."

Luka (LOO-kah): An old Turowan medicine woman known to Nagaro during his childhood at Averwin.

Lunani (loo-NAH-nee): A Torowan woman on Pakoa given to migraines, mother of Tobei and Kadi.

Luweda (loo-WAY-dah): A Turowan woman, younger daughter of Yuli and Ramu, the keepers of the Bay Tree Inn on Pakoa.

Madrel (MAH-drehl): Third month of the Edroviran calendar, equivalent to March.

Mahuk (MAH-hook): An adjective used to identify things from the Mahuk Baar, such as ships. Used ignorantly in Edrovir to refer to the tawny-skinned, black-haired people from the Mahuk Baar who are properly called Hashtep, or Mautep in the case of the warrior class.

Mahuk Baar (MAH-hook bar): The coastal country and islands to the south of Edrovir beyond Jinara.

Maramine Virden (mar-ah-MEEN VER-dehn): A Kelorin lady, guardian of Leyel Virden and victim of a fatal plot by King Elgurn, his Lore Master Dreigen, and others.

Matahi (mah-TAH-hee): A young Hashtep woman on Pakoa Island, older sister of Tenepti.

Mautep (MAOW-tehp): Hashti word for the Hashtep warrior class.

Medrin (MEHD-rihn): Fifth month of the Edrovirin calendar, equivalent to May.

Mendorel (MEHN-dor-ehl): A Kelorin shopkeeper and candle-maker from Kel Tierna. Also a slave freed from the *Fist of Death*.

Minowei (mih-NO-way): Princess Minowei to the Turowan people. A Turowan chief's daughter known from the story of her romance with the Kelorin lord Nevrath who founded the House of Loros. She became Nevrath's wife, the first lady of Loros Wared, and mother of Darion.

Mira (MEER-ah): A Turowan woman on Pakoa Island suffering from pneumonia.

Moraga (mor-AH-gah): A Turowan merchant seaman and former slave freed from the *Fist of Death*.

Nagaro (nah-GAR-o): Name taken by Leyel Virden after his escape from Lankura. It means "nameless man" in the old Turowan tongue.

nan (nahn): Hashti for "no."

Nanu (NAH-noo): A young Turowan man, a former slave freed from the *Fist of Death*, and inseparable friend of Chaheel.

Narei (NAR-ay): A baby girl of mixed Turowan and Kelorin blood, Jila's daughter. The name means "sea" in the Torowan language.

Naru (NAR-oo): The dark moon. Smaller and dimmer of the world's two moons, it travels a little faster than the bright moon, Talebra, at times ovetaking the larger moon and crossing in front of it. In Kelorin legend, Naru is a "ship that sailed between the stars, carrying the various human races and the "seeds" of all the plants and animals.

Neved (NEHV-ehd): A nine-year-old Kelorin boy living in Pakoa Town, injured by falling off a roof. Brother of Sali (Salinda).

Nevien (NEHV-ee-ehn): Princess Nevien, daughter of King Elgurn and Queen Semorel of Edrovir.

Nevrath (NEHV-rahth): A high-born Kelorin man (son of a Wared lord) who courted and married Princess Minowei. Founder the House of Loros and father of Darion.

Nondorin (NOEN-dor-in): Eleventh month of the Edroviran calendar, equivalent to November.

Obedo (o-BAY-do): A Turowan fisherman from Pakoa and former slave freed from the *Fist of Death.*

Obiari (o-bee-AR-ee): Master Obiari, a Jinari lore master whose works are much favored by King Elgurn's sinister Lore Master, Dreigen.

Olomi (o-LO-mee): A Turowan woman of Wotana. Wife of Jomo and mother of Taru, killed by Captain Urchak.

onam (O-nahm): That of which the material world is composed—matter, flesh.

opa (O-pah): A narcotic drug given in extreme cases for pain, but known for causing strange dreams or hallucinations. Probably opium or something related.

Ororu (o-ROR-roo): One of the Jinari islands.

Oteyin (o-TEHY-ihn): Eighth month of the Edroviran calendar, equivalent to August.

Pakoa (pah-KO-ah): Island off the southern coast of Edrovir, southern-most isle of the Lomoas. Pakoa Town is the island's only real town and it's port, located on Pakoa Harbor.

Panila (pah-NEE-lah): A young Turowan woman on Pakoa Island. (Coincidentally, there was a young woman of the same name in Wotana, of dubious reputation.)

Pavo Maat (PAH-vo maht): A young Hashtep fisherman's son, a former slave freed from the *Fist of Death*, and close friend of Nagaro and Taru.

Pedril (PEHD-rihl): Master Pedril, a Kelorin healer in Pakoa Town.

Pilo (PEE-lo): A young Turowan boy, younger son of Animara and Sudano.

Potero (po-TEHR-o) A Turowan slave on the *Fist of Death*, killed at Jaamra in the fight to take the ship.

Raak (rahk): A Mautep sea warrior, slave driver on the *Fist of Death*.

Ramu (RAH-moo): A Turowan man, keeper of the Bay Tree Inn on Pakoa, husband of Yuli.

reivinkor (RAY-vihn-kor): The Kelorin alphabet, used to write the Common Speech. The set of letters was devised by a woman named Reivin who was one of the founders of Kelornas.

rin (rihn): A small copper coin that is the basic unit of the Edrovirin system of currency. There are one hundred rins to the trokin, and one thousand rins to the dokan.

Roheed jir-Akaan (ro-HEED jeer-ah-KAHN): A young Mautep sea warrior who tried to help Nagaro during his time as a galley slave on the *Fist of Death*. Roheed did so because of a "blood debt" charging him to help men who were orphaned in infancy. Nephew of Lord Baalkir.

Rubo (ROO-bo): A Turowan former Fleet warrior and ship's cook.

saatif (SAH-teef): Hashti word for "lord."

Sar Tipaal (sahr tih-PAHL): A port city of the Mahuk Baar. Home to Lord Baalkir and site of his great shipyard.

Sedrin (SEHD-rihn): Ninth month of the Edroviran, equivalent to September.

Seftep (SEHF-tehp): A Hashtep slave freed from Lord Angkat's ship.

Semorel (SEHM-or-ehl): Queen Semorel. King Elgurn's Kelorin queen, mother of Princess Nevien.

shaku (SHAH-koo): Hashti word for "slave."

shaku raal (SHAH-koo rahl): Hashti for "slave dog."

Sheptuum (SHEHP-toom): God of the Hashtep and Mautep people of the Mahuk Baar.

sho abtaak (show ahb-TAHK): Hashti phrase meaning "Are you ready?" Literally "you (to be) ready."

sho naneef lashir-aan (sho nah-NEEF LAH-sheer-AHN): Hashti phrase meaning "You will not be harmed." Literally "you not harmed (will be)."

Shofeer (SHO-feer): Name of a Mautep warrior family and their House.

Shupti (SHOOP-tee): A young Hashtep woman on Pakoa, briefly courted by Pavo Maat.

Simion (SIH-mee-ahn): A young Kelorin see warrior formerly of the Royal Fleet and a former slave freed from the *Fist of Death*. A "crossed man."

Sodo (SO-doe): A Turowan man, keeper of the Red Cask tavern in Pakoa Town.

Solbrid (SOLE-brihd): The Leithian Mother Goddess. Ruler of earth and giver and taker of life.

sothiril (SO-thur-ihl): A tea-like infusion of Kelorin origin brewed from the berries of the plant of the same name. Also used to refer to the dried berries.

Sudano (soo-DAH-no): A Turowan kuma farmer on Pakoa, husband of Animara.

Sulani (soo-LAH-nee): A young Turowan woman, adored by Habu.

Taan (TAHN): Pavo Maat's older brother.

Takuma (tah-KOO-mah): Chief of the Turo dwelling around Kel Lankura during the Time of Fire and Water. Father of Minowei.

Talebra (tah-LEHY-brah): Name of the larger and brighter of the world's two moons. Often called simply "the bright moon."

Taru Nareyo (TAR-roo nar-AY-o): A young Turowan fisherman from Wotana, Nagaro's Turowan friend.

Tavo (TAH-vo): A young Turowan boy, older son of Animara and Sudano.

Tego (TAY-go): A Turowan merchant seaman and former slave freed from the *Fist of Death*.

Tenepti (tehn-EHP-tee): A young Hashtep woman on Pakoa, Pavo's sweetheart.

Timegar (TIH-may-gar): A Kelorin man from Pakoa, a former Fleet warrior.

Tira (TEER-rah): Respectful from of feminine address, roughly equivalent to "Mrs.", without implication regarding marital status. Used preceeding a given name.

tirka (TUR-kah): A short-sleeved upper garment, opening down the front and cut long enough to cover the hips. Generally worn over a long-sleeved shirt and usually belted.

tirkyl (tur-KEEL): A closed-front, shirt-like garment with long cuff-less sleeves, falling to the hips and usually worn belted.

Tobei (TOE-bay): A nine-year-old Turowan boy on Pakoa Island, son of Lunani and brother of Kadi.

Todrin (TOE-drihn): Tenth month of the Edroviran calendar, equivalent to October.

Tor (tor): Respectful form of masculine address, roughly equivalent to "Mr."

Tredhold Ferth (TRED-hold FURTH): A Leithian former ship's doctor in the Royal Fleet of Edrovir, and a former slave freed from the *Fist of Death*.

trokin (TRO-kihn): A silver coin worth one hundred rins. There are ten trokins in one dokan.

Tulara (too-LAR-ah): A young Turowan woman, first a tavern woman, then employed at the Bay Tree Inn in Pakoa Town. A romantic interest of Taru's.

Turo (TOOR-o): "The Turo" is the Turowan name for their own people. The word Turo also can mean a Turowan man. Turowa is the female equivalent.

Turowan (toor-O-ahn): A member of the brown-skinned, dark-haired people native to the coastal region and islands of Edrovir, also called the Turo. Also an adjective used to describe things relating to the Turowan people.

Ulapa (oo-LAH-pah): An aging Turowan man, former sailor, caretaker of the Fendorin house on Pakoa Island.

Urchak tok-Faar (UR-chahk toke-FAHR): A Mautep sea warrior under Lord Baalkir, captain of the *Fist of Death*.

Utabala (OO-tah-BAH-lah): A Jinari merchant's agent and interpreter, a former slave freed from the *Fist of Death.*

Vedorel (VEHD-or-ehl): Second month of the Edrovirin calendar, equivalent to February.

Vothra (VO-thrah): The Benevolent Spirit of the Kelorin people, teacher of the Path as set forth in the Writings. Not a god, but a joining of many human spirits, Vothra offers council, drawn from the wisdom of many lives, and guides a spirit after death through the void and into a new life.

Wared (WAH-rehd): Territory ruled by a Kelorin lord. Equivalent to a Leithian "Hold."

Wotana (wo-TAH-nah): A fishing village in Galenor Wared, twenty miles north of Lankura, on Wotana Bay.

yaah (yah): Hasti word meaning "go", in the sense of "commence" or "proceed."

Yuli (YOO-lee): Tira Yuli, A Turowan woman, wife of Ramu. They keep the Bay Tree Inn on Pakoa Island. Mother of Habu and Luweda.

Zirda (ZUR-dah): A respectful masculine form of address, roughly equivalent to "sir" in our modern usage. Used without an accompanying name.

Zirdyn (zur-DEEN): A respectful feminine form of address, roughly equivalent to "madame." Used without an accompanying name.

Zo-Hlan Tai (ZO-hlahn TAHY): A Hranji merchant beaten to death by the slave driver Raak on the *Fist of Death* because he refused to row.

Zomora (zo-MOR-ah): Tira Zomora. The Torowan medicine woman on Pakoa Island.

Acknowledgments

First I must thank all of the many people who gave me input on the manuscript while it was in development. Most significantly, this includes my test readers for the final version: Sherry Hintze, Suzanne Coulter, Anne Bannon, and Aubrey Lyons. Others read an earlier version: Kristie McCue, Marie Lim, my mother, my brother Paul, and my son Arthur. And of course there are the members of ScHoFan, a critique group under the auspices of GLAWS (Greater Los Angeles Writers Society) who gave me feedback on the early chapters. They include, in alphabetical order: Carol Ann Alves, Lee Bohannon, John Gwinner, Steve Graziano, Ken Hughes, Scott Kilburn, Katy Mann, Carmen Mendivil, Robin Reed, Taguhi Tavitian, Lynn Ward, and Garrett Weinstein. James Graetz and Christina Przybilla also provided comments on partial readings. There may be others who have slipped my mind, and if so, I very humbly beg their forgiveness.

I am also grateful for the support of my husband and the other members of my family, who not only continue to allow me to pursue this madness, but actually encourage it. My special gratitude also goes to three friends, Kristie, Anne, and Suzanne, who have believed in me and in my vision, now and, in some cases, over the long years it took me to get to the point where the vision is finally coming to fruition.

And finally, one last heartfelt acknowledgement to the person who is doing most of the work required to get my words into publishable form: my editor, book designer, file format wizard, and general partner in crime, Kristie McCue. I don't know where I'd be without her.

About the Author

Carol Louise Wilde is the author of the fantasy adventure series the *Nagaro Chronicle*. She long led a double life: biology research scientist by day, and by night, chief archivist for the nation of Edrovir and its neighboring states. The *Nagaro Chronicle* covers but one brief period in the long and eventful history of this world and its inhabitants. Ms. Wilde lives in Southern California with her husband of forty odd years. They have two sons to carry on the tradition.

Praise for Carol Louise Wilde's *Gift of Chance*:

"Our young hero awakens, stripped of his memories, in a strange and dangerous land. Something has pushed him tohis limits, and maybe it's better not to remember. As dreams help him piece his past together he discovers he's innately a man of honor. He is also a man of anger. *Gift of Chance* will appeal to lovers of world-building fantasy. Wilde's commitment to her characters lights every page with their passion, and hers."

— Petrea Burchard, author of *Act As If: Stumbling Through Hollywood with Headshot in Hand* and the novel *Camelot & Vine,* and instructor at the Story Kitchen.

"*A Gift of Chance,* by Carol Louise Wilde is the first of a fantasy series that centers around a young man who has mysteriously lost his memory. He's taken in by a kindly fisherman's family and because he can't remember his true name, he decides to call himself Nagaro, which means 'no one'. As the story unfolds, Nagaro is repeatedly plagued by terrifying dreams that show him glimpses of his past. He struggles to remember, but at the same time, he's afraid of what he might learn. The emotional heart of this book revolves around Nagaro's harrowing journey to the truth of who he is. He and his friend Taru, the fisherman's son, are tested in a most horrific way, and in the process, they both discover the breadth of their strength and courage. *A Gift of Chance* is a fine debut from a promising new talent in the epic fantasy genre. I, for one am eagerly awaiting the next installments in the series."

— Leslie Ann Moore—Author of the award-winning *Griffin's Daughter Trilogy* and the *Nuetierra Chronicles.*

"[...]Wilde has created a maincharacter who immediately comes alive in her story *Gift of Chance: Book 1 in the Nagaro Chronicle.* Nagaro is sure tocapture the hearts of fans, and he will stay with them long after the last pageis read. There is quite a bit to like about this book. [...]Readers willappreciate the extra material. The maps in the front provide an excellent pointof reference, while the terms in the back help with pronunciation and generalunderstanding of the rich and lavish world of this story."

— Writer's Digest Self-Published Book Awards reviewer's comments.

www.ingramcontent.com/pod-product-compliance
Lightning Source LLC
Chambersburg PA
CBHW070419170726
48291CB00002B/267
9781944492076